Hera Takes Charge

An Olympus Inc Romance

Kate Healey

Karen Healey

Contents

Content Description

Hera Takes Charge is primarily a romance with a guaranteed happy ending. However, there is some content you should be aware of, including references to past familial abuse and neglect, some on-page violence, and a brief on-page moment where a PoV character fears sexual activity continuing after consent has been withdrawn (it doesn't.)

Also, I know that while *Persephone in Bloom* and *Aphrodite Unbound* were my take on well-attested mythology, a relationship between Poseidon and Hera isn't one of the great Greek myths. But it's definitely where *this* story was always going. Don't @ me.

For Jessica Tai, who totally gets it.

Prologue

The evening before Hera married her husband for the second time, she opened her apartment door to find her brother-in-law waiting outside.

"Don!" she said. "This is wonderful! We weren't sure you could make it."

Don didn't return her smile. He looked travel-worn and rumpled in his plaid shirt and denim jacket. Hera hoped he'd brought something suitable to wear to the ceremony and reception, but the stained duffel bag he was holding didn't bode well. She made a mental note to contact her assistant, and renewed her smile.

"I didn't think I was going to," he said, his voice rough. Had he been drinking? There was a definite beer-ish aroma. But he looked steady on his feet.

"Well, come in and sit down for a moment," Hera said, stepping back from the door. "We kept your seat reserved, of course. Are you bringing a date? Do you have a hotel reservation, or are you staying with Hades?"

"Is Zeus here?" Don asked, unmoving.

"No," Hera said, blinking at him. "He's at his place. We're spending the night apart before the wedding."

"Romantic," Don said, his voice much grimmer than the observation warranted. But he stepped inside and laid his duffel bag down on the shining hardwood of her entrance, unlacing his work boots and stepping out of them.

One sock had a hole in the toe. Hera looked at the flash of pale skin exposed there and winced. Well, the rest of him looked well-cared for, if worn. Don was tanned and a little weather-beaten, and could probably stand to moisturize more often, but his burly frame moved easily and from the muscles pressing against his sleeves, he was clearly getting enough physical exercise. "How's life on the boat?" she asked.

"Ship," he corrected, and finally smiled at her. "When it's big, it's a ship."

Hera was well aware of the fact, but she'd been after the smile, not accuracy. "Did you come here straight from the airport?"

"From the docks," he said, and looked around her tidy living room. "This is a nice place."

"Thank you. We're moving into a penthouse downtown after the wedding, but I'm rather fond of this apartment. I thought I might keep it, and rent it out."

"Good call," Don said, back to sounding grim again.

Hera elected not to ask him more about that, and instead murmured a polite apology, excusing herself to the bedroom. A quick search through Zeus' drawer in her dressing room provided a pair of gray cashmere socks, still in their cardboard box. She returned to the living room and offered them to Don.

"Oh," he said, and covered his eyes with one big hand. "Thank you. A cast-off from Zeus?"

"Certainly not," Hera said. "Brand new."

"Won't he miss them?"

"He won't even know they were there." Hera frowned at him. Don was occasionally erratic, but he was acting more than usually unusual. "Is everything all right?"

He peeled off his worn socks and stuffed them in his pocket, and she found herself unaccountably disconcerted by his naked feet. There was a sharp tan line across the front, where his deck shoes had left the rest of his skin exposed. The pale toes looked oddly vulnerable.

"No," Don said.

"Sorry?"

"Everything's not all right." He took a deep breath. "I'm sorry. I wanted to say this sooner, but it had to be in person, and now the timing is terrible. But I think I'll be failing you if I don't say it."

Hera took a deep breath of her own and sat down on the couch beside him. She was fairly certain she knew what came next. "Well, go ahead," she said.

"Don't do it," Don said. "Don't re-marry Zeus."

"I appreciate your concern," Hera said. "But I've considered the situation carefully, and I've made the best decision for myself and my happiness."

It was a practiced spiel by now. She'd delivered it in the face of her mother's vague curiosity, Minerva's blunt disbelief, and Hades's gentle concern. Saying it to Don shouldn't have been harder, somehow, but she watched him flinch and felt guilty.

And then she felt annoyed at the guilt. She *was* making the best decision for herself. She'd thought it over many times before she'd come to her final conclusion, that giving Zeus a second chance was the right choice. For both of them, but especially for her.

She didn't owe anyone an explanation, least of all Don, whose timing really was atrocious. The night before the wedding was not the appropriate moment to raise the issue, however well-intentioned he was.

And she didn't doubt his intentions were good. She really did appreciate the concern.

It was just that he was wrong.

"Do you trust him?" Don demanded.

"Yes," Hera said, without hesitation. "I wouldn't be doing this if I didn't."

"And if he betrays your trust again?" Don said. "If he cheats again, what will you do?"

"Then I'll divorce him again," Hera said. "And Minerva wrote me a bulletproof prenuptial, so I'll be walking away much better off. But it won't happen, Don. I promise you. Zeus has changed." She laid her hand on his wrist, and he stilled under her touch. "Can you not admit the possibility? Do you not believe in second chances?"

"I know my brother," Don said. "He doesn't—Hera, he's not good at caring about people. It's not even his fault, not really. You know what our dad was like."

Hera shuddered. Saturnius Kronion had been a genuine monster, a poisonous old man who tainted everything he touched.

"Zeus has done the work," she said. "Hours of therapy, couples counseling with me. He's worked on developing empathy. We communicate so well now, Don, it's—he's a different man."

"Sure," Don said. "He'd do anything to get you back." He swallowed hard. "Who wouldn't? It's once he's got you that worries me."

Hera felt the first stirrings of alarm. She took her hand off his arm with studied ease and stood up, brushing down her skirt with unnecessary attention. "Let's get you something to eat."

"Hera," Don said. His voice was ragged.

"I know that you're just looking out for me," she said, and tried a casual little laugh. It fell flat. "Very brotherly of you."

"Brotherly," Don said. "Right."

"But I must ask that we stop discussing this. How have you been?"

"Do you love him?" Don asked, and stood up.

Hera made the mistake of meeting his eyes.

The Kronion brothers didn't look that much alike. Hades was lean and dark, taking after their father in looks, if nothing else, and his eyes were dark blue. Zeus was golden blond, with sky-blue eyes, movie star cheekbones and a winning smile. Don was blond too, but his hair was bleached lighter from sun and salt, and his eyes were a blue that was almost green. Those eyes bore down into hers, and she saw anger and fear and something she instinctively shied away from.

"Yes," she said quietly, holding his gaze. "I love him very much."

Don looked away first.

"Okay," he said, and walked towards her door. "That's all I needed to know."

"You don't need to go."

"I really do," Don said. His voice sounded normal, but he was facing away from her, bending over to pull his shoes on over his new gray socks.

"All right," Hera said, with more bite than she intended. "Then I'll see you tomorrow."

"Don't count on it."

"Don!" Hera protested. "You can't come all this way, and then—"

"I can't watch you do this again," Don said, and straightened, turning to face her. His face was blank, rigidly controlled rather than emotionless. "I hope you're right. I hope he's changed. I hope you get everything you ever wanted, for real this time, because you deserve the man you love. And I hope he loves you the way you deserve."

"But you think he won't." Hera felt heat flush her cheeks. Technically, it was Zeus Don didn't trust, but it felt as if he were doubting her too—her intelligence, her good judgment, her ability to control her own life.

"That's right," Don said, and opened the door. "Sorry to interrupt your evening. Congratulations on your upcoming nuptials."

He stalked out, and she closed the door behind him, with more force than was strictly necessary. The bang resounded through her quiet home.

This was just like Don. He'd turned up, ruined her equilibrium, and then run away again. Zeus, even in the worst times, when he'd barely troubled to conceal his infidelity, had never given the least indication that he meant to leave. Indeed, it was her own leaving that had finally shocked him into understanding, made him realize she *meant* it, that it was monogamy or nothing.

That, if she had to, she could live without him.

But now she didn't have to. Zeus had wooed her, persistent and patient, and she believed him. He'd changed. He'd never betray her again.

And tomorrow, they'd be back together.

Forever.

Chapter One

The evening before what would have been the sixth anniversary of her second wedding to Zeus—if she hadn't just finished divorcing him again—Hera's doorbell rang.

She'd been expecting it all day. Only pride had stopped her from reaching out to Don herself, but he would have remembered. She wasn't sure whether it would be comfort or recrimination he offered, but she'd take it either way.

Don had never once brought up the warning he'd given her before that ill-fated second wedding. Not when she'd first learned of Zeus's infidelity with Semele Cadmida and the child that had resulted. Not when she'd heard about the even worse betrayal of the threats Zeus had made to his former mistresses while pretending to *be* Hera herself. Don had been enraged on her behalf, and a supportive ally in her bid to wrest Olympus from Zeus's hands, but he'd never once said *I told you so*.

Now, perhaps, was the time.

She opened the door, already preparing her opening statement, and blinked in startled reappraisal.

"Surprise!" Aphrodite Urania sang out. Her slender arms were holding an enormous wicker gift basket, much larger than her entire model-thin torso. Beside her, Persephone Erinyes, beautiful and warm in a long floral dress, smiled a more tentative greeting.

Hera blinked.

Aphrodite apparently took this as an invitation to enter, because she walked in with no hesitation, stepping out of her high-heeled slides with the grace that had put her on hundreds of catwalks. "Guess what?" she said brightly, putting her burden down on the antique foyer table. It wobbled alarmingly. "Our boyfriends have totally abandoned us, and we're super sad."

"Heph and Hades are getting to know each other over a beer," Persephone translated. "Aphrodite suggested we come here instead." She glanced at Hera. "I would claim that I tried to talk her out of it, but I didn't. Did you have plans?"

"We can totally go if you have plans," Aphrodite said readily. "Or even if you don't, like maybe your plan was 'stay at home and not have visitors, thank you, please leave the basket'."

Hera laughed, surprising herself. "You're both very welcome. I was expecting... Never mind." She picked up the basket and guided both younger women further into the penthouse, away from the more public reception areas and into the sitting room she enjoyed the most, with its view over Ida Park. The mid-summer sun hovered above the horizon, flooding the room with golden light, warming Persephone's honey-toned skin and turning Aphrodite's red-gold hair into glittering flame.

Hera wasn't sure what she looked like, in comparison. Older, certainly. Tired, probably.

Sad?

Hopefully not.

"Did you know it was my anniversary?" she asked.

"Hades mentioned it," Persephone said, and pulled a bottle of champagne out of the gift basket. Water beaded promisingly on the label. "Aphrodite, seriously, how much of this do you just have on hand?"

"Lots," Aphrodite said happily. She fetched champagne flutes from Hera's sideboard while Persephone popped the cork. "Anyway, it's not your anniversary, right? It's your ex-iversary."

"I'm not sure that's an accepted neologism," Hera said, but she raised her glass when Aphrodite handed it to her, clinking it against those held by the younger women. "Cheers."

She surveyed them as they sipped, touched that they'd bothered to come. Well, Persephone was practically her sister-in-law, if one ignored both that she wasn't actually married to Hades, and Hera herself was no longer married to Zeus. Hera intended to ignore those inconvenient quibbles, because Persephone was a delightful person who thought the best of everyone and brought beauty into the world through her lush and astonishing art.

Aphrodite was a different matter. If Hera had followed the generally approved response of ex-wife to one-time-mistress, she should have dramatically barred Aphrodite from ever darkening her door. But Zeus's affair with Aphrodite had been years ago, when she'd been barely seventeen. Zeus had had plenty of cause to regret that ill-advised fling over the past months, as Hera and Aphrodite had presented a united front to news media and the social pages alike.

Also, hating Aphrodite would have been like hating a golden retriever that got mud all over your couch. If the couch had thrown itself at the retriever and demanded the paw prints. And if the retriever had been determined to make amends for the stains, with the kind of charm that could melt colder hearts than Hera's.

Hera let the increasingly tortured metaphor go, and smiled at them. "Well, thank you. I'd decided to leave the day unmarked, but I was having a hard time pretending it wasn't significant."

"I'm kind of surprised you didn't throw a party," Aphrodite said.

"I was tempted," Hera admitted. "But it might have looked gauche. And the shareholder meeting is next week." Her fingers tightened on the stem of her flute.

"Are they kicking Zeus out?" Aphrodite asked, as Persephone said, "Are they making you Olympus CEO?"

"I don't know," Hera said. She put the wine down before she spilled it. "I have forty-five percent of the shareholder vote firmly behind me—Hades, Don, and my own five percent. Zeus and whoever he sold those shares to is fifteen percent. The rest are...undecided."

She should have had ten percent, which would have made victory so much easier—she'd then only need one of the other shareholders to vote her way, however slim a margin of victory that gave her. But Zeus had sold half of his own twenty percent in Olympus Publishing before she could serve him divorce papers, which meant she was getting only half of what remained.

She swallowed acid at the memory. *Calm down. You don't get anything if they see you're angry.*

She was almost certain she had the support to oust Zeus as chairman of the board and CEO. Her carefully planned campaign had undermined his public credibility, which had an impact on the bottom line. And it helped a great deal that Hades was on her side. As Head of Finance and Chief Financial Officer, he held a lot of sway with the board, even if he was typically self-effacing about it. He very much disapproved of Zeus betraying her, committing fraud to pay off his former mistress from the company accounts, and assaulting Persephone in his office in an attempt to control the story. As he should.

Zeus losing control of Olympus would be some form of justice for his multiple misdeeds, personal *and* professional.

But the ultimate prize—and, if she were being truly honest, the ultimate revenge—would be taking the CEO position herself.

And she wasn't positive she had the votes.

"You'll get it," Persephone said confidently. "Has Minerva found out who Zeus sold half his shares to?"

For a dollar, Hera thought. That had been a contemptuous little message. "Not yet. My guess is that it's Samuel Janus, the Board deputy chair. He's always been Zeus's yes man. No doubt they have some sort of gentleman's agreement that he'll sell them back." She refocused. "But I don't mean to go on about this. How have you two been lately?"

"Great!" Aphrodite said. "I just finished recording the initial vocals for my character in the next *Binding* expansion."

"And Hades and I are all moved in to the new house," Persephone said. "Thank you so much for the rug, by the way. All those bright colors in the hallway are perfect."

"Oh, good. Don helped me pick it out."

"Is he still working at that interior design place?"

"Part time, I believe."

"Do you know if he's sticking around?" Persephone pressed. "Hades is worried that once the sale for his old house goes through that Don will wander off again."

Hera hadn't considered that. "Don will do what he feels best," she temporized. "I must admit, it's been nice seeing him more often."

"Mm," Persephone said, and took a sip of her wine.

"So," Aphrodite said brightly. "Now that you're officially divorced, are you planning to start dating?"

Persephone choked.

Hera waved the query away. "Oh, I'm not worried about that right now."

"Fair, fair," Aphrodite said. "Mind you, I thought I was done with dating, and then I met Heph, so stay awake to those possibilities!"

"I wasn't planning on hiring anyone for dating purposes," Hera said. "I can't expect to come out of that as well as you did."

"Shhh!" Aphrodite said. "That's a *secret*." She glanced around dramatically, exactly as if she hadn't told Hera all about her arrangement with Heph before she requested Hera's help in getting him back.

"And also, you'd met Heph well before that?" Hera said. "Yes. Because it was at the Olympus Winter Ball last year."

"That's right," Aphrodite said. "Maybe you'll find feelings for someone you've already met! That's an excellent point." She gave Hera a look of sunny approval.

"There was something magic at that party," Persephone said. "That's when I first asked Hades out."

"And I broke up with Ares and fell literally into Heph's lap," Aphrodite said.

"Well, I wish the magic had worked on me," Hera said, and sighed. "It was months afterwards that I found out about Zeus. At the ball, I was still a happily married woman."

Persephone made a sympathetic noise.

"Wasn't that the night Don came back into town?" Aphrodite asked.

"Oh, yes," Hera said, and smiled at the memory of Don's grin as he surprised them all. "You're right, that was good." She blinked back to the present, where Persephone was glaring at Aphrodite. "What is it?"

"Nothing," Persephone said, and took a hasty gulp of wine.

"Persephone is reminding me I wasn't supposed to push you into romance talk," Aphrodite said. "Or set you up with any of the multiple tech billionaires I keep meeting at parties…"

"Oh, please don't," Hera said.

"No set-ups, check," Aphrodite said, lazily untucking her feet from under her and stretching out on her sofa. The toenails of her long, fine-boned feet were painted with bright pink glitter, and she admired them for a moment. "But you're staying open to love."

"Hm."

"Staying open to good times with hot strangers?"

Hera laughed. "I wouldn't know where to start."

"Hera Rheczack," Aphrodite said, her feet hitting the floor as she sat up straight. "Are you telling me you've never had a one-night stand?"

"I've hardly had the opportunity."

"Not even in college?" Persephone asked.

Hera shook her head.

"Well, we've got to put that on the bucket list," Aphrodite said. "Let me know if you want any tips."

Hera grimaced. "I'm not sure any of that is going to be part of my life, going forward." And that was the first time she'd admitted that, to anyone.

Aphrodite and Persephone exchanged another glance, but they didn't let out any startled shrieks, so Hera supposed it wasn't that stunning a revelation.

"Aw, that's a shame," Aphrodite said. "Sex is fun."

"But not necessary. Look at Minerva. She's never felt the lack of sex or romance in her life."

"She's also, like, totally uninterested in both," Aphrodite pointed out. "That's not you."

"Well, when it comes to sex, I have a very good vibrator," Hera said, which startled a laugh out of Persephone and a "get it, girl!" from Aphrodite. "But as for romance... I've only ever loved Zeus."

"Really?" Persephone asked.

Hera shrugged. "Clearly a bad idea, in so many ways. Unfortunately, I just can't imagine feeling that way about anyone else. If it happens, it happens. But if not... Well. I think I've already demonstrated I'd rather be happy alone than miserable with someone else."

"Sing it, sister," Aphrodite said, and tapped her glass against Hera's.

Persephone looked anxious. "And you are happy now," she said, and it was almost a question.

"I'm getting there," Hera said, and her doorbell rang. *Don*, she thought, and her mood lifted. "Excuse me, ladies."

She took her glass with her as she went back to the front door, feeling pleasantly loose and giddy. How long had it been since she'd actually had a drink with friends? Minerva had been pressuring her for a cocktail for months, but she'd been so busy fighting for Olympus. Every social event was a battlefield where she held a glass she never sipped from, her senses alive to every nuance.

She wouldn't let Don say *I told you so*, she decided. She'd offer him a drink and delightful company, and they could just relax for an evening.

"I've been wondering when you'd—" she said, as she opened the door, and then froze.

The man in the doorway wasn't Don. He wasn't quite as tall, nor nearly so broad. His hair gleamed gold, his eyes sparkled the blue of a summer sky, and he grinned down at her with the same self-assured smile that had greeted her nearly every morning of her married life.

The only man she'd ever loved.

"Hello, Hera," Zeus said. "It's been a while."

***

"Why am I here?" Don asked, looking around the downtown bar his brother had dragged him to. It was all shiny, well-groomed people in suits meeting for cocktails after their corporate jobs. Even the bartenders wore ties. Hades fit right in with the crowd.

Don, not so much.

"You're being sociable," Hades told him. "Drink your beer."

"I'm being a social buffer, more like," Don said, and watched as Heph Smith came through the door, spotted Hades's wave, and began to make his way over, moving slowly through the busy bar with his crutches. At least he wasn't wearing a tie. "Talk me through this again."

"Aphrodite and Persephone are good friends," Hades said.

"That doesn't mean you have to bond with Aphrodite's boyfriend," Don observed. It was probably a positive step, now that he thought about it. The Hades who'd taken a six month leave of absence from

Olympus was a little more relaxed and a touch more willing to try new things, but he'd never be a social butterfly. Most of his friends were workmates or family members. Branching out into his girlfriend's friends and their attachments was a bold new move, relatively speaking.

He might not have chosen the taciturn IT consultant as first choice, but at least Hades had given up on trying to get him and Odysseus Turner to be buddies. Something about the man just rubbed Don the wrong way. He was too clever by half, and always looked as if he were amused by things you'd thought were secret.

Heph arrived, as Hades slid out of the booth and gestured him into it. "I'll get you a drink," he said. "What are you having?"

"Tonic and lime, thanks." Heph said, and pushed himself onto the bench seat, using his arms more than his legs to move along.

Hades took off, and Don eyed his retreating back suspiciously.

"Do you get the feeling we're being set up on a playdate?" he asked Heph.

Heph snorted. "Definitely. Aphrodite picked my outfit."

"Looks good," Don said. It did—Heph's light brown skin looked great against the warm olive of his short-sleeved button-up, and his biceps bulged impressively from the sleeves. Don's taste in guys ran more to the sleek and wiry type, but he could appreciate well-built muscle when he saw it. "I'm not really dressed for this place. I don't think they'd have let me in without Hades." He plucked the fabric of his faded blue T-shirt in emphasis. About the most you could say for it was that he'd picked it out of the laundry basket fresh that morning, and the holes around the hem weren't *that* obvious. His jeans were in even worse condition.

He hadn't really meant to come out. He'd planned to drop in on Hera after he finished work and see how she was doing with the anniversary.

But Hades had ambushed him on the way out of the Grotto. If Don leaned back and craned, he could see Hera's building diagonally across the street, so it wasn't as if he were far out of his way. It was just that he hadn't planned to delay his visit by sitting in a yuppie bar with a taciturn nerd, who was also looking dubious about the whole situation.

"So what do we talk about?" Heph asked. "Beer? Sports?"

Don perked up. "You like sports?"

"No," Heph said. "Well, e-sports." He noted Don's confusion and added, "Video game tournaments. Competitive gaming is called e-sports."

"I've played video games," Don said doubtfully. "But I didn't know there were tournaments." He picked at the label on his beer. "Travel? I do that a lot."

"I try to avoid it," Heph said, and Don nodded, conceding his point. Traveling with mobility aids was probably inconvenient

"Interior decorating?" he tried.

"No," Heph said, looking mildly startled. "But tell me about that. My sisters keep telling me I should do more with my space."

"I work at the Grotto," Don said. "It's an interior decorating and gardening store in the docks district, owned by a couple. I'm kind of the general dogsbody—painting, delivery, that kind of thing."

"That sounds interesting."

"Yeah, I like it. Never the same thing twice." He launched into a description of his day, which had involved repotting rootbound plants for a nice elderly couple, delivering furniture to an apparently-famous podcaster, and mixing paint samples for a stylist who'd given him her number with a smile he didn't think was strictly professional.

Heph actually looked interested. "And before that you did... Something with boats, right?"

Don swallowed a sigh. "I was second mate on a cargo container vessel for an international shipping conglomerate."

"Oh," Heph said. After a moment he ventured. "I guess you need a lot of experience for that."

Don decided that was an adequate summary of years of study and hard work, and nodded. "When that company went into receivership, they laid off most of their crews. I traveled some, and then... Hera invited me to her winter party last year. I thought, it's been a while since I've seen the family. Why not surprise them?"

"And I, for one, liked the surprise," Hades said. He put down three glasses and took the single seat on the end. "Heph, you're doing some contract work with Hesperides now, is that correct?"

"Yeah, rebuilding their network," Heph said, and, encouraged by Hades, began talking about network infrastructure. Most of it went well over Don's head, and, he suspected, Hades's as well, but it was interesting to see the normally reserved Heph get outright passionate about something, his big hands describing shapes in the air as he talked about off-site backups.

Don sat back and took a pull of his beer. Well, all right, maybe Hades hadn't had such a terrible idea. Heph wasn't a bad guy. He was clearly smart as hell, and he'd also pissed Zeus off, which raised him several slots in Don's estimation.

"You said you were thinking of redecorating?" he asked in the next conversational lull.

Heph nodded. "If I don't do it myself, I think Aphrodite and my sister Mellie will join forces."

"Drop by the Grotto some time," Don said. "I can help you out."

Heph looked surprised, then pleased, and Don decided his social duties had been fulfilled. Hades could continue the bonding on his own. He checked his watch, a heavy-duty device that had seen him through a number of late nights on board.

"Um, speaking of houses," Hades said hesitantly, and Don refocused.

"Is the new place not working out?"

"Oh, no, it's great," Hades said immediately, radiating the satisfaction of a man who lived in domestic serenity. "But um, the latest offer on the old house went through the broker today. It's nearly settled."

Ah, the old house. Where Don was currently living. The just-casual-drink made more sense now—Hades had wanted a relaxed atmosphere to convey what he feared would be bad news.

"You put up with me rent-free for months," Don pointed out. "Don't worry about it."

Of course, if he didn't bring in more money, he might have to tap his trust fund to pay rent, and he didn't like doing that. Hades had encouraged him to look at his inheritance as just compensation from dear old Dad, but it still felt faintly repulsive, as if some sticky aura of bad will clung to the cash.

Maybe he could ask Doris and Neron for more hours.

"Then you plan to stay in the city?" Hades said tentatively.

Don grimaced. He was willing to admit that Hades's tendency to treat him like a delicate little butterfly who might flutter away if startled wasn't completely unjustified, but it was annoying. He'd had good reasons for leaving, every time he'd left, even if he couldn't voice them to anyone.

"We'll get Hera elected CEO first," he said. "Then I guess I'll see."

"Cheers to that," Heph said, and clinked his glass against Don's bottle.

Hades's phone, disregarded on the table, beeped at them as if it were cheering them on.

"Not very social," Don said, grinning at his brother. It was fun to fluster Hades.

"It's from Persephone," Hades said, already tapping the notification. He glanced at the text and went still. "Oh, fuck."

Hades didn't curse often. Don went on high alert.

"She's at Hera's," Hades said, his eyes going dark and angry. "Zeus just turned up."

Don slid out of the booth and past his startled brother. "Pay for my drink," he said, over his shoulder, as he strode to the door.

"Don, wait!" Hades said.

"Nope," Don said, and hit the street. He wasn't running, quite, but he was big enough and moving fast enough that people got out of his way. He flung up a hand and dashed across the street without waiting for the lights, ignoring the chorus of honks.

They didn't matter. Hera needed him.

***

"What are you doing here?" Hera demanded.

"Tomorrow's the anniversary of our second wedding," Zeus said softly. "Don't you remember?"

"All too well," Hera said. "If only I'd been wiser." *If only I'd listened to Don, and Minerva, and everyone else who told me not to do it.*

But he'd been so convincing. There were still nights when she dreamed she was with him, oblivious to his infidelity, happily patronizing artists, managing events, organizing their home and planning their weekends, the social strategist to his business genius.

The worst part about those dreams was that she woke up feeling good. Before she remembered.

"I still love you," Zeus said, his eyes locked with hers.

Hera's treacherous heart skipped a beat. "I don't return the sentiment."

Zeus's mouth quirked, as if he didn't believe her. She wasn't sure she believed herself, which was so much worse. "You should go," she added, and that was better, something honest. Even her stupid heart wasn't foolish enough to actually want Zeus around; it just kept yearning after him in unhelpful and unhealthy ways.

"I think we should try again," he said.

Hera laughed in his face.

"I'm serious," he said. "I can go back to therapy. I should never have stopped."

"You should definitely go back to therapy," Hera said. "But it won't get me back. Nothing will. Goodbye." She tried to close the door, but he just stood there and as tempting as it was to smash the heavy oak into his nose, it seemed too needlessly dramatic. She attempted to take a more militant stance instead, planting her feet squarely and wishing she were taller. "Zeus, I mean it."

"I mean it too," Zeus said. "I want to come back and make a home with you, Hera. I know you love this place. That's why I didn't insist that we sell it and split the proceeds."

"I bought you out," Hera reminded him. "After a fair valuation." Several of the rooms were still half empty. She'd consigned Zeus's things to the movers, and never asked them where they were going. That wasn't her concern anymore.

"Hera," Persephone said from behind her. "Is everything okay?"

Hera shot a glance over her shoulder, to see Persephone and Aphrodite walking down the hall towards them. Hera hadn't quite forgotten they were there, but the reminder sent a heartening jolt of energy through her spine.

"Wow," Aphrodite said, her voice dripping amused scorn. "I knew you were scum, but this is some seriously scummy bullshit."

Hera had never really seen Persephone angry before. But it was clear she was furious now, her rage almost tangible, rising from her skin as she glared at Zeus. She'd stabbed him with his own letter opener, Hera remembered. It didn't seem so wildly out of character now.

"I didn't think we had an audience," Zeus said, sounding taken aback.

"Oh, yes, because I don't have a life outside of you," Hera said, and took a fortifying sip of her wine.

"Do you?" Zeus asked. "Because it seems like everything you've been doing lately has been about me."

Hera was abruptly so angry she couldn't move.

"Hera," Zeus said, and tenderly took her free hand.

Hera resisted the urge to tenderly take it back and punch him in the eye. *Vengeful women don't get companies,* she reminded herself. It was just possible that Zeus was trying to provoke her into violence, so that he could press charges and splash a crazy ex-wife story across the media right before the Olympus shareholder meeting. She wouldn't put it past him.

"I know I screwed up. Believe me, I know. That's why I tried to hide it." He gazed at her. "I didn't want to lose you."

"Then you should not have slept with your *intern*," Hera snapped, snatching her hand back. "You should not have tried to stop her from telling anyone about it, and you should not have tried to stop her from claiming paternity support by telling her that your *evil, vengeful wife* would *ruin her life*!"

"Is this about the boy?" Zeus asked, looking honestly puzzled. "I don't care about Semele's kid, Hera. I've been thinking about it, and you're right. We should have a kid of our own. I'm ready to adopt, like you've always wanted." He smiled at her. "Won't it be great to have a family?"

Hera had to throw all her willpower into not lunging for his throat. She reared back instead, choking on a scream. Aphrodite and Persephone stepped forward, flanking her, and she saw Zeus register the united front.

But he still looked confused.

"You impersonated Hera and threatened to destroy my career," Aphrodite said, all amusement gone from her voice.

"You physically assaulted me in your office to keep your awful secrets," Persephone growled.

"I'm trying to make amends," Zeus said, in a tone he obviously thought was soothing.

"Then get the *fuck* out of my *home*," Hera said, finding her voice at last. "Get away from Olympus. The best amends you can make is leaving me alone, forever!"

"But you don't want to be alone forever," Zeus said, and then the elevator bell chimed.

The doors parted and Don stepped out. He was wearing some horrible, paint-stained jeans, and a worn shirt she wouldn't wear to wash a dog, and he looked solid and reliable and utterly trustworthy.

Hera's knees weakened. *At last.*

Don summed up the situation with a single comprehensive glance. The muscles in his massive shoulders bunched, but he stepped past Zeus into the entrance hall without touching him and pivoted, neatly cutting off his view of Hera.

"Time to go," he told Zeus, his voice genial enough.

Hera wasn't going to peer around Don's reassuring bulk like a child trying to get a glimpse of a parade. That would be undignified. She strained her ears instead, and glanced at Aphrodite, whose height gave her a better view.

"Oh, so *now* you're talking to me," Zeus said.

"I don't have that much to say. Come on, Zeus. No one's having a good time here."

"Don't pretend *you're* not enjoying this," Zeus said, his voice acquiring that sneering edge it got before he and Don launched into one of their terrible fights.

Aphrodite bit her lip. It probably wasn't meant to look incredibly sensual, but that was just how her face worked. "Should we call the cops?" she murmured.

Hera wavered. Calling the police would be messy, but "messy" would also apply to the aftermath of Don and Zeus brawling in her foyer, and they seemed perilously close to it. She tapped Don's shoulder, about to deliver an ultimatum that Zeus had to go or face arrest.

The elevator chimed again, and this time she did yield to curiosity and peered around Don. It was her *other* ex-brother-in-law and Aphrodite's boyfriend, both of them looking a little worse for wear. Heph had obviously moved faster than he ideally should have, and Hades's height phobia made elevator rides difficult for him, but they were both there, looking angry and concerned.

Zeus had never liked being outnumbered. "All right," he said, and put his hands up with exaggerated care. "I'm going, okay? Everybody can calm down."

"I'll go down with you," Don said, not moving an inch, and Hera felt an alarm that was echoed in Hades's face.

"I'll go too," Hades said quickly.

Zeus rolled his eyes. "What is this, a brotherly intervention?"

"We just want to make sure you get where you're going," Don said, still eerily calm.

Zeus stepped back from the door. "Fine," he snapped, and made eye contact with Hera. "I'll be in touch, okay? Good luck at the board meeting."

Don stepped purposefully forward, saving Hera from having to come up with a reply, and closed the door firmly behind him.

Chapter Two

"You two are going to feel stupid about this when Hera takes me back," Zeus said, as Don stabbed the button for the ground floor. He folded his arms and smirked at his brothers. "The holidays will be awkward."

Hera and Hades will be sad if you kill him, Don thought. How sad, that was the question. Eternal grief, or momentary regret?

Hades shot him a warning look, and Don shoved his hands in his pockets, so that his younger brother's throat would be a little less temptingly easy to squeeze.

"Let it go, Zeus," Hades said mildly. "You've lost Hera for good, and you did it to yourself."

Zeus's face twisted for a moment, before he plastered the sneer back on, and Don felt a moment of unwilling sympathy. How would it feel to know that you'd lost Hera? That you'd never again get to see her smile in approval, or listen to her slice through a knotty problem with her incisive wit, or marvel at her energy and ambition?

Zeus had had much more than that, and he'd thrown it all away. Don could never forgive him, but he could appreciate the scale of the loss.

"You and your big-mouthed girlfriend did it to me," Zeus snapped at Hades.

Then again, sympathy only went so far.

"You know what, maybe we should have invited Persephone on this little trip," Don said. "I'm sure she'd be happy to stab you again."

Zeus's hand went protectively to his upper arm, before he forcefully lowered it and glared at Don. "You must be loving this. Finally, a chance to make your move. I wouldn't, if I were you. Hera never goes for second-best."

Don walked straight into Hades's arm, flung out like a bar to stop his lunge forward. It wasn't much of an impediment—Hades was too scrawny for that—but it gave him a moment for the red mist to subside.

"That's enough," Hades said, and his tone was sharp enough that Don took his eyes off Zeus's smirk. Hades actually looked angry. "*You* fucked up, Zeus. You fucked up with Hera, you fucked up with me, you most certainly failed Semele and Dio, and instead of manning up and accepting responsibility for any of it, you're blaming everyone around you. You're apparently incapable of dealing with the consequences of your own choices, and I, for one, am sick of it. You're an entitled brat who thinks he's a big man. Grow the fuck up."

Zeus stared at him, his mouth hanging open, as the elevator doors chimed open behind him.

"Yeah," Don managed, finding his own tongue. He moved forward again, and Zeus stepped out of the elevator.

The doors closed, for once before Zeus could get the last word in.

Hades sagged against the elevator wall and closed his eyes.

"Holy shit," Don said. "That was beautiful. How long have you had all of that pent up?"

"A while," Hades admitted. He had the handrail in a tight grip.

"You okay?"

Hades opened his eyes and focused on Don. "Do you want to talk about it?" he asked.

"About what?"

"About Zeus saying you had a chance to make your move?"

Don abruptly lost his enthusiasm for the conversation. "He was just being a little shit," he said.

"Oh," Hades said. "Well. If you ever did want to—"

"So when are you kicking me out of the house?" Don said.

"Thirty business days. Don, it's not necessarily a bad—"

"Shut up," Don suggested, and felt bad as Hades nodded and swallowed hard. Distraction helped him with elevator rides, Don knew, but he'd picked the one topic Don was totally uninterested in exploring.

They rode out the last few seconds in silence, and Hades stepped out of the elevator with more than his normal relief.

The door to Hera's place was closed, and Heph Smith was lingering in front of it. He relaxed when he saw it was only the two of them. "Everything okay?" he asked.

"More or less," Hades said, and knocked on the door. "Hera? He's gone. May we come in?"

Persephone opened the door, assessed Hades with one sweeping look, and nodded, apparently relieved. "Come on in," she said. "Aphrodite's trying to talk Hera into hiring her security company."

"Gorgon do good work," Heph said, and headed down the hall, following Persephone's head-jerk direction. He was moving carefully, leaning into his crutches, and Don wondered what it had cost him to stand sentinel at the door instead of immediately finding a place to rest. He'd done it, though. Good man, Heph Smith.

Persephone and Hades followed him, holding hands, and Don took a moment to make sure the door was securely locked.

So. Zeus suspected. And Hades might suspect something too, but as long as he didn't press the issue, Don could ignore that. His older brother could be discreet.

But he needed to get a better grip on himself, if they'd seen even a hint of how he felt about Hera.

It was proximity that was the problem. When he was away, he didn't have any trouble finding willing partners, and shipmates and fellow travelers didn't tend to expect a commitment he couldn't give, or be upset that he could never offer his whole heart. He'd had plenty of good times and sweet moments, and he'd long ago decided that was more than enough.

But the more time he spent around Hera, the more difficult it was to school his face and tongue. Over the last six months, as she'd divested herself from Zeus and become even more impressive, a shining blade emerged from its final tempering, it had been increasingly difficult not to throw himself at her feet and make all sorts of confessions.

Things like, *You're the most beautiful person in the world and you get more beautiful every day.* Or *I've loved you for years and I don't think I'm going to stop.*

One day, maybe, in five or six years, when her grip on Olympus was firm and she was steadier, he might gently broach the possibility.

But not now, when her emotions were raw and her divorce so recent. She needed to focus on Olympus. And she needed him to be Don, her friend and ally, loyal and reliable. Not some calf-eyed idiot tripping over his own feet to coo at her.

He'd waited for years, without hope or expectation. He could wait forever, if he needed to. If that's what it would take to keep Hera in his life.

And that, paradoxically, meant he needed to keep his distance. Get a little more space, so that he could get better control of the signs he was apparently showing.

He'd see if he could get those extra hours at the Grotto. And he'd find somewhere to live closer to work.

Resolution made, he stepped into the sitting room, which was furnished with Hera's usual bias towards pieces that were comfortable, but formal. No squashy giant sectionals for Hera. She liked antiques and vintage pieces from several different eras, and Aphrodite was sitting on a tapestried chaise lounge, looking like a bird-of-paradise flower that had somehow bloomed in an old-fashioned rose garden.

Hera had chosen a deep-buttoned leather armchair. Her back was ramrod straight, and two pink spots had appeared on her cheeks.

"I am not taking out a restraining order," she said.

Aphrodite threw her hands in the air. "Girl, I'm telling you, that man is not making sane choices."

"Then he won't pay any attention to a restraining order," Hera pointed out, with inescapable logic. "Besides, what do I have to offer a judge? 'Your Honor, my ex-husband came to my place of my residence, which I formerly shared with him, and he had to be asked several times to leave?' He's never acted violently towards me."

"I'd testify that he can get violent," Persephone said quietly. She was rubbing her wrists, her blue eyes darkening with the memory.

"Zeus would sue," Hera said. "And he'd have a case—he was the one who left your encounter bleeding."

"That was self-defense," Hades pointed out.

"Of course," Hera said, and put her glass down. "But unless Persephone wants to pursue charges on her own behalf..." she waited, and Persephone shook her head. "... then I don't think I'd gain anything from it. Quite the reverse."

"Then hire Gorgon," Aphrodite said. "They're the best. And total sweethearts, though I never know what Medea is thinking."

"I'll think about it," Hera said, with the bite that said she was repeating herself, and considered the repetition unnecessary. She looked unhappy and impatient. Was he imagining that her expression eased a little when she saw him? "Don, can I get you a drink?"

"I'm fine," he said, and started to take a seat near the door.

"Don should stay with you," Hades said abruptly.

As everyone in the room turned to look at him, Don wondered if he'd made murder plans for the wrong brother.

"Hera won't want me underfoot," he said.

"Oh, no, there's plenty of room," Hera said automatically. "But I wouldn't want to inconvenience you."

"You'd be doing him a favor," Hades said. "The house sale closed today," he added to Persephone, who grinned back at him. "Your mural bumped the price up."

"So it should," Hera said staunchly. "A Persephone Erinyes original already in the home?"

"Yes, and Persephone will probably want to touch it up," Hades said hastily. "Plus we've got to get the last of the furniture out, get the cleaners in... I might have to ask you to move pretty soon, Don."

"You told me I had another thirty days," Don said. Through his teeth.

"Hera needs to feel safe," Hades said, and to give him what credit he could, Don thought he was sincere. "And you need a place to live while you find your new digs. Seems like a win-win to me."

Aphrodite was watching them, her eyes flicking back and forth. "I think that's an *excellent* idea," she said brightly. "Heph, don't you think?"

"Um," Heph said, and then, when his girlfriend gave him a meaningful look. "Uh, yes, absolutely." After a second, he added, with more conviction, "It's better to take precautions than wonder what else you could have done when things go wrong."

Hera looked undecided, but it wasn't the flat no she'd given the other proposed measures.

"Could I talk to you for a moment?" Don said, and she set her glass down and came out to the hall with him.

"I don't want you to feel that you have to," she began, and Don shook his head.

"Do you want me to stay over?" he asked bluntly. "Even if it's just for a little while?"

Hera pursed her lips, and nodded reluctantly. "I would feel...more certain," she admitted, and Don thought about how much Zeus must have shaken her composure for her to acknowledge even that much. "I really don't want you to feel obligated," she added. "I know you have work, and other demands on your time, but in the evenings, when my staff aren't here—"

"Then I'm in," Don said, trying to push away the image of coming home to Hera every night, of being alone with Hera, of waking up to Hera. "The blue guest room okay?" The one furthest away from the master suite.

"Perfect," Hera said, and smiled up at him. She put her tiny hand on his wrist, and he hoped like hell she couldn't feel his heartbeat. "Don. Thank you. Really."

"No problem," he said, and they walked back into the sitting room, where everyone did a bad job of pretending that they'd been talking about something else. "I'm going to stay for a while," he announced, to general expressions of reassurance and relief.

Hades smiled at him.

Don glared back.

This was going to be a problem.

***

Hera woke up curled on the edge of her bed.

Her muscles had knotted while she slept, and she felt the ache in her jaw that meant she'd been clenching her teeth. She'd been alone in a large, dark space, with a voice she didn't know offering safety, always out of reach.

It was a familiar anxiety dream, and she tried to shake the blurry dregs of it out of her head as she rose and went about her morning routine. Ten minutes of stretches beside the bed. Shower, teeth, face. She ignored, as she had for months, the other side of the his-and-hers bathroom vanity, with its separate sink wiped clean.

In her dressing room, she dried her short hair, taking more than her usual care in making sure it fell into neat lines. Her latest trim had been three days before. Her stylist had offered to come and work with her on this important morning.

She'd thought about it. Professional hair and make-up artists were miracle-workers. But for today, it was even more important that her mind be in the right place, and the necessary chatter and bustle might distract her.

Don had understood. Without being asked, he'd told her that he'd be at work early, and would join her at Olympus.

This was a sacrifice Hera would not discount. Hades enjoyed his work in the Finance department, and Zeus had loved being the lord and master of Olympus, but Don hated the company that was the source of his family's fortune. As far as she was aware, he would be stepping foot inside the building for the first time in years. And he was doing it for her.

She couldn't waste that sacrifice by losing.

Hera sat cross-legged on her bed in her dressing gown, going over her notes and arguments. She'd memorized everything, of course, but it never hurt to refresh.

There was a light tap at the door.

"Yes?"

Hera's housekeeper pushed the door ajar. "Would you like some coffee?" she asked.

"Oh, thank you." Hera set down her tablet as Samia brought the tray in and set it on the small breakfast table Zeus had bought her for her thirtieth birthday.

She'd had most of Zeus's presents to her listed as chattels in his half of the settlement, not that he seemed to have noticed. But she really liked that table.

"You'll do great," Samia told her. She had been with Hera a long time, and could doubtless read the tension in her movement as she climbed off the bed and sat down.

"Thank you," Hera said automatically. As well as the silver coffee pot and china cup, Samia had included some toast, a selection of preserves, and a dainty bowl of yogurt, in what was most definitely a hint. "I'm not hungry, though."

"Can't drink coffee on an empty stomach," Samia said, shaking her greying head.

Hera took a spoonful of yogurt to please her, then sipped the rich, dark brew.

Samia withdrew without further commentary, and Hera went back to her notes. She had impeccable academic credentials—a double degree in Art History and Business Administration from Eleusis University and an MBA from Midaeion Graduate School, completed part time after Zeus's father had died and Zeus had thrown himself into running Olympus. He'd worked so hard, and she'd concentrated on her studies, happy to apply her insights when he came home to her, using her access to faculty and the library to unravel the many knotty problems his father had left behind.

They'd been young and unbeatable, the perfect team, united in energy and ambition.

And then she'd discovered that not all those late nights at the office had been spent working.

Hera was chewing her lip. She made herself stop. *Not relevant*, she told herself firmly. *Focus on what's coming, not what's past. What's next?*

Her charity and volunteer work included organizing benefits, fundraisers, gallery exhibitions, fashion shows, and educational programs. She was a well-known patron of the arts, with her finger on the pulse of new trends and exciting rising artists. She hadn't left the dirty work to assistants or underpaid non-profit workers either. She had essentially been an executive director and project manager for multiple simultaneous detail-dependent projects.

And she'd organized two sensational annual events for Olympus every year—the Midsummer celebration, aimed at employees, and the December Winter Ball, a glittering display of Olympus's unsurpassed superiority in matters of taste and taste-making.

There'd been no Midsummer party this year, and the eyes of the world were on Olympus, waiting to see if the Winter Ball would also fail.

Hera wouldn't let it.

The only possible flaw in her resume was that none of her work had been paid employment. She hadn't needed the money, and she'd never wanted to work for someone else, with all the contractual obligations that implied. And volunteering shouldn't be considered less worthy, but some of the more conservative board members might well regard her as a frivolous socialite, wanting to sit in the big chair without earning her place.

Hera straightened her shoulders against the self-doubt. She *had* earned it. She could do the job of the Olympus CEO, and do it well. *Without* abusing her staff or her expense account.

And all she needed to prove it was the chance.

And the votes.

With a start, she saw that she'd eaten everything on the tray. Samia always knew her better than she thought.

Right. It was time to dress, do her makeup, and go.

***

Hera's outfit had been the focus of two lengthy strategy sessions with Aphrodite and Penny Laconia, the head of Wardrobe at Olympus. She needed to look professional, but not staid, in style, but not slavishly on trend, classic, but not conservative. Fashion wisdom dictated that when you were in doubt, go with all black, and there would be plenty of that on display today. But black was too common. She needed to stand out.

But not look as if she were *trying* too hard.

A sleeveless cream silk shift dress with a subtle origami fold neckline from an up-and-coming designer had been the final choice.

Then they'd spent three hours on the accessories.

Hera sat in the backseat of her town car and concentrated on her breathing. She'd timed this carefully. She wasn't going to look too eager and linger before the meeting began, but neither was she going for the look-at-me drama of a late arrival.

"Right on time, Ms. Rheczack," her driver said as he held the door open for her, and Hera made a mental note to increase his end-of-year bonus.

Then she swung expertly out of the car, took three purposeful steps towards the Olympus building, and nearly tumbled headlong over a dirty teenager sitting on the pavement.

"Sorry!" the young person said, scrambling to their feet. They weren't wearing any obvious cues to signal gender, but Hera made an educated guess at female.

"Are you all right?" she asked.

"Yes, ma'am," the probably-girl said. "Sorry." She appeared to steel herself. "Um, do you have any spare change?"

"I'm afraid I don't carry cash," Hera said, her automatic response whenever anyone asked her for money on the street.

"That's okay," the girl said, and there was something in the way she said it, a mixture of despair and kindness, as if she didn't want Hera to feel bad for failing her.

"Wait a moment," Hera said, and hurried to the wide glass doors.

The security guard on duty was frowning at the teenager through the glass. "Sorry about that, Mrs. Kronion," he said. "She just got here and sat down like that. I was about to send her away—"

Hera took in the implications of that for later review, and went straight to her main point. "Do you have any cash on you I could borrow?" she asked.

He stared at her.

"I will pay you back, of course," Hera said. "With a fee for the inconvenience."

"Um, no," he said. "I mean, I'm not saying no to you, Mrs. Kronion, I just don't have any cash."

"Ms. Rheczack," Hera said, and while he stammered an apology, she mentally rifled through the possibilities. Obviously, the demands of a cashless society meant that her odds wouldn't be much better with anyone else within easy range, so she couldn't give the girl money.

What else did she need?

Well, she was rather dirty.

Hera hurried back outside. The girl was watching her warily, like a stray cat not sure whether she should creep closer or bolt.

"What's your name?" she asked.

"Leia," the girl said, and then looked annoyed at herself, presumably for either using her real name or for giving it up so easily.

"I'm Hera. Would you like a shower, Leia? And maybe a change of clothes, and something to eat?" She would have to call in some favors. Fortunately, she had a near unlimited supply of those at Olympus.

"Oh," Leia said. "That would be nice?"

"Then come with me," Hera said, and whirled back towards the door. After a few steps she realized she wasn't being followed, and turned back.

The girl was staring at her, hugging her backpack as if she thought Hera might take it from her.

"I have a *meeting*," Hera said with more bite than appropriate. She bit her lip and tried again, gentler this time. "I would like to help, but I don't have cash. If you come inside this building, I can get you a shower, something to wear, and a good meal. Please let me help."

"All right," Leia said slowly. "Thank you." She was clearly wary, which probably wasn't a bad character trait for someone in her situation, but was terribly inconvenient right at the moment.

But Hera didn't toss away tasks she'd already started, and she had a few minutes before she became actually late.

"Come on, then," Hera said, and Leia went through the revolving doors with her. The security guard stared at both of them as if he thought he should do something, but Hera walked with the young woman over to the elevator bank.

The security guard on duty there stood nearly to attention and said, "It's so nice to see you back, Ms. Rheczack," and Hera wondered if a linguistic survey of who in the building was still calling her by her married name might reveal some interesting data. It was a brief thought, though, driven out when Leia staggered against her shoulder in the elevator.

"Sorry," she said, backing away. "I'm just a little dizzy."

Hence sitting down in the middle of the sidewalk, Hera divined. "It's all right," she said. In the close confines of the elevator, it had become clear that Leia smelled unpleasant, the rank aroma of someone who had gone a hot summer week or two unwashed, in unwashed clothes.

"How old are you?" she asked.

"Eighteen."

Older than Hera had thought. But still far too young.

At eighteen, Hera had been on summer vacation. Her parents had gone on one of their romantic getaways for the summer, and had left her in the big house with plenty of money and the genial instruction to have fun. She'd done all her preparatory reading for her college courses instead. She'd gotten bored and restless, roaming the big house, swimming endless laps in the pool. Too much energy, nothing to do.

So on impulse, she'd rented a little cottage by the sea for a week, just for herself, and in the vacation home next door were three young men, also on vacation, and the youngest was her age and incredibly handsome, sky-blue eyes and golden hair...

"Are you okay?" Leia ventured.

"Hm? Yes. I'm sorry, I was thinking about something else. Here we are." She stepped off on the seventh floor, and walked through the wide wooden doors of the Wardrobe.

"Oh," Leia squeaked.

The racks and racks of designer clothing and wall storage crammed full of shoes, bags, and accessories were no doubt very impressive if you'd never seen them before, but Hera's target was a specific person. The nearest Wardrobe assistant was Diana, who looked up, audibly gasped, and hurried towards her.

"Is Penny here?" Hera asked.

"I'll get her right away," Diana promised. If she was curious about Leia's presence, she was wise enough to keep further questions to herself, and in no more than a minute or two, Penny herself appeared from the racks, wearing a daring vest and trouser two-piece, and a curious look.

It didn't get less curious when Hera introduced Leia and explained her offer.

"Of course," Penny said. "The bathroom is this way, Leia."

Leia cast a panicked glance over her shoulder, so Hera felt obliged to walk with her.

"I need to get to my meeting," she said, as Penny showed Leia the bathroom and took swift note of her shoe and clothing sizes. "But you're in good hands now."

Leia still looked a little like a startled fawn, but she nodded. "Thank you." Her face crumbled in on itself, then tightened. "Really. Thank you."

She walked into the bathroom, still clutching her ragged backpack, and closed the door. After a moment, Hera heard the shower start, and turned away.

"Hera," Penny said. "Could I talk to you for a moment?"

Hera didn't have a moment. But she did owe Penny the courtesy of more explanation. "She asked for cash, but I didn't have any money on me. I'm sorry, I do know I'm imposing on your time—"

"That's not an issue," Penny said. "What I want to know is what happens afterwards. She gets cleaned up, I find her something to wear, Hestia feeds her, and what next?"

"I'm...not certain," Hera admitted.

From Penny's look of horror, swiftly concealed, she hadn't expected that reply. Hera found it a little disconcerting herself. She was nearly always certain.

"I'll come back after the meeting," Hera said quickly. "I'll—" She crossed to the bathroom door and tapped on in it briskly. "Leia? It's Hera. You're free to go whenever you wish, of course, but you're also welcome to stay until I get back, and then we can decide your next steps." It sounded appropriately firm and businesslike, but there was a long pause on the other side of the door.

"Okay," Leia called back.

Penny eyed the door with some favor. Apparently, she appreciated the sense of that pause.

"I *must* go," Hera told Penny.

"Your dress," Penny said, and Hera followed her gesture to find the smudge on her shoulder, where Leia had brushed against her in the elevator. "I can get the stain remover."

It wasn't a large mark. But the brownish smear against the cream silk didn't belong. It wasn't *perfect*.

She would have to deal with less than perfect.

"I don't have time," Hera said, and went back to the elevator bank. She'd never minded her height, but just for once, she wished she had longer legs that could carry her faster.

***

Don sat back, and, under cover of the boardroom table, slid his jacket cuff back from his watch.

Hera was late.

Hera was occasionally tactically late, if she wanted to make an entrance, or needed to put someone off balance. But Don had been there when she'd decided to be exactly on time for this meeting, and now she was six minutes late.

He'd been watching for five days as Hera wound herself tighter and tighter, aiming at the meeting like an Olympic archer drawing on a target. She was absolutely focused, and even as he worried about what would happen if her focus slipped, he couldn't help but admire her adamant will and sense of purpose. He'd never in his life wanted anything as much as she wanted Olympus.

Well. Maybe one thing, but he couldn't have that.

Hades was sitting by the empty chair beside him, his back to the window. Don had spent the elevator ride up talking about how much he liked the mural Persephone had painted in Hera's penthouse, and Hades had actually been distracted enough that he'd looked faintly surprised when they arrived. Though he'd still shuddered when they went through the glass walls of the reception space, walking past Zeus's large, empty office as quickly as he could.

Without speaking, they'd left a chair between them for Hera. When she did arrive she'd be visibly flanked by two out of three Kronions, and their forty percent of the shareholder vote. This was probably the only time in his life that Don would be happy he had those shares.

He hooked a finger into his collar and tugged.

"Stop fidgeting," Hades murmured.

"I hate these things," Don said.

"We call them 'shirts,'" Hades said. He sounded dryly amused, but his own hand moved over his phone, checking for messages from Hera.

Samuel Janus, the deputy chairman, looked across the boardroom at both of them, his sparse eyebrows raised. He held four percent of the shareholder vote, and was a member of the old guard, the only remaining member of the board who'd worked with their father. Not a family friend, exactly—dear old dad had regarded people as enemies, useful tools, or irrelevancies, never friends—but at least a known quantity.

Unfortunately, what they knew was that he was focused on the bottom line, and Zeus had been very good for the bottom line. The empty seat beside him was probably reserved for Zeus, who also hadn't gotten there yet.

To be honest, Don had expected that. Zeus would definitely want to make an entrance.

And now Hera was seven minutes late. The other shareholders, most of them with one or two percent of the company, were taking their seats and looking settled.

Those were the people Hera needed. She'd planned to be here in time to greet them.

"Well," Janus said, jovially surveying the table. "Shall we get started?"

Hades looked up in alarm.

"I need a coffee first," Don said, aware that he sounded like an asshole, but not really caring. Being the family black sheep was useful, sometimes.

"Oh, Artie can get you that," Janus said, and turned to Zeus's senior assistant, who was taking notes for the meeting.

Don would sooner drink rattlesnake venom than anything Artie handed him. The woman was utterly dedicated to Zeus, and had actively helped cover for him. But she took a minute to pour and serve him a cup, and it turned out that was just enough time for Hera to arrive.

Don pretended to take a sip so that he wouldn't smile at her fondly or say "you look magnificent" or anything else that could incriminate him.

"Mrs. Kronion," Janus said. "I'm glad you could join us."

"Ms. Rheczack," Hera said. Whatever she'd been doing on the way to the meeting, it had put a snap in her step and a flash in her eyes. It had also ruffled her hair and put a smudge on the shoulder of her otherwise perfect dress. She scanned the minor shareholders and their crucial votes, smiling.

Most of them smiled back.

"Yes, of course," Janus said. His voice had an indulgent note that Don thought came very close to patronizing. Hera took her seat between Hades and Don, opposite the empty chair, and let her gaze skate across it with the slightest hint of a raised eyebrow.

If Zeus was planning a dramatic entrance, he was cutting it very fine, that eyebrow said.

"First order of business," Janus said. "Last night, I received and provisionally accepted the resignation of Zeus Kronion as both Board Chair and Chief Executive Officer of Olympus Publishing."

Hades made a muffled sound. Artie gasped, her hand going to her mouth in unconcealed horror. The minor shareholders looked various versions of shocked or curious.

Hera didn't move. The only indication that the news was a surprise to her was the movement of her foot, pressing against Don's. *Let me do the talking.*

From the way Hades bit back a question, Don assumed Hera was also nudging him. He had no reason to feel especially favored.

That extra warmth in his chest was just because he was wearing a suit in a warm room, probably.

Hera cleared her throat, and everyone in the room looked at her. "I move that we formally accept the resignation of Zeus, with thanks for his years of generally exemplary service to this company," she said.

"Seconded," Janus said promptly, and collected the unanimous yes vote by general acclaim. Don tried not to make his "yes" sound too grudging. Zeus *had* worked hard for the company. It just didn't, to Don's mind, make up for everything else he'd done.

But Hera now looked generous, not vindictive.

"I nominate Samuel Janus as Board Chair," she said, and Don wasn't sure how people reacted to that. Some of the minor shareholders looked surprised; perhaps they'd thought Hera had wanted to replace Zeus in both positions.

Janus himself looked pleased. Hera had told him of her intentions, but perhaps he hadn't been sure. "I accept the nomination," he said, and that also passed by general acclaim and no discussion.

"I nominate myself to the position of Chief Executive Officer," Hera said, which wasn't the timing they'd agreed on. She was moving ahead, reading the social currents in the room as easily as he could read the tides.

"Seconded," Don said, in chorus with Hades. Forty-five percent of the vote in favor of Hera. They just needed six more. Janus, plus one two-percenter, or two one-percenters. Or if, as Hera suspected, Janus had Zeus's proxy vote and those missing shares, they needed three two-percenters, or six one-percenters, or two twos and four ones, or...

Don's head spun. He was good at math. You couldn't navigate without it, even if the bridge computers did a lot of the work for you. It was the people here that he couldn't calculate.

"The floor is yours, Ms. Rheczack," Janus said, and Hera stood, smiled slightly, and began her presentation.

Don had heard it in rehearsal, several times, but he was still stunned by her accomplishments, by her resume, by her meticulous and detailed vision for the company.

How could anyone not be impressed by her? In fact, apart from Artie, who looked as if she wished she could shoot arrows out of her eyes to strike Hera dead where she stood, most people did look suitably impressed.

Just, also...wary.

"I look forward to leading Olympus Publishing to further heights of excellence," Hera concluded, and took her seat to muted applause.

Hades opened his mouth, ready to call the vote.

"Before we vote," Janus said, "I wondered if we might discuss the motion a little."

Hades hesitated.

"Of course," Hera said smoothly. "I'd be happy to answer any questions."

"No one could doubt your interest or dedication, Ms. Rheczack," Janus said. "And your vision for the company is...very appealing."

"And well-supported," Hades put in. "Finance department projections support Ms. Rheczack's proposals."

"Excellent," Janus said, though his expression suggested some doubt as to how neutral the Finance department was.

Which was fair enough, Don supposed, because Finance *wasn't* neutral in this dispute. Zeus had embezzled from the company. Accountants tended to frown upon that.

But they were also precious about their numbers and budgets. If Finance had judged Hera's proposals financially feasible, then they were.

"My only real qualm is your lack of experience," Janus said.

Hera's forehead creased slightly. "I believe I've outlined significant relevant experience."

"Of course your charity work is exemplary," Janus said, making it sound as if she'd sold cookies door-to-door. "But you've never headed a company before, and Olympus is a rather large starting point, wouldn't you say? These are difficult times for publishing. Perhaps Olympus would benefit from some more direct executive experience."

Don glared across the table at him. Was Janus planning to nominate himself? He'd need Zeus behind him, plus most of the minor shareholders, but it was just possible that Zeus intended Janus to step in until the heat died down and he could try getting Olympus back under his own control.

"I'd be curious to hear about your proposed alternatives," Hera said coolly. "Since with Zeus's abrupt resignation, I appear to be the only person willing and able to take on the job."

"We could advertise," one of the two-percenters put in.

Janus grimaced slightly. Advertising on the open job market instead of handing the job to someone through a series of back-room handshakes probably offended his sense of the appropriate.

"As Hera says, we have a qualified candidate right here," Hades said. To anyone who didn't know him, he probably sounded normal, but Don read the frustration in the set of his eyebrows.

"Have you considered standing for the position yourself, Mr. Kronion?" Janus asked, leaning forward. "Your experience as Chief Financial Officer would be invaluable, and of course you have the legacy of the Kronion name." The minor shareholders looked attentive.

Don turned a bark of laughter into a cough. Anyone who knew Hades knew he'd rather gnaw off his own leg than take on the wheeling and dealing of the CEO job.

"I'm happy to assist Hera, of course," Hades said carefully. "She'll have the benefit of my advice and experience as CFO. But I've never had any interest in the chief executive position."

Janus's eyes passed over Don without pause—well, that was fair, he wouldn't vote for himself either—and then went back to Hera.

"I do have a proposal," he said. "Perhaps we could appoint you as temporary CEO, Ms. Rheczack."

"I'd be willing to agree to a limited term to begin with," Hera said crisply. Not her ideal solution, Don knew, but a fallback position she'd already prepared. "Perhaps we could review in six months and then make the appointment permanent."

Several of the minor shareholders visibly relaxed, and Don had to stop himself from grinning. She had them. Six months with Hera at the helm, and they'd be falling at her feet to stop her from leaving.

"That does sound feasible," Janus allowed. "But six months is a long time in publishing, and Olympus's recent difficulties have attracted some attention." Those difficulties were caused by the CEO's self-destruction, but Janus left that delicately unsaid. "While you fulfil the six-month term, Ms Rheczack, might I recommend the board also appoint an assistant CEO with more executive experience?"

"Did you have someone in mind?" Hera asked.

"As a matter of fact," Janus said, "I know that Peter Atlas would be available."

The room inhaled.

Don was very clearly the only person who had no fucking idea who that was. He put on a face he hoped conveyed something smarter than puzzled ignorance, and paid close attention. Hades was frowning, but he didn't look horrified, so it wasn't a completely stupid idea.

"Peter Atlas," Hera repeated. "We've met, of course, but I thought he was based in London these days."

"He recently moved back to the city. He mentioned that he's been looking for a challenge. And the non-compete clause from his time at Titan has expired."

Titan Publishing was the only real rival to Olympus's market share. So Atlas had to have magazine experience, and from the expressions in the room, a good reputation.

Hera's eyes swept around the table, gathering information, gauging allies, opponents, and the undecided.

"I would be happy to work with Mr. Atlas," she said. "For the six-month period until permanent appointment."

Which was a nice bit of sleight of hand, because no one had officially agreed to that yet, but in a flurry of yes votes and relaxed shoulders, the deed was done. Hera was to be provisional CEO, and Atlas would be approached for assistant CEO, which Janus had obviously already primed him for.

Don did manage to note that no one came forward to be either Zeus's proxy vote or claim the missing ten shares. That fifteen percent was recorded as an abstention.

Hera didn't look triumphant or defeated. She looked politely, pleasantly blank as the meeting moved on to the next item on the agenda. Her hand went to the smudge on her shoulder, just once.

Don concentrated on not looking too obviously bored. When his knee started jumping up and down under the table during an interminable discussion of website advertising revenue, Hera put her hand on his thigh. He tried not to enjoy that, but as the meeting went on and she didn't move it, his world slowly narrowed to that small hand, resting just above his knee.

If they were anywhere else, doing anything else, perhaps he could imagine her hand sliding higher. He could imagine her turning to him, that full lower lip curving, her white teeth biting into the lush curve of it as she whispered his name.

Don jerked his leg away. Hera didn't react.

When the meeting broke up, she exchanged a few words with Hades, shook Janus's hand, and leaned into Don's space. He got a whiff of her perfume, a subtle grassy thing she'd had designed for her that she'd once explained to Don was supposed to evoke feelings of calm and control. It wasn't the perfumier's fault that the smell had automatically become an aphrodisiac for him, but he still resented it.

"Thank you," she murmured.

"I didn't do anything," Don said.

"You were here," Hera said, as if that was all that she needed. "*And* you wore a suit."

Don grinned, feeling more like himself. "Well, take a good look, babe, because you're never going to see this thing again."

Hera smiled back, and deliberately looked him up and down, making a game out of it. Then she did it again, slower. "Oh," she said, sounding surprised. "Well. That would be a shame." She stood up, and her hand went to the smudge at her shoulder again. "I'll see you at home?"

"You bet," Don said, and caught Hades's curious gaze.

Well.
Shit.

Chapter Three

Hera walked into the office that was now hers, stood in front of the enormous full-length windows, and looked out over the city without taking in a single detail of the magnificent view.

She could throw Samuel Janus out of that window and not feel a speck of guilt. He thought she needed a *babysitter*? Well, she was going to show that sanctimonious fence-sitter what she could do.

Behind her, someone coughed.

"Yes, Artie?" Hera said, without turning around.

"Mrs.— Ms. Rheczack—"

"Hera is fine." She turned to regard her ex-husband's assistant. Artie had worked with Zeus for nearly ten years. She was effortlessly fashionable, brutally efficient, and knew how everything at Olympus worked.

She would have been an incredible asset, if Hera could have trusted her at all.

"Please feel free to list me as a reference," Hera said. "I will be more than happy to speak highly of your outstanding work ethic."

Artie's eyes went hard. "You're firing me?"

"Yes," Hera said. "Surely you expected that? Your compatriot Polly jumped ship weeks ago."

"I didn't expect you'd *win*," Artie spat.

"That shows a lack of foresight," Hera said. "But I don't think we'd work well together, do you? You don't like me, and I can't rely on you."

Artie nodded reluctantly. "Do you mean it, about being a reference?"

"Yes. You were an exemplary employee. You'll receive your full compensation package, plus this year's bonus payment, pro-rated to the months of your employment. There's no need to work out your notice." She didn't need the woman sitting on the top floor like a malicious spider in her web, especially because there was no doubt Artie would be reporting everything she could to Zeus.

Hera *had* considered keeping Artie around just to feed her misinformation, but she couldn't do that and expect Artie to do her job, and a CEO needed effective assistants. She would appoint her own personal assistant to the senior assistant role, and draft another assistant from one of the Olympus departments.

"Fine," Artie said. "I didn't want to work for you anyway." She stalked out of the office, pausing in the doorway. "And anyway, you didn't get everything you wanted. You're only *temporary* CEO."

"Goodbye, Artie," Hera said. "Please refrain from trying to copy any files or take proprietary information on your way out. I would hate to have to call the Legal department."

Artie closed the door, with a violent motion that wanted to be but wasn't quite a slam, and Hera picked up the phone. Her first call was to the Head of IT, who took a moment or two to get over his confusion that she wasn't Zeus. But he didn't sound disappointed, and he promised to lock Artie out of the Olympus system immediately.

Her second call was to Mark Hermes, Head of Human Resources.

"Ms. Rheczack!" he said, his rounded British accent curving around her name. "Congratulations on the appointment."

Hera laughed. She'd always liked Mark, who combined his responsibilities to the company with a genuine care for its employees. "I see the Olympus gossip chain is still going strong."

"Naturally. How may I assist you?"

"I need a new senior assistant, and everything you know about Peter Atlas."

"I've already started compiling a dossier on Mr. Atlas," Mark said. "And as for an assistant... May I suggest Diana from Wardrobe? Penny has always spoken highly of her work."

"I'm heading to Wardrobe in a moment, actually," Hera said. It had been almost two hours since she'd left Leia there. She'd originally intended to get to work right away, but she couldn't do that now. She was a bit hazy on the etiquette of snatching young people off the streets and promising to help them, but it felt like a higher priority than getting an early start on her paperwork.

There *were* a few things that couldn't wait, though.

"I'll send you the draft of my first all-staff email in an hour or so, and would welcome your comments." It would be the draft she'd hoped she wouldn't have to use, the one that announced she was *temporary*—but phrased to suggest this was just a formality. "Could you courier the Atlas file to my home this evening, please? And make sure that whoever you have on it knows to be discreet."

"I'm undertaking the task personally," Mark assured her. There was a muffled sound, and then his voice came back clear. "Artie has just arrived."

"Then that's all for now. Thank you, Mark."

"Thank *you*, Ms. Rheczack," Mark said, and she thought it was sincere.

"Hera is fine," she said. She was going to be repeating that a lot. Zeus had been Zeus to the staff, but she'd been *Mrs. Kronion,* attached and apart. She needed to establish herself as herself. But not too formal, not too stand-offish.

She looked around the office again, and shoved every memory of every other time she'd been here firmly away from her conscious mind. This was a time for new beginnings.

***

Leia was still in Wardrobe, tucked into the corner of Penny's office with a large, empty plate balanced on her knees. Scraps and crumbs suggested she'd eaten well.

"It's not that I'm not *thankful,*" she was saying to Penny when Hera walked in.

"What's the problem?" she asked.

"Penny won't give me back my clothes," Leia said.

"I didn't say I was keeping your clothes," Penny protested. "I said they weren't worth the effort of washing. Some of those stains aren't coming out, and that shirt might not even make it through the wash cycle."

Leia stuck her chin out. "I didn't say you had to wash them. You can just give them back to me. They're *mine.*"

Cleaning up and getting some food had apparently given her more confidence. Under the dirt, she had a face that was all points and angles. High cheekbones, pointy chin, sharp little nose. She had probably naturally pale skin with a light tan and hair that had looked dark brown before, but was, once it was clean, revealed to be light brown and fine, drifting around her face. The center parting didn't suit her. No split ends though, and an even length to the shoulder. Leia's hair had been cut recently, though not by any stylist Hera would trust with her own look.

Penny threw up her hands. "I got you new clothes, Leia. If you're worried about not having a change, that's not a problem, either. You're basically sample size, and I have a lot of sample sizes."

Leia said nothing, her mouth in a stubborn line.

"What are we not understanding?" Hera said, taking the other chair.

Leia looked at her, considering. "I'm honestly grateful," she said. "I don't want you to think that I'm not—"

"Just tell us," Hera suggested.

Leia sagged. "I can't wear this stuff to the shelter," she told Hera. She sounded resigned, not angry, which was somehow more heartbreaking. "The first night there, one of the other ladies took my jacket, and it wasn't anything special. These clothes are way too fancy."

Hera assessed her outfit. Penny, as always, had chosen well. Leia was wearing jeans and a rust-red tank top, with a boxy linen jacket slung around her bony shoulders. Her long feet were encased in white leather sneakers. Other than the dirty backpack, tucked beside her feet, what she was wearing was stylish, suitable to the season and the weather, but unremarkable.

Or unremarkable to Hera, at least. When she took a mental step back and surveyed the quality of the craftsmanship, the designer tags, and the likely price point of each item, she could understand Leia's concern.

Penny blew air through her mouth. "She's got a point," she admitted. "We don't really specialize in...not fancy."

"I could rub some dirt on them," Leia offered. "That might help."

Penny jerked upright, her mouth opening in what Hera was sure would have been an indignant rebuttal. She interjected before Penny could voice it. "The problem is that wearing these clothes to the shelter would attract undue attention, correct?"

Leia nodded. "But I can wear them for, like, trying to find work and stuff," she told Penny anxiously. "This really is a big help."

"You can stay with me tonight," Hera said.

Penny winced. Leia stared at her.

"You don't have to," Hera said. "Penny will give you your clothes back, and I'm sure she can find you something less conspicuous, but if you would like a place to sleep tonight where no one will steal your things, I can give you one."

"Why would you do that?" Leia asked bluntly. "You don't know anything about me. I could be a thief, or a serial killer or something."

Hera looked at Penny's cluttered desk, then at the carpet. "I'm not really sure," she admitted. "I just... I donate to many causes and I do plenty of charity fundraising for facilities that might be able to assist you, but that doesn't help you right now. I would like to help you, right now. Perhaps tomorrow I can place some calls and help you find work."

"Okay," Leia said, though she still looked a little doubtful. "And once I have a job, I'll pay you back for the clothes. I'm eighteen. I can work."

"Don't worry about it," Penny said. "All of that is old stuff."

Hera had seen those shoes on a ready-to-wear runway show three months ago, but she kept silent.

Penny signaled through her window at her assistant and Diana poked her head through the door. "Diana will take you to get your old clothes," she told Leia, and turned to Hera as soon as the door closed behind them.

"Don't," Hera said. "I know it might be a terrible plan, but I'm doing it anyway."

"No, I think giving her a night to relax is a good idea," Penny said. "I wanted to say, congratulations on your appointment."

"Oh. Thank you."

"And I'll put some other pieces aside for Leia tomorrow morning." Penny looked faintly abstracted. "Maybe I can pull something from that department store collaboration, or some of the leisurewear selection... Anyway. Glad to have you in charge."

"For the meantime," Hera said. It just slipped out. She hadn't meant to reveal that the impermanency of the position was on her mind.

"You'll nail it," Penny said confidently.

"Yes, I will," Hera said, gathering herself again. "Oh, by the way, I'm stealing your assistant."

"I know," Penny said mournfully. "I may never forgive you."

***

After the meeting, Don had gone for a run.

This hadn't necessarily been a good idea. The afternoon was scorching hot, and he was sweating like a stallion ridden hard by the time he'd gotten halfway round the Ida Park loop. But he'd needed *something* to get his mind off Hera's hand on his thigh before he saw her again, and exercise had worked in the past.

When he got back to her place, he swung into the kitchen to grab a bottle of water.

There was a small person sitting at the marble counter, watching Hera rummage through the pantry. "I know Samia keeps the ingredients for chocolate chip cookies around," she was saying, sounding flustered.

The small person stared at Don.

"Hi," he said. "I'm Don."

Hera whirled, narrowly avoiding hitting her elbow on the pantry door. "Oh, hello! This is Leia. She's staying here tonight."

"Hi, Leia," Don said. "Are your parents big *Star Wars* fans?"

"No," the kid said, with the careful patience of someone who was used to explaining this. "My full name is Basileia. It's just Leia for short."

"*Star Wars*," Hera repeated. "Oh, yes. The science fiction film."

Don grinned at her. "Sometimes I think you're from a galaxy far, far away."

Hera looked politely uncomprehending. Don walked past Leia to the massive chef's refrigerator, and felt more than saw her instinctive flinch away. Some internal alert was flashing at him. In her neat jacket and ironed jeans Leia could have been the nearly-grown kid of one of Hera's friends, but he'd met most of those kids at the various functions Hera had hosted or taken him to in the last six months, and none of them would have ever carried the shabby backpack sitting on the stool beside her.

And while Hera entertained often, she wasn't in the habit of hosting sleepovers.

He leaned against the fridge, and took a long swallow, half-emptying the bottle. Her eyes tracked the motion, and then flitted to the door he'd walked in and the other exit, out to the dining room. Checking her escape routes.

He would have sworn she'd been relaxed with Hera before he walked in, so she didn't distrust everybody. Big men she didn't know, that was a different story.

"Don is my…" Hera said, and hesitated minutely. Don watched her with interest. She couldn't say "brother-in-law" anymore. "Ex-brother-in-law" required a lot of backstory. Hades had taken to calling her his sister, but Don hadn't followed suit, because his feelings for Hera were not in the least fraternal, and he wasn't prepared to lie that much.

"…my friend," Hera finished, and smiled brightly.

Leia gave Don a small, provisional nod. He nodded back.

"Want a water?" he offered.

"Sure," she said, after a moment, and then, "thanks."

He tossed it to her, rather than getting any closer, and she caught it easily, then took a long drink, never quite looking away from him.

"Samia left us dinner," Hera said. She pulled out a plastic tub with a quiet noise of triumph. "But I thought we could have a treat."

"Do you know how to make cookies?" Don asked. The tub contained flour, sugar, chocolate chips, vanilla, and other ingredients, but he couldn't see any instructions.

"I know how to look up a recipe online," Hera said tartly. "I suppose you're going to tell me you have hidden baking talents?"

"I do," Leia offered. "I mean. Not talent, but I know how to bake. I know a good chocolate chip recipe."

So did Don, but the kid had straightened a little bit on her stool, and he wasn't going to take that away from her.

"That would be lovely," Hera said.

"Yeah," Leia said, and slid off the stool. "So I'll make cookies and you can talk about me in the dining room." There was challenge in her voice, and Don recognized it. She was waiting for them to lie to her.

"Sounds good," he said equably, and tossed his emptied bottle in the recycling bin. Hera followed him into the dining room and closed the door, while Leia, looking satisfied, started rummaging for bowls and utensils.

"I'm sorry," Hera whispered. "I thought about texting you, and then I thought it would be easier to explain in person."

"It's your house," Don pointed out. "You don't owe me any explanation. But sure, if you want to."

Hera wrinkled her nose, a gesture that always had the unfortunate effect of making Don want to kiss the tip of it. "I hardly know where to begin," she started, and then told him anyway, her voice confident on the details, and wavering when it came to the reasoning behind them.

"And I thought... I don't know." She shrugged. "I don't think I thought. I *felt*. I wanted to help her."

Don thought he could see it. Hera, who loved solving problems, had been presented with a problem. Hera, who was instinctively kind, had been given an opportunity for kindness. And also because she was Hera, she wasn't able to let it go.

"So, because you didn't have any cash on you, you dressed a street kid in high end fashion, fed her a gourmet meal, and brought her home to your penthouse apartment."

Hera sighed. "Yes."

"How old is she?"

"Eighteen."

Don would have guessed sixteen, tops, but some eighteen-year-olds did look younger.

"And what's her story?" Don asked.

Hera blinked. "Sorry?"

"Where did she come from. Why is she on the street. That stuff."

"Oh," Hera said. "I didn't ask. I thought it would be impolite. I don't think she's been living rough for very long, though. Her hair and teeth are well-cared for."

"Hang on," Don said, and went back to the kitchen. Leia straightened from where she was leaning over the counter. She'd finished mixing the dough and had started scooping cookies onto a tray, working much faster than Don would have expected. The oven was heating.

"I'm nearly done," she said defensively.

"They look great," Don said. "I just wanted to ask what you were running from. Family stuff? Bad partner? Trouble with the law?"

Leia hunched over her tray.

"For me, it was family," Don told her, and her head came up, surprised. "My dad was a real asshole. One afternoon, we got in a really bad fight and I told him some things he didn't want to hear. He kicked me out."

"What did you do?"

"I had some money, but I didn't really know how to spend it wisely, and that went quick. I slept rough for a couple months, and then my older brother got some money to me. He made sure I had enough, and it never got that bad again. I was lucky."

Leia nodded, although Don wasn't sure whether that was agreement with him being lucky, or a nod of general recognition.

"And you're big," she said.

"Yeah. I was big then, too. And I had a temper. That was both good and bad."

"Why both?"

"People usually didn't want to mess with me. But if they did, I'd always try to mess back. It got me in trouble a few times."

He could feel Hera behind him. When he glanced over his shoulder, her face was the careful, pleasant mask she wore to conceal what she was thinking. Her hand was balled into a fist at her hip.

Leia snorted, and started working on the second tray. "I don't get in trouble. If someone tries to mess with me, I give them what they want, or run."

"That's smart."

"That's *weak*," she said, and then stopped, apparently startled by her own vehemence. "I mean I know self-defense. I just didn't *use* it."

Don nodded. "Your instructor should have told you that the most effective defense is always avoiding the fight in the first place, right?"

"My instructor told me that if you let someone take what you've got, they'll keep taking," Leia said.

"Only if you stick around," Don said. "Running is everybody's best option. You should only fight if you can't run."

The oven beeped, and Leia looked at it.

"That means it's finished heating," Don said.

Leia opened the oven, and Don handed her the trays. She slid them in and closed the oven door again, her back to them.

"It was family for me, too," she said, without looking around. "Three weeks ago, I hitched a ride into the city. I thought I could find work here. But I didn't have a phone number or address to give anyone, and it's been so hot, and it was hard to keep clean..." She turned around. "Some nice ladies told me about a youth shelter, and I hoped they could help, but when I said I was eighteen they told me I had to go to a different place, and that wasn't so good."

"One of the women there stole your jacket," Hera said, the first thing she'd said for a while.

"Yeah." Leia scrubbed at her face impatiently. "She wasn't even mean about it. She just told me to hand it over, and I didn't want to get kicked out of the shelter for fighting, so I did. I just... I'm not dumb, you know, but I don't know anyone, and people look through me all the time, and I couldn't get enough money together to do anything. No one has cash."

"And there's no one where you came from that could help?" Don asked. He was working to keep his voice level, but it still came out strained.

Leia laughed, a sound without any humor at all. "Oh, they all know me there. No. No help."

Don didn't ask where she was from, both because he was sure she wouldn't tell him, and because if he had an address, he might be tempted to pay them a visit and start knocking heads together.

"Were you planning to go to college?" Hera said. "Because Financial Aid might be available to—"

"College?" Leia said, sounding bemused. "No." She looked at them. "Um, if you don't mind me asking, what do you do?"

Don watched her as Hera talked about being the new CEO of a magazine publishing company, and thought it interesting that Leia didn't react to any of the titles Hera named. Maybe the teens these days didn't care so much for print media, but most people had at least heard of *Luxe*.

Hera noticed her incomprehension, of course, and smoothly transitioned to a discussion of the Wardrobe and how it worked, which Leia seemed to find more exciting. When the oven alarm went off, Leia busied herself pulling the trays out. Hera found plates, and Don poured glasses of milk, and they sat around the breakfast bar, drinking and munching in silence.

They were good cookies.

Leia yawned hugely after she'd finished her third cookie, and Hera looked at her wilting where she sat, and glanced at the kitchen clock and said, "Why don't you go take a nap before dinner?"

"But I haven't done the dishes."

"I'm eating Hera's ingredients and your skill," Don said, taking another bite. "That means I'm on dishes."

Leia looked at him as if he was an amusing alien, which was a lot better than looking at him like he was a threat. "Okay," she said, a touch indulgently and wandered into the hall. A moment later she passed the dining room door again, shaking her head.

"She's in the cloud room," Hera said. The "cloud room" was Hera-speak for the guest room with a gray and white color scheme. Don had spent a satisfying couple of days piling Zeus's possessions into boxes and storing them in there before the movers came. "It's mostly empty at the moment. I didn't want to overwhelm her."

Don looked around the dining room, at the light cream walls, at the long, hand-made beechwood table, at the chairs, upholstered in gold and cream silk, and then finally at the gigantic mural Persephone had painted on the wall.

"Well, fine," Hera said, a touch exasperated. "More than I had otherwise." She folded her arms on the table and dropped her head onto them. "Have I made a terrible mistake?"

Don knew he was privileged to be one of the few who ever got to see Hera less than composed and self-assured. That didn't mean he liked knowing she was doubting herself.

"I don't think so," he said. "She strikes me as a nice kid who's had a tough time. Now, taking me in off the street, that would have been a bad idea."

"Oh, it's worked out so far," Hera said pertly. She sat upright, then, and grimaced. "I didn't know things were that bad for you, before. I'm sorry."

"It was a long time ago."

"Still. I wish I'd known. I wish you'd asked me for help."

Don had thought about it. Well, daydreamed more than thought, because he'd known he'd never actually do it. But he'd imagined hitching a ride, or walking if he had to, all the way to Eleusis, and knocking on Hera's dorm room door, grinning at her with as much insouciance as he could muster and saying, *so, had a fight with the old man...*

She'd been a freshman then, with Zeus, both of them so young and perfect and in love, but he'd known even then that she would have taken care of him.

What he hadn't known was that what he was feeling wasn't just a crush, because he'd known her for six months, and because when he was twenty he'd wanted so many people. He'd felt that pull to everyone with energy or confidence, everyone with a set of the jaw or a tilt of their hip that said *I know who I am and what I'm worth.* Hera stood out, because she'd always been exceptional, but he hadn't known it was forever. He'd just known that he couldn't make a move on his little brother's girl, and that if he knocked on her door, he wouldn't be able to stop himself.

"I asked Hades for help," he said. "Well, kind of. I sent him an email and told him I'd run out of money. I couldn't quite bring myself to ask him for some, because I was an idiot, but of course he gave it to me anyway."

"Bless Hades, then," Hera said.

"I didn't tell him I'd been sleeping rough, though," Don added. "I, uh, haven't told that much of the story before."

"Oh," Hera said. "I'm honored." She touched his hand, and Don held his breath. There was something in her face, something in the way she was looking at him, in this still, safe space she'd made for herself at the top of the world. He couldn't call it attraction, or interest, couldn't fool himself that far, but he hoped, he hoped...

Hera's doorbell rang.

"Oh," Hera said, and made to get up.

"I'll get it," Don told her. "Just in case."

But when he looked through the peephole, the man at the door wasn't Zeus. He had rich brown skin and was wearing a suit in charcoal grey and lavender stripes. Don took note of the color combination—might look good in a kitchen—and opened the door.

"Oh, hello," the man said, rocking back on his heels and smiling. British accent. "Is Hera in? She asked me to bring her this file."

"Hello, Mark," Hera said behind him, and Don shifted slightly so that she could reach past him and grab the file. "Thank you. That was very quick."

"I thought speed would be of the essence."

"Absolutely," Hera said. She was holding the file like she'd been tossed overboard and he'd thrown her a line. "Anything in particular you think I should look at?"

"Nothing that especially jumped out. Sort of...interestingly bland."

"Ah," Hera said. "Good to know. Don, have you met Mark? Head of Human Resources at Olympus."

"I don't think so," Don said, and thrust out his hand.

"Mark Hermes," the other man said. His palm was warm, his grip brief but firm. "Actually, we were briefly introduced at the Winter Ball last year."

"Oh, right," Don said, as if the reminder had sparked a memory. "Of course, Mark. How are you?" Most of that night was a blur. He'd barely made it at all, still wondering even as his car pulled up if he was making an awful mistake. And then Hera had whirled to face him in the reception line, and he'd known the answer was both yes and no.

Mark twinkled a smile at him, and Don thought he'd probably seen right through the social fiction. "Oh, I'm very well," he said. "Though I'd best be on my way." He nodded at Don, smiled at Hera, and walked away.

Don closed the door slowly. "What's in the file?"

"Hm?" Hera said, and looked up from it. "Oh. It's on Peter Atlas."

"Okay," Don said. Whatever had passed between them in the dining room had been buried for now, as Hera refocused her attention. He hoped it wasn't gone for good. "How about this? You head to your study and get started, and I'll bring you dinner at eight."

"Oh," Hera said, and her head turned towards the back of the apartment. "But Leia—"

"I can take care of Leia too," Don said. "Trust me."

Hera beamed at him. "I do," she said simply.

And when she walked away, Don had to close his eyes and breathe for a second, because his chest was too full and he couldn't take it.

He had to get out of Hera's apartment.

But he wasn't sure he could bear to leave.

Chapter Four

Hera sat cross-legged in her bed and spread the Atlas file out again.

This was the third time she'd looked at it—a quick scan, mentally pulling out items of interest, a detailed probe into the areas that had caught her attention, and now, the final read-through before sleep, to lock it into her memory for good. She'd started using the technique for important information in college, and it had carried her through hundreds of final exams, committee meetings, and reception lines.

She'd intended to join Don and Leia in the dining room for dinner, but when she'd gone out there, they'd both finished eating. Don had pushed the table to the side of the room and was giving Leia an impromptu self-defense lesson. Hera had watched them for a moment, then crept back to her study with her plate.

So. Peter Atlas.

He'd been brought up in an affluent suburb on the outskirts of the city. His parents, both deceased, were a lawyer (husband) and an accountant (first wife). His stepmother had been his father's administrative assistant—Hera paused to snort at the cliche—and was now happily retired in California. Hermes reported that the relationship between Atlas and his father's widow was cordial, but not close.

Atlas had been educated at a private boys' prep school, then gone to Eleusis and Midaeion, much like Hera herself. He'd worked in the finance division of Spartan Industries for a few years, then as a Vice-President of Sales at Hesperides, a luxury goods brand, and then had transitioned into head of Sales and Marketing at Titan Publishing. He'd remained there for eight years, building his reputation and making Titan a lot of money. Then the Titan CEO had retired, and Atlas put his name forward for the position. Unlike Olympus, where the Kronions held a controlling interest, Titan wasn't family owned. The shareholders elected a board of directors, and the directors chose the CEO.

They hadn't chosen Peter Atlas.

And Atlas had walked away. He'd graciously given a full twelve months' notice, moved to London, and set up as a private sales consultant and motivational speaker. In January, he'd been the keynote speaker at the Olympus employee retreat, the first time he'd been able to do any work for his previous competitor. So, yes, his no-compete clause had expired.

Hera couldn't recall much of that keynote speech. She'd spent the first part of that retreat furious at Zeus for bullying Hades. Oh, she'd clapped and smiled and nodded at the appropriate parts, but Peter Atlas hadn't been able to cut through that haze to grab her attention. A competent speaker, but perhaps not a charismatic one? That could be useful information.

She flipped to the part about Atlas's personal life. He'd been married once, divorced ten years ago. A no-fault divorce, jointly filed. Irreconcilable differences, no disputes, apparently amiable. His ex-wife still lived in the city and had remarried an Economics professor. Hermes had helpfully included a list of her associates, some of whom Hera also knew. Good.

Political inclinations: Centrist conservative. Collection interests: Rare first editions and Impressionist art. Hobbies: Racquetball, golf, and polo. Vices: None known.

Hera tapped her lips, thinking. Mark was right. This was almost suspiciously dull. On paper, Peter Atlas wasn't an innovator or a genius, and he certainly wasn't a self-made man. He was a competent strategist who'd come from money, learned how to use money, made money, and expected to leave money when he died.

But not to his heirs. Hera flicked back to check. Yes, his marriage had been childless, and there were no rumors of children outside it. Though she knew all too well that men like Atlas had ways of silencing those rumors.

Stop it, she told herself. Peter Atlas wasn't Zeus, and she shouldn't act as if he were. It was wise to collect information on him and assess his possible motivations, but she didn't need to jump straight to thinking he was an enemy with a closet full of skeletons. He might just be exactly who he appeared to be—a good manager who knew the business of publishing and had the executive experience Samuel Janus thought she lacked. If so, she'd work with him and learn everything he knew. In six months she'd give him a case of his favorite Scotch—Lagavulin, according to Mark—a nice performance bonus, and a flattering speech at his final board meeting before she took over as permanent and uncontested Olympus CEO.

And if he was more than he appeared to be, she'd crush him without hesitation or mercy.

In the meantime, she needed to be thinking about Zeus. No doubt most of the board had regarded Zeus's resignation as a tacit acknowledgment of final defeat, but that would have been the worst kind of wishful thinking. She recognized a tactical withdrawal before a surprise attack.

Tomorrow, she'd start shoring up her defenses.

Tomorrow, she'd find out what she could do for Leia.

Tomorrow, she'd start working with Peter Atlas, and see what kind of man he really was.

She put the file on her nightstand, where she'd see it first thing in the morning and kickstart the memory cascade, turned her bedside lamp off, and slid under her crisp, white covers, deliberately spreading her limbs to feel the freedom of all that space.

As she slipped into the cool waters of sleep, a thought drifted up.

Really, it was too much bed for one.

***

Don was an early riser, but he wasn't surprised to see that Leia had gotten up before him. She'd made a full pot of coffee and was mixing a batch of pancakes. She wasn't referring to a recipe. Like the cookies, this was something she'd done often enough to stick.

He made sure that he shuffled a bit, making some noise even in his bare feet. Leia had loosened up some when he'd shared his own story, and even more when he'd shown her how to punch, but he didn't think she'd react well to someone sneaking up on her.

She turned to see him enter and chirped "Good morning!" Chipper as hell, and clearly on a mission.

"Hi," Don said, and poured himself a coffee. "This smells amazing."

"Thanks!" She ladled three servings of batter into the greased pan and expertly tilted it. "This is a really great kitchen. I'm not even sure what all these gadgets do."

"Me either."

Leia flipped the pancakes, and pulled a plate out of the warming drawer. "So I was thinking, about getting a job," she said. "Maybe I could do chores for Hera? I know how to cook and clean."

"Hera already has staff," Don said. "Her housekeeper, a private chef who delivers from his commercial kitchen, catering and cleaning staff on call for events."

Her pointy little face fell. "Oh." She rallied. "Well, does she maybe know someone else who needs chores done?"

"Maybe," Don said, because it never paid to underestimate Hera. "Or she'll find you something else. But I figured you could come to work with me today."

Leia put the stack of pancakes in front of him, along with a glass of freshly squeezed orange juice, a tiny china plate with a glistening pat of butter, and a sauce boat of warm maple syrup.

"You don't need to cook for me for me to help you," Don said, because he thought it needed to be said, and then he picked up his knife and fork and cut into the stack because he also thought that the pancakes looked incredible.

"Good, right?" Leia said, watching his face. "Mom always says— I mean, pancakes are one of the things I do well."

Don nodded, pretending that he hadn't heard her verbal slip, and then Hera came into the kitchen, and the bite lodged in his throat.

He'd been staying with her for six days now, and on every other morning, he'd either been at work before she emerged from her suite, or she'd come out fully dressed, hair styled and make-up pristine. Beautiful, of course, but untouchable.

This morning, she was wearing a navy blue silk dressing gown pulled tight around her waist. Her bare toes were tipped with pale pink nail polish, and her ankles looked impossibly delicate as she padded in, looking curiously at the stove. Two locks of dark hair were standing upright at the crown of her head.

She looked sleep-rumpled and relaxed and all Don wanted to do was take her back to bed and slide all that slippery silk off her so he could touch the warm, living woman underneath.

"Good morning," Hera said, and Don tried to respond, but his throat closed on pancake and he choked instead.

"Oh no," Hera said, bending over him, and the neckline of her dressing gown gaped and he saw navy silk and creamy lace underneath. She was wearing a negligee, or maybe one of those camisole and shortie pajama sets. That would be all right, more layers for him to unwrap, while she laughed and smiled at him...

He reared back before she could touch him and make a terrible situation a thousand times worse, and sputtered and coughed until he got the pancake down his throat. He chased it with a long drink of juice, and when he lowered the glass, both women were staring at him.

Hera looked concerned. Leia looked...carefully blank.

"I've got to get ready for work," he said, and left the rest of the pancakes on his plate. "Ready, Leia?"

They took the bus to the docks district, because Don hadn't bothered getting a car. He'd originally only planned to be in the city for a few weeks. Leia asked a few questions about the Grotto, and if the owners were nice, and then fell silent for the rest of the journey. It wasn't until they were walking the last stretch that she said, carefully casual. "At first I thought you were Hera's boyfriend."

Don didn't miss his footing, but it was a near thing. "Nope," he said, with what he hoped was cheerful finality. "I'm just staying with her for a little while. Her ex-husband caused some trouble a few days ago."

"Oh," Leia said, and he hoped that digesting that would take all her attention, but then she said, "Her ex is your brother, right?"

"Right. Do you have any experience with gardening?"

"Some," she said. "How long have you and Hera known each other?"

"We met the summer before she started college," he said. "Me and my brothers. We'd rented a holiday house for the summer, out at the Hippocampus." It had been Hades's idea. Looking back, Don thought it had been because he was worried about them, worried about Don's fights with their dad over Don's unsuccessful sophomore year, worried about Zeus going off to college with their father's expectations in his head. At the time, Don had only seized upon the promise of escape.

Unbidden, he remembered Zeus, looking up from where he was sprawled on the leather couch in the den, his face alive, saying, "And Don can teach me to sail!"

He'd started to. Just the two of them, out on the bay in the Sunfish, with the sky and sea. Zeus was different with no one to boast to or show off for. He paid attention to everything Don taught him and obeyed when Don told him to duck or shift his weight. By the third day on the water he was starting to have the makings of a decent sailor.

And then that tiny, reserved, brunette girl had rented the cottage next door, and Zeus had lost all interest in sailing.

"Oh, wow," Leia said, stopping stock still, and Don banished the memory. She was staring at the Grotto, looking intimidated and delighted. "You work *here*?"

The Grotto was housed in a converted warehouse that had been constructed back when warehouses were built to last, made out of red brick and a high, slanting, corrugated iron roof. Doris and Neron had cut skylights into the roof and enlarged the windows on the sides. They'd first walled up a small space in the interior and filled it with the items Neron had brought home from his stint in the Merchant Marines. Then they'd expanded, and expanded, until they filled the whole warehouse with an eclectic mix of on-trend and vintage, classic second-hand pieces and vivid pop art.

Leia wasn't seeing any of that, though. She was looking wide-eyed at the way in. It thrust out from the wall, sculpted in concrete, painted to look like a rocky cave entrance. Doris had filled every depression and cranny with soil and planted moss and vines and trailing plants. Neron had installed a water feature, so that the sound of trickling water and the smell of fresh green things reached out for them as they approached.

The neon letters above the cave flashed THE GROTTO in bold, fuchsia pink, and Don grinned up at them. He'd been looking for something bright and funky, something that might lift the cold, lifeless monochrome of Hades's old house. The second he'd seen that sign, he'd known this was the place to find it.

"Come on," he said. "I'll introduce you to the boss."

Doris was in the gardening section, doing something arcane with the orchids. She straightened when Don coughed, and tossed her iron-grey braid back over her shoulder. She was a tall woman, raw-boned and plain-faced, eyes and forehead showing the weathering of her sixty-some years.

But when she smiled, as she did when she saw Don, you could see why Neron had loved her for decades. A smile like that made the world turn.

"There's some repotting waiting for you out back," she said, and raised an eyebrow at his companion.

"This is Leia," Don said. "She's staying with Hera for a while."

Leia threw him a startled look at the last bit, but mustered a shy smile and said, "Very nice to meet you, ma'am."

"Ma'am!" Doris said, and chuckled. "Ma'am's for old ladies, honey. You call me Doris, like everyone else."

"She was hoping to find some work," Don said. Doris and Neron ran the Grotto by themselves, but they hired a series of cheerful temporary workers who came and went. At five months, he had the most longevity of any of them.

"Oh, goodness, it's the beginning of September. There's plenty of work," Doris said, and cracked her knuckles. "Any retail experience, Leia?"

"Yes, ma'am—Doris. I worked in a general store, over the last year."

Doris waited a moment, probably expecting some more information, like the name or location of the store, but Leia had clearly said as much as she planned to, and Doris picked that up without a beat.

"Well, you go take care of that potting, Don, and Leia and I will see what else needs to be done," she said. She put her arm around Leia's shoulder and threw Don a wink over her head. "Now, would you be named after the movie?" he heard her ask as she ushered the girl away.

Don grinned to himself and headed to the workshop out back.

***

Hera didn't know why Don had choked on Leia's pancakes. They'd tasted perfect to her. She let the mystery drop from her mind as she walked into Olympus, bright and early—but not too early. Long hours at the office could signify a business in trouble, and she wasn't going to give those signals.

Her long hours would be completed at home.

Cyd Dippe, her personal assistant, was already setting up at Artie's old desk when Hera arrived. She flipped open her notebook as Hera walked in. "First things, boss?"

"I need meetings with the key staff in Finance, Sales and Marketing, and Events, in that order," Hera said, opening her office door. Cyd followed her in. "Then a general meeting for all the department heads—that had better be after lunch. Mid-afternoon."

"Catered?"

A mid-afternoon energy boost was always welcome. "Tea, coffee and cake for thirty, with vegan and gluten-free options. Hestia might want to do something, but if not, organize outside catering. Check with her first, though."

Hestia probably didn't care who was sitting in the top office, as long as they let her run Kitchens unimpeded, but she was justly proud of her work. It was even odds as to whether she'd be unhappy about extra tasks added to her schedule, or annoyed that Hera would bring *outside* baking into her domain. Asking which she'd prefer was a courtesy the Kitchens Head might remember.

Cyd was scribbling busily.

"Schedule an editorial meeting for 5 p.m. I want all editors and assistant editors there, but do stress that it will be brief. I'll be meeting with them all individually this week."

"Do you need me to source the proofs for upcoming publications?"

"Anything publishing in the next two weeks can go out as is, but I want everything else after that sent to me as a matter of course. You can make that one of Diana's responsibilities. She'll be joining you shortly."

Cyd raised an eyebrow. "So I don't have to do everything myself?"

Hera smiled back. "I don't doubt that you could. But let's leave a little room in your schedule for breathing, hm?"

"Why?" Cyd asked. "You don't." She flipped through the pages. "Anything else?"

Hera scanned her outfit. Black slacks, white short-sleeved blouse, shiny black pumps, braids neatly coiled. Cyd looked clean and polished in an appropriate outfit for Hera Rheczack's personal assistant. But not for the senior assistant at a publishing house that showcased the world's greatest designers and best new talent.

"Ask Diana to set up a meeting for you with Penny for a wardrobe update," Hera said. "Anything she can't supply in-house, we can call in from designers."

"*Yes*, boss," Cyd said, grinning ear-to-ear. "Finance, Sales, Events, all-hands department heads, editorial, and Operation Makeover for me. Is that everything?"

"That's all for now, thank you."

"Got it." She headed for the door, then paused. "Did you want me to loop Mr. Atlas in on these meetings?"

Time to be gracious. "Certainly, when he arrives."

"He's already here."

Hera raised her eyebrows. "Where?"

"He took that meeting room in the far corner of the floor. His assistant came in yesterday to oversee the move."

A very speedy acceptance of a job offer he'd only just received. Well, she already knew that Samuel Janus must have sounded him out before he even proffered the alternative.

Hm. The meeting room in the far corner was a corner space with good views and natural light, even if it didn't have quite the same spectacular drama as her own office. It was near the auxiliary elevator, which meant people would be able to go and meet him without her knowing about it.

Don't assume the worst.

He'd arrived early, which was important, and he hadn't waited for her to arrive, which might indicate that he didn't think she was important enough to wait for, or simply that he wanted to get to work right away. Hera had much more experience with Olympus, after all, even if it was the *volunteer* work Janus didn't seem to think was worth anything.

"He asked me to call when you arrived," Cyd added. "So that he could come and meet you, when it was convenient."

"Now is convenient," Hera said. She stowed her purse and inspected her desk while Cyd made the call. Zeus had used this gigantic carved and wooden monstrosity despite all her efforts to steer him in a more modern, minimalist direction. Well, now it was her office, and she'd decorate it as she pleased, in light woods and harmonious shades.

And she'd ask Don for advice. He'd know how to make this space professional, but not dull, and elegant, but not stiff.

So many things she had to be, so many tightropes to walk. Hera opened her laptop and started scrolling through the financial projections Hades's second-in-command had sent her last night. When Peter Atlas knocked on the door and walked in, she was genuinely absorbed in her work.

Although she had also, of course, been listening for his entrance.

"Hello," she said, rising to her feet and smiling across her desk at him.

He smiled back, and something rippled through her.

Oh, she thought. *Oh my.*

Peter Atlas had dark hair, with attractive silver wings at the temples, and strong, even teeth. His brown eyes crinkled at the corner, and he had the just-weathered-enough look of a man who made sure he got outside at least once a week, rain or shine. Hera had known all of this. She'd met Peter before, and even if she'd forgotten his face, Mark Hermes had diligently included a selection of recent photographs in his briefing.

What Hera hadn't anticipated was the warmth that seemed to spread from the touch of his brief and cordial handshake, or the way her skin prickled when he followed her to the sitting area.

Peter Atlas was an attractive man.

And for the first time since Hades and Persephone had told her what Zeus had done, Hera felt attraction. Maybe that part of her wasn't over forever. It was probably cause for celebration, but she was mostly irritated at the catastrophic *timing*.

Aphrodite is going to love this, she thought, and then firmly recentered her attention on what Peter was actually saying.

"—really impressed by your vision," he said.

"Thank you," Hera said. "I'd welcome any suggestions you might have."

Peter nodded and began to speak again, then stopped. "Look," he said, and his voice struck a note of honesty that hadn't been part of the flattering pleasantries. "I can't imagine you're that happy to be saddled with me."

Hera could have laughed, and said something polite. "Not really," she said instead. "I don't blame you personally, of course. I'm just not convinced your presence is necessary. I wouldn't have put myself forward as CEO if I didn't believe I was ready for the position."

Peter sighed. "I told Sam Janus that when he asked me to consider the consultancy. I said that Hera Rheczack, of all people, wouldn't need me hanging around."

Hera raised an eyebrow at him.

"And yet, here I am?" he asked, and spread his hands. "Well, a buddy asked me for a favor, and I've known Sam for a while." He leaned forward, and his knee brushed the hem of her skirt. "And to tell you the truth, I could use the credit on my resume. I'm getting tired of the one-man show. I'd like to get back into publishing. That's where my passion really lies."

Hera could certainly sympathize with that. "At Olympus?" she asked.

"Maybe," he said doubtfully. "Though there isn't much space at the top." He grinned at her and Hera tamped down on the answering spark in her belly. "No, there are a couple of European houses that have people on the way out. Or there's Moloch, in Australia. But you know what it's like." He steepled his fingers and pursed his lips in an uncanny impression of Samuel Janus. "Well, Peter, you have some impressive credentials, but what have you done for us lately?"

Hera laughed without meaning to. Damn the man. She didn't want him to be charming. "So you work here for six months, get the credit for guiding the neophyte, and then every success Olympus has for the next couple of years, you get to point at it and say, 'I taught her that?'"

"See, this is why they say you're smart."

"They say that because I am," Hera said, and why was she glinting at him like that? Far too close to flirtation. "I'll make a deal with you, Peter. You teach me everything you know, and I'll sing your praises. The next company with room at the top will be begging you to fill that space."

"Deal," Peter said, and held out his hand.

Hera shook to seal their bargain, and allowed herself to enjoy the contact. "My assistant is calling in the troops. How would you order the meetings?"

"Finance first," he said promptly. "Then Sales and Marketing, maybe PR or Events, depending on what's coming up. You'll need a general all hands meeting with the department heads, and editorial should at least get a glimpse of us soon."

Hera smiled. "Peter," she said. "I think we're going to get along just fine."

***

Repotting monstera plants could take a fair amount of muscle, and these two were so rootbound that Don had to gingerly break their ceramic pots with a hammer and maneuver the pieces away from the compact mass of root and soil. He hoped Doris had told the owner that might be a possibility. The new pots were better — large enough for the root ball, and not so large that they'd increase the risk of transplant shock.

Don guided the plants into their new homes and carefully covered the roots with the new potting mix. He still didn't get why people hired the

Grotto to do something they could do themselves. It was a thirty-minute job, tops.

True, he was only doing this single-handed because he was big enough to make it work.

And also true, someone like Heph Smith wouldn't be able to easily manage this.

Maybe he shouldn't be a reflexive gardening snob, especially since whoever this was had paid the Grotto enough to handily cover his wages for the whole day.

He watered the plants, checked the soil pH level, and straightened up. His lower back clicked, pulling on a tight muscle at the base of his spine. "Hope you appreciate the new digs," he told them, rubbing at the sore spot.

"See, I knew you'd talk to them eventually," Doris said from the workshop doorway. "They're good listeners."

"Not great conversationalists, though," Don said, and looked past Doris. Leia was in the kitchen herb section, earnestly explaining something to a short, dark-skinned customer who was nodding seriously.

"Is Leia doing all right?" he asked.

"She's a good little worker, and real bright," Doris said. "How long is she staying in town?"

"I'm not sure."

"Well, she's welcome at the Grotto while she's here. Weekends would be best, and we can probably do some evenings, too." Doris washed her hands, scrubbing under her nails. "Where did you say she's from?"

"I don't know, actually," Don said.

"Hm," Doris said, and Don wondered what Leia might have let slip about her hidden origins. Doris had a way of getting things out of you.

"She knows a lot about herbs." She slid Don a glance under her stubby eyelashes. "Should I be putting her on payroll, or paying in cash?"

"Cash might be best," Don said blandly, and pointed at the repotted plants. "Did you need me to deliver these?"

"This afternoon, yes," Doris said.

"I was wondering if you could use me to work some extra hours," Don said. "I'm moving out of my current housing, and my rent's probably going up." From zero.

"Mm-hmm," Doris said and smiled at her husband as he walked in. "Perfect timing, love."

Neron was short and wiry, with longish white hair and a scraggly beard. His stringy arms and legs were covered in tattoos, some of which Don recognized. The compass rose, the nautical star, and the swallows all marked various rites of passage from his time at sea. The double-tailed whale blowing a spume of water up a pin-up girl's skirt while she glanced coyly over her shoulder was...less traditional.

"You tell him yet?" he asked his wife.

"Let's go into the office," Doris said, instead of answering the question, and Don followed, curious and slightly alarmed.

Once they were in the dusty room, Neron moved a stack of invoices from a wooden straight-backed chair and made Don sit in it, while Doris put on her glasses and peered at her computer monitor.

"So, Don," she said. "How long've you been working here?"

"Nearly five months." He didn't think he was being fired. Was this their idiosyncratic version of a performance review?

"And you've been doing pretty well, wouldn't you say?"

Don shrugged.

"Good with the customers," Neron volunteered. "Reliable. Only have to tell you something once."

From a usually taciturn man, that was the equivalent of a ticker tape parade. Don sat a little straighter. The chair creaked under him.

"Well, truth is," Doris said. "I want a holiday." She swiveled her monitor around to show him a cruise ship, nosing its way through an ice field. "In Antarctica."

"Only fair," Neron said.

"Damn straight," Doris said, leaning back in her chair. "Twenty-six years I've been running this place. This one—" a jab of her thumb at Neron "—gets to go off to foreign ports and find new things, and I stay and mind the shop. Well, now we're both going." She nodded firmly.

"Congratulations," Don hazarded.

"Right. Thing is, we were going to close the place up while we were gone, from January to March next year."

Oh. So he was being fired, or at least being given four months' notice that he'd be out of a job, which was actually really generous.

"Thanks for letting me know," he said. Hera would have a good grip on Olympus by then, and she could find something for Leia somewhere. He could give Hera his proxy vote, and find work on a cargo ship.

Just a short contract, though, a couple of years max. She'd need that breathing space to get over the divorce, and then maybe he could drop by and see how she was doing.

"Well, we were thinking, maybe we wouldn't do that after all," Doris said, peering at him through her glasses as if she were having doubts. "How would you like to run The Grotto while we're gone?"

"Uh," Don said, and sat there for a second, his brain stalling out while he rapidly shifted gears. *I'll have to buy a car*, he thought, and then, *they'd actually trust me with this?*

"Yes," he said. "I'd really like that."

"Good!" Doris said. "So you'll be working full time, which ought to help with the rent. And as manager, we can pay you an extra five dollars an hour." She beamed at him.

Neron coughed.

"Six dollars more an hour," Doris said, her smile unchanging. "With a bonus if the shop hasn't burned down when we get back."

"That seems fair," Don said. It was better than the living wage, which was what he was paid now. Neron had firm views on the value of labor, while Doris had firm views on solvency. "And I could always email you if I have questions."

Neron grunted.

"No," Doris said. "We'll show you how everything works, and then you'll be in charge. The only email questions I want to get are 'How many penguins did you see today?' and 'Was the magician cute?'" She smiled at him. "I'm glad you said yes, hon. We were worried you were getting itchy feet. Neron said you were the wandering type."

"Nope," Don lied. "Steady as a rock, that's me."

Chapter Five

Driven to perfection by the mention of potential Outside Cake, Hestia had performed miracles, all the more impressive because Hera was positive that she'd also kept up with the rest of her workload. And yet, the tray after tray of freshly baked goods brought into the fourth floor meeting room by the Kitchens staff went well beyond the stipulated cake-for-thirty.

"Is the catering always this good?" Peter said in Hera's ear, as she took a bite of dainty lemon pastry. She'd forgotten to eat lunch, and the combination of sweet and tart exploded over her tongue.

"The test kitchens are excellent," she murmured back, ignoring the shiver caused by his breath on her cheek.

"We could have used these brownies to sweeten the Events meeting," Peter said, and Hera nodded back, both of them carefully not looking over at Joy, the Events Head, who was glowering like a sulky child in the corner. Hera had asked to see her plans for the Winter Ball, which was always the third Thursday in December. When Hera herself had organized the ball, she'd had general plans and a venue booked by February. She'd tightened up the details throughout the year, and made final decisions in October. November at the latest.

It was the beginning of September, and Joy's planning had barely gotten beyond "let's have a party." Olympus hadn't even booked a venue, because Joy hadn't wanted to go ahead without Zeus's approval.

It seemed that a great deal had been waiting on Zeus. New hires, new equipment, new policies and procedures... Olympus had been in a holding pattern for six months, and six months was a very long time in publishing. It wasn't a disaster, not yet, but Hera couldn't imagine what Zeus had been thinking. Unless he'd planned to hand her a poison pill and watch her choke on it, before he heroically swept in to save them all.

Some departments didn't need much input from Zeus and had kept moving in their groove without him. Some department heads had shown initiative, doing end-runs around Zeus when possible and finding alternatives when it wasn't. But Events had clearly suffered, and Joy hadn't done enough to address the problem. Hera wasn't impressed, and she'd let that be known.

At least Joy, unlike Artie, was someone Hera could probably work with, if she could get over her affront and do her job. Hera sincerely hoped she would try.

The department heads drifted away from the laden tables and to the meeting room seats, lapsing into thoughtful silence as they munched. Hera noted that Hades hadn't come himself, but sent his second-in-command. She and Peter had visited Hades in his own lair for the Finance meeting, where he was still settling into his new office on the eighth floor. By necessity, he'd asked Odysseus to present, and Hera had been favorably impressed by Hades's wily second-in-command.

But this was a heads of department meeting, and she'd wanted all of them there. That was why she'd specified the fourth floor, so that she wouldn't be dragging Hades up to the boardroom.

Well, something to discuss with him later.

She waited three minutes past the appointed time and stood up.

The room went obligingly silent, although quite a few people were glancing at the man beside her.

"Hello," Hera began. "Most of you already know me, but I'm delighted to introduce myself to you in my new capacity as Olympus CEO."

Penny began a round of applause, and others picked it up with gratifying swiftness. Hera smiled and waited for the noise to die down. "I'm very much looking forward to getting to know all of you in this context, as we work together to make Olympus the best it can be." She gestured at Peter. "This is Peter Atlas, who you may have encountered previously in the guise of the competition…" Peter pulled a face, and people smiled, good. "He's joining us as assisting CEO until the end of February. I'd like you all to welcome him to Olympus. He is, of course, an expert in the field, but he won't be as familiar with the way we've done things around here. Let's start with introductions."

She sat down again and nodded at Mark Hermes, who smoothly picked up the cue. Hera watched, asked questions, and listened to people's voices as much as what they said. She gauged the mood as cautiously optimistic.

They couldn't get much actual work done in this first meeting, but even so, quite a few of the department heads seemed remarkably unprepared to answer very simple queries. She gained the impression that they didn't really take a general heads of department meeting seriously. There could be a few reasons for that, but nobody here was actually negligent or incompetent, so…

"How often do these all-hands meetings usually take place?" she asked.

"We met three times a week with Z— the previous CEO," Augie Pelopson said. "8:30 am Monday, 2 pm Wednesday, and 5 pm Friday. Fridays were catered."

Hera had heard her ex-husband refer to the Friday meetings as "cocktail hour" more than once, which argued against their efficacy—at least for the stated purpose. "You can say his name," she said. "Were those frequent meetings a good use of resources?"

Hestia snorted. Penny rolled her eyes. Odysseus minutely shook his head.

There were arguments in favor of team-building and regular checking in before problems arose, but there were arguments against wasting the time of busy people who already had very full workloads. And people who expected to attend another meeting in a few days would find it easier to skip one or two, for increasingly minor reasons. After all, they could always catch up at the next meeting.

Hera suspected that Zeus had used the meetings to perform the role of Great Leader and bask in the admiration of his staff. It wasn't necessarily a bad idea, because Zeus did need external validation to do his best work. It was part of his management style.

But it wasn't part of hers.

"All right," Hera said. "Does everyone here read their email?"

Her staff exchanged puzzled looks. They were managers at a publishing house.

"I mean genuinely *read* your email," Hera said. "Not glance over it and wait to be reminded of the content later, but internalize the information and alter your schedule and prioritize task lists accordingly."

Odysseus was sitting up straight. He, at least, could see where she was going with this. "I'm sure we could all make a more concerted effort to do so," he said.

Hera nodded. "Good. Then these all-hands meetings will be every two weeks from now on. Cyd will schedule a regular time slot. Don't schedule anything that clashes with that time. And they will be *all-hands* meetings. I expect to see every department head there and prepped, barring genuine emergency." She would happily accommodate Hades on a lower floor, but running Finance did mean he had to overcome his social reluctance and turn up to *some* meetings, no matter how competent Odysseus was. "Penny?"

Penny hadn't quite raised her hand as if she were an eager student, but she was making sustained eye contact. "Could I suggest a mid-morning time slot? Those of us with childcare obligations will find it easier to avoid clashes."

"Excellent idea," Hera said, and glanced at Cyd, who nodded and scribbled in her notebook. "I will note that this only works if you do read and respond to email, and if you flag any causes for concern before they become concerning. No concealment. No surprises." She looked around the room, making eye contact. Most people met her eyes, a few nodding. She wasn't sure that Cleon from IT understood much of what was happening, but he seemed willing to go along with whatever she said. Augie was scowling, but that was his default expression. Joy looked at her shoes.

"Then that's everything I think we need to cover right now," Hera said. "But before we all go, let's express our appreciation for Hestia and the Kitchens staff."

The applause this time was genuine and unrestrained. Hermes nudged Hestia, grinning widely, and she inclined her head.

For Hestia, that was the equivalent of a triumphant bow.

"That went very well," Peter said, as they went back to the top floor together.

"I thought so," Hera said absently, already focusing on the next thing. Editorial meeting in thirty minutes, and she would need to call Hades to remind him she was his boss as well as his 'sister,' and—Oh no. She'd completely forgotten about finding something for Leia. And she needed to investigate the possibility of college for her, perhaps with an intensive foundation course beforehand. It would be a late admission, of course, but she had plenty of pull at Eleusis. One of the buildings was named after her great-grandfather.

"Something wrong?" Peter asked, and Hera smoothed out her frown.

"Just thinking about the next steps," she said, and stepped out into the foyer.

Gary, the receptionist, was at his desk, practically standing to attention. "Ms. Rheczack, Mr. Atlas," he said. "What do you want us to do with the deliveries?"

"Deliveries?" Hera said, already moving through to the assistants' outer office. She stopped in her tracks.

Diana and Cyd were standing by their desks, which were overflowing with gift baskets, large, elaborately wrapped boxes, and more bouquets than the average florist stall. "What on earth is going on?" Hera asked.

"Hiccup in the mail room," Cyd said, staring at a floral arrangement of lilies and peacock feathers. Perhaps a reference to the mural Persephone had painted in Hera's dining room? "These were supposed to be delivered to your office as they came in, but with Artie gone, no one was quite sure what to do with them."

"I said they could bring it all up," Diana said, looking a little overwhelmed. "I'm sorry, I didn't realize it would be so *much*."

"But what *are* they?" Hera asked.

"They're welcome gifts," Cyd said. "For you. And for you, Mr. Atlas," she added, in what was clearly an afterthought. "Designers, brands, celebrities, industry heads. Practically everyone who's ever advertised in an Olympus publication. A lot of gifts from your friends too." She pointed to a box that was wrapped in paper emblazoned with the Hesperides golden tree logo. "That one is from Arethusa Hesperides personally."

"And that flower arrangement is from Gaia," Diana said, with frank awe. "*The* Gaia."

The elevator chimed again, and Hera stepped out of the way as a mail room clerk wheeled in a laden cart. He gave Hera a respectful nod and started unloading onto the floor by Diana's desk, that being the only space left.

"You have a lot of messages, too," Diana said. "Like, a *lot*."

"Right," Hera said, her mind shifting back into gear. She could just tell Cyd and Diana to deal with it, and they'd work it out. But Diana was looking skittish, and part of good leadership meant giving your people guidance when they were lost. "Diana, set up a spreadsheet, and start itemizing what's come in and who it's from. Stick to general categories, and don't try to list every item in a gift basket. Non-perishables can be stored in the back room with an inventory. With flower arrangements, you can remove the cards for later reply. Keep one or two up here and redeliver others to the heads of department. Draft Gary to help you.

Clothes, shoes and accessories can go down to Penny, but you're the Wardrobe specialist up here, so you can put aside anything you think I should be wearing."

Diana was making a bullet point list, refocusing as Hera broke it down for her. "What about food?" she asked. "There's a ton of fruit baskets and luxury chocolate."

"Take what you want for yourself—and Gary and Cyd—and the rest can—Hm." Hera tapped her lips. "Where's the nearest shelter for unhoused persons?"

"I don't know," Diana said. "But I can find out."

"Good. Then inquire whether they could use them. If yes, the delivery is on us, of course. If they don't want the food, ask Hestia if she'd like them for the staff cafeteria." She turned to Cyd. "I need you for the Editorial meeting, but afterward, please assist Diana. You know who I'm close to. Anything that's from personal friends or is personalized from the head of a business instead of the PR department will need my attention. For everything else, please draft a brief note of acknowledgment and thanks for my signature."

"I'll send my guy over to help," Peter said, looking fascinated by the entire process. "What about the booze?" He gestured at a tall, narrow box, prominently stamped with the logo of an exclusive whiskey distillery.

Hera picked the box up and placed it in his hands. His fingers brushed hers as he took it, and she didn't have to force her smile.

"Oh, we're keeping the booze," she said. "I think we're going to need it."

***

Don had gotten a few brief texts from Hera throughout the day. It was enough to know that she was happy and busy—which were often the same thing, for Hera—and he figured that if she made it home for dinner at all, it would be late. So he took Leia to his favorite pizza joint, and watched her eyes glow as she ate garlic knots and talked between mouthfuls about how great Doris was and how much fun it would be to work at The Grotto.

When they arrived home, Hera was standing in the kitchen, dictating a long list of tasks to her assistant and rummaging through the refrigerator for the watermelon and roast chicken salad her chef had delivered earlier. She was wearing a grey pencil skirt, and her butt flexed as she reached into the lower shelves, but at least she was fully clothed.

"—and set up a call with Arethusa tomorrow or Thursday to discuss better brand integration on our luxury titles," Hera said, and turned around. "Oh, hello! I wondered where you'd gone. Thank you, Cyd, that's everything. Enjoy your evening."

Cyd left, winking at Don as she went past.

"Sorry," he told Hera. "We would have waited, but I figured you'd be eating at the office tonight, so we went out for pizza."

"Peter asked me to dinner, but I wanted to hear how things had gone today," Hera said. "Don said you had fun, Leia?"

"Peter?" Don said, at the same time that Leia said, "Yes!"

"Peter Atlas," Hera said, and smiled. "You know, I think I'll be able to work very well with him after all." She picked up the salad container and began walking towards her sitting room. "Come and tell me all about it, Leia."

Don followed them into the living room. Leia told Hera about the unusual herbs Doris included in the kitchen garden section and Don sat on the couch and tried to think normal, good friend thoughts about the way Hera had smiled when she said *Peter Atlas*. It was *good* that she got along with the guy. It was *good* that a driven, successful man who shared Hera's interest in publishing had appeared on the scene to help her approach the most important challenge of her life.

It was *good*, and he was *not* petty and jealous, and he absolutely *wouldn't* automatically distrust the guy for no reason.

"—and Don said it would be all right if I stayed here tonight, but is it?" Leia said, and Don shook himself out of his funk, alerted by the note of hopeful anxiety.

"Oh, certainly," Hera said. She started to say something else, and then hesitated.

"I just need to save enough for rent," Leia said. "But Doris said she could pay me for this week's work on Friday."

"Then let's say you can stay until Friday, and we can discuss what happens next then," Hera suggested. "Oh, Penny gave me some clothes to bring home for you. And there's another surprise in your room."

Leia jumped to her feet, and scrambled out of the room, looking all of thirteen.

Hera looked at Don and exhaled. "I was going to tell her she could stay as long as she liked," she said, her voice low.

Don winced. "Don't do that unless you're absolutely sure."

"No, I know. I won't. But she won't make enough for a deposit by Friday."

"I don't think she's thought about the deposit. Or furniture, or utilities," Don said, having listened to Leia chatter about her plans for independence on the bus ride home. "She doesn't seem to really know how renting works."

"Well, she's young," Hera said, but she was frowning slightly. "Do you think that college might—"

"This is for me?" Leia said, bursting back into the room. She was holding a dark wooden box, lined with black velvet. Nestled inside were various items that, after a confused moment, Don realized were not actually jewels, but makeup and perfume in cases designed to look like jewelry, light glinting off their faceted edges.

Leia hesitated, then closed the box and held it out to Hera. "You didn't need to give me a present. You've already done so much for me."

"It's the Hesperides summer line, and those are not my colors," Hera said. "I was given an awful lot of things today, and I can't even use half of them. My assistants are trying to figure out where to put everything, and you'd be doing them a favor if you took it." She nodded towards Don. "He has surprises too."

"Oh, cool," Don said. "Thanks, Hera."

Leia gave him a sidelong look, but seemed reassured by his easy acceptance. "Well, thank you," she said, and sat down cross-legged on the rug, opening the box. "I don't really know how to use this stuff," she said, touching a gold-plated lipstick. No, it was more of a stroke, her fingers lingering in longing.

"You don't need to," Hera said. "But would you like to try?"

Leia screwed the bright pink lipstick out, and then back again. "Maybe later," she decided, and pulled out a brochure that described the various perfumes. "Ooh, this one has bergamot."

Don nodded towards the glossy brochure, which featured Aphrodite in an artful swathe of poison green gauze, vintage emerald earrings, and very little else. "The model is a friend of Hera's."

"She's pretty," Leia said politely, and went back to sniffing the perfumes.

Hera looked up and met his eyes over her head, and he knew the same thought was running through her head. What teenage girl didn't recognize Aphrodite Urania?

Later, when Leia had taken her new prizes back to her room, Don wandered to his own room to find his own surprise. Given that Hera had selected the gift for him, he expected to be happy about it, but he still stopped in his tracks when he saw the characteristic green box on his nightstand.

"I thought you'd like it," Hera said behind him. "But let me know if it's not right?"

"You got me a Rolex?" Don asked. He picked up the box.

"Rolex got you a Rolex," Hera said. "Well, technically, I think they got it for Peter, but there weren't any names on the card, so I didn't quibble at swiping it. Besides, he already has one."

Don noted and disliked the part where she'd paid enough attention to Peter to notice his watch, but it was hard to concentrate on anything but the box in his hands. He raised the lid and stared at the contents, nestled in the cream velvet.

"A Submariner," he breathed.

Avarice wasn't normally one of Don's vices. The restless greed that had consumed his father had been enough of a warning, if he'd ever been tempted to indulge. But he appreciated fine workmanship and good craft, and he was a seaman to the bone. He had a perfectly serviceable nautical watch that he would have replaced in a couple of years. But this...this was much more than serviceable.

He reverently lifted the shining thing out.

The Submariner wasn't a useless frivolity. The silvery ring of the bezel was not actually silver, he knew, but scratch-resistant ceramic. The watch was shock-resistant, water-resistant to 300 meters, and luminescent in dark water environments.

The practicality wasn't why his mouth had gone dry with want. There were more technologically up-to-date watches, with more functions.

But none of those were this beautiful. The Submariner was perfectly balanced and cunningly devised. Even the weight of it settling into his hand felt just right. The dark face gleamed up at him, catching the light from his bedside lamp.

"Here," Hera said, and she was a lot closer to him than he'd thought, holding her hand out, palm up.

Don gave her the watch.

She worked the clasp open and looked at him expectantly, and Don held his left arm out for her, feeling as if he were in some kind of dream. She slid the watch over his hand, her fingers deft and delicate against the tender underside of his wrist as she worked the clasp. He had big wrists, but the watch's fabled expanding adjustment mechanism clicked smoothly out until it settled neatly into place.

Hera made a small, satisfied sound, took his hand, and turned his wrist over to admire the watch face.

Don felt desire pool at the base of his belly.

Hera looked up, her dark eyes gleaming at him. There was a faint question in her expression, and he realized he hadn't said anything since she touched him.

"Thank you," he said, and if his voice came out hoarse, it also came out steady. "I'll treasure it forever."

"It looks good on you," Hera said, and tilted his wrist again.

Don gently pulled his hand away from her light touch, pretending to admire it himself. It was nighttime, and the lights were dim, and they were standing very close together, right next to a bed. He'd had a lot of dreams like this one.

They had not been wearing so many clothes, in his dreams.

"I'm going to be managing the Grotto for a while," he blurted.

Hera blinked twice, and then smiled widely. "Don, that's wonderful!"

"Not forever," he said quickly. "For a few months, from January, while Doris and Neron are on a cruise."

"Oh, good for her," Hera said. "Are they doing the Antarctic trip?"

"When did you talk to Doris long enough to learn about her vacation dreams?" he asked.

"About a week after you started working at the Grotto," she said, and looked unruffled by his startled response. "Well, really, Don, it's important to know who you're doing business with."

"You weren't doing business with her at the time, as far I know." Hera *had* bought a few things from the Grotto, to replace some of the pieces that had been relegated to Zeus in the separation of assets, but that had been months after he'd got the job.

"Potential business," Hera conceded. "But she was employing someone I care about. Of course I was interested in knowing more." She smiled at him, before he could get his breath back. "I'm glad you're going to stay."

"At least until March."

"Well, that's more certainty than we normally get," she said, and hesitated.

"Say it," Don told her.

"Zeus hasn't tried to come here again," she said in a rush. "And the doormen know not to let him up anymore, and if he does come up I won't answer the door, so I don't really think that's a problem. And I know you know all that and you've only stayed over to make me feel better, but—"

"You want me to leave?" Don asked. He didn't like the stab of disappointment, but it was probably for the best. "Sure, that's fine."

Hera looked at him as if he'd grown another head. "I want you to stay *longer*," she said. "I didn't want to say it because it's *selfish*. Olympus is in more trouble than I thought, and I'm going to have to work terrible hours to get it stable again, at least at first. It would reassure me so much to know that you were here, and that Leia had someone to talk to. Of course, you'll see her at work, but I don't like the idea of her coming home to no one. Or of you living alone in some shabby apartment." She was frowning, her thumb running lightly over her fingers.

"What about you?" Don said gently.

Hera blinked at him.

"You don't like living alone," he pointed out.

Her laugh was brittle. "Oh, I'm not that co-dependent, am I?"

"No, not at all. You're independent and self-reliant and I admire the hell out of you." Shit, no, he was getting too close to things he couldn't say. He redirected. "But you've spent most of your adult life living with the man you loved. And before that, you lived with your parents."

"Well, they left me alone a lot," Hera said.

"Exactly," Don said.

Hera frowned. "You think I want you to stay because my parents were the case studies for benign neglect?"

"I don't think it was that benign," Don said, but they'd talked about this before, and it had never ended well, so he backtracked. "But I mean more that you naturally like to be around people. You like moments of solitude and time to reflect, but you also like company and the presence of others."

"So I'm needy?"

"So you want to live with people, which is a rational and normal desire you don't need to feel bad about," Don said, exasperated. "It's all right to want that, Hera. It's all right to want things."

Hera put her hands on her hips. "I want lots of things," she said, and there was a note of challenge in her voice, daring him on.

Don had never been able to resist a dare. "Oh yeah?" he said. "Like what?"

Her dark eyes caught on his, alive and dangerous, and he froze. She was looking at him. Really looking at him, and he felt something spark, an electric crackle that had never been there before. He held himself completely still, not even daring to breathe. If she made one move, if she took one step forward, or tilted her head, or said his name, then he was going to kiss her and fuck up his entire life.

And it might be worth it.

Hera looked away first. "Olympus," she said, her voice cool and businesslike. "I want Olympus."

"Of course," Don said, thumping back to reality.

"I haven't exactly made a secret out of it," she added. "I don't think you need to reassure me about wanting things."

Don swallowed disappointment. He'd done it a million times, and it still tasted bitter. "That's true."

"And I want you to stay," Hera said, and finally looked at him again. "Maybe you're right, maybe I want that for me too."

"Okay," Don said, feeling dizzy again.

"But if *you* don't want to, I understand."

He should walk away, Don knew. He should get that little apartment by the docks district, keep his distance and maintain his grip on his increasingly fraying composure.

But who was he kidding? This was Hera. He could never deny her anything she wanted. "Then I'll stay," he said.

"Thank you," Hera said.

He shrugged. "The perks are good," he said, and flashed his watch-hand at her. "Thanks again."

"You're most welcome," she said, a little stiff, and walked out of his room.

Don's knees abruptly gave out under the strain. He sat down hard on the edge of his bed and gasped for air, letting it out in a long, controlled exhale.

Hera.

Well, she'd always been able to snatch the wind out of his sails.

Nothing has changed, he told himself. *She's still not interested. She likely never will be.*

But she'd looked at him with tenderness and exasperation and that tiny, flickering spark of something else, and he was finding it harder and harder to tell his heart what it really didn't want to hear.

Chapter Six

When one was a highly accomplished woman, successfully channeling the restless spirits of a neglected company into new purpose and drive, it was entirely foolish to keep thinking about a brief encounter in one's guest room that had taken place nearly a month ago.

It was totally unnecessary to bring to mind, two or three times a week, how powerful Don's wrist had felt in her hands, how the weight of the corded muscle and heavy bone had spoken so clearly of his strength. It was ridiculous to consider the way he'd flinched when her fingers had brushed the tender underside of his wrist and wonder what it meant.

It meant she'd tickled him and his response had been an involuntary biological twitch with no significance whatsoever.

Obviously.

There was absolutely no need for the memory to keep leaping into her head, for her to wake up morning after morning, hearing *Oh, yeah? Like what?* echo from her dreams.

She hadn't lied. She wanted Olympus. It was her ultimate desire and greatest ambition.

It was just that, occasionally, she wondered about whether it might be all right to want *more*.

"Definitely that one," Aphrodite said, and Hera brought her attention back to the here and now with some noticeable effort.

She was sitting on a cream leather chair in the lavish dressing room of an exclusive boutique, while Leia posed in a tightly fitting royal blue shift dress and Aphrodite Urania scrutinized her choice with an expert eye.

"It's pretty tight," Leia said, tugging at the neckline.

"It's supposed to be," Aphrodite told her. "But if you don't like it, we'll find something else."

"I do like it," Leia said, sliding her hands down her hips and inspecting herself in the mirror with growing confidence. "What do you think, Hera?"

"I think you look great," Hera said.

Leia rolled her eyes, which was both annoying and a reassuring indication that she was beginning to think of Hera as someone who would care about her even when she was annoying. "You say that nearly every time!"

"You look great nearly every time," Hera responded, which got another eyeroll *and* a disgusted sigh.

It wasn't untrue. Leia was mid-height and slender, which meant, with some judicious hemming, most of the clothes made in these stores had been made to fit a frame like hers. More to the point, with Hera and Aphrodite picking out clothes for Leia to choose from, she was getting nearly fifty years of cumulative fashion expertise. There weren't many bad selections to *make.*

Hera had snatched a free Saturday for this shopping trip, planned two weeks in advance, and had invited Aphrodite, Persephone, and Persephone's young lawyer friend to join them.

She was privately congratulating herself on a successful strategic approach. Aphrodite was energetic and charismatic, Persephone was warm and cheerful, and Hecate was slightly sarcastic, a little gothic, and undeniably cool. Leia had bonded with them immediately, like a duckling looking for someone to imprint on. She was making friends with her workmates at the Grotto, but there wasn't any harm in widening her understanding of what thriving women could look like.

"We have some of the new winter collections out back," the store assistant put in. She was looking at the number of clothes in the keep pile with the unabashed joy of someone who got commission bonuses. "They've just been delivered."

"Ooh, coats," Aphrodite said. "Leia, you need coats. There's this fit and flare silhouette I walked in the fall shows that would be perfect for you."

"We have the Prada and Bottega Veneta versions of that," the assistant said eagerly, and headed towards the back. Another assistant smoothly stepped into her place, offering everyone a selection of sparkling waters. Either Hera Rheczack or Aphrodite Urania appearing in the boutique would merit the star treatment. Both of them at once had triggered the full luxe experience.

Actually, Hera didn't go out shopping very much. Most of the time, when she chose things for herself, she chose from runway catalogues or couture lookbooks. Cyd made sure everything was tailored to her proportions and Samia organized her wardrobe. It was rather nice, to slip out of the changing room and drift through the racks with a glass of lemon-lime water, considering her options.

Persephone was standing by a rack of white t-shirts, looking pensive.

"See something you like?" Hera asked. "Today is my treat."

She realized her mistake as soon as Persephone smiled ruefully at her. "Hera, do you really think anything here would fit me?" she asked.

"I'm sorry," Hera said. Penny's predecessor in the Wardrobe had done a great deal to expand the consideration of which bodies deserved fashion, and Penny had continued her work, pointedly showcasing designers who included more than the thin, white, able-bodied ideal in their design sensibilities.

Zeus had approved, largely because it had proved good for the bottom line. Hera had never really had to think about whether that had translated as neatly into brick-and-mortar stores.

She thought about it now, frowning around the store. "I would have expected more size options."

"Maybe if we were in a department store," Persephone told her. "Although even there, often the plus sizes are on a separate floor, or in their own corner. But places like this still don't have those sizes, even if the designers they stock have expanded their lines."

"Well, that seems both unnecessarily alienating and economically foolish," Hera said. She hadn't had to raise her voice; the assistants in earshot were so obviously noting everything she said. "Shall we go somewhere else?"

Persephone looked wry. "Maybe next time?" Obviously disinclined to discuss the matter further, she headed back to the fitting room.

Hera scanned the boutique, lips pursed. This felt like the sort of thing the CEO of Olympus could do something about. She didn't have the weight—yet—to change the entire fashion world, but she could at least put her thumb on the scale. She pulled out her phone and added a note to her to-do list for tomorrow before heading back to the fitting room herself.

Leia was twirling in a pink and black houndstooth coat with deep sleeve cuffs and a full skirt, an obvious hit.

"Okay, so once we find a lot of things you like, we can start nailing down your style," Aphrodite told her. "Honestly, finding your style points is the most important thing. It makes your whole look coherent and saves a bunch of shopping time. Now, obviously I wear whatever I'm told to wear for work, and my brand deals mean I've got to wear stuff from their lines. But those brands want me partly *because* of my style so their products usually work with what I choose myself, which is lots of skin, lots of drama, hems either full-length or really high, and jeans with heels. Also, I've never met a metallic I didn't want to marry." She did a little shimmy, and the bronze cowl-necked top she was wearing glimmered into motion.

"I don't think that's my style," Leia said cautiously.

"No," Aphrodite agreed cheerfully. "I'm extremely high-maintenance. Like, there are three people helping me maintain this. Now, Hecate is much more low maintenance, because she has a uniform."

"Hey," Hecate said mildly.

"It's a good uniform," Aphrodite assured her. "Black is boring, but stylish. No offense."

"Offense taken," Hecate said, touching her Armani blazer cuff protectively.

Aphrodite turned back to Leia, who was squinting seriously at her, obviously taking mental notes. "Hecate goes for shift dresses and tailored pantsuits, always black, always designer, always classic lines. Then she accessorizes with those big statement necklaces. She doesn't actually have that many clothes, but because she's sticking to the color scheme, she can mix and match her options, she looks classy, and no one notices that blazer is six years old."

"Except you," Hecate grumbled.

Aphrodite buffed her fingernails. "Hey, I'm a professional."

"What about Persephone?" Leia asked, and they both turned to scrutinize Persephone, who smiled back at them.

Recalling their recent conversation, Hera felt a flutter of unease, but kept her peace. Persephone was more than capable of changing the conversation herself, if she wanted to.

"Not a uniform," Aphrodite said. "Persephone goes for a variety of styles, but she favors flowing lines, lots of color and lots of patterns, especially florals. She's not big on accessories, so she lets her clothes make the statement."

"My tattoos are basically an accessory, anyway," Persephone said, holding out her bared arms for Leia to admire the bright floral designs twining from shoulders to wrists.

"She sometimes gets a pattern clash that doesn't work, but most of the time, Persephone looks gorgeous and vibrant," Aphrodite said. "And hot as hell."

"Yes, I do," Persephone said. "Thank you for noticing."

"And Hera?" Leia asked, and Hera found herself standing under their scrutiny, not quite knowing what to do with her hands.

"You try," Aphrodite said. "What does Hera wear, and what does that say?"

"Um...she mostly wears dresses or skirts and tops. She doesn't wear many patterns. Not much black, but the colors are kind of... I don't know how to describe it. They're not like Persephone's colors."

"Muted or rich shades, no brights or pastels," Aphrodite said crisply. "You're doing great."

"Her going out dresses are really nice, colors like teal green or deep purple. Her clothes always look like they're brand new and they've got like, lines. Structure. And she wears really high heels."

"And what does all of that tell you?" Aphrodite asked.

"Hera always looks perfect," Leia said. "But not like, beautiful-perfect, not like you. Even though she does look beautiful. But she looks really strong. Bigger than she actually is. Powerful."

Hera, to her intense pique, blushed.

Aphrodite clapped delightedly. "Exactly! Now, a lot of that is personality, because no one in their right mind is going to fuck with Hera Rheczack. But the structural lines and subtle shoulder pads help present that vibe, and so do the spike heels. Most of the time people don't even stop to think that, in reality, they could pick her up and put her in their pocket."

"Excuse me?" Hera said.

Leia was still scrutinizing Hera. "And I've been living with you for nearly a month, but I've never seen you wear the same thing twice. Except your PJs."

"I do have *some* repeats," Hera said.

"Part of Hera's job means that she can't be photographed in the same thing twice, unless it's clearly on purpose," Aphrodite told Leia. "And she can't be sure when she's going to be photographed."

Leia looked appalled. "Isn't that a waste?"

"I don't actually buy that many clothes," Hera said. "For special occasions, for example, I'm usually lent something in return for the designer getting credit in the event photos. Those clothes go back to the designers afterwards."

"What happens to the clothes after that?"

"Well, if it's unique, a gown might go in the designer's archives. Otherwise, it'll eventually go to a sample sale, or perhaps a fashion renting service."

"Or sneaked out to a consignment store, if an assistant needs to make rent," Persephone said, and then added hastily, "I've heard."

Leia still looked alarmed. "But all that work."

"Perhaps I should repeat items more often," Hera admitted. "As Aphrodite says, it is possible to do that in a purposeful manner." She was trying to remember what Leia had been wearing when she'd first encountered her. A black t-shirt, and sturdy walking pants, she thought. Well worn. Leia often wore the jeans Penny had given her, but Hera had assumed that was because they were more appropriate for her work in the garden center section. Perhaps it was instead a gravitation towards rewearability.

Aphrodite had apparently come to the same conclusion. "Sustainability," she said, snapping her fingers. "That's a style point for you. How do you feel about linen? Merino? Natural colors? That's a muted palette and various shades of beige, by the way, not 'all the colors in nature.'"

Leia shrugged. "I guess?"

"I'm going to take that as a no. Thrifting? Vintage?"

Leia's nose wrinkled. "Is that like hand-me-downs?"

Aphrodite earnestly took Leia's unresisting hand in both of hers. "Ah, my young apprentice," she said. "You have so much to learn." She looked at Leia's keep pile, and then beamed at the closest assistant. "I'll take all of those, please. And this coat."

"Oh," Hera said, reaching for her purse. "Let me—"

"No way," Aphrodite said. "This is the most fun I've had in *weeks*."

"Look," Hecate said in a stage whisper to Persephone. "Mom and Mom are fighting over the check."

Leia giggled, her cheeks pink, and Hera conceded with as much grace as she could muster. The happy assistants packaged everything up, promising to have it all delivered to Hera's apartment by the end of the day. Hera and Leia had already agreed that Leia would be responsible for unpacking and hanging everything herself. That way Leia would know where everything in her closet was located, and they'd both avoid getting on Samia's bad side, a crucial element of maintaining domestic harmony.

"Okay," Aphrodite said, spinning back towards them and tucking her credit card back into her skintight back pocket. "I know *exactly* where we need to go next." She strode towards the door, her glittering hair streaming behind her.

Aphrodite's security consultant, Gorgo, had spent the last hour standing in the corner, apparently ignoring them, but situated so that she had eyes on the street, the front door, and the women in the changing room space. She stepped forward now and handed Aphrodite a baseball cap and a pair of oversized sunglasses.

"Will that really work?" Hecate asked.

"For about twenty minutes, if we keep moving," Aphrodite said, bundling her hair into a messy ponytail and pulling it through the back of the cap. "Okay, let's go!"

Hera let herself be swept up in the storm as Aphrodite's driver took them to the next location, a narrow street in one of the bohemian neighborhoods off Ida Park, where artisanal candle stores, hip cupcake dispensaries and crowded thrift stores vied for the attention of the crowds.

Gorgo didn't like the mob, and had the driver illegally park right outside Aphrodite's chosen target. The younger women tumbled out of the car under Gorgo's stern eye, and Hera trailed behind them, thinking.

What did Leia's style say about her? It was fairly quiet, but self-assured, like the girl herself. She liked color, but not bold explosions. She had an eye for fabrics and prints that would wear well season after season, though it was difficult to tell how much of that was genuine interest and how much was learned reflex.

And if was reflex, where had she *learned* it?

Don had been evidently and annoyingly right about how much better Hera felt to be living with others again. Seeing Leia every morning for breakfast was starting to feel less like a nice surprise and more like a good and natural part of her day. Don's off-tune humming as he brewed coffee, Leia's delighted reports on her work at the Grotto, the cheerful trash talk while the two of them played video games—even if Hera was in her study or bedroom, trying to finish revising proofs or approving the Winter Ball theme proposal, she kept the door open so that she could hear them. It made the apartment feel alive.

It made her feel alive.

The Friday Leia had asked for had come and gone three weeks ago, and after confirming that she was happy to have Leia stay longer, Hera had carefully avoided asking when that might end. Because she didn't want her to go. Leia was bright, effusive, kind, and open about everything—except who she was and where she'd come from.

More than once, Hera had been tempted to set her considerable resources to work on tracking Leia's past, but that would be a betrayal. Besides, Don had warned her not to do it, and on matters related to family estrangement and living rough, Hera had decided to defer to him.

Hera had never been tempted to run from her own family. Her parents had given her everything she'd ever asked for. She'd been safe, sheltered, financially supported, expensively educated, and ridiculously privileged in ways she still didn't always recognize.

But she hadn't been loved. Not really. Her parents had used their limited capacity for that on each other.

Hera had wondered if Leia might have possibly come from something similar, at least as far as parental interest went. But there were other, interesting hints for any reasonable observer.

Leia hadn't known who Aphrodite Urania was. She hadn't known how to use makeup or a smart phone, although she'd picked both up with commendable speed, and was exploring a whole new world of dramatic eyeshadow. The internet wasn't a complete mystery to her, but her access had clearly been limited. She *could* cook, clean, garden, and sew—the last, Hera had discovered when she'd ripped the cuff of her own blazer, and Leia had repaired it in a couple of minutes, with tiny, near-invisible stitches.

Don had let slip that at work her math skills were great, and she was comfortable around all the workshop tools, but couldn't talk about TV or movies with the other young part-timers. She was familiar with classic literature and read voraciously, but anything published in the last fifty years was new to her. Don had taken her to the public library with proof of address, and watching Leia learn she could access library books from her phone had been one of Hera's best moments in the last month.

And yet, she'd showed no interest in applying to colleges. Perhaps that was just her pragmatism; without proof of identity or any academic transcripts, it would be very difficult to secure her a place anywhere. But it seemed more as if she'd never considered it a viable pathway.

Hera had some thoughts, a few educated guesses and a theory or two she was keeping in reserve. But until Leia offered any information herself, Hera had resolved not to inquire any further, no matter how incredibly frustrating it was not to know everything about any given situation, immediately. Possibly, this was personal growth.

Walking into a second-hand clothing store probably counted too.

Persephone had immediately brightened when she'd spotted the well-stocked plus-size section, something Aphrodite had probably considered in her choice of destination, and had disappeared into a changing booth with Hecate and an armful of polka dots and florals. Aphrodite and Leia were hunting through the Americana section. There were no attentive assistants here, only a couple of gloomy cashiers in their early twenties who had obviously recognized Aphrodite immediately, and just as obviously decided that caring about the presence of the world's most renowned supermodel was completely beneath them.

Hera herself wasn't in any disguise, but she also wasn't quite as recognizable. She wandered over to an accessories display, and had picked out a 70s bracelet with chunky resin beads that Aphrodite might like when the first paparazzi motorbikes arrived.

"Incoming," Gorgo said, and Aphrodite straightened and sighed.

"Okay," she said, looking resigned, and looked at Leia. "The photographers are here. They can't come in or take photos of us inside the store, but they're going to start shooting the second we hit the street. Just follow Gorgo and go straight to the car. If there's any talking, Hera or I will do it, okay? If anyone asks you a question or shouts something to get a rise out of you, just ignore them."

"Do we have to go right now?" Leia asked. She was holding a denim jacket covered in patches, looking dismayed.

"Nope, but the longer we wait, the more there'll be," Aphrodite said. "Up to you."

Hecate and Persephone had emerged from the fitting room. Persephone looked worried. Hecate...looked like a lawyer. That could be helpful.

"We have a website, if you want to look at stuff online," one of the cashiers volunteered, looking sympathetically at Leia.

"Thank you," Leia said politely. "I'll take this, please."

Hera held her tongue while Leia pulled out her own wallet and paid for the jacket in crisp twenty-dollar bills. She clearly wanted to feel as if she had some control over the situation, and Hera couldn't blame her. Media attention had been a useful tool in her campaign to take Olympus, but it was the kind of tool that could turn in the user's hand, cutting deeply at a moment's notice.

Aphrodite shook her hair out, adjusted her cleavage, and flashed Hera a bright smile. "Let's do it," she said, and they followed Gorgo out.

There were perhaps eight reporters there, and they all began shouting at once, the flash of their cameras an annoying assault on the eye. Leia had been tucked in between Persephone's reassuring presence and Hecate's sharp aggression. She flinched at the wall of sound, but kept going. Hera, bringing up the rear, smiled impartially.

"Aphrodite! Any news about the new *Binding* chapter?"

"Hera! Why is Zeus's brother living with you?" Hera had expected that one would come up eventually. She didn't break stride.

"Aphrodite! Why are you shopping with Hera? Is it true you two are hooking up?"

Hera hadn't expected that one, and hoped her face didn't show it.

Aphrodite grinned. "Sorry to disappoint you, Derek," she said breezily. "You know I'm a one-man girl these days."

The photographer grinned back at her. "Who're your other friends?" he asked.

"No comment," Aphrodite said. "Come on, man, I'm allowed to have friends. Don't be a dick."

"That's Persephone Erinyes, Demeter's daughter," someone else said, and a red-haired man pushed forward. "Persephone, is it true your mother cut you off? Is your mom a psycho?"

Persephone ignored him, but Leia looked astounded, and Hecate's head came up in a sharp gesture that promised nothing good for that reporter.

"Move aside," Gorgo said, and jerked the car door open. Hecate motioned Persephone in first, and Leia after her, while Aphrodite flirted with the cameras, answering questions for the reporters who could stay civil and pointedly ignoring the ones who couldn't. Hera abstractly admired her poise.

There was one reporter standing to the side of the pack, her camera dangling from her hand. A younger woman, with black hair and pink cheeks, who looked vaguely familiar. Persephone stared at her as the car started to move and the paparazzi scattered.

"Who's that?" Hera asked.

Persephone shot her a quick glance, then looked away. "Semele," she said quietly.

Semele Cadmida. Zeus's former mistress. The mother of his son.

"Oh," Hera said, and turned determinedly back to the group in the car. "Well. I think we all deserve ice cream back at my place. What do you say?"

Chapter Seven

By the beginning of October, Hera felt that the bi-weekly all-hands meetings were working well enough that she could make them permanent best practice. She kept an additional weekly meeting with Mark Hermes, though, because he wasn't just up-to-date with his own department, but shockingly knowledgeable about what was happening everywhere else. And, to her immense gratitude, he was willing to share the information, always scrupulously clear about what he knew was real and what was only hearsay.

Hera had thought herself an expert in networking, until she'd seen Mark at work. Now she had Cyd sit in with them, so that Hera could focus on the torrent of information while Cyd took notes.

"The interns have finished their first rotation," Mark said. "No resignations, and they're suitably terrified by the scope of their task. Which brings me to the final point today. The deferment was a good idea, but Persephone can't stay an ordinary intern."

Hera arched an eyebrow at him.

"She's too good," he explained. "She flusters the others, because she knows who everyone is and how the place works. She's not perfect, but she's much more like someone nearing the end of the intern program than someone starting out. With your permission, I want to try something different."

"Hm," Hera said, and held her hand up to call for a pause while she thought. Persephone had some entirely understandable qualms about nepotism, both perceived and actual, and some less understandable fears that she might not truly deserve the praise she received for her artistic skill, sunny demeanor, and excellent work ethic. Less understandable, that was, unless you'd met her mother, which Hera unfortunately had.

"Take it to Peter," she decided.

"Excuse me?"

"Your proposal. Your something different. Take it to Peter Atlas, present the case. Without naming Persephone, if you can. Tell him that you have an intern who unfortunately had to suspend her involvement part way through the program last year, but is now back, and ask him to approve whatever you want him to do."

"And if he declines, and says she should serve out her term?"

"Then that's the decision," Hera said. "Persephone knew that being an intern again would be awkward, but she's still determined to work for the best. And unless I'm much mistaken, that's still us."

Mark smiled. "Yes, it is."

"And, Mark, once Peter leaves, you might need to be the final arbiter on Persephone's future with the company. She's too closely entwined with Hades and myself for me to even pretend to neutrality."

"I...wasn't sure you'd care about that."

"I like to think I have a little more sense of the appropriate than Zeus did," Hera said dryly. "But no, as it happens, I don't have any particular problem with doing good people favors, and Persephone is good people.

However, she doesn't feel the same way about favors, and I respect her desires in this matter."

"Noted," Mark said and picked up his laptop. Hera got to her feet, but he stayed sitting a moment, frowning.

"Something else?" she said.

"Have you checked in with Events since the last general meeting?"

Cyd looked up.

"No," Hera said. "Should I?" At the last all-hands meeting, Joy had reported that planning for the Winter Ball was well underway. The most crucial bookings had been made and Events would have a final budget proposal ready for approval soon. Joy had sounded confident and professional, and Hera was deliberately trying not to micromanage, so she hadn't inquired further.

"I don't have an intern in Events," Mark said. "Joy requested we not send them any until January. So this is only hearsay, but the rumor is that she's taking on a lot of the Winter Ball organizing herself. Her people haven't seen much of the planning."

"Ah. Thank you, Mark. Talk to Peter about Persephone and have a good weekend."

"You too," Mark said, and left, looking considerably lighter now that he'd taken a weight off his own shoulders and laid it on hers.

"Should I get Joy on the line now?" Cyd asked.

"I suppose so," Hera said, sounding unenthusiastic even to her own ears.

Joy, predictably, was both defensive and suspicious about the call.

"It's all fine," she said, in response to Hera's delicate inquiry. "I have the Minos Center booked, and we've put the deposit down for the caterers."

"The same caterers as last year?" Hera asked.

"Yes," Joy said, a little snippily. Last year, Joy had insisted on using heavy platters that hadn't been pre-approved by the catering manager, and he'd refused to have his staff use them, citing health and safety concerns. Joy had drafted the interns instead. It had not gone well.

"The musicians?"

"We're in the final negotiations. I'm taking care of that personally." Joy paused. "I'm taking care of a lot of this personally," she said, sounding calmer. "I want to do a good job, Hera. I know the Winter Ball was your baby, but you're CEO now, and I've got this. Can you just trust me?"

That was the problem. Hera wasn't sure she did.

But she *should*. Joy had made a few mistakes, but she was otherwise competent and experienced. There was no reason not to extend the same trust Hera herself had wanted from the Board; recognition that while she might not be their personally most desired choice, she was more than capable of the job. It made sense that, in a bid to prove herself, Joy was managing a lot of the work herself.

"Yes, of course," Hera said.

"Thank you," Joy said, sounding surprised and pleased.

Hera bit her lip. She wanted to say "Please keep me informed of any problems." Instead, she said, "Thank you, Joy," and hung up.

Cyd, who had hovered in the room, ready to take notes or leap into action, smiled at her. "And now you can go home."

Hera slumped and rubbed her eyes. "Now I have this gallery opening."

Cyd eyed her. "Or you could have an early night?" she suggested.

"Do I look that bad? No, I can't. I'm chair of the Emerging Artists Trust." She blinked up at Cyd. "You know that. You wrote most of my speech."

Cyd put her notebook down. "Yes. And your speech for the Opera House refurbishment fundraiser, and the opening remarks for the Young Designer awards. Then I researched the guests at the Unhoused Youth Center fundraiser, which wasn't previously on your list, so that you knew who to talk to about getting on their board."

"Well, they need someone on their board who can target big sponsors," Hera began, and saw Cyd's face. "You're saying I'm doing too much."

"I'm saying that for ten years you ran charitable trusts and boards all over this city as if it was your job. And now you've got a job. And a kid."

"She's not my kid," Hera said, a little more sharply than Cyd deserved. "She's an adult woman who's staying with me for a while. Besides, if I were a man, would anyone ask if I were neglecting my kid for my job?"

"You don't neglect Leia," Cyd said. "But you're running on what, four hours of sleep a night so that you *can* spend time with her *and* do all your charities *and* run this company?"

"Cyd."

"Hera," Cyd said. "*Listen to me.* I have been working with you for years, and I have never seen you run yourself so ragged. You're going to get sick."

"Oh, nonsense, I'm as healthy as—"

"Or you'll make a mistake," Cyd went on, and Hera's blood ran cold.

She couldn't afford to make a mistake. Not a single one, not while the CEO position was still *temporary.*

"All right," she said. "Make a list of all my non-Olympus commitments. I'll cut some." No, that was too vague. Goals needed to be specific. "I'll cut a quarter of them."

"Well, it's a start," Cyd said, and mercifully left.

Hera's personal cellphone rang, and she picked it up, wondering if Persephone had been able to sense she'd been talking about her earlier. "Hello, Persephone."

"Hi, Hera. Hades won't be able to make it to the thing tonight. He's come down with that bug that's going around and asked me to call to let you know. I'm going to stay home and baby him, so I'm out too."

"Oh no," Hera said. "Well, I hope he feels better soon, but I must admit I was looking forward to catching up. At least, before you two hid somewhere quiet to do inappropriate things to each other."

"That was one time," Persephone protested.

"I only caught you one time," Hera said. "Aphrodite's told me stories." She'd been working such hours that she'd hadn't seen Hades anywhere but at work. And she'd only seen Persephone when she'd trooped up to Hera's office with the other interns for the official greeting from the boss, where she'd assiduously avoided Hera's eye, and Hera had just as assiduously ignored her.

"I miss you too," Persephone said, sounding genuinely regretful, without a single and-who's-fault-is-that note in her voice, exactly as if Hera hadn't declined three invitations in a row to Aphrodite's variously themed girls' nights. "I had an idea, though. Why don't you take Don?"

"I don't think Don's very interested in the fine arts," Hera said.

"He might surprise you," Persephone said. "We had some good conversations while I was working on Hades's mural."

"How is the one in the new house going?"

There was the faintest of pauses, then Persephone said, "It's done. I finished last week. I texted you a couple of photos, but I think you must have missed them."

"Oh," Hera said. "I'm so sorry."

"It's okay, Hera. We all know you're busy."

"Nevertheless," Hera said. Maybe she'd cut a third of her non-Olympus commitments. "I'll call Don."

"Oh, great," Persephone said, sounding very cheerful, even for her. Hera was a little suspicious about that, but when she called Don, he sounded amenable, but not knowing, so she put aside the idea that they might have conspired together for some kind of surprise.

Hera started on the financial report review, and paused.

When had she lost her taste for surprises?

Probably the moment you learned Zeus had not only slept with his intern, but had a son, she told herself tartly. *What a fun surprise that was.*

Dio, Semele's son. Hades had set up a trust for the boy and his mother. Hera had the impression he'd met the boy a few times, but he hadn't discussed that with her. She wasn't sure whether that was out of respect for her feelings, or Semele's preference.

Diana came in, with a garment bag carefully slung over her arm and a printed list in the other.

"Cyd asked me to give you this," she said, looking curiously at the list.

Hera took it. All right, so there were quite a few names when you put them in bullet points. She was probably due for a review.

"And Lionel from Beauty is on their way up to do hair and makeup," Diana said. "Um. Are you feeling all right?"

"Did Cyd tell you to ask that?" Hera asked, and when Diana looked surprised, and a little scared, she held up her hands. "Never mind. I'm sorry. Let's get me into this dress."

She sent Diana home after she was zipped in, and Lionel had departed after their usual excellent work, so she was all alone in the office, the last of the sunlight gleaming through the windows, when Peter Atlas knocked on her door.

"Working late?" he said, and then looked at her in open admiration. "That's a hell of a dress."

"Hello," Hera said, smiling at him. Peter looked good, last thing on a Friday, with his tie loosened and his dark hair attractively ruffled.

"Hi," he said, smiling back. "I was going to ask if you wanted to go and get a drink, but obviously you have plans."

"A hot date with an emerging artists exhibition opening at the Rainbow Gallery. I was just looking at these latest proofs for *Luxe*."

"I have no idea how you do it all," he said. "Rain check on the drink?"

"Of course. I think next Thursday evening is free."

"Then it's a date," Peter said, and departed for the main elevator, whistling.

Hera checked the proofs for *Luxe*'s main story—a tell-all interview with Aphrodite and Heph that actually told very far from all—and looked up.

"Date?" she said, out loud, and the word echoed in her empty office. Peter hadn't meant—had he?

"Oh, hell," she said, as her phone beeped. She had to call for her car, swing by their building to pick up Don, and then go and be charming to her guests. She didn't have time to pee, let alone ponder whether Peter had meant a *date* date.

"That's a hell of a dress," Don said. He was aware he was staring, but it was difficult not to. In the dim light of the town car he hadn't been able to see it, but now they were under the icy lights of the Rainbow Gallery he could barely take his eyes off her. Hera was wearing a forest green one-sleeved cocktail dress that wrapped tightly around her petite body in a thousand tiny folds. The neckline was demure, but the hem stopped halfway down her thigh, exposing a ludicrously tempting expanse of bare leg.

"Thank you," Hera said, and then looked at him curiously. "You know, you're the second person to say that to me."

"Get ready for more of it," Don told her. "You're the hottest person in this room."

"Oh, nonsense," Hera said, but she looked pleased, so Don simultaneously counted that as a win and mentally scolded himself.

He'd been doing a lot better lately. Hera had stayed out of his room, which helped, and he'd been working a lot at the Grotto, which helped more. He'd been gratified by how much of his shipboard experience translated to management. Stocktaking, supply chain logistics, using charm to get what he needed—those had all come pretty easily. Even the accounting wasn't too hard. He wasn't up to Doris's rigorous standards, but he could manage a balance sheet, and he could always ask Hades for help if he got really stuck. Hades thought break-even analysis tables were *fun*.

He hadn't been working as hard as Hera, though. She nearly always made it home for dinner, but afterwards she would sequester herself in her study, while Don and Leia watched TV or played the video game Aphrodite had told them about. Lately, though, Leia had made cautious friends with some of the other casual workers at the Grotto. Two weeks ago, she'd gone out to dinner after work, and come home bubbly and happy. The week after that, she'd gone to a board game evening Jasmine had invited her to. Tomorrow, she was going to a movie with Jasmine and Amir. (Don had suspicions about Amir's intentions. He spent a lot of time asking Leia for help with the herb section, which was at least a better tactic than trying to explain stuff *to* her.)

Don could foresee a day in the very near future where Leia had her own social circle, maybe moved out into a roommate situation, and Hera didn't need to worry about leaving her alone.

And that would be great. That would be a really good thing.

It was just, then there'd be no more excuse for him to hang around.

Typhon from Titan Publishing, technically a rival but also one of Hera's ten thousand friends and acquaintances, dropped by to say hello and compliment her dress. Hera did what she did best and talked a donation out of him for the Emerging Artists trust. His companion nodded at Don, and Don nodded back.

"Are you on eye candy duty too?" he asked.

"Pretty much," the man said, looking more interested. "But I do like the exhibit. Have you had a chance to look at it yet?"

"No," Don said, and Hera said, "Oh, let Carlos show you around while Typhon and I talk shop."

Carlos turned out to be an arts journalist and a pretty interesting guy, and under different circumstances, Don might have done some flirting, but since they were both there as someone else's date, he kept it strictly friendly. The exhibit was interesting too, an eclectic collection of works by new artists. Other than their newness, there wasn't a coherent theme that Don could recognize, but each artist was sequestered in their own little white rooms, so the clash of media and ideas wasn't immediately apparent.

There were some moody monochromatic photos of streetscapes that Don didn't think much of, and some colorful abstract acrylic paint splashes he liked, but Carlos thought were less conceptually developed. All of those had red dots beside the placards, indicating they'd sold already. Then things got weirder. There was a series of miniature mixed media pieces, where the artist had carefully stitched crumpled shopping lists and notes she'd found on the bus to the center of bleached linen squares, embroidering an intricate border around each grubby piece of ephemera. There was a collection of Barbie dolls pinned inside shadow boxes like butterflies, where the artist had hollowed out their smiles and painstakingly inserted tiny teeth—sculpted from real human teeth, the placard said. A couple of these also had red dots. Don wouldn't have wanted shopping list art or Barbie teeth in his own house, but he could kind of see the appeal.

The installations were obviously not going to be sold, unless you wanted a series of green shower curtains forming a tunnel that led to a single papier-mâché mask on a pedestal made out of sculpted wax. In the room next to that, paper cut-outs of crayon-drawn houses hung from the ceiling while an old gramophone played voice mail messages from the artist's grandmother. Carlos explained the Portuguese portions of the voice mail to Don, and they went into the last room.

There were no white walls here. They were covered in quilts.

At first, Don felt as if he was being visually assaulted. The quilts were a riot of color, texture and abstract shapes. He tried to focus on them one at a time, which helped. On the first one, bold vertical stripes in red and black met a succession of different squares marching up from the bottom and dissolved into a corner of wavy horizontal curves. For some reason, it made him think of skyscrapers, and when he checked the wall placard, the artist had called it "City II". It was far more interesting than the black-and-white streetscapes in the first room. The quilt next to that was smaller and square. It had an applique velvet rose in the center, each petal outlined in red beads. The petal shapes were repeated around that center, increasingly exaggerated with sharper and sharper lines and a greater variety of colors until a succession of hectic triangles were crashing into the border.

"Typhon doesn't think these are art," Carlos said. "But I kind of like them."

"Typhon is wrong," Don said. The next quilt, partially obscured by the exploding rose, was a collection of blue curves on one side and brown and green squares on the other. He stared at it for a full minute, trying to understand why it tugged at him, and then moved on. The quilts were incredible, but the frenetic activity of all of them piled on top of each other was starting to give him a headache.

Further along was another large piece, layers of textured fabric shapes pieced together to suggest a garden. The wall placard said that it was the result of the artist's interest in plant-based fibers and dyes, and Don crouched down to look closer. There was a tiny scrawl of yellow and black almost covered by a giant purplish flap, and Don realized he was looking at a small bumblebee embroidered in life-like detail, tucked behind an abstract lavender bloom. He laughed out loud.

"This is *great*," he said. "Is it for sale?" There were no red dots here.

There was a quiet gasp, and Don turned to see a short, round, brown-skinned girl with enormous glasses in the corner. She was wearing black slacks and a long black tunic style shirt with sleeves that hung over her hands. Her fingers were fretting at the cuffs, fraying the threads.

"Um, yes," she said. "They're for sale. You can talk to Iris, the gallery manager." Then, on a gasp, "*Really?*"

"Really," Don said. "These are your work?" He read the placard again. "You're Ara Kaney?"

"Yes," she said, in a voice so small it was almost a whisper.

"I like the one that looks like a garden a lot," he told her. "I know exactly who I'm giving it to." Leia, he was pretty sure, was going to flip her lid.

Ara looked like she was going to faint, so Don nudged Carlos out of the room and they found their way back into the lobby.

"You're seriously going to buy it?" Carlos said.

"You bet," Don told him. For this, he'd happily break into the trust fund, not least because his father would have *hated* it. For Saturnius, art was about price tag and brag value. He wouldn't have given textile art a second look. But Don liked things that were beautiful and useful, that added color and comfort to a home, and Ara's quilts did all of that. They'd look even better when they weren't all piled together.

"There's Iris," Carlos said, pointing to a tall, dark-skinned woman in a rainbow-striped silk gown, and ten minutes later, Don was the proud owner of not one, but two art quilts that would be his once the exhibit was over. He hadn't even had to break into the trust fund—Ara's work was priced in the high hundreds to low thousands, which Don thought was way too cheap.

Iris agreed, rolling her eyes. "You just can't talk the young ones into valuing their own work," she said, sounding frustrated, and then strode into the white-walled maze with a sheet of red dots in hand, ready to give Ara the good news.

Don caught Carlos glancing at his Rolex, the tailoring of his suit, and the ease with which he'd just bought fine art, and realized he was doing a quick reassessment.

"Oh," Carlos said. "Don *Kronion*."

"That's me," Don said, repressing the urge to roll his eyes. "The black sheep middle brother."

"Huh?" Carlos said, and then shook his head and refocused. "No, you're at the Grotto, right?" There was a barely suppressed excitement in his voice. "Are art quilts a niche you're looking to explore there?"

Carlos wasn't looking at Don as the useless scion of a wealthy family, Don realized. Carlos was wondering if there was a *story*.

"I bought those for personal use," he said. "But the Grotto's always on the lookout for innovative and eye-catching work in home design."

It was true. And he could tell Neron and Doris about Ara's work. He was going to be manager, at least for a while. He *should* be thinking about where new statement pieces might come from.

"I'm just going to catch up with Iris," Carlos said. "Nice to meet you, Don. Hope we can talk again soon." He hurried after Iris, looking intent. Maybe he'd give Ara a promotional boost. Don hoped so.

It was weird, to think Don had any influence. But he did. He wasn't any kind of interior design expert, but he made recommendations, and customers listened. He was apparently building a reputation.

It made him feel...restless.

He grabbed a glass of wine from one of the roving servers and scanned the lobby, now a lot busier. They must be getting close to the part of the evening where Hera made her speech.

Don caught sight of Demeter Erinyes, resplendent in red, her hair piled up on top of her head in a way that resembled her daughter. She was staring daggers at him. His one encounter with Persephone's mother had not been positive, but this was Hera's night, so he raised his glass and nodded. She turned her back and began animatedly talking to the man beside her. Don couldn't see his face, but he was tall and blond and...

Zeus.

Hera was all the way across the lobby, surrounded by admirers. Don moved towards her, and people melted out of his way until he was by her side.

"Heads up," he said in her ear.

"I saw him," she murmured back. "Phoebe! So good of you to come." She seemed unconcerned, but Don caught the tension in her grip on the silver velvet clutch purse, and resolved not to leave her side for the rest of the event.

***

Hera wasn't sure she'd done Cyd's speech justice. It had been hard to summon the necessary composure for a good performance while her ex-husband was in the front row, smirking at her, and his brother was off to one side, glaring daggers at him.

It was definitely comforting to know that Don was there, looking rakish and dangerous in his suit, like a lion someone had accidentally placed in a kitten enclosure. But if Zeus chose to make a scene, Don couldn't actually stop him by any method except violence.

Hera contemplated that briefly.

It wasn't an *entirely* unappealing thought.

Nevertheless, as the guests applauded her and the young artists the trust had sponsored for the show, and Iris stepped forward to give her remarks as gallery owner, Hera decided discretion was the better part of avoiding a fraternal ruckus. At the first opportunity, she slipped away to the ladies' room.

Unfortunately, Demeter Erinyes was already in there, touching up her lipstick.

"Hello, Hera, darling," she smiled, into the mirror. The smile wasn't reflected in her eyes. "What a splendid event. So *interesting* of you to choose a textiles artist."

"Hello, Demeter," Hera responded. She didn't want to go into a stall with Demeter lurking, so she began to ostensibly check her mascara, knowing that her own smile was just as fake. They'd never really been friends, though they'd moved in the same philanthropic circles for years. Recently, however, she'd heard enough about Demeter's appalling, controlling behavior toward Persephone to place the woman on the 'minimal contact only' list. "Thank you for the compliment, but the trust committee chose the artists this year. I'm only here to say nice things about them."

"I had hoped Persephone might be here," Demeter said mournfully.

Hera made a non-committal sound.

"I *barely* see her these days. The other night she hung up on me!"

Good for her, Hera thought. It seemed that Persephone was getting better at boundaries. "Oh," she said. "Hm."

Demeter's eyes glinted. "And how is the Winter Ball progressing?"

"Very well," Hera said brightly. "But I can't take any credit for that either, I'm afraid. As CEO, there are other claims on my time."

"Oh, of *course*. Well! We can hope there won't be any terrible incidents like last year, can't we?"

"Lovely to see you, Demeter," Hera said, and stepped out again. There'd be another bathroom somewhere else. Or if not, she'd be prepared to invade the men's.

While she was hunting—unobtrusively—for an alternate bathroom, Zeus caught up with her in a quiet corridor. "Great dress," he said.

"Oh, not you," Hera said.

Zeus blinked at her. "Nice to see you too, Hera."

"It is not at all nice to see you," Hera said impatiently. "It is never going to be nice to see you. You did awful, unforgiveable things, and I will never forgive you for them."

Zeus held up his hands. "Okay, okay. I just wanted to ask how Peter Atlas was working out. As a shareholder, I can ask that, right?"

"Feel free to put your query to the next shareholder meeting," Hera said tartly, and then wrinkled her nose. If any other shareholder had asked... "He's working out just fine." She remembered Peter's look of honest admiration, the way he'd said "it's a date", the spark that leapt between them sometimes, and smiled, quite involuntarily. "We get on very well."

Zeus's eyes narrowed.

"Excuse me," Hera said, and he stepped to block her path.

"Hera," he said, his voice dark with emotion. "I love you."

"Get out of my way," Hera said, but she was painfully aware of her racing pulse and flushed cheeks. Zeus looked unfortunately good in his designer suit, debonair and perfectly groomed. He was wearing the cologne she'd bought him three years ago, the one she'd learned to associate with good times and hot sex.

She should have demanded the cologne in the settlement.

Zeus's pupils were dilating, and he smiled, that slow, sexy smile that had always done terrible things to her insides.

"Don't bother looking for my date," he said. "I didn't bring one."

"I wasn't looking," Hera said.

"Because it's only you," he said. "I promise. Hera, this time, I promise I can do it. I'll win you back, and you'll see—"

"Get away from her," Don said flatly, and Hera took advantage of Zeus's startle reaction to duck around him and stand beside Don. She'd watched Don stalk silently down the corridor behind Zeus's back with enormous relief.

She didn't think Zeus would hurt her. But she didn't want to listen to him lie to her anymore, or, worse, try to kiss her, especially when she couldn't be one hundred percent absolutely certain that she wouldn't have yielded at the crucial moment. Probably she would have shoved him away.

Probably.

"Hello, Don," Zeus said. "Finally dressing like a grown up?"

Don ignored him. "Ready to go?" he asked Hera, and she nodded, tucking her hand into his arm when he offered it to her.

Under the crisp cotton of his sea-green shirt, Don's forearm muscles were tight with rigid control. They left with deceptive speed, smiling and exchanging pleasantries with a few people on the way. One of the young artists, who Hera mostly remembered because they were nearly the same height, thanked Don just before they stepped out the door, effusively and nearly incoherently.

"What was that about?" Hera asked, as her driver brought the car round.

"I bought some art," Don said. "Are you okay?"

"Yes," Hera said, and squeezed his arm. "Thank you. I'm very glad you were there."

"Literally any time," Don said, and smiled at her.

Hera blinked hard. It was probably a trick of the street lighting, but his eyes were glowing green and gold, and his smile seemed deeper than usual. It was heartfelt. Perhaps even tender.

The car pulled up.

"Let's go home," Hera said faintly. "I really need to pee."

Chapter Eight

Two weeks after the Rainbow Gallery event where Don had nearly put his brother's face through a wall, he was looking over the Grotto Saturday delivery list when a name snagged his eye.

"Huh," he said.

"Huh what?" Leia said, putting down a seedling tray. The muscles in her arms moved smoothly under her tanned skin and Amir, standing behind her with another tray, watched admiringly. Then he caught Don's eye, put his tray down, and scuttled out.

"Huh what?" Leia repeated, eyes on the prize.

"I'm supposed to be delivering to Hades and Persephone this afternoon," Don said, and showed her the list.

Leia brightened. "Oh, cool. Can I come?"

"Sure."

"Can I drive?"

"No."

"Why not?"

"Because you don't have a license."

"Yes, but I can *drive.*"

"And that'll be a very helpful thing for the cops to know when they pull you over, but you'll still get booked for driving without a license."

Don gave her a look. "Which brings me to something I want to talk about, actually."

"I should be helping Amir with—"

"Leia. I know you don't want to talk about your family or what got you living on the streets, but we're going to have to do something about your paperwork at some point."

Leia hunched into herself, a gesture she'd almost stopped doing, and Don felt bad about it, but he was still right. "Doris doesn't mind paying me in cash," she mumbled.

"Doris doesn't mind stiffing the IRS," Don conceded. "But future employers aren't going to be that relaxed. You need a social security number and a birth certificate to do all kind of stuff, including getting your driver's license or a passport."

"Passport?" Leia said, and then her eyes widened. "I could get a passport!"

"Yeah, if you want to travel—"

"I do!"

"Well, then we need to tackle your documentation." Don held up his hand. "I'm not trying to pry. Right now, I just want to know if those things exist in your name, or if we'll have to start the process from scratch, maybe start dealing with Immigration."

"I'm pretty sure I have a birth certificate," Leia said. "I mean, I was born here. My parents and grandparents were born here." She bit her lip. "I— My family weren't *bad* to me, okay? I don't want you thinking that. They just wanted things from me I couldn't give, and the only way out was leaving."

"Do you want to get back in touch?" Don asked, feeling his way through the conversation. "Let them know you're okay, maybe see about getting these documents?"

Leia shook her head, looking sad and thoughtful. "Not yet. Maybe...maybe next year?" Then, in a rush, "Could I send them a letter that they couldn't work out where it came from? To tell them I'm safe?"

"Sure," Don said, and then thought about how they could make that happen. "We could go out of town, maybe, take a weekend trip, and send it from there. We need an excuse to get Hera away from the office anyway."

"*Yes*," Leia said emphatically. "Every time I get up in the night to pee, her light is still on."

"It's a plan. I'll ask her, and you be prepared to spring the guilt trip if it doesn't work."

"Okay," Leia said, and Don went to tell Doris he and Leia needed a weekend off.

She was frowning over import invoices in the office, but her frown transferred to him with no appreciable effort. "Both of you, for a whole weekend?" she said, voice quavering. "I don't know if we can manage." She sounded like a frail old lady, and Don rolled his eyes.

"I like you a lot, Doris, but you are ruthless," he said. "I'm giving you three weeks' notice and you've got a platoon of part-timers to call on. You'll be fine."

"You'll learn when you have to manage the schedule," she said ominously, reverting to her usual tough-as-nails tones. "Go on, then, take that weekend off. And that reminds me. From next week, you need to spend less time in the garden department, and more learning the ropes in interiors. Fall is all about nesting and textiles. You're going to be up to

your ears in women looking for something cozy for the reading nook."
She looked over the rims of her glasses at him. "Come to think of it, they
might want to put you in the trunk."

"What did you think of that quilt artist I told you about?" Don said,
sounding diffident even to his own ears.

She leaned back, looking thoughtful. "I looked at her website. She
might not be the best fit for our clients. But I've emailed her an offer to
show a couple of pieces, on commission."

Don grinned.

"Don't get cocky," she said, and went back to the invoices. "You've still
got a lot to learn."

"Yes, ma'am," he said, and escaped, collaring Amir to help him load
the delivery van.

***

Don cheated on the delivery schedule to make sure Persephone and
Hades were their last delivery. They lived further out of the city in what
was essentially an oversized cottage, a small wooden house painted a soft
white that had faded into a genteel grey. The house had porches front
and back, deep windowsills, sound but creaky floorboards, and doors
that had stuck a lot until Don took his planer to them. It was the furthest
thing imaginable from the cold, corporate house Hades had been living
in when Don first moved back to town.

From sheer necessity, some of Hades's expensive monochrome furniture had made it inside, but as time went on, Don privately predicted
that it would all be replaced. Then his older brother would settle into

colorful, eclectic bliss with his lovely, loving girlfriend and Don couldn't think of two people who deserved it more.

Don backed the truck up the driveway. He ignored Leia's grumble that at least she could have done *that*, there weren't any cops in the *driveway*.

Persephone was sitting on the front porch, under the lush weight of jasmine vines that curled around the faded white trim. Her blonde hair was piled on top of her head in the messy bun she wore in work mode, and she had her graphics tablet and stylus out, but she set them down as the truck arrived and jumped to her feet.

"Hello!" she said, beaming uninhibited warmth and joy at them.

Don had had some initial qualms about his brother falling so fast and hard for a woman fifteen years his junior. He didn't have them anymore.

"Hi, Persephone!" Leia said, sliding down from the truck. "You took my advice on those citrus trees!"

"It was good advice," Persephone said, and gave Don a quick hug, which he enjoyed. Persephone was extremely huggable.

"Is Hades over that cold?" he asked.

"Completely recovered," Persephone said. "So, of course, he's gone to work today."

"Of course he has," Don said. "At least you have the sense not to work weekends."

"Mm," Persephone said, looking guiltily towards her tablet.

"Or maybe not," Don said. "What's that for?"

"*Agora* website redesign," Persephone said, cheering up. "They're letting me design some of the accent graphics. I am now a *senior* intern, permanently assigned to Art and Design."

"I didn't know that was a thing."

"I think they invented it for me," Persephone admitted. "But Mr. Hermes explicitly said it had nothing to do with my connections."

"Excuse me, Persephone Erinyes, the celebrated muralist? They'd be idiots not to appreciate you. And Olympus isn't known for harboring idiots. Where do you want these pots?"

Persephone pointed. "The citrus trees either side of the back porch steps, and that one in the corner of the living room. "Do you two have time to stay for a drink of something cool?"

"That'd be great. You're our last stop." Don deputized Leia to follow her inside with the smaller indoor rubber plant, and got out the hand truck to trundle the lemon and lime trees around the back of the house.

It was one of those bright autumn days with a deep blue sky and a warm wind rattling through the leaves that still clung to the huge maple tree in the backyard. The lawn was cheerfully overgrown, and surrounded on all sides by deep garden beds, blooming with the last flowers of the season. There were weeds sprouting up everywhere, which Leia would probably start clearing, given half a chance, but Hades was dragging his feet on hiring a gardener. Don suspected his brother just liked the excuse to get his own hands in the dirt.

Persephone came out with a tray holding three glasses and a bucket of ice, and Leia followed her with a glass pitcher of lemonade.

"Maybe we can make lemonade from our own lemons, next year," Persephone said.

"Maybe the year after," Leia said, squinting professionally at the trees. She jumped down the steps and tugged the lime pot a fraction of an inch to the left. "Did you want me to take a look at your herb garden while we're here?"

"It's more Hades's herb garden, but yes, please. He's getting anxious about the rosemary."

Leia nodded seriously and headed around the side of the house.

Don took the drink Persephone poured for him and sipped. Sweet, with a tang.

"So," Persephone said, sitting on the porch steps and tucking her legs under her vivid floral maxi-dress. "How was your date with Hera at the art gallery?"

Don choked on his lemonade.

"It wasn't a date," he said, when he'd got his breath back.

Persephone smiled. "Didn't you want it to be?"

Don wanted to throw the glass at the adorable cobblestoned garden path, so instead he carefully placed it on the worn wooden railing. "Okay, so Hades told you what Zeus said?"

Persephone blinked at him. "No?"

"Then...what are you doing?" He stared at her helplessly. "How did you find out?"

"Oh, Don," Persephone said, her surprise transmuting into sympathy. "Did you think it was a *secret*?"

Don felt the world drop away underneath him. He sat down on the porch steps before his knees gave out. "Is it obvious?" he said urgently. "Does Hera know?"

"It might only be obvious to people who know you?" Persephone tried, though she sounded doubtful. "But no, Hera doesn't know. It's literally the only thing I've ever seen her be obtuse about." She looked at him, the exasperation sitting strangely on her kind face. "Don't you think you should *tell* her?"

"Oh, right," Don said. "I just say, 'hey, Hera, I've been in love with you for twenty years, sorry it's never come up before, please pass the salt.'"

"*Twenty years?*"

"More or less. Twenty-two, actually." He frowned at her. "Why? What were you thinking?"

"I thought you must have discovered your feelings after they remarried," Persephone said weakly. "You mean you loved her the whole time she and Zeus were married? And then they divorced, and then you watched her get married *again* and you never said anything?"

"Of course not," Don said, ignoring the part where he had very nearly blurted out his whole sad confession on the eve of their second wedding. But Hera had told him she loved Zeus very much, and he couldn't tell her after that, even though he'd been absolutely positive Zeus was going to hurt her again. It would have been such a dick move. He should have said something earlier, but he hadn't, and then it was both too late and too soon. "Anyway, I didn't watch her get married again. I was too much of a coward to make it to the ceremony."

Persephone was still staring at him. When he defiantly looked back at her, he saw tears welling up in her dark blue eyes.

"Hey," he said, alarmed. "Don't—it's okay. I'm used to it."

"I'm sorry," she said, and gave him a tremulous smile. "It's just sad."

"Sure. But it's only a little bit sad. I've seen people whose lives have been destroyed. People with nothing. Loving someone who doesn't love you the same way isn't even close to a tragedy."

"But it still hurts," Persephone said, and he saw the weight of her own history pressing on her back, her mother's shadow in her eyes. It wasn't at all the same thing. Her mother *should* have loved Persephone the way she deserved. Hera was under no such obligation. But Persephone knew what she was saying.

"Yeah," Don said, and dropped his gaze back to his hands. "It does hurt."

They let it sit there for a moment, and then Don raised his head. "Don't tell her."

"I won't," Persephone promised. "But I really think you should. It's not fair to either of you, otherwise."

"I was thinking I'd give her a couple of years," Don began, and Persephone's jaw dropped. "No?"

"No," she said. "Definitely not. Don, someone's going to let it slip before then. It's a miracle it hasn't already happened."

Don's muscles tensed. "Really?"

"Really," Persephone said. "Aphrodite knows, for one thing, and she's not really celebrated for her impulse control. I've managed to sit on her so far, but that's a woman who's been known to blurt."

"Oh, hell," Don said, his thoughts skittering around his brain like a frantic dog. "I don't... I had a *schedule*."

"Schedules change," Persephone said. "She deserves to know, and you deserve to have it said. And Hera plays things very close to the chest, but I honestly think you've got a shot."

"Really?" Don said, hating how pathetic he sounded.

"Yes. She looks to you first. She leans on you the most. And Hera doesn't lean easily. I'm not saying it's a done deal, but I truly think she hasn't let herself consider the possibilities. Once you make them clear..." Persephone spread her hands. "Who knows?"

Don sat very still and Persephone seemed content to let him mull it over in silence. Above them, a bird let loose a series of trilling notes, and a gust of wind tore a flurry of leaves off the maple.

Hades and Persephone had had a rough start, but here they were, making their lives work together in their own version of paradise. Maybe he could reach for his. Before he could think better of it, he pulled out his phone.

Hera picked up immediately. "Hello, Don," she said. "I might be home late tonight, I'm afraid—some of these proofs need a lot of revision."

"Well, that's kind of what I wanted to talk to you about," Don told her. "You've been working non-stop, and you need a break."

"I don't disagree," Hera said cautiously.

"Leia and I both have a weekend off in three weeks. Can you get away? I thought we could go to the Hippocampus."

"Goodness," Hera said. "That brings back memories. Are you planning to teach Leia to sail?"

"If she wants. Or you and I could go for a ride."

"Horses," Hera said, the same way an arachnophobe might say 'spiders.' "You may consider that a low probability."

"But can you come? I should warn you that if you don't take a break soon, I think Leia might stage an intervention."

"Oh, *Leia* might," Hera said, her voice warm and teasing. "Yes, I think I can leave Olympus to its own devices for 48 hours. I'll have Cyd calendar it in on Monday. One moment." He heard the muffled sound of her voice, further away from the phone. "Come in, Peter," she said, and he couldn't tell if her voice had the same warmth, and then she came back to him. "Sorry, I have to get back to it."

"See you tonight," Don said, and hung up.

Persephone was looking at him hopefully. "A nice romantic trip?" she said.

"Maybe," Don said, and took a deep breath. Something was stirring in him, a hope he hadn't dared nurture. "Maybe it's time."

***

"You look happy," Peter said, as Hera hung up and smiled a welcome at him.

"I may actually get a weekend away from this place."

"Girls' trip?" he asked, taking a seat.

"No, I'm heading to the Hippocampus with Don and Leia."

"Huh," Peter said. "I've been meaning to ask. What is the situation there?"

"Situation?"

"Are you and Don..." Peter made a back-and-forth gesture.

"Oh, no," Hera said. "He's my...well, we're very good friends. I don't think about him that way."

Except two or three times a week, remembering the weight of his wrist in her hand, or the snap in his eyes as he'd moved towards Zeus and she'd known she wasn't on her own.

Or the way he looked in a suit, that contrast of tousled hair and crisp tailoring. Or the way he looked in his work clothes, massive shoulders swelling under worn cotton T-shirts, tattered, loose jeans that couldn't conceal the outline of his thighs.

But that didn't count. Don was an attractive man, and she was just appreciating the view. She was head of a magazine publishing house, for goodness's sake, of course she was primed to notice a healthy masculine specimen when he was living in her home and making her coffee every morning.

"Good to know," Peter said, and laughed, looking a little embarrassed. "I mean, I figured. It'd be weird to shack up with your brother-in-law right after the divorce went through. People would talk."

Hera's stomach tightened. "Would they?" she said, on a light laugh.

"Oh, definitely. But don't worry. I'll put the word out." He gave her a reassuring smile.

"You don't normally come in on the weekends," Hera said.

Peter nodded. "I think we've got a problem."

"How so?"

Peter crossed his legs at the ankles. His cuffed slacks rode up slightly, exposing the bare, tanned skin of his ankles above his loafers. "Dammond Argive was planning to get married last weekend, to a girl called Cressida O'Brien."

The Argives were an old and prominent family in the city. Dammond was in his early twenties, the apparent heir to his grandfather's real estate empire, and in Hera's considered opinion, a spoiled brat. "I know Dammond, of course, but I don't recognize the girl's name." And she hadn't been invited to the wedding, which was either a snub or an attempt at diplomacy, depending on whether or not Zeus *had* been invited.

Peter looked a little grim. "You wouldn't. Her stripper name was Chrissy Bee. According to the rumor, Dammond met her at work. The bride-to-be was a couple of months pregnant when the nuptial preparations began. It was supposed to be a quiet affair, but of course Dammond wanted a blowout for the bachelor party, and they ended up spending a ton on the venue and reception."

"Goodness," Hera said, picturing Dammond's grim and conservative grandfather. "I can't imagine Adrestus Argive was happy about any of that."

"Nope. But he was even less happy when Cressida told him to choke on his money and left Dammond, the night before the wedding."

"She sounds like a sensible girl," Hera said, and Peter grinned.

"Well, maybe. But Adrestus picked up the bill for most of the wedding preparation, and he is not happy. Especially because a day or two after she split, one of Dammond's college buds pointed him to a column in *Agora*."

Hera called up her mental file. *Agora* was an Olympus title, with a monthly print copy and daily digital content. Aimed at mid-twenties to mid-thirties young professionals, with a seventy percent female readership. Funny, smart, feminist, not high-fashion, but a good sell to quirky and sustainable advertisers, with a number of advice columns that brought decent convertible clicks to the website.

"Get to the point, Peter," she said.

"I thought you'd enjoy the backstory," he said. "Anyway, one of the weekly advice columns, by an anonymous writer, is called "Ask Cassandra." A pseudonymous reader who is definitely Cressida O'Brien wrote in to ask whether or not she should go through with the wedding. The columnist told her to dump the fiancé. Cressida didn't use his real name, but again, it's identifiably Dammond to those in the know."

"Ah," Hera said. "And Dammond blames us for Cressida taking that advice?"

"I saw Adrestus at racquetball this morning, and he was spitting mad. He's pushing his grandson to sue. And since Cressida O'Brien sure as hell doesn't have any money, Dammond thinks he can get something out of *Agora*. Which is to say, out of Olympus. At the very least, he wants the columnist fired." He shrugged. "I tried talking Adrestus out of it, but he was not willing to listen."

"He's planning to sue because the fiancée didn't go through with it?" Hera said. "That's ridiculous. I know it used to be possible to sue over a broken engagement, but surely not now."

Peter sighed. "Yeah, but even a nonsense suit can be an expensive pain in the ass. We should probably think about firing the Ask Cassandra columnist, just to smooth things over. Do you want me to be the one to make the call to Sam? I might be able to soften it a bit."

"Who?"

"Samuel Janus. The Board Chair needs to be informed when we get sued."

"Only if it's really happening," Hera said, her brain ticking over. "Has a lawsuit actually been filed?" If it had, and that hadn't been immediately flagged for her attention, she was going to have a strong word with Legal.

Peter looked uncertain.

"Find out," Hera told him. "And if not, I'm going to call Dammond Argive in for a little chat. We'll see if I can sort this out without any legal bills. And *certainly* without firing one of our columnists, who really hasn't done anything but her job."

Peter looked at her admiringly. "You're incredible, do you know that?"

"I do," Hera said. "But thank you."

For a brief moment, Peter looked taken aback. Then he laughed. "Which brings me to our next problem. You canceled Thursday drinks on me."

"I am sorry," Hera said contritely. "I'd completely forgotten that I'd committed to the ballet opening night."

To be completely honest, if only with herself, the fact that she'd forgotten concerned her more than having to cancel. Cyd kept a meticulous diary for her, of course, but Hera had always been able to carry a calendar in her head of her tasks and appointments. Cyd hadn't said anything when she'd pointed out the clash, but she *had* looked meaningfully at the corner of Hera's desk where the list of her non-Olympus tasks sat, still unedited.

Peter crossed his arms in mock-outrage, a gesture that made Hera notice his bare forearms, exposed by the rolled-up cuffs of his green button-up. She was used to seeing Peter in business attire. He wore well-cut suits, of course, but he didn't have to be fashion-forward in the same way she did. It was...interesting to see him more relaxed.

"To make it up to me, you can say yes to dinner," he said. "Monday night."

"I—"

"I already checked your schedule," he added. "You're free."

"Oh," Hera said, not sure whether she liked the presumption in that. On the other hand, it was nice to have the burden of checking removed. "May I ask a question?"

"Of course."

"Is this—I don't wish to presume, but is this a date?"

"Yes," Peter said, lips curving. "I'm asking you on a date."

"Oh," Hera said. "Well. Won't that complicate our business relationship?"

"I don't think so," Peter said easily. "I'm leaving Olympus in four months. If it's a bad date, we can laugh it off and continue working together. If it's a good date, we can see where that goes."

There was a heat in his eyes that Hera allowed herself to enjoy. "May I consider it?" she asked.

"Certainly," he said. "I'll keep the evening free, either way." He got up and inclined his head at her, not quite a bow. "See you Monday morning. Let me know then?"

"I will," Hera said, just a touch breathless. It *was* nice to know someone was interested.

After he'd gone, it was unusually difficult for her to focus on layouts, even though *iHearthit*'s December issue needed a serious refocus on cute and cozy instead of kitsch. The market trend research had been very clear.

She wrote "NO" on a post-it and slapped it on a story about ironically ugly holiday blankets, a trend that had been thoroughly covered last year and was currently fodder for satirical social media. She tried to run an internal cost-benefit analysis on whether it was worth it to source a new textiles story, then put her pen down and sighed.

After a moment, she searched "Dammond Argive" and then "breach of promise." The internet did not give her sufficiently clear information at first glance. Well, when in doubt, call the experts.

Minerva answered the phone herself. She, like Hera, did not expect her assistants to work weekends.

"Are you in the office?" Hera asked, turning in her chair. From her desk, she could see the shorter red-brick building that housed Eule and

Spindle, Attorneys-At-Law if she squinted, though she'd need binoculars to make out a tall figure in the top office.

"Yes," Minerva said. "Are you?"

"Yes," Hera said. The sun was fading over the city, one of those bright October days which promised warmth now, but was going to bite as soon as the last of the light was gone. "I need some legal advice. I don't think it's a real problem, but I don't want to involve the Olympus legal team to check, because then I'd have to tell Samuel Janus about it and he'll patronize me."

"I am intrigued. You can tell me all about it over a cocktail this evening. We haven't seen each other in months."

"I invited you to my last gallery opening," Hera protested. "We could have seen each other then."

"I don't want to look at black and white photos of street lamps in the rain. I want a cocktail—or three or four—with my best friend."

Hera stifled a laugh. "To be fair, only one of the young artists exhibited black and white cityscapes."

Minerva made a rude noise. "Non-official legal advice in exchange for your company. That's my offer."

Hera looked at the pile of proofs on her desk. No one else was going to do anything about them until Monday. She could get it done tomorrow.

"I'll pick you up in an hour," she said.

Later, sipping a martini with the perfect measure of vermouth, she had to agree that Minerva had been right. It was much more relaxing to explain the situation to her friend over a private table at the Happy Isles. It had also been gratifying to walk in, back straight and head high, and hear a young woman whisper behind her "That's Hera Rheczack!" in tones of awe.

Minerva was a good listener, and Hera could see her agile mind sorting through the details as Hera explained the situation. "This is all third-hand," she warned her at the end. "Adrestus to Peter to me."

"Then I would say first task is find someone who can give you the story at only one step removed," Minerva said. Her German accent got stronger when she was working on a problem.

"I can probably find out who did the wedding planning," Hera said. "They might be willing to tell me something. People say a lot of things in front of servers without noticing."

"I have noticed this," Minerva said, and they both paused as their waitress drew near.

"Are you ladies all right with these drinks?" she asked.

"Everything's fine, thank you," Hera said.

"We will both have another drink," Minerva said, and held up her finger as Hera made to protest. "Thank you." She waited until the young woman left, and then leveled her finger at Hera. "The good news for you is, breach-of-promise suits can no longer be adjudicated in this state. And even when they were, they were only successfully laid against *men* who broke engagements. The basis of the argument was that the reputations of the abandoned women were materially damaged, thus inhibiting their hopes for future prosperity and stability in the only job good girls were supposed to have.

"Marriage."

"Precisely. So Dammond Argive, being a well-funded young man, has no precedent and no case. Now, in these enlightened times, he may well be able to successfully sue the young woman herself for emotional distress and financial damages, especially if he can prove purposeful or reckless conduct and outrageous behavior. Perhaps if she never intended to go through with the wedding at all, and was foolish enough to tell anyone that. But no civil court in the state would hold Olympus responsible. Drink your martini."

"Isn't her writing to Ask Cassandra for advice proof that Cressida O'Brien originally intended to undertake the marriage in good faith?"

Minerva lowered her glass. "Not necessarily. And also not your problem."

"If he sues her, Olympus is bound to come up in the tabloids," Hera said. "Even if it's not actionable, wouldn't it be better for the company if he never tried anything at all?"

"Hera the hero. You can't save every young woman from the consequences of an ill-advised liaison, you know."

"Can I save this one?"

Minerva eyed her narrowly, then sighed. "I'll have one of my people put together a quick brief. Probably Hecate. I believe she had an affair fail recently, and she's moping around the office without her usual vigor. Perhaps she needs to be reminded that things could be much worse."

Sometimes, Hera was reminded, her best friend could be ruthless. "Speaking of affairs," she said. "Peter Atlas asked me out. On an honest-to-goodness, old-fashioned dinner date."

Minerva raised an eyebrow. "Did you say yes?"

"Not yet."

"Are you going to say yes?"

"I'm thinking about it," Hera confessed. "He's much more likable than I expected. And good at the job. Not spectacular, but solid."

Minerva snorted. "Oh, to have been able to make it to his position by being merely solid."

"There is that," Hera agreed. "I keep looking at him and thinking, 'I had to be exceptional, and you just had to be you.' He says all the right things, though. He appreciates that I'm good. And there's a zing, you know?"

"I do not know," Minerva said. "But I can exercise my imagination. Well done?"

"There's the ringing endorsement I was looking for."

Minerva shrugged. "You know I'm not the right person for romantic girl talk."

"Which is very funny, given how many people fall instantly in love with you."

Minerva smirked and twirled her olive stick around the glass. "I am rather magnificent."

"Yes, you are," Hera said, and clinked her glass against Minerva's. "I love you. Thank you for blackmailing me out of the office this evening."

"I love you, too," Minerva said. "Now! Shall we get drunk?"

***

Don checked his watch again. The hour hand, gently luminous in the dim light of the kitchen, showed it was after midnight.

Even for Hera, that was taking working late too far. He picked up his phone again, put it down again, ate one of Leia's cookies while he walked a restless lap of the kitchen island, and nearly had a heart attack when the doorbell rang.

Hera was there, beaming up at him and supported by a very amused Minerva Eule.

159

"We had drinks," Minerva said cheerfully. "Hera is drunk now."

"You're a bad influence," Don said severely, and Minerva laughed.

"Noooo," Hera said, and reached up to pat his arm. Her movements were loose and uncoordinated. "Minerva is my friend, Don. Don't be mean."

"I was joking," Don assured her. "I'm glad you had a night off." He held his arm out for her, but Hera pushed herself off Minerva and stood something close to upright.

"It was an enjoyable evening," she said, trying for dignity, and then smiled widely at him. "I had a martini with a chili pepper in it."

"Yes," Minerva said. "It was disgusting, but we had a good time. Good night, Hera."

"Good night," Hera said, and Don backed off so she could walk in under her own power, then closed the door behind her.

"I'm not that drunk," Hera said immediately.

"Oh, I think you are," Don said, not even bothering to hide his smile.

"I had the same number of drinks as Minerva," Hera said, listing gently to one side. "I counted."

"Minerva Eule is nearly six feet tall and built like a brick shithouse," Don pointed out. "You...are not."

"I'm so short," Hera agreed mournfully. "It's terrible. Models are like trees." She wobbled a few steps down the hall, and then folded up to sit on the floor. "I need to take my shoes off," she explained, and then fumbled at the straps. "Hm. This is hard."

"I've got it," Don said, and knelt by her. Even sober, the fiddly little buckles were a challenge, but he used his thumbnail as a lever and pried them loose.

"Ah," Hera said, and wriggled her toes happily. Then she froze. "Shh. Don't wake Leia."

"Leia's dead to the world until her 3 a.m. pee break. It might be time for you to go to bed too."

"Not yet," Hera said, and tugged at his arm. "Sit down. I never see you. Tell me things."

Don squeezed gingerly into the space between her and the antique wall table. "You see me every day," he said.

"Yes," Hera said, and her head tipped against his shoulder. "That's good. Your shoulders are very wide, did you know?"

"I'm aware."

"Good, good," Hera said. "What did you do today?"

"I took some trees to Persephone's place," Don said cautiously, thinking of the sun-drenched back porch and the quiet epiphany he'd had there. This wasn't the time, obviously, but...

"I like Persephone. She's a very nice girl."

"Yes."

"Sometimes I wish I was nice," Hera said wistfully.

"You don't need to be nice," Don said. "You're fierce and uncompromising. You know who you are and what you want, and you don't let anyone get in your way."

"I don't know everything I want," Hera said. She snuggled a little closer to him and looped her arm in his. "I didn't know I needed to live with other people until you told me. You see things I don't."

"Mm," Don said, and cleared his throat.

"You never talk about your love life," Hera said, apparently at random. "I don't think I've ever met one of your girlfriends."

"Or boyfriends," Don said.

"Oh!" Hera said, and then patted at his arm. "Well, that's what I mean! I didn't even know about boyfriends! I mean, not that you're obliged to tell me or anything. Do I sound like an asshole?"

Don laughed. "No. It hasn't been a secret since I was twenty. It's just never come up."

"Right! Yes! My point!"

"And you haven't met anyone, because there's never been anyone serious," Don said.

"Well, I should hope you'd have told me that!" Hera said. "I should hope you'd never conceal someone you *loved*!" Her attempt at indignation was spoiled when she yawned immediately afterwards.

"Okay," Don said, and rolled to his feet, crouching beside her. "Bed for you."

"We were having a nice chat," Hera protested, and then she let out a short, high yelp as Don slid his arms under her knees and behind her shoulders and lifted.

Hera was small. It was hard to remember, sometimes, because of her drive and poise and her absurdly high heels, but here, in his arms, staring up at him with startled dark eyes, she was light, a weight he could carry with no effort at all.

"Oh," she said and wrapped her arms around his neck as he carried her down the hall to her bedroom. Don felt a painful squeeze in his chest, as if she'd instead slipped her delicate hand around his heart and squeezed.

But his heart had been hers for a long time. He let himself meet her wide-eyed stare as he opened the bedroom door. Her pupils had blown huge and black, and he realized, in a triumphal rush, that she was looking at him with desire. He wasn't imagining it. The attraction was real.

It would have been so easy to kiss her. Her breath was coming fast through her parted lips.

But she was drunk and he was sober. It wasn't even a real temptation—just a flickering wish that she'd had two or three fewer drinks.

The housekeeper had already turned down the covers, and he slid her under them. Undressing her would be a step too far. She could sleep in what she was wearing, or figure herself out once he left.

"Okay," he said, and went to get her a glass of water from the ensuite.

When he came back, she was sitting up, propped against the bedhead. "You scooped me," she said accusingly.

"Well, you're very scoopable," he said. "Drink your water."

She held the glass in both hands and sipped, her eyes still locked on his. "Peter Atlas asked me out."

"Oh," Don said.

"I texted him from the cab. I said yes." She put the glass down on the nightstand a little too hard. Some of the water sloshed out, and Don made a movement towards it.

Hera caught his wrist, and then tugged his hand into both of hers.

Don closed his eyes. "Hera."

"Should I have said no?" she said, and it sounded as if her voice was coming from far away.

Don's stomach was churning. He wanted very badly to say, *turn him down, don't do it, tell him you changed your mind.*

Tell him you want me.

"I guess that's up to you," he said instead, which was the mature and responsible choice of a grown man who understood women were whole beings who made their own decisions. When he opened his eyes again Hera was looking at him, her face blanked out in the mask she used when she didn't want to show her feelings. She could have been relieved or outraged or deeply disappointed. Even drunk, she was so controlled he just couldn't tell.

It only emphasized how free and open she'd been, just moments before.

"Thank you for looking after me," she said politely, as if he'd been entertaining her at a tea party. "Good night."

"Good night," Don said, and went to his own room, feeling very certain he'd made a mistake, but not at all sure what he could have done differently.

Chapter Nine

Hera didn't want to speak to Peter Atlas, so of course he popped his head into her office first thing on Monday.

"Thanks for the late night text," he said, grinning at her.

"Sorry about the typos," Hera said. "I was a little worse for wear."

"So I gathered, from the timing. But I'm pleased you said yes." He came into her office properly. "Are those the *iHearthit* proofs?"

"They're not ready yet," Hera said, feeling surly. She'd spent Sunday morning asleep and most of the afternoon hiding in her bedroom, embarrassed, and not a little hungover. Chasing down what had really happened at Dammond Argive's rehearsal dinner, and then convincing Cressida O'Brien to talk to her had occupied some hours. When she'd emerged, it was time for dinner, and really too late to go to the office, especially since Hecate had dropped by with the brief she'd put together on her day off.

At least Don hadn't made any references to her making an utter fool of herself. Really, what had she been thinking? Staring at him, pawing him, asking him about his love life, asking him if she should have turned Peter down, hoping he would say *yes*, practically *begging* him to kiss her and put his big hands on her body and slide into her bed... It was a wonder he hadn't packed his bags and walked right out.

Instead, he'd just been quieter than usual.

She was grateful. Really, she was.

"You're a little flushed," Peter said.

"It's warm in here," Hera said. "Did you have a specific inquiry?"

"I was just going to say that I could take the proofs off your hands," Peter said. "I mean, you don't really need to oversee every publication. That's what we have editors for."

"I'm only focusing on the problem areas and the big sellers," Hera said. "Our market research shows that *iHearthit*'s potential readers think it's getting stale. We need this holiday issue to be on trend."

"You're the boss," he said, holding his hands up.

And she was. But her to-do list wasn't getting any smaller, and she needed to check over *Luxe* again. Xanthe White was new to the editor-in-chief position of Olympus's flagship title—the previous editor had been poached by Titan right before Hera had taken over Olympus. "All right," she said, reaching a decision. "You take *iHearthit.*"

Peter picked up the spiral bound book with a nod that was nearly a little bow. "I've booked a table for two at the Augean at eight," he said. "I've got an afternoon appointment, so I'll meet you there?"

"Yes, that sounds good."

He smiled at her. "I'm looking forward to it."

"Oh," Hera said, and felt heat come to her cheeks again. "Thank you. Yes. Me too."

She reviewed the *Luxe* proofs. Xanthe had taken her suggestions, and improved on them in a couple of places in ways that suggested she only needed more time and confidence to grow into her role. Hera sent the book back down to her, via Diana, with her compliments, and settled down for a departmental review before the all-hands meeting.

There was a minor flurry of activity in the outer office as a blond young man came in, and Hera ignored it. Cyd knew what she was doing.

Sure enough, five minutes later, she tapped on the door and came in, closing the door behind her. "Dammond Argive is here. Want him to wait another five minutes?"

"Mm. Let's make it ten," Hera said, and started an email to Joy, asking for the revised Winter Ball budget. She'd been trying very hard to be hands-off with Joy, but they really did need those numbers.

In the outer office, Dammond had been seated on a low beige chair, where he was trying, and failing, not to sneak envious glances at Hera's luxurious office space. Cyd and Diana were seated at their desks, doing a very good impression of ignoring him completely, though Hera suspected they were both on their private chat channel. Hera had angled herself behind her monitor so that she could look at Dammond without appearing to do so. She caught the moment he slumped in the chair and took out his phone, and buzzed Cyd through her headset.

Taken off-guard, Dammond startled when Cyd spoke to him, and was ushered into Hera's office a little less cocky than he'd arrived. He had a deep reserve of arrogance to draw on, so he was very far from appropriately humbled, but it was a beginning.

"Hera, I have Dammond Argive for you," Cyd said blandly, and withdrew to the outer office.

"Hello, Dammond," Hera said. "How is your mother?"

Dammond had been in the process of sitting down, but at this reminder of Hera's social connection to his family he hesitated. "Um, she's fine," he said.

Hera graciously indicated the chair he'd been heading towards. "Please," she said, and now when he sat, it was at her invitation and with her permission. He was so bad at this that Hera could have felt sorry for him.

But she'd spent much of yesterday talking to Cressida O'Brien, and she didn't have much sympathy to spare.

"What is it you would like me to do for you?" she asked.

"Fire the Ask Cassandra writer," Dammond said promptly.

"No," Hera said, just as promptly. "Anything else?"

Dammond looked taken aback. "She slandered me! That's defamation!"

"She responded to an anonymous letter outlining your character—also anonymous—and gave her opinions and advice on the information received," Hera corrected. "She couldn't have defamed you, because she had no idea who you were. Also, I believe you're trying to claim that she committed libel. Slander is spoken."

Dammond scowled at her. "Whatever. If you don't fire her, I'm going to sue for damages and emotional distress."

"I note that you don't have a lawyer with you today," Hera said.

Dammond held up his phone. "I have one, and I have him on speed-dial," he said smugly.

"That's nice," Hera said. "Olympus has a whole legal department, four floors down."

"Look, we think we've got a good case for damages," Dammond said, his voice a little more cautious. "Ask Cassandra told Cressida to leave me at the altar and she did. The venue, the flowers, all that stuff—it cost a ton."

"Well, let's see," Hera said, swiping over her tablet. "I have the relevant part of the advice column right here. Ah, here we go: 'Leave him. Leave him now. Leave him yesterday. In fact, I'm going to amend that to "leave him as soon as you can safely do so" because from what you have told me I do not trust this entitled baby-man or his evil patriarch not to start something as you go, so please check out the list of resources and safety plans in the sidebar. This man is not going to be a good husband or father, and as long as dear old pale, stale granddad keeps covering for him with this boys-will-be-boys bullshit, your soon-to-be-ex fiancé has no reason to change.'" Hera laid down her tablet. "Is that accurate?"

Dammond had flushed dark red. "Yeah. That's what she wrote."

"And this Ask Cassandra column was published on the *Agora* website on the 1st of June. Your wedding was scheduled to take place a week ago."

"Yeah."

"So, in fact, Ms. O'Brien did not take the columnist's advice to 'Leave now'."

"She took it *eventually*."

"Even if I were to concede that, which I do not, from all reports, she *eventually* took action after your grandfather got drunk at the rehearsal dinner and told her that she was a—" Hera checked her notes "—moneygrubbing little whore who would never be worthy of his family and that as soon as she popped out his heir, he'd make sure she never soiled their house again."

"She *was* a—sex worker."

Hera looked at him. "Yes. Is that not how you met?"

Caught by her gaze, Dammond nodded.

"So," Hera said. "Even if we were to ignore the derogatory reference to Ms. O'Brien's occupation, what we have here is a woman who was, essentially, threatened by her fiancé's grandfather."

"It wasn't a *threat*."

"Exactly how *is* someone supposed to interpret 'I'll make sure you never soil our house again?'"

Dammond grimaced. "Look, I'll admit that Grandfather was maybe a little over the top, but he didn't mean it."

"And what did you say when Ms. O'Brien said that she didn't feel safe?"

"I don't remember," Dammond mumbled.

Hera checked her notes again. "Sit your ass down and stop being so fucking dramatic, Chrissy." She put her tablet down. "So."

"How did you get that?" Dammond asked. "How do you *know*?"

"I know a lot of people," Hera said. "They talk to me, and they're willing to talk to the courts. As it happens, you're very fortunate that Ms. O'Brien wants nothing more to do with you or your family, or I would be encouraging her to lay suit, you miserable little tick."

Dammond jerked in outrage. "*What* did you just say?"

"Dammond, look at where you are," Hera said. She gestured at the window, and the wide world below. "Understand who I am. Do you think I got here by being nice?"

Unbidden, she remembered telling Don that she sometimes wished she was nice, and his immediate, gratifying response. *He* didn't expect her to be nice. Don thought she was fierce, and from his tone, he very much approved.

"Now *you're* threatening *me*," Dammond said triumphantly.

"Not even close," Hera said. "Here's the situation. We will not be firing the Ask Cassandra columnist. We will not print a retraction or an apology. If you attempt to sue Olympus Inc, I will set my lowest-ranked legal staffer on it, and as your frivolous suit inevitably founders, I will set my *highest*-ranked legal staffer on the counterclaim for malicious prosecution and abuse of process. Your grandfather will not only be paying your legal bills, but mine, which will be *very* expensive. Incidentally, you should remember that whatever your grandfather spends on this is coming out of your inheritance."

She tapped the black folder beside her, the one emblazoned with *Eule and Spindle* in gold letters, and Dammond's eyes fastened on it. He was finally beginning to look appropriately intimidated. "If your grandfather wants to waste a great deal of money and effort for a negative return, that's his decision, but you might want to remind him of the sunk cost fallacy."

Dammond looked at her in confusion.

"Oh, Dammond, really," Hera said. "Did you learn nothing from your Business degree? Review your notes and talk to Adrestus before he empties your trust fund." She turned back to her monitor. "My best regards to your mother."

Dammon sputtered something she ignored, and sat awkwardly for a moment, which she also ignored. Then he got up, and stomped out of her office, a move that came across less as "righteously furious" and more as "tantrumming toddler."

Hera caught movement in the outer office, and watched as Peter Atlas walked past. He greeted Dammond, and they exchanged one of those elbow gripping handshakes. Dammond said something, pointing his chin towards Hera, and Peter laughed and said something back.

Cyd and Diana were exchanging looks.

Peter escorted Dammond out, presumably to the reception desk and the elevator bank beyond, and then came back, looking pleased with himself.

Hera gave him a raised eyebrow through the glass, and he came in.

"What was that about?" she asked.

"Oh, I told him what he wanted to hear. Soothed his ego."

"His ego doesn't need soothing," Hera said tartly. "It needs eradication."

Peter laughed. "Well, you certainly cut it back some." He held up the *iHeartbit* proof book. "All done. Do you want to see it?"

Hera did. But she'd accepted Peter's offer to handle it, and he truly did know what he was doing. "Diana, can you please take that down to Editorial?" she called instead, and Peter waved her a jaunty salute and sauntered back to his end of the floor.

Perhaps they could talk about any changes he'd made over dinner.

***

Don had taken proud possession of a second-hand 2005 Toyota Camry. It was reliable, safe, beige, only a little sun-blistered, and totally out of place in the parking garage of Hera's building, which otherwise mostly housed gigantic SUVs, but also contained more than one cherry-red Porsche, a couple of Lamborghinis and a bright pink Mini Cooper.

Don approved of the Mini, because it was owned by Mrs. Berkowitz on the ninth floor, and she called him "that nice young man." The other cars seemed to be sneering at his Camry every time he got into it, but the joke was on them, because his car got out five or six days a week, and they had to stay in the garage most of the time, being status symbols instead of actual vehicles.

"We're going to be late," Leia pointed out.

Don stopped anthropomorphizing his car and backed them out of the parking spot. Leia was slumped in the passenger seat, staring at her phone, looking exactly like a surly teen ignoring an embarrassing parent.

"You're quiet," he said.

"Amir asked me out, and I said no, and now I'm worried things are going to be weird," Leia said.

"Huh," Don said. "Did you want advice?"

Leia slumped further down. "Not really."

"Okay," Don said, and got them onto the freeway route towards the docks. The Camry's CD player was broken and it had never heard of Bluetooth capability, but the radio still worked and 87.5 Classic Rock was a reasonable soundtrack for the commute.

They were halfway there, and midway through a Queen medley, before Leia broke. "But what do I do if he's weird?" she asked.

Don stopped humming along to "Killer Queen." "If he keeps asking you out, or gets mad, or whines at you, tell me, and I'll kick his ass."

"Will you really?"

"No, probably not. I'll have a word with him, and he'll back off, because I am manly and strong."

Leia's eye roll was exaggerated enough that he caught it even in his peripheral vision. "I don't think he'll *harass* me," she said.

"I don't think so either. He seems like a nice kid."

"But what do I do if he's *weird*?"

"Are you asking what to do if he's sad, or quiet, or doesn't want to talk to you so much?"

"Yes!" Leia said eagerly. "What do I do then?"

"Nothing."

"What?"

"Nothing. I mean it. Amir is allowed to have his emotions, and it's not your job to do anything about them." He took the freeway exit and pointed the Camry down the main road to the Grotto. "When he took his shot, he knew that rejection was a possibility. Let him feel what he feels about that."

"But doesn't that mean it might be awkward between us?"

"Oh yeah. It's definitely going to be awkward."

"Don!" Leia squawked.

"Leia, there is absolutely no way to get through a human existence without awkward and uncomfortable moments. It's part of the package. You just need to wait it out." He swung into the Grotto parking lot and eased into his usual spot closest to the delivery truck.

"Did you and Hera have an awkward and uncomfortable moment?" Leia asked, and Don braked just a little too hard, jolting them both forward.

"Okay, let's get to work," he said, unclipping his seatbelt.

"Because you were both weird and quiet yesterday and she wasn't home when I went to bed on Saturday night and I eavesdropped on you and Persephone that afternoon and I know you're in love with her," Leia said, all on one breath. "Sorry! I didn't mean to spy. But did you ask her out?"

"We're not talking about this," Don said, staring straight ahead.

Leia jerked, and he looked at her and realized she wasn't just being nosy. As far as she knew, the stable friendship that had provided a place for her to find her footing was about to crumble.

"Hey," he said, more gently. "You know I'm on your side, right? And Hera is too. Whatever I do, or she does, we're not going to just drop you, okay?"

"Oh," Leia said. "Thank you?"

"And no, I didn't ask Hera out. As it happens, she has a date tonight."

"With someone else?" Leia said, sounding faintly scandalized.

"Yes. And that's her choice, okay?"

"Okay," Leia said, but she still looked wobbly, and Don made a decision.

"I got something for you," he said, and got out of the car, heading for the trunk. Leia followed him curiously. "I meant to get it giftwrapped, and I was wondering if I should give it to you for your birthday, but since you won't tell me when your birthday is..." He pulled out a large paper bag and handed it to her. "Here. Happy whenever."

"What is it?" Leia asked, but she was already pulling the folded fabric free and shaking it out. "It's...is this a quilt? I've never seen one like this before!"

Don put "has seen a lot of quilts" in his mental file on the mystery of Leia, and held the top of the quilt for her so she could pull out the bottom and look at the whole length.

"It's a garden!" she said, sounding delighted and all of eight years old.

"See if you can find the bee," Don said.

"There's a *bee*?" She leaned over it, marveling, and then looked up at him. "Don, this is so great. Thank you so much."

"You're welcome," Don said, and suddenly found himself with an armful of teenager, hugging him tight.

He gently squeezed her back, absurdly touched. Leia wasn't physically demonstrative—even with him and Hera, she kept up a protective aura, a psychic no-touch zone around her. For her to break through it and hug him spontaneously meant something, something important.

Whatever happened, he was going to keep this kid in his life.

***

Hera got home at nearly eleven and opened her front door in a quiet and thoughtful mood.

There was a promising scent of spice and apple wafting from the kitchen, so she dumped her bag on the hall table and wandered that way.

The oven was humming, the light inside showing an expertly crafted pie turning golden brown.

Leia was sitting on a stool at the breakfast bar, her long jeans-clad legs wrapped around the wooden bars. Her light brown hair was braided back out of her face, and she was scrolling through her phone, the light from the screen illuminating her sharp features.

She hadn't noticed Hera yet. Hera leaned in the kitchen doorframe and watched Leia's eyes flicker, the intensity with which she was consuming information, and thought, *oh no, I love her.*

"You're up late," she said quietly.

Leia jumped. "I wanted to make a pie," she said, when she'd recovered from the momentary surprise.

"You know you don't have to bake for us," Hera said.

"I know," Leia said. "You might have noticed that I don't cook breakfast anymore." That was true; Don had taken over that chore, with every evidence of enjoyment. "But I like baking," Leia concluded simply. "And Samia doesn't mind, I asked her." She smiled. "Actually, she asked for my chocolate chip recipe."

The housekeeper could just have been being kind, but having tasted Leia's cookies, Hera suspected the gesture was one of respect towards a fellow master.

"I wanted to ask you something," Leia said.

Hera climbed up onto the stool beside hers. "Go ahead."

Leia squared her shoulders. "Last week, Don talked about me getting ID papers and stuff, and I said maybe next year."

Hera nodded. "I'm glad he brought it up."

"Yes, but after that I realized that I'll probably need ID to rent an apartment and get utilities and stuff, right?"

"Probably, yes."

"And I didn't want to just assume that I could live with you for months—"

"You can," Hera said. "You can stay as long as you like. And I really mean as long as you like."

Leia sucked in a breath.

"I should have said it sooner," Hera said. "But I wanted to make sure that it was true. It is."

"Well, that makes the rest of this speech kind of out-of-date," Leia said, looking both touched and daunted. "Do you mind if I give it to you anyway?"

"Go ahead."

"Okay. So, I say the thing about not making assumptions, and then, I say, if that doesn't work for you, I understand, and I'm very grateful for everything you've already done for me. If you are willing to let me stay, I want to be clear that I appreciate it very much. But I don't want to take you or your home for granted. I'd like to start paying rent." Her shoulders relaxed a little. "And I was looking up rent for places in this area and then you walked in just as I was working out I definitely can't afford anything close to market price."

"I should think not," Hera agreed. "And I really don't need the money, but I think this is more for your sense of independence than any financial distress on my part, correct?"

"Right."

"And of course we'll need a rental contract, which gives you some legal protections that don't depend upon my continued good will. Yes. It's a very good idea."

"I didn't even think about the contract part," Leia said. "But I'm glad you agree. I thought you might say no, and then I'd feel..." She frowned. "I don't know how to say it. Not ungrateful, because I am grateful, but I don't want to *have* to feel grateful."

"Obligated?" Hera suggested.

"Yes, I think so. I didn't want to feel obligated." Leia's face wrinkled. "My parents...they aren't bad people. But they expected us kids to recognize what they'd given up for us, how much work they'd put into keeping us safe. We were supposed to be grateful, and that gratitude was supposed to make us agree with them. I stopped agreeing with them and after that I stopped being grateful, and..." She shook her head. "Well, never mind."

Hera had been holding her breath in case she interrupted the flow of this unexpected confidence. She let it out in a slow exhale.

"Don said you would always be on my side," Leia said.

"I will."

"He said that he'd be on my side, too."

"He will. You can always trust Don to keep his word." She smiled at Leia. "He's reliable."

"That's right," Leia said, sounding unusually firm. "How was your date?"

"It was nice," Hera said. Good food, good company. Peter had asked that they not talk about work, which had been a little difficult, but they'd been able to find common ground talking about art and music. He'd been very well-informed about several of her charity ventures. And he thought Puccini was a better composer than Verdi, which was the correct and right opinion.

"Just nice?" Leia asked, getting up to check on the pie. Hera couldn't see her face, but her voice was neutral.

"Maybe better than nice," Hera said, remembering Peter kissing her good night. Afterwards, she'd said, "Let's take it slow" and he'd said, "I know, but I had to," and there'd been that zing again, so she'd kissed him that time, and it had been good, the brush of firm lips against hers, the masculine scratch of late-evening stubble against her cheek.

Her ridiculous brain had chosen that moment to bring up a sense memory of Don picking her up, how he'd moved so effortlessly with her in his arms. It was probably bad manners to kiss a man while you were inadvertently thinking about another one. Especially when the other one had more or less told her to date this one.

"We had dinner, and we went for a walk. I enjoyed myself, and I think he did too."

"Will you see him again?" Leia asked. "Um, for a date, I mean. Not at work."

The pie had come out of the oven in a rush of heat and heavenly smelling steam, and Hera sniffed appreciatively.

"Yes. We're going to dinner next Saturday."

"Oh," Leia said, and this time her voice was very flat.

"Would you like to meet him?" Hera asked.

"Maybe," Leia said, but she sounded doubtful. "Can I show you something? Don got me a present."

Hera followed her down the hall to her bedroom, thinking that it was a pleasant enough guest room, but would really need to be made over for Leia to stay long term. Don could doubtless come up with some ideas about what would work with Leia's preferences.

And then Hera walked inside and understood that he already had.

The quilt was spread on Leia's bed, replacing the gray Egyptian cotton comforter that had previously occupied the space, which Hera now realized had been dull and muted, totally inappropriate for Leia's green thumb and vibrating intensity. The quilt had no repeating pattern or clear form, but exuberant curves and strong lines hinted at a garden, thrumming with energetic life. Hera had seen it on the gallery wall, but there, beside so many other works, it had seemed hectic and overdone.

Against the neutral walls and clean lines of her guest room furniture, the quilt was a joyous explosion.

And Don had seen what she hadn't, and brought it home for Leia. Not to be hung on a wall and admired, but to be put to use, to keep her warm and sustained with color.

"Oh my," Hera said, and suppressed the temptation to grip the door frame. "Will you even be able to sleep under that?"

Leia grinned. "I'm pretty good at sleeping."

"I'm not," Don rumbled, and Hera turned to find him behind her in the doorway. He was wearing pajama bottoms and a worn white t-shirt, and his hair was mussed. His feet were bare, flexing against her polished wooden floor, and she could feel the heat of his body radiating through the thin cotton.

"I'm sorry," Hera said, and stepped backwards into Leia's room. "Did we wake you?"

"I wasn't really asleep," Don said. "Looks good, doesn't it?" He nodded at the quilt.

"You have an excellent eye," Hera told him.

"Everyone at work thought it was great," Leia said proudly. "Jasmine wrapped herself in it and sang, and Javier videoed the whole thing."

"We'll be viral in no time," Don said, and glanced at Hera. "Good night?" he inquired calmly.

"Yes," Hera said, her voice equally calm. "We went to the Augean, then a walk after dinner."

"Classic choice," Don said.

"There's pie in the kitchen," Leia offered.

Don shook his head. "That's all right. I'm going back to bed. Night, ladies."

"Good night," Hera said, and went to her own room, where she showered and got into her silk camisole set, and then stared at her crisp white bed with her hands on her hips.

The first thing she'd done on the day she'd discovered Zeus's betrayal—well, the third thing, after changing the locks and drinking an unconscionable amount of gin—had been ordering a new bed and mattress, express delivery. She'd envisioned herself spreading out in cool white sheets, entirely unmarked by either love or betrayal. And it had been what she'd needed, on that night and for the six bitter months it had taken to procure her divorce and make her bid for Olympus.

Now she had the divorce, and her grip on Olympus was growing firmer every day.

Maybe it was time to add a little more color to her bedroom. She wouldn't want the wild energy of Leia's quilt, but perhaps something more muted would be nice. A textured navy throw, or a few sage-green cushions. Maybe even a pop of orange or lemon, for verve.

After that night, she'd thought she'd never drink gin again, but Minerva had gotten those martinis into her with shocking ease, and she hadn't even thought about it until she was halfway through the one with the chili pepper.

Come to think of it, she'd gotten a lot drunker the night she'd kicked Zeus out. Don had been with her then, too, and she hadn't made any embarrassing gestures in his direction on that occasion. She'd wept all over his broad shoulders, and torn Zeus's clothes out of their closet, but she'd never once considered climbing his brother like a tree. Instead, she'd let Don tell her everything was going to be all right—not now, but one day.

One day might have arrived.

What did Don's bed look like? She hadn't gone into his bedroom since the day she'd clasped the watch around his wrist.

Hera firmly dismissed the little voice at the back of her head that suggested she go and find out, right now. She clambered into her cool, white bed instead, trying to ignore the delicious slide of silk against her skin.

She was sex-crazed, that was the problem. Or sex-deprived, really. She needed to do something about it, before she completely lost her mind.

Chapter Ten

J asmine had gone viral.

The video of her twirling in the quilt, singing, had been picked up by a couple of design influencers just as the temperature had dropped into the crisp, bright days and chilly nights of mid-fall. It was perfect weather for nesting on the sofa, tucked under something warm.

Then Carlos, the arts journalist Don had met at the gallery, had run a story both on the viral quilt story and on Ara herself. He'd used an interview that made Ara sound like a slightly baffled and very endearing genius, which Don was pretty sure she was. Excerpts from the interview had also gone viral.

Over the last four days the Grotto had been inundated with people wanting art quilts. Ara Kaney quilts, in particular. This was a problem, because Ara's supply had been rapidly depleted. Doris had ruthlessly raised the price on the last few, and declared the Grotto the exclusive retailer. Ara was frantically finishing quilts that had tops but no backing, and had turned out a pile of half-completed projects abandoned before the patchwork was done. She was only one woman, but she was sewing as fast she could to make the most of this unexpected bounty.

Fortunately, if people couldn't get or afford a genuine Ara Kaney, they'd happily browse the homewares section of the Grotto, looking for something similar. Doris had sent her minions into every homeware store in the city, looking for things that approximated Ara's bold shapes and lack of obvious pattern, and was right on the verge of asking for anyone who'd ever done an improvised quilt workshop to get in touch with the Grotto. Don had been stuck in textiles all week, talking fabric choices and measurements and color schemes until his jaw hurt.

"Do you think I could order two of these the same?" a customer asked him. "I have twin boys."

"They're all unique pieces," Don said. "Some have similar color schemes and forms, but there aren't any two exactly the same."

The blonde woman frowned.

"Like your boys, I bet," Don added. "They might look similar, but you're their mom. You know they're not actually identical."

The woman softened around the eyes. "That's true. Although that won't help when they both decide one of the quilts is the best and start fighting over it."

Don laughed. "That sounds right."

"You're a twin?"

"Middle boy of three."

"Ah," she said, and gave him another look. "Well, maybe I should forget the boys for a minute and get something for myself. What do you think?"

Don was pretty sure they were no longer talking about quilts. "I think you deserve a treat," he said.

"Yes, I do," the woman said, and drifted off to look at coverlets, smiling at him over her shoulder.

Don had long ago acknowledged that he was into women who knew what they wanted and were a little bit distant. He wasn't surprised when she returned and bought two (identical) pillowcases and a fluffy throw from him and put herself on the waiting list for the next Ara Kaney.

"I'm Tyro," she said.

"Don."

"Nice to meet you, Don," she said, and underlined her phone number on the waiting list form, giving him another meaningful smile.

At that point, Amir appeared, looking a little ragged, and probably sleep-deprived, but not desolate or desperate. Don hadn't had much time to observe him, but Leia hadn't reported him bothering her, and their public interactions appeared to be friendly, if a little subdued. Don was therefore prepared to give him the benefit of the doubt.

Tyro wandered a few feet away, ostensibly looking at curtain samples.

"Can I ask you a favor?" Amir said.

Don leaned on the counter, keeping half an eye on Tyro. "That depends."

"Leia and I are down to do deliveries this afternoon," Amir said. "I don't know if she told you that—"

"Yep," Don said.

Amir winced. "Okay. Well, I don't want her to feel weird about being stuck in the truck with me. Do you want to go with her instead, and I take over here?"

Amir probably also didn't want to be all alone with the girl who had turned him down for a solid couple of hours, but Don appreciated the approach. "Check with Doris," he said. Tyro had fished her phone out of her handbag and was frowning at it, typing rapidly with her thumbs.

"I did. She said it was up to you, because you needed more experience making decisions, and also she was too busy trying to source anything that looked anything at all like an Ara Kaney quilt, and that was your damn fault." Amir took a breath. "So. Will you swap places?"

Tyro was striding out of the store, looking purposeful. She didn't spare a single glance over her shoulder, much less a smile. A woman who knew what she wanted.

Don swallowed a sigh and turned back to Amir. "Yeah, okay."

Normally, they would wait for the after-lunch rush to dwindle, but after an hour, it didn't show any signs of doing that. Then Ara called, frantically wondering if anyone could go to the fabric store for her. Don left Amir earnestly explaining the history of the Gee's Bend quilters and their influence on Ara's work to a customer and yanked Leia away from the garden center.

They made a good team at the fabric store, with Don grabbing colors and prints he thought would work for Ara, while Leia inspected labels and felt fabric weights and told him what to put back.

"You've made quilts?" he asked, when they were back in the van.

"Sure," she said. "My mom and grandma have made more." She grinned at him. "None of them are as cool as the one you got me."

An idea was percolating in the back of Don's head. "Could you teach someone else how to make them?"

"Probably? I couldn't teach them how to make Ara's, but I know how to do piecing and inset seams."

"Hm," Don said, and pulled back out into the flow of traffic, listening to the directions Leia read him off her phone.

Ara was delighted to see the fabrics they'd selected, but was obviously far too busy to chat, blinking at them from behind her giant glasses as if they were strange visitors from another world. She did stammeringly thank Don for bringing her all the new attention, and then absently closed her front door in the middle of his explanation that she didn't need to thank him, that it was all due to her own talent and hard work.

"I think she's distracted," Leia observed.

"Oh, you think?" Don hefted the bag of quilts that Ara had handed over in exchange for the fabrics. "All right, where next?"

Next was a trip all over the city, from the pricey suburbs on the outskirts, to the boho apartments downtown, to the buildings of the rich and powerful in Hera's neighborhood. Most of what they were delivering was small stuff, ordered from the Grotto's online store by people who couldn't or wouldn't make it out to the docks to collect. There was some heavy cast iron garden furniture in the back, though, that Don was supposed to bolt together whenever they got to their destination. Leia had put that last on the delivery list.

"If you get rid of the really heavy stuff first, we use less gas," he told her.

"I forgot," she said glibly, and Don eyed her, but she went back to reading out the directions, and Don realized after a few turns that he was following a familiar route.

"This is Hades's old neighborhood," he said, navigating the meandering roads with ruthlessly manicured lawns.

Leia stared at the McMansions out the window. "This doesn't feel like his kind of place," she said doubtfully.

"We're passing by his old house on the right," Don said.

Leia twisted to look over her shoulder, and stayed looking until they turned a corner. "Ew," she declared. "How did you live there?"

"I started making changes pretty much immediately."

"Good. Oh, it's this one."

Don reversed into the property, and eased the truck backwards down a long driveway, lined by stiff rosebushes.

"Now, don't get mad," Leia began, which was a really promising start, "but this is Peter Atlas's house."

Don hit the brakes. "Leia," he said, and then stopped. He had no idea of what to say next, just that this was so clearly a terrible idea.

"I saw the order come in and thought we could check him out," Leia said. "Make sure he's a good guy."

"I'm sure he's fine," Don said. "Hera has good judgment."

"Aphrodite says she has good judgment in everything except men, and Persephone says we can't tell that from a sample size of one, but it's a very troubling sample. And Hecate says there's no point in pursuing romantic happiness when all things end in entropy, but she's having a tough time at the moment." She read his face and added, "They added me to a group chat."

Don closed his eyes. "Please tell me it's not their main group chat."

"Not the one where they talk about sex, no," Leia said, sounding faintly disgruntled. "This one's called GLOW UP AND GROW UP and it's about teaching me things."

"This is what they're teaching you?"

"Come on," Leia wheedled. "We're already here."

Don tried to think it through. It was the middle of the afternoon, so Atlas wasn't going to be there. They could put the furniture in the backyard, drop the rest of the stuff off at the back door, and go.

And if there was anyone at the house, maybe they could talk to them and get another take on Peter Atlas.

"All right," he said, and took the truck the rest of the way, parking just outside the flashy triple garage. Leia scrambled down and knocked on the back door. A gray-haired woman came out, wiping her hands on her apron. Housekeeper? Private chef? Cleaner? Most of the people on this block had at least one.

"Delivery?" she said. "You can give that to me."

"I need to assemble the furniture," Don said, pulling out the toolbox.

"There are a few boxes, ma'am," Leia chirped. "I can take them all in for you while Don gets that furniture set up."

"Oh, thank you," the woman said, exactly as if Leia were a nice kid and not a spy determined to unearth as much dirt as she could find on her employer. Leia grinned at Don from behind the cover of the truck, picked up the first box, and followed the woman into the back room.

Don stripped the protective wrappings off the black cast iron tabletop and started bolting the curved legs in place. The back room windows were all fitted with Venetian blinds, and he thought he saw one of them crack open a little. The housekeeper, checking up on him? Leia, trying to signal? He shook his head and concentrated on putting everything together, securing each bolt three-quarters of the way before moving to the next, and then methodically tightening all of them in turn.

He set the table on the patio and gave it an experimental nudge. No rocking, solid and secure. It was a small table, sized for two, and there were only two chairs in the truck. Did Atlas picture himself sitting out here with Hera, drinking wine and laughing over office mishaps?

Leia came out to get the second box, wide-eyed, and mouthed something at him with her back to the house. Don frowned at her and walked towards the truck—ostensibly to grab the chairs—then realized what she was trying to tell him.

Coming out of the back door was a tall, distinguished man in a tailored suit, with dashing silver wings in his dark hair, and a broad smile that probably owed a lot to subtle and expensive dentistry. He looked like... Well, he looked like a male version of Hera. Composed, pleasant, perfectly coiffed, expensively dressed and nearly impossible to read unless you knew them very well.

"Don Kronion!" he said heartily. "I thought I recognized you!"

Don made the split second assessment that anyone Hera thought was competent wouldn't be dumb enough to think Don hadn't realized whose house he was at. "Peter Atlas, right?" he said. "I saw your name on the list, but figured you'd be at work. Good to meet you." He held out his hand.

Atlas had to look up to meet his eyes. It gave Don a mean little thrill of satisfaction, but Atlas's grip was firm and sure and he didn't try any hand-grinding power games, which meant Don couldn't either.

Don caught the glint of metal at his wrist, and realized that Atlas was also wearing a Rolex.

"Nice, isn't it?" Atlas said, tilting his wrist so that Don could get a better look at the burnished orange gemstone face. Tiny diamonds flashed. "Day-Date in carnelian. An indulgence, I know, but you look like a man who appreciates fine craftsmanship." He nodded at Don's left hand. "Submariner's a good choice. A real workhorse."

As opposed to a thoroughbred? "That's me." He nodded at the garden table. "You're getting settled in to the city, then. Not going back to London when your time at Olympus is up?"

"Ah, home is where the heart is," Atlas said easily. "How about you? Hera said you were staying with her until you got your feet under you."

Don was fairly certain Hera hadn't said anything that made him look like a supplicant at her table, but he nodded. "Yeah, she's putting me up for now."

Atlas was all smiles and genial small talk, but the hairs on the back of Don's neck were prickling. He told himself that it was because he was jealous. Because this man, whether he knew it or not, was a rival. But when Leia walked past them and picked up the last box, Don didn't call her over to be introduced, and from the way she kept her head down, he thought she was moved by the same instinct.

"Generous woman, Hera," Atlas said. With another pointed look at Don's watch, the fucker.

"Very generous," Don said, and decided to go for the attack. He could play the just-good-buds game too. "Did she give you the afternoon off? Or are you playing hooky?"

Atlas chuckled. "No, I had a business appointment. Not everyone wants to come into the office. Will I see you at the November shareholder meeting?"

Don shrugged. "Probably not. Hera has my proxy."

"The Winter Ball, then," Atlas pressed.

"Wouldn't miss it," Don said, and smiled at him. Or, at least, bared his teeth in an approximation of a smile.

Leia came out again, and hovered at the edge of Atlas's eyeline. Don saw him register her presence and dismiss her, before he moved forward and clapped Don on the shoulder. "Good, good," he said. "Well, I'd better let you get back to it."

"Yep," Don said, and watched him saunter back into the house through narrowed eyes before he moved to the truck and grabbed both of the chairs. You were supposed to move them one at a time, but he wanted to get the hell out of there.

Leia came up behind him. "Don," she said quietly, her voice tense.

"Not yet," he muttered. "Get in the truck." He jumped down, a cast-iron chair under each arm, and maneuvered them into place, one on each side of the table.

The housekeeper had come to the back door, and she wasn't pretending to do anything but watch him. He didn't think it was out of appreciation for his muscle. He forced himself to nod and smile at her anyway, and saw the same twitching movement of the Venetian blinds. Then he hauled himself up into the truck cab, waved at the housekeeper through his window, and took the truck down the driveway at a nice, even pace.

"Well," Leia said, after a moment. "What did you think?"

"I didn't like him," Don said. "Did you expect me to?"

"No, of course not," Leia said impatiently. "But what was he *like*?"

Don thought back, trying to draw conclusions stripped of animosity. "Confident, bordering on arrogant. Plays status games, and was annoyed I wouldn't play along. But not dumb enough to make anything explicit. He didn't try to crush my hand."

From the look Leia gave him, that last had been too obscure. "Some guys like that—polo guys, lacrosse guys—they'll shake your hand and automatically squeeze too hard, trying to show you that they're stronger. That they can hurt you. It's kind of a pretend-polite wrestling."

"Who'd try that on you?" Leia said, making a vague wave that was probably meant to indicate "you are a mammoth."

"Well, idiots, obviously." Don said. "But a lot of rich guys are idiots. Peter Atlas is not one of them." He thought more. "He didn't expect to see me, and he wasn't happy that I was there, but he adapted fast. He can think on his feet."

Leia was bouncing in her seat. "Did you see the other guy?"

"Just Atlas and the housekeeper. What other guy?"

"He was talking with someone when I went in," Leia said triumphantly. "Then they both went quiet. Atlas went out to meet you, and the other guy stayed in the study. I tried to get a look at him when I went in to unpack some of the cushions."

"Cushions in the study?"

"I know, but I couldn't think of another reason."

"He said he had a business meeting."

"The other guy looked like a businessman," Leia conceded. "He said hi when I went in, but he didn't say anything after that. He was just flipping through a magazine. I thought about trying to get a picture of him, but I figured he'd notice that."

"Good call," Don said fervently. "Please don't try and take photos of strange men."

"I *said* I didn't," Leia said.

"What did he look like, this guy?"

Leia made a face. "White, blond, business guy. Younger than him. Younger than you."

In other words, exactly the kind of man Peter Atlas was most likely to be meeting, and one of thousands in the city.

"I'd recognize him if I saw him again," Leia said. "Maybe if I do, I can point him out to you, and you can identify him!"

"Wait," Don said, and parked the truck. "Leia, what are we doing? This isn't a grand conspiracy. Atlas was meeting a guy who didn't want to come into the office. It's probably some kind of confidential deal about printing paper or something."

"They had beer on the table," Leia said.

"It might surprise you to know how many people drink while doing business," Don said dryly, and turned the key in the ignition. "But maybe it was a friend. Maybe Atlas really was playing hooky, and didn't want me to rat him out. We're speculating because we don't like him."

"But you don't think Hera should go out with him, right?"

"Hera is a grown and capable woman who can make her own choices," Don said. "But no. That guy is a snake."

Leia nodded. "So what are you going to do about it?"

"Nothing," Don said, and ignored Leia's arguments and rationalizations all the way back to the Grotto.

***

Hera, after mature and deep consideration, and another date where Peter had kissed her good night again, had decided that if she couldn't talk to Minerva about sex and romance, she would go to the women who could. Cutting her obligations by a fifth—not *quite* a quarter, yet, but she'd get there—had meant that she'd been able to say yes to Aphrodite's "I Can Cook Now!!" dinner party invitation.

"It won't be pretty," Aphrodite had warned her. "I'm still learning."

And indeed, the roast chicken and salad had been plated inexpertly, and the flavors were perhaps a trifle unbalanced, but everything was still tasty, and Aphrodite was deservedly proud of herself.

She'd also made chocolate mousse, and after dinner they sat in Aphrodite's pink living room, looking at Persephone's exuberant mural of pink and red roses, and ate the mousse with fresh whipped cream and chocolate curls.

"So I think I'm going to sleep with Peter Atlas," Hera said, and licked a smear of whipped cream off her thumb.

"Peter Atlas?" Aphrodite said. "Really? Him?"

"He's smart. He's nice."

"*Nice*," Aphrodite said, as if the word tasted foul. "Babe, you can do much better than nice."

"Well, nice is what's on offer," Hera said. "I think I'm going to try it out. And it's not as if either of you can tell me not to date at work."

"I wasn't in Hades's direct line of report," Persephone said applying herself industrially towards her second helping. "And we talked to HR."

"Heph and I explicitly dissolved our contract before anything sexy happened," Aphrodite said, and then grinned. "Anything *too* sexy, that is."

"Maybe you should wait out the rest of his contract?" Persephone asked.

"Hm," Hera said, and put her spoon down on Aphrodite's rose-patterned china saucer. "The problem with that is that I really need to get laid."

Persephone choked on a mouthful of chocolate. Aphrodite flung her arms in the air, tossing a blob of whipped cream in an arc that landed somewhere behind her. "Fuck yes!" she whooped. "Hera's gonna get some!"

Hera got up to find the paper towels. "He's leaving in February," she said. "That's both too long to wait and short enough that if things go terribly wrong, it's unlikely to matter very much." She made to kneel down by the cream droplet on the rug, but Aphrodite swiped the towels and did it herself.

"So you don't think he's a long term possibility?" Persephone asked.

"No, not really." Hera went back to her chair. "For one thing, he wants to run a media company somewhere else. For another... No. I don't think so." She frowned. "You have to understand, when it was good with Zeus, it was really good. We were head over heels. We truly loved each other so much. Marrying him the first time wasn't a mistake. But even now, when I know all the things he's done... There was so much between us. I'm not sure I can let myself have that with someone else."

"It's the good things that trap us with people who are bad for us," Persephone said quietly. "We stay because there really is something good, something that draws us to them. My mom could be so generous. She could make me feel like the most important person in the universe. I was the only person who could understand her and support her, and that made me special." She made a face. "I know it's not true, but it *feels* true sometimes, even now."

"With Ares, it was the sex," Aphrodite said, toying with her fork. "Really, really good sex. And the constant drama was exciting, even though I got sick of it. He was arrogant, and really unpredictable, and I thought I wanted that." She looked at them both. "But also, the explosively great sex."

"We get it," Persephone said. "Although I know for a fact that Heph's no slouch in that department, because you keep texting updates to the naughty group chat."

Aphrodite grinned. "I *do*. And you and Hecate have to support me, because I'm developing my literacy skills!"

Persephone leaned forward. "But you *can* get great sex with the *right* person, Hera. I promise."

"I would settle for reasonably good sex with a right-for-now person," Hera said, on a sigh. "I feel...itchy. I keep looking at men and wondering how they'd be in bed." She let out a little laugh that sounded false, even in her own ears. "The other night, I looked at *Don*."

Aphrodite sat up straight. "*Hello.*"

"Really?" Persephone said.

"Tell us all about that," Aphrodite encouraged. "Don't leave out any details."

Hera shook her head. "There aren't any details. I was a little tipsy, he put me to bed, and there was a...moment. That's all." And there had been a moment before that, with the watch, and another one after, when he'd stood behind her in Leia's doorway, the warmth of his skin reaching out to hers like a caress.

Both of those times, she'd been stone-cold sober.

But all of that just went to show that she needed to sleep with Peter Atlas and get all of this crazed lust out of her system. Perhaps she was entering menopause. Forty was early for that, but they did say it could turbocharge one's sex drive.

"He put you to bed," Aphrodite repeated. "How did that happen, exactly? What did he say? How did he look at you? Did he kiss you?"

"Oh, goodness no," Hera said. "He was a perfect gentleman. I was the one making a fool of myself." She could feel her cheeks flushing. "Not that I said anything, or did much more than make eyes at him, but it's not really the mark of a good hostess, making unwanted advances at your guests."

Aphrodite took a deep breath.

"Aphrodite, can I talk to you for a minute?" Persephone said.

Aphrodite gave her a glittering smile, and said, "Not now, babe. Hera's telling us about how Don took her to bed."

"*Now*," Persephone said, with a tone of voice she rarely employed, and was thus very effective. Aphrodite pouted, but got up obediently and they both trooped into her bedroom.

Hera ate another spoonful of chocolate mousse.

When they came out, Aphrodite looked chastened and Persephone serious. No doubt Persephone had told her friend to stop teasing Hera about her drunken escapades.

Hera wasn't as delicate as all that, but it *was* embarrassing. She smiled gratefully at Persephone and put her spoon down in her empty dessert bowl. "This was lovely, Aphrodite, but unfortunately I must be going."

"You barely got here," Aphrodite protested, and then, off the look Persephone gave her, "but we know you're really busy and thanks for your time."

Hera laughed. "I'll have more time soon," she promised. "Really. I think Olympus is nearly out of the teething issues, and Cyd keeps making noises about my resigning from more boards."

"Good," Persephone said firmly. "I thought my mom did a lot of charity work, but you're spread *way* too thin."

"Well, I still want to get involved with the Youth Shelter Committee," Hera admitted. "They're all lovely, competent people who know what they're doing far better than I do, but they don't have any connections to big donors."

"Hello?" Aphrodite said, spreading her hands.

"Why don't we talk about that later?" Hera suggested.

"Check out my hot, rich friends, doing good and looking fine," Persephone said. "How do I get to join these hallowed ranks?"

Hera smiled at her. "Marry Hades," she said, and left while Persephone was still sputtering.

***

Three nights later, Peter signed the receipt with a flourish and sent the waiter off looking very happy. One of the things Hera liked about him was that he always tipped well and treated service staff with respect. Zeus had once snapped his fingers at a waiter, and she'd walked right out of the restaurant and refused to talk to him all the way home.

Unlike their two other dates, Peter had reserved a table at a boutique hotel restaurant this time. The hotel wasn't especially known for its food, but it was renowned as a discreet and luxurious retreat for the city's wealthy and powerful.

Hera had accepted the venue for their date without the flicker of an eyelash. She'd known exactly what he was doing, of course, but she appreciated his delicacy.

The restaurant lighting was dim, with only candlelight at the table to illuminate their features. Around them people spoke in hushed voices, while a piano trio played quiet jazz standards.

Hera had spent most of the meal ignoring the food. She'd watched Peter's mouth as he talked and imagined how his lips might feel on her skin. Her body was thrumming, not with flaming desire, but with a simmering heat.

He leaned across the table and took her hand in both of his, lightly drawing his fingers down the delicate underside of her wrist. Hera shivered, and met his eyes.

"I didn't want to assume anything, but I've reserved a room upstairs," Peter said. His voice was low and intimate. "Would you like to come up with me?"

He was handsome and intelligent and there was that unmistakable zing. "Yes," Hera said. "I'd like that very much."

They didn't touch in the elevator, only smiled sly-eyed at each other as the couple ahead of them chatted about the lobster and got out on the sixth floor. Peter had reserved a room at the top. Exactly the move she would have expected.

When they stepped out of the elevator, he tucked her hand in his arm, and walked with her down the hall. She swayed against him, and felt the attraction charge between them.

Zing.

He opened the door without flourish, guided her in under his arm, and then Hera found herself on her tiptoes, kissing him for all she was worth in the narrow entranceway. He laughed against her mouth, and she laughed back, breathless.

Peter's hands settled on her waist, a tentative touch, and Hera said, "I'm not breakable."

"No, you're not," he murmured, and kissed her again, walking backwards into the room and reeling her in after him until they stood at the end of the bed. Then he kissed the hollow of her collarbone, exactly the same spot Zeus had always targeted, and she froze, the automatic desire mingling with a queasy surge of memory.

Peter didn't seem to notice. He kissed his way back up her throat to her mouth, and it was good again. Hera liked the careful slide of his tongue through her parted lips, and his hands were good too, very nice, though maybe she should be feeling something more than *nice*. He was gently pulling off her blazer and moving up under her silk blouse. His touch was warm and confident as his fingers curved around her ribs and slipped higher, cupping her breast in his palm.

Hera hitched a breath, and abruptly realized she was standing there like an idiot and letting him do all the work. She applied herself to his shirt buttons with determination, and then his fingers unhooked the back of her bra and she froze again, this time flinching back.

He noticed that time. "Everything okay?" he said, but without any real alarm.

"Yes, it's fine, I'm fine," Hera said, and moved back to his mouth, trying to chase the spark.

But their tongues were just wet muscle moving on muscle, and when Peter slid his hand down her ass and squeezed, she felt like she was meat being prodded at the butcher.

"Let's get on the bed," she said. Maybe it would be better if they equalized the height difference.

He stripped his shirt and slacks while she clambered onto the bed, still in her skirt and panties, her bra hanging off one arm until she impatiently tossed it aside. He had a perfectly nice body, and she focused on the gym-toned muscle in his arms and chest as he crawled up her body, framing her with his hands and knees, and there was something there, something good, and then he kissed her and lowered his weight down on her and she was abruptly trapped and suffocating.

"Get *off*," she said, and shoved at his shoulders with both hands, knowing it was rude, but needing to be out from under him, needing to *breathe.*

He kissed her neck again, and there was a brief moment when she thought *he didn't hear me* and then an even briefer moment when she thought *he did hear me, and he's not going to stop*, but as ice poured through her veins and she went rigid, he rolled off her and lay on his back.

"Okay," he said. "Do you need a minute?"

Hera scrambled off the bed and picked up her bra. "No," she said. "No, I'm sorry, I think I made a mistake."

Peter propped himself up on his elbow, and looked at her. He was probably trying to look patient and understanding, but he was simmering with frustration, and not a little annoyance. "Hey, if you don't want to do this, then you don't," he said after a moment. "But I think I can be forgiven for thinking otherwise."

"Yes, of course," Hera said, almost at random, as she located the rest of her clothes—how had her blouse gotten all the way over *there*?—and stepped back into her heels. She felt better covered up. Back in her armor. "This isn't your fault."

"It's not you, it's me?" Peter said, sounding tired. "Well, I guess that's a classic for a reason."

"It really is me," Hera said. "And I really am sorry. But I have to go now, and I don't think we should try this again." She pulled her dignity around her and met his eyes. "I do hope this won't affect our relationship in the office."

"I wouldn't have started this if I didn't think we could both be professionals," Peter said. His smile was wry, and Hera remembered why she liked him.

But she absolutely didn't want to have sex with him. Or spend another moment in this room.

"Well, then," she said. "I'll see you tomorrow. Good night."

"Good night, Hera," Peter said, and she was grateful he didn't try to walk her to the door or escort her down to the lobby, or any of the gentlemanly courtesies she might have otherwise expected from him.

She straightened her clothes and reapplied her lipstick in the empty lobby bathroom, and then locked herself in a stall to have some privacy while she cried, great, silent sobs that shuddered through her entire body. When it was over, she dabbed at her face with a wad of toilet tissue, and then emerged from the stall to find a round young woman in a designer silver mini dress leaning into the mirror, inspecting her teeth.

The woman startled and spun around. "Where did you—" she started, and then looked at Hera's face, no doubt mascara-streaked and tear-marked. "Oh, honey. Whoever he is, he's not worth it."

"It wasn't him," Hera said, hearing the wobble in her voice. "I left my husband in March, and I thought I was ready to do this and I'm not, and I feel *broken.*" She gulped, and took a couple of deep breaths, while the young woman pulled a mini pack of tissues out of her black leather purse and pressed them into Hera's hand.

Hera nearly wept again from the sheer kindness, but she pulled herself together and looked in the mirror. She was in even worse shape than she'd thought. Her red-rimmed eyes were underlined with deep black smudges, the lipstick she'd reapplied had smeared again, and her foundation was half-scrubbed off, making her skin look mottled. "I can't go home like this," she said, appalled. She'd scare Leia, and Don would probably demand to know who'd made her cry.

"Honey, I have got you," the young woman said, and proceeded to unload the contents of her purse onto the vanity. She had wet wipes, condoms, more tissues, a flashy cellphone, a small bottle of lubricant, two sets of keys, a travel toothbrush set, hand sanitizer, mints, deodorant and, right at the bottom, a small black pouch which proved to be full of sample-sized cosmetics. "I'm Anna, by the way."

"Hera."

"Nice to meet you," Anna said cheerfully, and steered Hera to the white leather bench which was probably placed there for women to sit while they gossiped with a friend in the stall. She wiped the wreckage off with gentle fingers, and then made Hera up again with practiced efficiency. "There! All done."

"Thank you very much," Hera said. "Really, I'm so grateful."

"My pleasure," Anna said, and winked at her. "And don't worry. I'm not going to tell anyone I saw Hera Rheczack crying. What happens in the ladies' bathroom stays in the ladies' bathroom."

"I appreciate it," Hera said. "I wasn't sure if you'd recognized me."

"You bet," Anna said. "I saw your Gaia interview, the one with Aphrodite. And even if I hadn't, well, I'm a big *Luxe* fan. Buy it every month. So great to see more women on top, you know?"

"Well, thank you," Hera said, relaxing a little. "And what do you do?"

"I'm an escort," Anna said. "Speaking of women on top."

"Oh," Hera said. "Well, usually my follow up is, 'That sounds interesting,' but perhaps that's rude?"

Anna smiled. "It *is* interesting. Probably not my forever career, but it's paying the bills." She rolled her shoulders. "And it's much better than waitressing."

"I can imagine," Hera said, although imagination was where it stopped. She'd never had to pick up any kind of service job. She checked her face again. Thanks to the wonders of white eyeliner, her eyes looked clear and bright again. No one would guess she'd been a weeping wreck ten minutes before. "You're a miracle worker."

"That's what they tell me," Anna said. She repacked her purse, somehow finding space for everything in a bag the size of a hardcover book. "I better get back to my date. And hey, don't worry about it, okay? Maybe this wasn't the right guy. But you're not broken. There will *be* a right guy." She left, and Hera gave her a minute before she followed.

She caught a glimpse of Anna in front of the concierge counter, linking arms with a tall woman and laughing up at her, and then Hera was out of the hotel and standing on the street in the desolate, rain-swept night. She called a car and went home.

Don and Leia were watching TV in the media room, some reality TV home makeover thing. Leia was absorbed, but Don glanced up as Hera paused in the doorway.

"Good night?" he asked cautiously.

Hera thought about Peter, and then about Anna.

You're not broken.

"On the whole, yes," Hera said, and went to her office, ready to get back to work.

Chapter Eleven

Don was stacking wicker baskets inside each other when he heard Jasmine whisper to another part-timer.

"Holy shit," she said, her voice a little strangled. "Is that Aphrodite Urania's boyfriend?"

"Looks like him," Celestia said, sounding impressed. "Did you see the costume he made her for Halloween?"

"Yes! So major. Should we ask him if he needs help?"

"You ask him, Jaz."

"Tia! What if *she's* here?"

"No, that's definitely the vibe of a man shopping alone. Go on."

"*You* go on."

Don rolled his eyes, walked past the whispering young women, and rounded the shelves. "Hey, Heph."

"Hi, Don," Heph said. He was using his chair today, big hands resting on the rims. "I thought I'd come see you about that stuff for my house."

Don thought the silence behind him was faintly tinted with outrage. "Sure," he said. "What's your style?"

"Aphrodite says it's normcore shabby chic," Heph said doubtfully. "Which I think means boring."

"Yeah, pretty much."

"Mellie told me to take photos and show you," Heph went on, and pulled his phone out of his messenger bag.

Don flicked through the pictures. Heph wasn't as tragic a case as Hades had been. The kitchen was good. He'd obviously had it refitted so that he could use it with his chair, and there was a deep red backsplash that indicated at least some interest in color. His living room showed signs of personality in the decoration—framed sci-fi posters, family pictures, a few nerdy figurines and a ton of books—but the furniture situation was definitely more shabby than chic, and the upholstery was all various shades of tan and beige, the kind of thing stores tried to sell as a neutral palette. The problem was that unless you matched shades exactly or added some color, everything just looked...muddy.

"Did you tidy up before you took the shots?"

"No. I'm always tidy. I need clear space to move."

"Great, so we're definitely not going for a maximalist thing." Don eyed Heph. Jeans, long-sleeved T, sturdy black leather shoes that looked like orthotics. "What's your favorite item you're wearing right now?"

"Uh. Oh! My bag, if that counts."

It was a sleek black messenger-style bag, reinforced with leather, and made out of some sort of strong canvas that had a bit of texture to it.

"Aphrodite gave it to me," Heph said.

It wasn't Aphrodite's style at all, so she'd obviously thought about what Heph would like, and delivered that. Don reasoned that he could probably trust her judgment as a starting point, and steered Heph towards a few Scandi look books that focused on clean lines and wood, furniture that was practical as well as good-looking. After consulting Heph's budget, they agreed that his coffee table could probably last another year, if it was polished, but new bookshelves were a priority, and he definitely needed a new sofa and armchairs.

Upholstery was easy—once Heph was prompted to think about the colors he actually liked, he went for plain chambray blues and sage greens, warm, dusty shades that would go well with the wood. He paid careful attention to the furniture dimensions, and they crossed several sofas off the list for being too low or too high for him to get in and out of without irritating his hips, before finding the perfect three-seater.

"And a throw or blanket of some kind," Heph said. "Something soft."

Heph, Don thought, was not an art quilt kind of guy. They had some cashmere throws in textiles, and when he brought out the biggest one, a gray-and-cream tabby weave that would look good on the sofa fabric, Heph reached for it immediately.

"This one," he said, as his hands sank into the folds.

Don escorted him to the cashier's desk, where Heph handed over his credit card without blinking at the total. Business must be going well for Vulcan Consulting. Don put the throw in a paper bag for Heph to take home with him, but everything else would have to be ordered and delivered.

"We can get things sent directly to you as they're ready, or they can come here and we deliver them all at once," he told Heph.

"That one," Heph said immediately. "And these bookshelves, they need to get the shelves inserted at the heights I want, right?"

"Right. Do you want us to assemble them?"

"Yes," Heph said, and Don noted that on the system. With a pang, he realized he wouldn't be the one doing assembly. The furniture wouldn't arrive until January, and he'd be in charge then, unable to leave the shop.

"You're really good at this," Heph said, and Don shook his head.

"I mean, it's my job," he said. "Doris and Neron are the real experts."

"Seriously," Heph said, and there was something in his voice, something that made Don look at him and realize he meant it. He wasn't flattering Don as a social nicety.

"Thanks," he said, and risked a further step. "I like it a lot. Making homes for people."

Heph nodded. "You should come over once it's all set up," he said. "I'll introduce you to e-sports."

"That sounds fun?" Don said dubiously. Well, it could be. He'd picked up *The Binding* at Aphrodite's recommendation, and that was fun. Heph grinned at him, his solemn face suddenly awash with good humor, and Don realized why Aphrodite was head over heels for him. "I'd like that," Don said, with more sincerity, and when Heph had left he went out to the garden section to let Doris know about the big sale.

"Good work," she said crisply, and then, as he loitered, "what?"

"I was thinking," he said. "Maybe we should run classes?"

"Classes," she said, and he had no idea what she was thinking, so he rushed into the gap.

"Quilting classes, maybe. Gardening demonstrations. Upholstery. People are interested in doing things for themselves. Our paint sells well."

"People teach themselves things from the internet, these days."

"Not always. Some things, you have to learn in the doing. And it's better with someone else showing you how."

"Hm," Doris said. "Well, put together a proposal and we'll see."

"Really?" Don said. "I mean, thanks!"

"It had better pay for itself," she said. "And you'll be the one running it, if we say yes. Yours to deal with, failure or success. And I mean it about the proposal, Don."

"Right," Don said. "Yeah. I think I know someone who can help me with that."

***

Hera decided that, in future, if she was going to walk into an all-hands meeting completely enraged, she needed to make sure that Hades wasn't in the room after all.

She knew her own face was perfect. She was wearing a pleasant, neutral mask that neither offered any comfort nor expressed any anger while Joy stammered excuses. But Hades, who knew her well, couldn't control his face, and he was wincing and grimacing as the story of Joy's incompetence compounded.

And the other department heads were taking note, and leaning away from Hera as if she were a time-delayed explosion. Augie Pelopson actually looked apprehensive, and for Augie to respond to an emotional atmosphere, it had to be a thunderstorm.

"So, we're still looking at alternatives, but I'm sure we'll have a solution soon," Joy said, her voice getting more strident instead of weakening. Joy was the kind of person who dug her heels in when others thought she was in the wrong, found ways to blame anyone but herself for her mistakes. "We might need to extend the budget in order to secure a venue at short notice—"

"Thank you, Joy," Hera cut in. "We'll discuss this after the meeting."

Hades winced again.

Mark Hermes looked at Joy, and then at Hera, and Peter sitting beside her. His face showed nothing, but Hera could make a fair guess at what he was thinking. Well, he'd tried to warn her, and she'd tried to act on the warning. She should have pressed Joy harder, but the woman had been so sure she had everything under control. And Hera knew she had a tendency to micromanage, knew that her perfectionism could turn into taking over instead of letting people do their jobs.

This time, she should have seen that Joy wasn't doing hers.

The rest of the meeting went quickly. Everyone was eager to get out of there. Hera crooked her finger at Joy and she stayed seated, shoulders slumping, but chin still defiantly raised.

Hermes lingered at the door, eyebrows raised in inquiry.

"Could you please close the door behind you, Mark," Hera said, and his eyebrows jumped even higher, but he left obediently enough.

Joy barely waited for the door to close. "If Zeus had just approved it in time," she started, and Hera threw up her hand.

"Stop," she said, her voice very quiet. "Joy, can you please confirm that we have nowhere to hold the Winter Ball?"

"I thought the Minos Center might drop a booking when—"

"Joy. It is November the 11th. The Winter Ball is in just under five weeks. The invitations which went out last week—already alarmingly late—named a venue that you knew for a fact we had not secured."

"Hera," Peter said. "You might be coming on a little strong, here."

Hera glanced at him. "I believe these are statements of fact. Joy?"

"It was more in the vein of a save the date. The Minos Center was really a placeholder. I thought we could notify the guests when we got another venue."

"Well, yes," Hera said. "We'll have to."

"You can't blame me for Zeus not approving in time!"

"I don't. I blame you for the fact I only discovered there was a problem when Demeter Erinyes called me two hours ago, wanting to know if I was aware that she'd already booked the center for that Thursday." Hera could still hear Demeter's voice in her head, sweet and faux-concerned, *just wanted to let you know, dear, I'm sure it's just a silly mix-up…* Hera had heard the gloating underneath.

Hera couldn't blame the Minos Center for opening up the slot during their prime season when Olympus had failed to either confirm the time or pony up the deposit, but she could and would blame Demeter for booking the center for the third Thursday night in December. That was *her* night, and had been for years. Demeter had known exactly what she was doing.

"You told me you could do this," Hera said.

"I *can*," Joy said. "I promise I can make it work."

"Why didn't you tell me there was no venue?"

Joy darted a beseeching look at Peter, then looked back to Hera. "You were so mad I hadn't got the plans underway," she mumbled. "I thought you'd be annoyed again."

"No," Hera said. "On my first day, Joy, I was clear that there should be no surprises. You should have brought this issue up weeks ago. Instead you told me everything was being handled. You told me to trust you. And I did, and you lied to me."

"I thought another woman would have more *understanding*," Joy said.

"I think I understand all I need to," Hera said calmly. "Just so we're clear, your employment is being terminated not because you didn't secure a venue, but because you lied about it."

Joy went chalk pale. "I'm being fired?" she said.

"Yes," Hera said. "Obviously."

"But I've worked here for years!"

"And now you will work somewhere else," Hera said, and shut her teeth on the suggestion that Joy not list her as a reference.

Now that her anger was cooling, Hera was feeling faintly sick. She should have had Mark sit in on this meeting, or met with him beforehand to discuss how best to go about it. She shouldn't have followed up with Joy at the all-hands meeting. She'd wanted to make Joy's mistake clear to the heads of department, before the rumor mill inevitably started turning out more outlandish stories to account for her termination right before the most important event of the year.

And, she had to admit, if only to herself, she'd been vengeful. The Winter Ball had been *hers*. She'd handed it to Joy because it was no longer her role, and Joy had tossed it in the garbage.

But the public meeting had been a mistake, disconcerting her staff and cutting Mark out when it was his right and duty to be more involved. Neither was a mistake she could afford.

At least she could avoid compounding her errors. "Mark Hermes will be in touch regarding the process from here," she said, and stood up to signal the end of the meeting.

Peter stood too, a little more slowly. He hadn't tried to dissuade her from the course of action she'd proposed, but perhaps he had regrets too.

Joy grabbed her bag and rocketed out of her chair so fast it nearly fell over. "I'm *glad* I slept with Zeus," she spat, and stormed out of the room.

Hera sat down again, somewhat abruptly. "Huh," she said blankly. "I didn't know she had."

Peter was shaking his head at the door. "We're better off without her."

"Yes, but not *now*," Hera said. Not five weeks before the biggest event in Olympus's busy social calendar. For all she knew, Joy might have been counting on that to save her job. She sighed, and rotated her shoulders, dropping her head to stretch the back of her neck. "Now we have to work out what to do with the Winter Ball."

"We could cancel," Peter suggested, and when Hera's head came up, he held out his hands protectively. "I know, you don't want to."

Cancellation would be beyond a mistake. It would be a disaster that marked her as incompetent. She was only *temporary* CEO and the waverers on the board would be severely alarmed by no Winter Ball. Perhaps if the invitations hadn't already gone out—*why* had Joy done that?—they could have instead sent a "save the date for next year." That way they'd appear prudent in a time of transition, while promising bright days ahead. But it was impossible now.

"I can only see one alternative to cancellation." Peter went on.

"Do tell," Hera said.

"You run the Winter Ball."

Hera frowned.

"You're the only one who could possibly pick it up at this stage. There's no one more familiar with the process, and you know every vendor in the city. And if *you* can't find a venue within a couple of days, I will eat my shoes."

Everything inside of Hera was shouting *yes, mine!* She tried to distance herself enough from that greedy elation to think through the proposal.

"You'd have to take on a lot of work too," she warned him. "If I'm focusing on the Ball, I won't be able to do everything else."

"I can handle it," Peter said. "I've been running under a very light load so far. Let me show you what I can carry." In his eyes was the glint of humor that she'd liked from the start. It was a week after their disastrous attempt in the hotel, but, as promised, he'd behaved perfectly professionally at work. She thought she had too. It helped that her attraction to him had been as abruptly severed as if it had been cut by a knife.

"All right," she said, and squared her tablet and notebook together. "Let's get to it, then."

In the outer office, Cyd and Diana were fielding calls. Even the unflappable Cyd was looking a little rattled, but she jumped to Hera's side as soon as she entered, scrolling through her tablet as they walked into Hera's office.

"Calls from Mark Hermes and Cleon in IT," Cyd reported. "A call from a society reporter at *Halcyon Days* wanting your comment on the Winter Ball being canceled—"

"That was fast," Hera said, placing her bag neatly on her desk.

"Is it? Canceled, I mean?"

"No."

Cyd looked at her. "Are you running it personally?"

"Yes."

"Then you need to cut almost all of the events from your charities list," she said. "Right now."

"Almost all of them? I'll cut some, of course, but does it really need to be—"

"Hera, this is your calendar for the next five weeks," Cyd said, and spun the tablet to show her. Yellow for Olympus meetings and appointments, red for her volunteer work, green for time at home or with friends. With the holiday season fast approaching, there was almost more red than yellow. She was scheduled for end of year meetings, dinners, parties, fundraisers. The green was disappearing, a few slivers here and there. But this evening and all of the weekend were blocked out with green, and for a moment, Hera couldn't remember why.

Wait. She and Don were taking Leia to the Hippocampus. She'd been happy about that just this morning, as she left a note asking Samia to pack for her, but now...

"Can you get Don for me, please?"

Cyd didn't move. "Don't cancel your weekend," she said. "Drop the dinners instead."

"I'm technically your boss," Hera reminded her.

"Sure, and part of my job is managing your schedule. You need that break."

Hera dropped into her office chair and massaged the bridge of her nose. Even her bones felt tired.

Diana burst into the office, grinning. "I have Mellie Smith-Freeman on line one," she said triumphantly, and Cyd smiled approvingly at her.

Hera felt her heart lift. Mellie was one of the best events planners in the city. "I'll take that now," she said. "Cyd, keep the unhoused youth shelter appeal, and please send my apologies to anything else you think I can reasonably miss." Cyd's understanding of *reasonable* was going to encompass more than her own, but she really did need that time. "After I speak to Mellie, I'll need to talk to Mark and—who was the other?"

"Cleon. From IT."

Hera felt a vague stirring of alarm, but she could worry about that shortly. "Diana, let Events know nobody else is in any danger of unemployment, but I need them to scramble and get me everything they've got for the Ball, ready for a meeting at my earliest convenience."

"And Don?" Cyd said, still not moving.

The red. The yellow. The Winter Ball...

A drive out of the city, to a peaceful retreat, where she could laugh with Don and watch Leia learn to ride.

"Please ask him if leaving an hour or two later will be inconvenient," Hera said, and picked up her phone. "Mellie? Hera here."

"So, what's going on?" Mellie said. Hera had known Mellie since her modeling days. She'd never been a true supermodel like Aphrodite, but she was smart, hard-working and beautiful, and had avoided most of the snares that tried to entrap the young people who entered that world. She was also Heph Smith's oldest sister, which Hera regarded as another tick in the positives column.

Hera outlined the situation in a few brief sentences, and heard Mellie's breathing change.

"Shit," she said finally.

"Precisely," Hera agreed. "Can you help? I will pay a truly extortionate fee, of course."

"I'm fully booked," Mellie said, with real regret. "Winter weddings are huge this year, and Demeter Erinyes hired me for her December thing, so I'll be busy on the night."

"Of course she did," Hera said.

"Honestly, I'd much rather work for you, but in this business keeping your promises is everything."

"I understand," Hera said.

"But I can maybe free up a few hours for consultation," Mellie said. "And I've got a few thoughts on venues. Can I get back to you on Monday?"

Hera felt her shoulders loosen for the first time in hours. "That would be amazing."

"You say that now," Mellie said cheerfully. "But wait until you see my bill."

They exchanged pleasantries and hung up, and Hera allowed herself a small sigh of relief.

Then Cleon burst into her office, Cyd right behind him.

"She took the files!" he cried, looking more upset than Hera had ever seen him.

"You can't just walk in—" Cyd began, but Hera waved her off and pointed Cleon to the chair in front of her desk.

"Who took what files?" she asked, although her shoulders were already tightening again.

Cleon took the seat, his fingers drumming against his thighs. "Joy! She downloaded all the Winter Ball files into a drive and *took* them. Not just this year's files. *All* of them. All the planning and the guest lists and vendor deals. *Everything* that's ever been done on *any* Winter Ball."

"Oh no," Hera said, her stomach dropping. She sat there for a moment in the full knowledge of her failure, and then took a deep breath. "Cleon, I do apologize. This is my fault. I should have followed the termination procedure and asked you to shut Joy out of the system before I spoke to her."

"No, you don't understand," Cleon said, which was not a thing Hera was used to hearing very often. "I messaged Maria during the meeting and told her to suspend Joy's access, because it definitely looked like she was getting fired. She downloaded the files before the meeting."

"She must have suspected it was coming," Hera said. "Well, that shows more foresight than I would have expected from Joy. Cleon, thank you for bringing this to my attention."

She waited until he'd left, and then asked Cyd to connect her to Mark Hermes. She had more apologies to make. And she had to find out what the rumor network had said about Joy's activities before the meeting.

***

It was nearly an hour past the extended time she'd given Don and really, unforgivably late, before Hera put her tablet down, rubbed her stinging eyes, and acknowledged there was nothing more she could do that night.

The Events staff had been eager to prove they hadn't known about Joy's negligence, and Hera thought this was probably true. Joy wasn't a woman who confided in others.

Unfortunately, while Joy had run away with years of successful Winter Ball files, she hadn't left them much to work with *this* year. All her assurances about working hard and taking care of things personally had been a cover for gross incompetence. The guest list hadn't been updated, and several key people had been left off it, some of whom would already be resenting the snub. Several important planning documents, which Joy had been "working" on in her office, turned out to be shopping lists, some bizarre fiction about a talking plant, and a ranked list of who in her staff she liked the least, updated daily.

"She looked so busy," said Daphne, the second-in-command. She was taking Joy's betrayal very personally, not least because she'd headed the list most often. "She was always at her computer."

"And the computer files would have looked like real work, unless any-one actually read them," Hera said grimly. IT kept records of everybody's workstation activity, and would have been alerted if Joy hadn't been logging in or saving work. But they had no reason to be suspicious of someone who was doing the hours and providing them with documents to save and back up. They didn't *open* those files.

Following a hunch, Hera had asked Daphne to check directly with vendors, and an hour later an ashen-faced Events assistant had reported that Joy had personally booked the musicians and caterers, only, it turned out, she hadn't.

At that point, Hera had moved her call to Legal several points higher up the priority list, because the disaster was starting to look a lot less like incompetence, and a lot more like deliberate sabotage.

But what was in it for Joy? She'd lost her job and her reputation. Could she really be motivated purely by spite?

Hera had sent Diana home two hours ago, but Cyd was still in the outer office, possibly to make sure that Hera herself left. Hera walked out to dismiss and thank her, and saw Peter approaching down the corridor, looking as tired as she felt.

"Is everything all right?" she asked. She'd dumped most of her afternoon's workload on him, and he'd evidently taken longer to get through it than she'd budgeted for herself.

"Long day," he said, around a yawn. "What time are you coming in tomorrow?"

Cyd sat straight up at her desk.

"I'm away this weekend," Hera said, trying to sound brisk and matter-of-fact, and not as if she were asking for forgiveness.

Peter frowned. "The Hippocampus trip? You're still doing that?"

Hera winced. "I know it's the worst possible time, but—"

"She promised Leia," Cyd said.

"I did," Hera agreed, her spine straightening.

Peter's lips thinned. "Well, okay," he said, sounding as if it wasn't okay at all. "I guess I'll keep the fires burning then."

Hera wavered. Was she being unfair, leaving him with Olympus at a time of crisis while she gallivanted around the countryside?

But she'd never broken a promise to Leia.

"Thank you," she said. "I really appreciate it."

Peter nodded, but he still looked mad.

"Your driver is ready downstairs, Hera," Cyd said. Her words and tone were perfectly appropriate, but her eyes promised that she would forcibly march Hera out of the building if she had to.

"Thank you, Cyd," Hera said, and left for her vacation, knowing she was going to have an absolutely miserable time.

Chapter Twelve

The drive up the coast to the Hippocampus was beautiful in daylight.

Even now, on this still, clear night, with a half-moon rising over the winding hills of the coastal road, Don could have really enjoyed the drive, if it weren't for the woman sitting in the passenger seat beside him, tense and unhappy.

Behind them, in the Camry's back seat, Leia snuggled deeper under the quilt she'd insisted on bringing with her. She was leaning her cheek against the window, her neck tilted at what looked like an uncomfortable angle, but since she'd been snoring quietly for the past ten minutes, Don was pretty sure Leia couldn't feel it.

"Do you want to talk about it?" he asked the woman beside him.

"I'm very sorry I was so late," Hera said quietly.

"You already said that," Don reminded her. "It's fine. We ordered burgers and Leia kicked my ass in *The Binding*. No big deal."

"I know. I just..." She let her breath out in a long exhale. "I made so many mistakes today. I hate that making us late for the trip is one of them."

She said it as if it were a crime. Maybe it was, for Hera. "Tell me about what happened," Don suggested. "We've got a couple of hours to go."

Hera half-turned. "Leia?"

"Sleeps like a log," Don reminded her. "And we'll be at the cottage before her pee break. I'll probably need a crowbar to get her out of the car."

"I fired Joy, from Events," Hera started, and Don nodded as if he knew who that was. He kept his eyes on the road and his hands firmly on the wheel, but half his attention was on Hera.

Don didn't give a crap about Olympus or the Winter Ball, except insofar as those things were important to people he cared about. But he was alarmed by Hera's voice, tight and miserable, wearily telling over her litany of errors. It was clear that she thought she'd failed the company, perhaps endangered her CEO position, and that in order to address the damage she'd taken on a mammoth task.

Out of the corner of his eye, he caught the glint of moisture on her face, and realized that she was crying, big, solid tears rolling silently down her face.

"Oh, hey," he said, and hit the indicator. They slid to a halt on the shoulder.

Hera opened the door and clawed at her seatbelt, and Don understood that she didn't want Leia to see her lose it. He went out after her, careful not to slam his door, and caught up with her a few feet down the road, outlined in the headlight beams, facing away from the car with her hands pressed over her mouth.

"Hey," he said again, and reached out, careful not to touch until she took a stumbling half-step towards him, and then he wrapped his arms around her and let her stifle her tears in his shirt. The storm of sobs lasted only a minute or two. "It'll be okay," he said, when it was over, and he thought she'd be able to hear him.

"I might lose Olympus," she said, her voice hitching.

"No, I don't think so," Don told her. "But even if you do, you'll still be okay."

She pushed herself away and glared up at him, and he spread his hands. "I'm not saying it won't suck. It'll definitely suck. But I'm saying that you'll still have all the people who care about you. You'll have people you care about and causes to champion. And you'll still be yourself. Hera fucking Rheczack, queen of the world."

Her smile was a little wobbly, but it was there. "My crown's a little tarnished today."

"Everyone makes mistakes," Don said. "You don't have to be perfect."

"I do, though," Hera said, and the exhaustion in her voice was deeply alarming. "For a woman to be where I am, she has to be perfect. And even then, it's not enough."

"If it's not enough, why wreck yourself over it?"

"You don't understand."

"I don't understand what it is to be a woman in your position, that's true. But I don't want to watch you destroy yourself to meet an impossible standard that still won't satisfy whoever you're trying to satisfy. Because they can't be satisfied. Because they're idiots who aren't worth a second of your effort in the first place."

He wasn't sure if any of it had got through, but she snorted, and her face relaxed. "I would love to see you say that to Samuel Janus's face," she admitted.

"Babe, you want me to do that, and it's done."

She gave him a sly look under her lashes. "It would definitely make the next shareholder meeting more entertaining."

Don didn't have to pretend his horror at the thought, but struck a noble pose. "For you, I'll go."

"Even if I want you to wear a suit?"

"Oh, I see. You just want me in a suit."

She smiled at him. "You do look very good in a suit."

There was a moment that stretched, that could have been something, and then Hera looked away.

"Besides, I'm not some big corporate guy, but I don't think leaving your HR guy out of one firing is that much of a crime," Don said, for lack of anything else to say. "I mean, I've committed actual crimes."

Hera blinked at him. "Truly?"

"Mm-hmm. Pleaded guilty and everything." He pulled a face, and felt the familiar tug of self-disgust that came up every time he thought about it. He kept his voice light, for Hera's sake. "Knocked a guy out in a bar fight, got arrested and charged, did time-served and paid a fine."

Hera patted his arm. "You're right," she said. "That's much worse than me."

Don burst into laughter. Hera giggled.

It had been a long time since he'd heard her laugh.

"You cheered me up," Hera said. "I thought it was impossible, after the day I've had, but look at that. How do you always know how to do that?"

Don had a plan. A bistro brunch reservation on Sunday, for just him and Hera. He had a speech he'd prepared, a careful revelation of how his feelings had deepened for her, how if she didn't share them he would understand, but did she think that maybe, once she'd thought about it...

Now she was beaming at him in the headlights, relaxed and laughing, and they could have been the only people in the world.

And then Leia stumbled out of the car, bleary-eyed. "What's wrong?" she called. "Is something wrong with the car? I can take a look at it."

"Just stretching our legs," Hera said smoothly, and headed back to the Camry.

But before they got moving again, she laid her hand on Don's, resting on the gear stick, and squeezed, just once, and he felt that phantom touch all the way to their destination.

***

The Hippocampus was an unusual place. Technically, it was Hippocampus Bay, a wide, deep curve carved into the coastline as if some giant had taken an enormous bite out of the hilly coastline. A natural sandbar protected the bay, and it had built up with soil and plant matter over the millennia until it was a long, skinny peninsula, just barely connected to the land. The most exclusive summer homes and resorts in the Hippocampus were located on that sandbar, and Hera had visited several times, but she'd never wanted to stay long. It seemed like a precarious sort of place, as if the sand might wash away underneath them. Indeed, during storm season, the buildings there often risked damage and destruction.

For once, she'd left all the details of the trip to someone else, both because she hadn't had time and because she was confident Don could handle it. He hadn't booked them a spot in one of those exclusive sandbar resorts, but rented a lovely cottage nestled in the deepest curve of the bay, halfway up a hill, with a stunning view of the sea.

Hera had woken in the quaint brass bed, listened to the birds in the pine trees behind the cottage, and felt as if her bones might melt into the very comfortable mattress.

Of course, two minutes later Leia had knocked at the door wanting to know if Hera was awake yet because Don had said they could go get brunch and she was *starving*, but the tranquility had been nice while it lasted.

It was a windy day, with a bite in the air, and white clouds scudding over the bright sky. Too cold to sit and eat outside, really, but Leia had clearly fallen in love with the bay at first sight. While planning the trip she had decided, after much deliberation, that she'd rather learn to ride than sail, but now her heart was in her eyes, watching the little dinghies from the local yacht club tack across the waves.

And she was oddly jittery on top of that, sneaking glances at Hera and Don that she obviously thought were subtle. Whatever was worrying her, she didn't seem satisfied by what the glances told her.

Or maybe she was just worried about the letter beside her plate, held down by a spare fork. The envelope had been resealed twice and was now stuck down with tape, so she'd obviously thought and rethought about what she told her family. Hera had resisted the temptation to offer her help with composition or drafting, and Leia hadn't asked for it, covering pages of plain notepad paper with her neat, loopy script.

Don pushed his plate away and sighed, a sound of deep satisfaction.

"You'd think you'd never been fed," Hera observed. "A bystander certainly wouldn't guess you were an excellent cook yourself."

"It's not the same as eating eggs someone else made," Don said. "Reminds me of life on board."

"You didn't cook, when you worked on the ship?" Leia asked.

"Nah, that's a specialist job. If you want to keep all your fingers, you don't walk into the galley uninvited and start messing around with Cook's supplies. The food was good, though, and there was always plenty of it. Quickest way to lose your crew is to feed them badly."

"Huh," Leia said, sounding thoughtful. "Do you need much school to be a cook on a ship?"

"A culinary institute or cooking school diploma, for starters. And some restaurant and sea time, usually."

"How did you start working on ships, anyway?" Leia asked.

Don grinned. "Deck hand. I'd got some work at a dock, helping with unloading, and was there when a cargo vessel needed someone who could sign on immediately. I had a passport, sea time, and I was physically able. They were in a hurry, so that was good enough. They hired me for the one voyage. And kept me on after. After a year or so, the second officer suggested I look into training as an officer cadet."

"Cargo vessels must be different from pleasure craft," Hera observed.

"Very different," Don said. He finished the last of his coffee, and got up to use the facilities.

"Hera," Leia said urgently. "I think I want to go sailing."

"You and Don are already booked at the stables," Hera said. "We haven't booked a boat."

"There's a sailing club offering walk-up lessons," Leia said. "I checked. I could go talk to them after brunch and see if they have room for me today. I can pay for it."

"Hm," Hera said. It was Leia's money, and Hera should probably be supporting her independence. It was a little rude to change her mind at the last moment, but after her terrible lateness yesterday, Hera wasn't sure she had much standing to point that out. "And what's Don supposed to do?"

"He could go riding with you!" Leia said triumphantly.

Behind her, Don was coming back from the bathroom. He met Hera's eyes, looking faintly resigned, and shrugged.

"Horses," Hera said. "I'm not great with horses."

"You told me that you used to have a horse," Leia said.

"It wasn't the most positive experience," Hera admitted. As a teenager, she'd been eager to ride. Many of her boarding school classmates were equestriennes, and she'd read all the sugary sweet books about the true bond between girl and equine. When she'd finally asked her parents for a horse—after all, their estate did have a stables—she'd prepared a detailed presentation on why having a horse would teach her valuable lessons about responsibility, vulnerability and trust.

In the event, she hadn't had to use any of it. She'd said, "Daddy, can I please have a horse?"

He'd taken his adoring gaze off her mother long enough to say, "Of course, honey."

And then, instead of doing any of the work a parent might reasonably do, he'd asked his assistant to get Hera a "really good horse" and the most exclusive trainer she could find.

Hera had ended up with a nervous thoroughbred sport horse who should never have been matched with an inexperienced rider, and a trainer who yelled at both of them.

Don was looking at her. She'd told him all about Starshine—ridiculous name, what had possessed her?—a few months ago, and his response had been cold fury at both her trainer and her father. And sympathy for

Hera and Starshine. Apparently there really was something to the whole bond between human and horse that she'd missed out on.

"It'd be different," he said quietly. "I chose the horses; they're steady, with good manners. And this stable has a great reputation. They wanted references and an interview before they'd let me out with two of their mounts and no guide."

"Or I could stay in the cottage and rest while you ride?" Hera suggested.

"They definitely won't let me ride solo," he said ruefully. "I think you're stuck with me, whether you stay in or go out."

Oh, no. She couldn't stay in with Don. She'd nearly kissed him last night, when he'd made her laugh. She'd thought he might have kissed her back, if she had. If she were alone in a cottage with him for hours with no wi-fi, she might be tempted to test the theory.

And they had such a good dynamic, so stable, so good for Leia. She'd be a fool to push their relationship in a different direction.

Besides, he probably didn't feel the same way. Don was so forthright and confident; if he'd the slightest notion of the thoughts running through her head, he'd have said something months ago.

Unfortunately, she realized, as Leia went to post her letter and check the sail club availability, that meant she was stuck with the horses.

***

"She's very tall," Hera said doubtfully.

Don already had a grudge against Hera's parents, but it flared into actual fury when he watched her hold her palm out to the elegant brown

230

mare he'd selected for her and obviously steel herself for a poor reception. The mare delicately picked the piece of apple out of her hand and munched.

"Tall is good," Don told her. "Big horses don't tend to dance around much."

"Is she an Arabian?" Hera asked, looking at the high, curving neck.

"They're usually smaller," Don said, eying the pedigree certificate on the stall door. "No, she's a Shire Quarter Horse cross."

"We think the Quarter Horse half might have some Arabian blood," the stablemaster volunteered.

"What's her name?"

"Cyllarus," Don said. "Which I think means 'pretend she's an expensive import instead of from a breeder in Kansas'."

The stablemaster snorted agreement and looked at Don with more approval.

Hera smiled, as he'd intended her to, and took the reins with more confidence, walking her mare out to the yard.

Don's own horse was already waiting there. The stables had re-named him Xanthus, another ridiculous name for the short, wide-set gelding. Don had satisfied himself that Xanthus had good manners, and would set an excellent example for Cyllarus. He checked the tack on both horses. The stablemaster had already done it, but it was an automatic gesture, and Hera looked more assured by the moment.

"Did you do a lot of riding, while you were away?" she asked.

"Here and there," Don said. "If you're months at sea, you're also months off."

"Well, I suppose we should get going," Hera said, and put her helmet on. She struggled with the strap, and Don avoided the urge to adjust it for her, but when she looked around, obviously searching for a mounting block, he couldn't resist.

"Let me help you up," he said, and walked behind her, bending to place his hands lightly on her hips. He didn't think he was imagining the hitch in Hera's breath as she went still. "Left foot in the stirrup. Good. Okay, now jump on three. One, two, three!"

Hera jumped. Don lifted. There was a scrambling moment, when she nearly kicked him in the chin, and then she was settling into the saddle, her right foot finding the other stirrup. Don handed her the reins, and mounted his Xanthus.

Hera gazed across at him, her eyes wide and dark. He could still feel the soft pressure of her hips against his palms. After a moment, Hera smiled. "I must say it's interesting to see you from this angle."

Don grinned at her. Xanthus was just over 15 hands, and Cyllarus nearly 18. The horses didn't entirely equalize the height difference between them, but Hera was a lot closer to his eye level than she normally got.

"Is that horse big enough for you?" she added. "It looks as if he could walk out from under you, if you put your legs down."

"Not quite," Don said, and nodded at the stablemaster, who opened the gate for them. He nudged Xanthus with his knee and the horse walked forward.

The trail wound up and down through pine-covered hills. The woods were spacious, not the close-quarters that might have made a horse edgy. Between and beyond the pines, Don caught glimpses of the sea, until they were behind the hills, into low scrubland. The horses were obviously accustomed to the route and Don barely needed to touch his reins. It was a quiet, gray day, and Don was happy to ride behind Hera in near-silence, listening to birds in the low bushes chirp the occasional sleepy notification of the big mammals passing through. Hera was drinking in the serenity of the surroundings, taking deep breaths of cold, pine-scented air. Her seat was good, and Cyllarus was surefooted and docile.

"We could try a trot?" Hera suggested.

"When was the last time you tried to sit a trot?" Don said.

"About fifteen years ago."

"Then no, we could not try a trot. Not if you want to be able to move tomorrow. Besides, that's the picnic spot."

The horses were already heading for the small pasture and the water trough inside it, with clear expectations. Don dismounted and offered his hands to Hera, and she slid down into his grip.

"Oof," she said, as her feet hit the ground and took her weight.

"Do some stretches," Don advised. He took care of their mounts, then investigated the insulated saddle bags for their lunch. A charcuterie spread, flavored soda water, and two brownies that looked promisingly dense and fudgy. No alcohol, of course. The stable wasn't going to risk their horses on drunk riders.

By the time he'd laid everything out, Hera was part way through a fluid yoga routine which made it clear just how flexible she was. When she bent in half and wrapped her arms around her calves, Don had to look away so he wasn't caught staring at her ass.

"It's chilly," Hera said, coming to join him at the picnic table. "You weren't kidding about dressing warm." Under Leia's borrowed rain jacket, she was wearing a gray cashmere sweater that had probably cost more than Don was paid in a week, but at least she didn't look cold. In fact, there was a flush in her cheeks and a brightness in her eyes he hadn't seen for a while.

Don pointed at the jagged mountain peaks in the distance, just visible through the cloud cover. "In a month, those will be covered in snow."

"Winter snuck up on me so fast. I feel as if I haven't been outside for months," Hera said wistfully. "I'd say that I must make more time for the outdoors, except the next five weeks are going to be... challenging."

"Can you really pull the Winter Ball together in five weeks?" he said.

"If I can secure a venue on Monday," she said. "Tuesday at the latest. If that doesn't happen, I will need to cancel. Otherwise... it will be tight. But I can do it." Her voice firmed on the last phrase, allowing for no doubt. Not that Don was inclined to doubt her. "I'm considering a theme change. Joy had put forward An Evening Among the Stars, which would have been workable, but then she didn't do any actual work on it."

"If you change the theme, won't people need new outfits?"

"It's not a costume ball," Hera said, amused. "Most of the time, people go for a tuxedo or a glittery formal gown. You were there last year, remember?"

"Yes. You wore that royal blue column dress. It wasn't glittery, but it had a kind of sheen to it."

Hera looked taken aback. "It was raw silk," she said. "And you wore your tuxedo. With no bowtie."

Don shrugged. "I couldn't find it."

"I'll make sure you have one this year." She smiled at him, and gestured at their surroundings. "Everything feels very peaceful here. Like the world is getting ready to sleep."

Don nodded. "It's conserving energy, getting ready to wake up again."

"What a lovely thought." She turned to face him. "Thank you for making me come out here."

"I'm not sure anyone can make you do anything."

"No. But I do listen, when people insist. Thank you for insisting."

"You're welcome," Don said. There was a deep calm to this place. Perhaps he should confess now, while they were both relaxed and happy together. Sure, if she said no, the ride back might be a little awkward, but they'd have something to concentrate on, and a good excuse to ride single file.

"Hera," he said, and leaned across the picnic table.

Something cold and wet splattered on his head.

Hera was holding her palm face up, frowning at the sky. "Is that... ?"

"Rain," Don said, as another heavy drop hit the picnic table, leaving a dark circle on the worn wood. He got to his feet, already castigating himself for not paying attention. The forecast had been for calm and overcast, with rain falling further inland, but the wind had changed. The mountains in the distance had vanished now, and the clouds that were rolling towards them were fast and dark. "We'd better get moving."

Hera nodded, and packed up their lunch debris, while Don got bridles and reins back on their mounts. The rain was sticking to occasional fat drops, but he really didn't like the look of those clouds.

"Is it going to be bad?" Hera asked.

"We might get damp," Don said, momentarily wishing he had access to a ship bridge. Once you'd navigated meteorological instrumentation, using your own human senses was a definite step down. But he still should have been more alert. "No thunder or lightning."

Hera shuddered. "That would be bad."

"Yes," Don agreed, and boosted her onto Cyllarus, too worried to enjoy it. "I'll take the lead, okay?"

The drops got lighter, but faster as they left the scrubland, until they were riding back through the hills in a thin drizzle. Don kept twisting in the saddle to check on Hera. The rain fell harder. Cyllarus snorted her discomfort, once, then twice.

Don moved his lower legs away from Xanthus's sides, and the gelding was already stopping before he put any pressure on the reins. He dismounted and helped Hera down. Cyllarus shifted from side to side. Xanthus whuffled reassurance at her.

"I think we'd better wait it out," he said. They were probably only forty minutes away from the stables, but forty minutes with a restless mare in what was fast shaping up to be an actual rainstorm wasn't an option for Hera. He scanned the woods for something solid the horses could put their tails against, and spotted the bare rock of the hillside through the sparse tree cover.

Two minutes later he was tying down the horses under the overhang at the edge of the clearing. The horses could be confident nothing was coming up behind them, and they had enough line of sight that the reduced visibility wouldn't be too frightening. There was even a thick hemlock tree to the right of the clearing that would make reasonable cover for the humans in the party.

He checked the knot on the tie down ropes, and then disconnected the reins. "Give me your rain jacket?"

Hera stripped it off without comment or question and handed it to him, wrapping her arms around herself. Don nodded at the big hemlock. "It'll be driest close to the trunk," he told her.

Hera ducked obediently under the low branches.

Don tied their jackets over their mounts' saddles. Wearing saddles through the storm would be a little uncomfortable for the horses but they'd be much more uncomfortable if he tried to put wet saddles on wet skin afterwards, and they'd still have to ride back. By himself, he might have put them both on a leading rope and walked, but it would be a real hike for Hera.

He talked softly to the horses as he worked; it didn't matter what he said, so much as the tone of voice. Cyllarus stepped nervously when a gust of wind howled and rain spattered on the overhang, but Xanthus stayed calm, and the mare took her cue from him, quieting down again.

Don checked the ropes one last time, and ducked in under the tree.

The tree cover was thick, holding off most of the rain, so that the soil beneath them was merely damp. He had to bend, but Hera was standing at her full height by the trunk, blinking owlishly at him through her wet bangs. Don took his helmet off, and went to his knees. "Are you okay?"

"Yes," Hera said. Her eyes were huge and dark, tracking his movement as he knee-walked towards her. "I'm very well. And you... you're wonderful."

"Hera," Don said, with absolutely no idea of what he'd say next.

Hera looped her hands around the back of his neck. Her body was pressed against his, all that thrumming energy and intensity barely contained by her delicate bones. Her eyes were electric, her touch was lightning, and Don had just enough time to think *yes, now* as she pressed her mouth to his.

"I had a schedule," he said, mostly to himself, and then he gave in to the inevitable and kissed the woman he loved with everything he had.

***

Hera wasn't thinking at all.

It felt as if every time she came up for air, or thought *what am I doing* or *this is Don!,* every time her brain tried to sabotage her with careful consideration or a rational approach, her body pushed her back under. Any feeble appeal to reason was being drowned out by the sheer physical wonder of what was happening to her, what she was causing to happen, here and now.

Here, Don's hands were tight on her waist, easily lifting her so she could lock her legs around his torso. She bent down to him, cradled his face in her hands, and nipped at his mouth in teasing little bites until he growled.

Now, Don was lowering her onto her back, kissing her so tenderly she thought she might die from the sweetness of it. He knelt over her, his mouth gentle while his hands roved hungrily over her body, skating the slight curve of her breasts, the trembling muscles of her thighs.

Here, she was tugging at his sweater, needing it off, *off*, breathless with joy and gasping with need, unable to understand why their clothes hadn't just melted away. He kissed her throat, and she sighed. He kissed the bared skin of her stomach as he tugged her riding pants down her thighs and calves, and she moaned and that brought him panting back to her mouth.

Now, finally, she was touching bare skin, broad shoulders and strong chest, all of him so big and sure and powerful. His body wasn't unfamiliar. She'd seen him bare-chested a hundred times. But not like this, not with license to stroke and tease, not with permission to feel his nipples harden under her fingers. She'd never been allowed to palm his cock through his underwear and hear him groan in her ear.

Why had she wasted all this time? Why hadn't they been doing this forever?

For a moment, something uneasy stirred at the back of her mind, like a shadow in a doorway.

But *here*, Don's mouth was at her breast, and *now*, his fingers were stroking her slick folds and *here*, she was pushing at his shoulder until he rolled onto his back and *now*, he was helping her climb on top of him, his hands tight on her waist, and *here* he was, long and thick in her grasp and *now* she was sliding him inside her and *here* they were finally moving together, *here, here, now.*

***

Don swallowed a groan as Hera rocked above him, her wicked eyes locked on his. She was smiling, that sharp, wild grin that almost no one saw, the smile that said she was winning, and knew it.

They hadn't had time to talk. Don wasn't sure they'd really had time to breathe. One minute they'd been kissing and rolling around on the damp earth beneath the hemlock tree, and in the next he was moving with her, thrusting up as she rolled her hips down.

It could have been a dream. He'd had dreams like this. But the quiet whuffling of the horses, the sound and smell of the rain, and most of all, Hera clenching around him, hot and wet—all of that was too real.

He grabbed her hips to keep her steady and sat up, still inside her, holding her close against him.

"Oh," she said. "Don. This is so good. I never thought—"

This wasn't a time for talking. He thrust up harder and she lost the rest of the sentence, her eyes going glassy.

Her hands were on his shoulders, small and strong, and she lifted one and laid her palm against his cheek, her smile softening.

"I love you," Don said.

It was a mistake. He knew it the second he'd said it. Hera looked blank for a second, as if she hadn't really heard him, and then comprehension and alarm flooded into her eyes.

He kissed her before she could say anything, and felt her respond to that, felt her weight shift as she changed her angle, taking him deeper, felt her shiver and pulse around him as the orgasm rolled through her.

And then he was gone too, his vision whiting out with the intensity of his own orgasm. He was gasping and shaking when it was over, feeling as if he'd been rung out. Hera was quiet, sitting in the circle of his arms as if she wasn't sure how to react to any of it.

"Are you okay?" he asked, when he got his breath back.

"Yes," Hera said, and then kissed him fiercely. "That was wonderful, Don. Really." She hugged him, a reassuring squeeze, before she unfolded her legs and carefully got to her feet, naked and pale and perfect in the dim light that filtered through the willow tendrils. Her skin was smudged with dirt, and her hair had tangled, but she still looked like a queen.

"I'll check on the horses," Don said. He clambered back into his pants and boots and walked out. The horses were fine, of course. As long as it didn't present a threat to them, they'd be totally unconcerned with the strange behaviors of the other mammals under the tree.

But he sure as hell needed a moment.

What had happened? What had he done?

He flashed back on Hera laughing in his ear as she cupped his cock through his underwear, and bit back a curse. She'd been right there with him, passionate and joyous and fierce, a miracle he'd only ever imagined, and far better in reality than he could have ever dreamed.

And then he'd opened his stupid fucking mouth.

The rain had dropped away until it was barely more than a drizzle. The horses wouldn't be happy, but they could ride home in this. They'd better, before it picked up again.

He turned back to the tree, just as Hera emerged, fully dressed. She held out his shirt and undershirt, and he pulled them back on.

Her cheeks were very pink.

"We should probably talk," she said carefully.

"Just forget I said it," Don said desperately. "Please."

Hera went even pinker. "Not that. Although—no, I meant, we didn't use a condom."

"Oh, fuck," Don said, and closed his eyes. "You're right. I'm so sorry. I didn't think."

"I'm on birth control," Hera said determinedly. "And my last checkup didn't show any concerns, and I haven't...engaged in anything since."

"I'm clean, too," Don said. "I'm usually pretty careful, believe it or not."

"I believe it," Hera said, and smiled at him. "I'm assuming people don't usually climb all over you at the drop of a hat. But maybe I'm wrong."

This was probably his cue to say something playful back, but he wasn't in the mood for banter. He felt sick and shaky, as if he might fall apart.

"Don?"

"I'm all right," he said, which was such a fucking lie he could barely stand it. "Let's just get back to the stables. Leia will be wondering where we are."

***

"What *happened*?" Leia asked.

Hera blinked and turned to her. Don had pleaded exhaustion and gone to his room for an early night. Hera had been staring down the hallway after him like a hormone-struck teenager.

Of course the *actual* teenager in her life had noticed.

"You came back all quiet and dinner was weird," Leia continued, staring at Hera. "Did you have a fight?"

"No," Hera said.

She'd thought that she and Don had done a pretty good job of concealing their mutual unease. The ride back to the stables had been excruciatingly quiet, with none of their usual easy rapport, but as soon as Leia had met them at the cottage, they'd both focused on her, asking about her sailing adventures.

But in the middle of gushing about her time on board, Leia must have been observing them too. Now she frowned at Hera.

"So you didn't have a fight, but you're not really talking," she said, and then her face changed. "He told you, didn't he?"

"Told me what?" Hera demanded, and Leia actually clapped her hands over her mouth, her eyes darting guiltily down the hall.

"Let's go down to the boardwalk for dessert," Hera said with more volume, and beckoned Leia out to the Camry. She didn't take them to the boardwalk, though, only drove two blocks away and parked. "Told me what, Leia?"

"Told you that he...likes you," Leia admitted.

Hera's stomach fluttered. She'd been drowning in sensation, barely able to breathe from the piercing sweetness of Don moving with her. She'd been happy, so happy, and she'd put her hand on his cheek and he'd said—

She tore away from the memory. He hadn't meant it, of course. People said strange things in the middle of sex, as the chemicals raged through their brains. If he'd meant it, he would have said something earlier. He'd even told her afterwards, *Forget I said it.*

Don didn't conceal things from her. Not the important things.

But when he had said what he'd said, she'd felt so strange. Elated, then alarmed. And whatever her face had done in response would have totally killed the mood, if they both hadn't been so close to that earthshattering orgasm.

These were not appropriate thoughts to be having right now.

"Don't you like him back?" Leia asked.

"Of course I like him!" Hera said strongly. Too strongly. "Don is one of my oldest friends, Leia. I like him very much." And that afternoon she'd fucked him senseless. No, she'd been the senseless one, leaping on top of him the moment he'd come under the tree with her. What had he said when she'd first kissed him? *I had a schedule.*

What schedule?

"Leia, has Don said anything to you about...liking me?" she asked.

Leia bit her lip. "I think we shouldn't talk about this anymore," she said. "I mean, you and me. I shouldn't have said anything in the first place."

Hera took a deep breath. "Yes," she said. "You're probably right. I won't press you to betray a confidence."

"He didn't confide in me," Leia said quickly. "I overheard—it doesn't matter."

Hera knew exactly why she responded so badly to secrecy, surprises, and other people knowing things she didn't. It was partially because she handled uncertainty by gathering as much information as she could and creating plans and back-up plans ready to implement, and mostly because her ex-husband had cheated on her and lied about it on multiple occasions, and had also *had a son* he'd kept her from knowing about.

Recognizing the source of the emotion didn't actually make it any more pleasant, but it did mean that later that evening, she knocked on Don's door with a certain amount of quiet restraint.

He opened it, fully dressed. So much for an early night.

"May I come in?" she asked.

"Sure," he said, equally politely, and stood back to allow her entry.

His bed was made, but rumpled, as if he'd been lying on top of it. Possibly staring at the ceiling while his brain turned anxious circles, but perhaps she was projecting.

"So," she began, perching on a chair in the corner, as far from his bed as she could get. "I think I do want to discuss what you said while we were...intimate."

Don nodded, and sat on the edge of his bed, keeping his distance. She wasn't sure if he was avoiding her eyes, because she wasn't quite able to make eye contact herself. "I thought you might bring that up," he said quietly.

Hera had prepared a careful, gentle interrogation with a few conversational gambits that would subtly lead to the information she wanted. She opened her mouth to begin and blurted, "Did you mean it?"

Don looked at her then, and she lost her breath at the intensity of feeling in his eyes. "I have never meant anything more."

"I—for how *long*?"

He shut his eyes, then opened them again, looking bleak. "A long time."

"Months?" She bit her lip. "Before the divorce?"

"Oh, Hera," Don said. "I've been in love with you for twenty-two years."

She stared at him, utterly bereft of speech.

"I never brought it up because it didn't seem like there was any point. You and Zeus were so happy. And then you weren't, but anyone could see you weren't over him. And then you married him again."

Hera thought back to the night before her second wedding, when Don had visited her with a warning. In the light of this new information, she could see the way the conversation could have gone, back then. But she'd said she loved Zeus. Which she had. And Don had elected not to tell her his own feelings, the night before the wedding.

It was most certainly the right and correct move, she told herself, and stamped out the wistful thought that maybe things would have been different if he'd confessed then. Past-Hera had been very sure of Zeus's reformation. She would have been appalled at Don, seen it as an attempt to wreck her wedding day, and she would have told him so in no uncertain terms.

And then, perhaps, he wouldn't have been there for her, over this past difficult year. Her chest squeezed painfully. It had been so very hard. But without Don...it was unthinkable.

"Oh, Don," she said, realizing something else. "Please tell me that's not why you went to sea."

He gave her a wry smile. "It wasn't the whole reason. I did genuinely love the work. It made more sense to me than anything else ever had."

"But it was some of the reason?"

He shrugged. "Sort of. I'd come back, see how things were, and then go away again. Except this last year, I haven't been able to leave. And spending so much time with you, *living* with you... I knew it was a bad idea. I couldn't keep my feelings hidden."

"But you still didn't tell me," Hera said, her voice breaking.

"I was going to," he said. "Tomorrow morning, at brunch, I was going to broach the subject."

"Your schedule."

"Yes. But we kind of jumped the gun this afternoon." He held up his hand. "And before you start, that's not your fault, okay? I was right there with you."

"I'm so sorry, Don. If I'd known..." she trailed off. Would she have exercised more self-control if she'd known how Don would feel about it? Well, now she'd never know for sure.

"I thought I knew you," she said. "But you kept this from me."

"Can you blame me?"

"No. No, I understand why you didn't tell me. But I can't help how I feel about secrets and concealment."

"I understand," Don said steadily, and the worst thing was that she knew he did.

"Can't we just forget?" Hera asked, knowing it was a foolish question even as she asked it. "I mean, not forget, exactly, but put it aside and go back to the way we've been?"

"I will never forget making love to you," Don said, his voice raw. "I will remember it until I die. And I don't think there's any going back. Hera, I need you to say it, okay? You need to tell me you don't feel the same way."

Hera's thoughts were scattered, like so many pieces of driftwood on the beach after a storm. She couldn't put them together. Could she even say it? Could she tell Don she didn't love him?

"I care for you very much," Hera said. "But I don't—" She quailed at the awful look on his face. "I've never *thought* about it, Don. I mean, I've been thinking about—I didn't kiss you out of nowhere." She pressed cool hands to her burning cheeks. "I was thinking, perhaps it might be worth exploring the possibility. But you love me? You've loved me this long? And I had no idea? It's too much!"

"I know," Don said.

"I just—I can't say anything right now. Can you give me a little time?"

"I don't know," he said helplessly. "I don't understand what's happened. Yesterday I would have told you I'd wait forever and be content, but now I don't think I can. I think, one way or the other, I need to know soon. Once and for all."

"It's not *fair*," Hera burst out. "I should have fallen for you *first*."

Don buried his face in his hands. From the way his shoulders were shaking, Hera thought for a terrified moment that he was crying. But when he lowered his hands again, she saw that he was laughing silently, his face caught on the knife's edge between hilarity and despair. "Of course it's not fair," he said. "But here we are. How much time do you think you'll need?"

Hera wanted to reach for him. Instead, she clasped her hands together, pressing tightly.

"I have the Winter Ball coming up," she said.

"Right," Don said, his face smoothing over. "You've got a lot of important things on your mind."

"No, I don't mean—Don, the ball isn't more important than you."

Don blinked at her. "It's not?"

"Of course not," Hera said, exasperated. "But what I mean is, that's in five weeks. Can you give me five weeks? The day after the Winter Ball, I'll...we'll have another conversation."

After a long moment, Don nodded. "All right," he said. "And in the meantime, I'm moving out."

"You don't need to—" Hera began, and then reconsidered. He really did.

Don gave her a complicated look. "Hera, I'm already packed."

"Why?" Hera asked, sincerely baffled. If he'd been planning to broach the subject of their relationship tomorrow morning, why would he have bothered to pack before he knew her answer?

Then she realized, and put her hand out to stop him before he had to say it.

He'd never expected her to say yes.

"All right," she said, her voice wavering. "I'll...we should explain things to Leia."

Don nodded. "We can do it on the ride home," he said. "Do you mind if we leave earlier than we'd planned?" He tried to smile. "I guess I can cancel my brunch reservation."

Horrifying herself on every level, Hera burst into tears.

Don jumped to his feet and reached for her automatically, then hesitated, his own face contorted.

"Don't," she said, hiccupping on the word. If he touched her, if he gave her comfort, she'd take it. And that wasn't right. She got up and stumbled out of the room.

Chapter Thirteen

Don let Hera take the lead on telling Leia that he was moving out for a while and focused on driving. As far as he could tell, Leia took it well.

"So you're not getting together?" she said, when Hera asked if she had any questions.

"Probably not," Don said, at the same time Hera said "We're not sure yet."

That was startling enough that he glanced quickly at her, before getting his eyes back on the road.

Don't hope, he told himself. In five weeks, Hera was going to sit him down and tell him, very kindly, that she'd considered it, and while she loved him as a friend, a romance wouldn't be possible.

What his next step was after that, he wasn't sure. A year ago, he might have run. But now he was tied to the Grotto, at least until March. And even if he hadn't committed to that, he'd made a home here, for the first time in a long time. He liked spending more time with Hades. He knew what time he needed to leave for work to avoid the morning rush hour and which newsstand made the best coffee. He wanted to start those DIY classes and find more artists like Ara.

And there was no way, no way at all, that he could run from Leia. Sure, she was technically an adult. Sure, Hera would take care of her.

But he loved the kid, and he wasn't going to run away from that.

"Where are you going to live?" Leia asked, her face young and vulnerable in the mirror.

"Somewhere cool, obviously," Don said. "You'll have to come over after work so I can kick your ass at the new *Binding* content."

Leia snorted. "As if," she said, but that brief, haunted look was gone. She pulled out her phone. "Well, okay. Thanks for letting me know." Her thumbs started moving. Don didn't ask what she was doing, because he was pretty sure she was talking to her group chat, and he didn't want to know.

He was achingly aware of Hera sitting beside him. On the ride up, she'd been tense and miserable, but she'd let him comfort her then. Last night, she hadn't.

Everything was different. He knew what Hera tasted like now. He knew how the soft skin of her breasts felt against his fingertips. He knew the way her mouth fell open and her breathing hitched when orgasm approached.

His body was interested in repeating the experience, as soon as possible, as often as it could.

Don told it not to lay any bets.

"Could you find a radio station?" he asked Hera.

She jumped, and then reached obediently for the dials. After some fumbling, she found a classical station playing a concert of choral pieces. It wasn't his style at all, and normally he would have teased her, or asked her to explain more about the work, depending on his mood.

Today he shut up, let the voices climb over and over each other in the background, and concentrated on getting them safely home.

They arrived just after noon.

"Help me with the bags, Leia?" he said, and she stuck around while Hera went up to the foyer to check the mailbox.

The second Hera was out of sight, Leia hugged him. His knees buckled for a moment, and he rested his hands gently on her shoulders. "Thanks, kid," he said.

"It'll work out," she said.

"Yep," Don said, though he was pretty sure they meant different things by that. "And you and me, we're cool, right?"

Leia rolled her eyes. "Of course."

"Sorry about the crappy vacation."

"It wasn't crappy," Leia said, her eyes suddenly shining. "I got to sail."

Okay, he definitely needed to blow some of his trust fund money on sailing lessons. From the way she'd taken to the dinghy, she'd be ready for keelboats before he knew it.

He grabbed the bags, gave Leia the picnic basket, and followed her up the stairs to the foyer. Hera was standing by the wall of mailboxes, a sheaf of white envelopes in her hand, but she wasn't alone.

A man perhaps ten years older than Don was approaching her, holding out a piece of paper. Don caught a glimpse of a photo that had been printed out. Hera's face, looking at the picture, went from politely bland to guarded.

Leia followed the direction of Don's gaze and went absolutely still. Don stepped in front of her automatically, and then hesitated, torn. He couldn't help Hera from here, but he couldn't desert Leia.

The doorman was watching the drama unfold, frowning slightly. He'd caught the strange tension too.

"Excuse me, ma'am," the man said to Hera. His voice was polite, but his manner abrupt. "Are you the lady in this picture with my daughter?"

Hera obviously couldn't deny that she was in the photo. "Can I help you?" she said instead, her voice cool.

"Yes, ma'am. You can tell me where my daughter is."

Don took a step back, intending to get Leia back into the stairwell, out of sight. But he heard her take a wobbly inhale, and then she stepped around him.

"Hi, Dad," she said. "I'm right here."

Leia's father spun round and scanned his daughter. The first expression on his face was clearly unalloyed relief to see her safe, and Don relaxed a little. Then it was replaced by a stony anger, and Don's shoulders tightened again. He walked with Leia, one careful step behind the pace she set. He was ready to act, if he had to, but he wasn't willing to start anything. Leia's dad was a slight man, with his daughter's light bones, but he also had the weathered look of a man who did physical labor, and a brawl in the lobby wasn't going to do anyone any good.

"Hera, Don, this is my dad, Joseph Graham," Leia said. "Dad, Hera and Don have been helping me out."

"You've been living on charity?" Mr. Graham asked, eyeing the expensive, tastefully decorated foyer with evident distrust.

Leia squared her shoulders. "I have a job. I pay rent."

"Nice to know all that worrying me and your mother have been doing went to waste," Mr. Graham said dryly, and shot Don a look. "Sir, were you aware that this girl was a runaway?"

"I left you a note!" Leia protested, before Don could decide whether the truth or a lie was a better option.

"That you did," Mr. Graham said grimly. "You sure said your piece."

"And I sent Mom a letter yesterday, telling her I was okay," Leia continued. "I guess she won't get it for a couple days, but I can tell you what was in it."

"You can tell me on the way home," Mr. Graham said. "Is this your bag?" He reached for the bag in Don's hand. Don tightened his grip.

"I'm not coming home, Dad," Leia said.

"You'll do as I say, Basileia Graham."

Hera frowned. "Mr. Graham, I'm sure she appreciates your concern, but Leia is an adult. She is legally entitled to make her own decisions."

Leia flushed bright red and looked at her shoes, and Don grimaced, knowing what was coming. Leia had always been just a little too insistent that she was eighteen.

Graham let out a short laugh. "Is that what she told you? She's sixteen years old, Mrs...."

"...Kronion," Don said, and stepped forward, hand outstretched. "Don Kronion. Nice to meet you."

Hera blinked.

Graham shook Don's hand, looking mildly surprised when he felt the strength in the grip. Don prayed Hera would let the deception continue. He was betting that this was a man who would be more willing to listen to a married couple than...whatever he and Hera were.

"Let's go upstairs and talk about it," Don suggested, and shot a significant look at the doorman, who was avidly listening. "If Leia's leaving with you, she'll need to pack."

"No if about it," Graham said, but he looked uneasy about continuing in public.

"Yes, this way, please," Hera said, all gracious hostess, and she ushered Mr. Graham towards the elevator banks.

Leia grabbed at Don's arm. "Don't let him take me," she whispered, her eyes pleading.

"Not a chance," Don muttered. He would have tried to get more information out of her, because it would be nice to know what the hell they were dealing with, but Leia's father looked over his shoulder, clearly unwilling to let her out of his sight, and Don sped up the pace.

Graham seemed taken aback by the obvious luxury of Hera's penthouse, but determined not to be intimidated. Hera ushered them all into the sitting room and Samia produced waters and coffee, looking askance at the man sitting awkwardly on Hera's antique chaise lounge.

Hera sat across from him, on the sofa with Leia beside her. Don picked a chair to the side, where he could easily throw himself between the women and Graham if he had to.

Graham was wearing jeans, a flannel shirt, and a padded jacket. Don couldn't tell if he was armed. He hoped not. If it came down to a physical confrontation, a weapon would dramatically change the odds.

"Well," Hera said brightly. "Perhaps Leia can tell us why she found it necessary to leave."

"There was no *necessary*, ma'am," Graham said stiffly.

"Yes, there was," Leia said. She'd got some of her color back. "Hera, my family are survivalists. They live in a commune with some other families, and they all think that civilization will collapse in the near future."

Don met Hera's eyes and saw the same lack of surprise there. Leia's skillset definitely indicated an education that focused on practical survival rather than scholarship.

Graham folded his arms. A muscle was jumping in his jaw.

"I got a job and made some friends outside the commune, and I saw what life could be like, and I didn't want to live that way anymore," Leia said, and shrugged with one shoulder. "I said I wanted to leave. I said it a lot, and no one listened to me. So I left."

"Did she tell you we mistreated her?" Graham demanded. "Because that girl has been cared for since the day she was born."

"No," Don said. "Leia has been very clear that abuse wasn't a factor in her choice to leave."

"Her *choice*," Graham said, sounding disgusted. "She's not old enough to make that kind of choice. Leia, we made sure you had food, shelter, education and a safe place to stay when everything goes to crap. And this is the kind of gratitude you show?"

"I wanted to go to high school, and you wanted me to get *married*," Leia said.

Hera tensed, and Don gritted his teeth.

"Caleb Kirtlan is a good man, Leia. I thought you liked him well enough."

"Not that much, Dad!"

"We've got something of a mismatch here," Hera said calmly. "You claim Leia's not adult enough to make her own choices, but you think she's adult enough to marry? Sixteen isn't even the age of consent in this state."

"She can marry before that with her parents' consent, and we gave it," Graham said, and then sighed. "Leia, we can talk about all this back at home. If you don't want to marry Caleb, then you know you don't have to. We don't do things that way."

"Are you going to let me go to a real school?" Leia asked. "Are you going to listen to me the next time I say I want something different?"

"Your mom's taught you much better than the nonsense they'd teach you at the high school. You already got a bunch of stupid ideas from those girls at the store."

Leia threw up her hands. "You see?" she said.

Graham stood up. "All right, let's go."

"No," Leia said.

"Basileia Graham, you pack your things, say thank you and goodbye to Mr. and Mrs. Kronion, and get in the truck."

"No, Dad," Leia said, and crossed her arms. "Maybe you can take me. But you'll have to call the cops to make it happen, and I know you don't want to do that. And you need to know I'll run again."

"Leia!"

"Dad, I mean it. I don't want to stay in Narrow Flat. You've been preparing for the end of the world since before I was born, and it hasn't ended yet."

"We are preparing to *survive*," Graham said.

"Well, I've survived so far! If you take me home, I'll run again. I'll go somewhere different, and then you'll have to spend *more* resources tracking me down."

Graham frowned.

"And I won't be dumb enough to stay with people who get followed by photographers next time," Leia added, and shot Hera an apologetic look when her father wasn't looking. "You won't find me nearly as easily."

It said something that Leia didn't seem to be afraid that she'd be locked away, deprived, or otherwise pressured into changing her mind. It appeared that in this case, "commune" wasn't a code word for "cult." But Don still didn't want her returning to a place that didn't offer her a future she wanted.

"Leia would be welcome to stay here, where you know how to contact her," Hera added. "And she *is* paying rent."

"I can't leave you here," Graham said, eyeing Hera's antiques and artwork. "Cities are killers when shit hits the fan. You know that."

"Hera has a fully-stocked safe room," Leia said triumphantly.

Graham gave Hera a doubtful look. "That true, ma'am?" he asked.

"Certainly," Hera said, and Don had a panicked moment wondering how they were going to convince this man that he didn't need to inspect the non-existent safe room. But Hera stood up and gestured Graham towards the kitchen. Don followed, so that he could be at hand when things went wrong.

Hera went past the walk-in pantry and straight to a door that Don had always assumed led to a utility closet. But behind that door was another, much more serious looking one, in a steel frame with an impressive lock. Hera opened it and stood aside.

"Huh," Graham said, and walked in. A few minutes later, he walked out again, looking grudgingly impressed. "It's a nice set up, ma'am, but it's short term. You've got three months of supplies there, tops."

Hera had *three months* of supplies in a safe room? Don tried not to crane too obviously, and caught a glimpse of a surprisingly big room, fitted out with stainless steel shelves holding plastic containers.

"Yes," Hera said crisply. "I've been thinking about that, and it occurs to me that we might have a mutual solution." She waved her hand dismissively at the city. "Obviously, if things get bad, we'll need to get out of here."

She sounded absolutely natural, as if the near-future collapse of civilization was something she thought about all the time. Don kept his mouth shut and nodded calmly when Graham looked at him.

"But our jobs are here," Hera went on. "I was considering buying some land, but I think it would be much better to have a community instead. What do you think, Mr. Graham, about all three of us coming to join you if need be?"

Graham looked taken aback. "The resources—" he began, and Hera gave him her most understanding smile.

"Of course we'd need to buy our way in," she said. "I quite understand that you can't take just anyone who wanders by. We can make a deposit now, contributing to the resources of the community, in return for consideration of our future admission. Perhaps you'd like to talk it over with your wife before we commit."

"What kind of deposit were you thinking?" Graham asked, and Hera named a sum that made Graham's eyebrows fly into his receding hairline.

"You could get those new solar panels and expand the orchard, Dad," Leia said.

Graham gave her a forbidding look, and turned back to Hera. "You can't buy my daughter, ma'am."

"I wouldn't try, Mr. Graham. I think Leia's made it clear that it's not easy to keep her where she doesn't want to be."

He grunted, but Don could see that he was weakening.

Hera stepped a little closer to him. "Frankly, I'm very glad that you came," she said. "I did believe that Leia was eighteen and able to make her own choices, but she hadn't told us much about where she came from, and I was quite concerned that she hadn't been in touch with her people. I didn't want to think of her family worrying." And there was the implication that if she *had* known Leia's origin, she would have contacted the Grahams earlier.

"Hera helped me write the letter," Leia added, which Don knew to be a bare-faced lie. "Dad, please?"

"I don't like rewarding this kind of behavior," he said.

"I know," Leia said, doing a fair impression of looking apologetic. "But I did try to tell you, Dad. You know I did. And I'm nearly seventeen, so I could leave in a year anyway, and I *really* don't want to marry Caleb Kirtlan."

"Well, that was more of your mother's idea," Graham admitted. "I'll need to talk to her, you know."

"Of course!"

"So you come back with me and we'll all discuss it."

Leia folded her arms again.

"Could I talk to you for a minute, Mr. Graham?" Don asked, and ushered the man out into the hallway. He flapped his hand behind his back, hoping Hera would get the message to move Leia somewhere more secure.

"I'm sorry about all this," Don said. "I know you must have been worried about her. Kids, huh?"

Graham looked slightly less harassed. "She's a trial. Her older sister was much less trouble."

"The truth is, Hera's pretty fond of her," Don said. "She might kick up a real fuss if she thought you were taking Leia back for good, and then I'm in the doghouse, you know?" This appeal to masculine sense in the face of feminine whim was gross, but if Hera could compromise her principles with a bribe, he could compromise his with some man-to-man buddy-buddy talk.

Graham cracked a smile. "I know what that's like. But I'm in the doghouse if I don't bring her back, Mr. Kronion."

"Oh, hey. It's Don."

"Joe," Graham said, relaxing a little further. "Look, I don't know what Leia's told you and your wife, but we're not some crazy cult. We've just been paying attention to the state of the world. If the power grid fails, or there's civil unrest—"

"Oh, we know," Don said, making a gesture towards the kitchen and the safe room inside. "Believe me, Joe, I'm a practical man." He refocused the conversation before Graham could ask him more. Don had a decent grasp on outdoor recreation skills, but he didn't think that would satisfy a true survivalist.

"Anyway," he continued, "my point is that Leia's safe here for now. You know where she is. If you take her back, even with the intention to talk over our offer, she might get it into her head that you mean for her to stay. And if she runs again, none of us knows what could happen."

He grimaced at the idea, and that, at least, wasn't a lie. He had a very real understanding of some of the dangers Leia had avoided. "You raised a smart, stubborn girl. Even if she's acting out a little right now, isn't it better to know she's someplace safe?"

"Safe," Graham repeated, glancing uneasily at the walls.

It must have cost him something, Don realized, to come into the city to look for his daughter. The sharp stab of sympathy was unexpected. This man had raised Leia, looked after her, and, he thought, genuinely loved her.

But Leia really didn't want to go back with him. And in this situation, what Leia wanted was what counted most.

"She's safer here than the streets," Don said, going for broke. He'd apologize to Leia later. "That's where Hera found her."

That got through. Graham's head snapped back.

Don nodded soberly. "There are youth shelters," he said. "She'd have been okay there, but she told them she was eighteen and they wouldn't let her stay."

"Why would she say—" Graham started, and then his shoulders sagged. "Because she was afraid they'd send her back."

Don kept his face neutral.

"I knew she wasn't happy," Graham admitted after a second. "Her mother said it was just the teenage years and she'd settle down once she was married."

"I'm…not sure that's the case," Don said carefully.

"No, maybe not." Graham sighed. "Well, I guess here is a lot better than that. I'll talk it over with Suzanne and see where we land. If you don't mind putting Leia up in the meantime…"

"Not at all. Besides, like Hera said, she's paying rent."

The look Graham gave him was shrewd. "What kind of job is she doing that she can pay rent on a room in this place?"

Don grinned. "Well, it's not exactly market rate. But she's working in the garden store I manage." He didn't mention the interior design aspect. Joe Graham wouldn't be impressed by that.

"She always did like the garden," Joe said, and Don thought the past tense was a sign that he might be coming round.

"Let's go find the ladies," Don said, and walked Joe through to Leia's bedroom, keeping up affable man-chat as they went. Leia's door was closed, and he heard a quiet murmur of voices. He was ninety percent certain that door was locked, so he rapped on it politely. "It's Don and Joe," he said. "Can we come in?"

"Just a minute, Minerva," he heard Hera say, and then she opened the door, her cellphone in one hand. Leia was sitting on the bed, looking tear-marked, but determined. She essayed a smile at her dad.

"Did you boys work it out?" Hera asked.

"Can I speak to my daughter for a moment?"

"Well, of course," Hera said, and stepped out into the hall with Don, closing the door on father and daughter.

Don had put aside his feelings in the face of this crisis. Now he stared down at Hera and knew that if he hadn't already been head-over-heels for her, he could have fallen in love with her for how well she'd handled this. Joe Graham had gone from wanting to bundle Leia into his truck immediately to being willing to let her stay. He knew she was an incredible judge of social cues, but she'd matched the mood so smoothly, with this man who was so far outside her personal experience that he could have been living on another planet.

Or maybe not that far outside.

"Safe room?" he asked quietly.

"I didn't tell you about that?"

"No," Don said. "I would have remembered."

"Well," Hera said, then, after a moment, "There was a storm a few years ago that knocked out power to this side of the city. We had enough food and water on hand, but only barely. Afterwards, I had the room installed. Zeus laughed at me." She shrugged, looking defensive. "But you know me. I like to be prepared."

"I think your preparation just saved Leia's butt," Don said, and nodded to the phone. "You've got Minerva on the line?"

She lowered her voice. "We're discussing legal emancipation."

"Hold that in reserve?" Don suggested. "I think he's going to let it happen."

"According to Leia, her father is not the biggest problem," Hera said, even more quietly.

"Yeah, I got that vibe." Meeting Leia's mother would be interesting, Don thought. But the immediate priority was keeping Leia with them, and it looked like they'd done that. "You're amazing," he told Hera. "Completely incredible."

She looked at him, her dark eyes crackling. "I was just thinking the same thing," she said.

Don wasn't sure who moved first. The distance between them disappeared as Hera reached up and he reached down and their lips met. It hurt, oh, it hurt as they clung to each other, hurt as he lifted her off her feet, hurt as she cradled his face in her palms, hurt as he set her down again and she settled back on her heels, her hands sliding down to clutch his forearms.

"I have to go," Don said. "I *have* to."

Hera bowed her head. "I know." She stepped back from him, and it felt as if something was tearing in his chest. "Leia's birthday is December 28th. Even if—I mean, we'll know by then."

"I'll be here for her birthday," Don said, as steadily as he could. "Whatever you decide."

An hour later, Graham was gone, Leia had finished apologizing for lying about her age and thanking them for standing up for her, and Hera was researching high schools with her in the sitting room.

Don stopped by the sitting room on his way out, duffel bag in hand. He'd pick up the rest when he had a place to move it to.

"So... 'Bye," he said.

Hera looked up, her face drawn. "Goodbye," she said formally.

Leia jumped to her feet. "Okay, I'll say it! This is *dumb*. You're both being *stupid*."

"Yeah, maybe," Don said. "If you need anything, you call me. Understand?"

"Yes," Leia said, her jaw setting stubbornly.

"I'll see you at work, then," he said and left before he looked at Hera again. If he did, he wasn't sure he'd be able to walk away.

The drive to Hades's place took thirty minutes, but afterwards, Don couldn't remember a single second of it. He walked to the front door with his bag slung over his shoulder, feeling unutterably exhausted.

Hades opened the door before he could even knock, a world of sympathy in his gaze.

"Hey," Don said.

Wordlessly, Hades hugged him.

Safely held, Don let go at last. "She doesn't love me," he choked out, and then tears swallowed the rest.

Chapter Fourteen

"**I**s something wrong?" Peter asked on Monday afternoon.

Yes, Hera thought. *Don didn't make my coffee this morning.*

"No," she said. "Thank you for working this past weekend."

"Not a problem," he said. "Did you have a nice break?"

"Yes," Hera said. "All right, the Winter Ball. I'm making decisions as required, but there are a few things I'd like your input on."

"I'm honored," Peter said sincerely.

"Venues. This is my top choice." She spun her tablet around.

Mellie Smith-Freeman had come through. She'd unearthed places Hera would never have thought of, listed pros and cons for each, estimated hiring costs, and added her own comments. Hera had received the report with more than her usual appreciation for a job well done.

"The Midaeion University atrium?" Peter asked. "Won't it be cold? I remember that place being an icebox in winter."

"We'll have free-standing heaters," Hera said, finding the line item in the budget. "That, plus the body heat of our guests will be more than adequate, I believe."

"Catering?"

"There are three cafes already on the premises, and two of them have full kitchens. We can either pay a fee to hire the facilities and use our own caterers, or hire the cafes directly and take our chances with their staff. My preference would be for the first option."

"You're in charge," Peter said. "But it's definitely easier to get good service from people you've dealt with personally."

Hera nodded. "My preferred caterers are unavailable, but I'm scheduled to meet two other possibilities tomorrow afternoon. The atrium also offers some bonuses to the decoration. It already has that wonderful cast-iron and glass roof, and if we can get lighting up there, the effect should be rather lovely. On the ground floor, the university recently replaced those awful concrete planter boxes with wooden ones." She tapped the picture to expand it, showing Peter the publicity shots of happy students leaning on raw wooden benches, while behind them, black olive and fiddle leaf fig trees reached for the glass ceiling.

"That wood won't be kind to evening wear," Peter said somberly.

"True, but we can offer other seating options. And those old planters were covered in graffiti."

"So they were. Did you ever add anything? I recall scrawling a 'Pete was here' between lectures."

"H + Z, 2getha 4eva," she said lightly. "Ungrammatical *and* inaccurate, as it turns out."

"I wish I'd known you in grad school," Peter said. "I bet you were a firecracker."

"Mm," Hera said. "I wish we had enough time for the fireworks approval process. They'd look spectacular through the ceiling."

"Maybe next year," Peter said.

Hera blinked at him. He wouldn't be at Olympus next year. "I'll make sure you get an invitation," she said, and flipped to the next item. Ah. "Budget," she said. "Looking less positive."

"You need an increase?"

"Yes. The items Joy didn't actually book still had deposits disappear from the funds."

Peter looked genuinely shocked. "She embezzled?"

"It appears so. Legal and Finance are on it."

"Seriously?" he demanded. "What a stupid—I mean, that's ridiculous! She must have known we'd find out."

"She didn't appear to mind burning her bridges," Hera said, mildly taken aback by his fervor. "Stealing our files was arguably even more aggressive."

"Speaking of that," Peter said, regaining his equilibrium. "I had a few of my old contacts from Titan get in touch over the weekend."

"Ah," Hera said, and put her stylus down. "May I assume Joy went to them?"

"I'm sorry, Hera," Peter said soberly. "I'd like to say that they won't make use of the files, but we both know that's not true."

"I'd anticipated that," Hera admitted. The rival Titan party had always been her biggest competition for the event of the season. She'd engaged in some underhanded tactics herself to discover and upstage their own plans, and could hardly complain about them taking advantage of the situation.

On the other hand, if Titan had decided to take corporate espionage to a new level and had actually hired Joy to sabotage this year's Ball, she was going to sue them into oblivion. "I've been working on a new theme. It's not solid yet, but I'm thinking Dryad's Dream."

"What does that mean?"

"Draperies, lots of green and silver, perhaps some projections on the atrium glass. An enchanted glade in winter, when everything is sleepy and sad outside, but there's warmth and light within."

Peter looked skeptical. "I'm not sure sleepy and sad is the image we want Olympus to project, Hera."

"It will be romantic," Hera said firmly. Was she projecting? Maybe a touch. "The dryad is dreaming of a bright future."

"I'll make sure to work it into my speech," Peter said.

Hera swallowed her first impulse, which was to ask "what speech?" She'd envisioned herself making the traditional end-of-year speech, with more delicacy than Zeus's usual bombastic self-praise, but still highlighting the strengths of her takeover.

But Peter was arguably entitled to speak too, even if he was leaving at the end of February. "Ah, yes," she said. "So speaking order should be Sam Janus, you, and then me to wrap up."

"Age before beauty," Peter said, and smiled at her again.

Hera put her stylus down. "I wish you wouldn't flirt," she said. "I thought we were doing very well at being professional."

"Force of habit," Peter said, and waved it away. "I'll behave. Did you really do all of this today?"

Hera looked at her desk. It was covered in fabric samples, post-it notes, sketches and catering menus. She'd run Cyd and Diana ragged all day and moved half the Events team up to her floor, stashing them in the boardroom, where they were still working on the recreated guest lists. "I feel like I've done nothing," she said helplessly. "The invitations must go out by the end of the week at the latest, which means the guest list and theme need to be finalized by then and the design brief at least partially complete, I need to prepare a new budget for Board approval and I haven't even *thought* about the musicians."

"It's still not too late to cancel," Peter said.

Hera didn't bother to reply. She stretched her arms up, felt something catch in her back, and lowered them more carefully. She needed a massage and a bath and a nice yoga session, except she didn't have the time for any of them.

That's what you get for having sex under a tree, she told herself, but even given the aftermath, it was hard to feel truly bad about that. Her body practically purred with the memory.

"There," Peter said. "As long as you can still smile, you know it'll be okay."

"Was I smiling?" Hera said. "Hm."

When she got home later that night, with the musicians still unconsidered and the guest list perhaps three-quarters complete, the light from Leia's room was spilling out of her open door into the hallway. It felt like a signal-call, and Hera dredged up her last reserves of energy to answer it.

"Hello," she said.

"Hey," Leia said. She was lying on top of the quilt Don had gifted her, fiddling with one of the textured linen sections.

"Hello. How was your day?"

"Not good. I got a coffee with Jasmine and Amir and told them I was sixteen," Leia said. "Well, I said, 'almost seventeen,' but then I said I had to quit day shifts to go to high school, and I don't think that helped."

"How did they take it?"

"Jasmine said she didn't care, I was still a cool kid. Amir was really mad."

Hera sat down on the edge of the bed, gingerly taking her shoes off. Racing from the Events war-room-cum-boardroom to her office several times an hour was proving hard on her feet. "Well, he saw you as a potential romantic prospect. It must have been a shock to learn that you were really too young for that. He's twenty?"

"Twenty-one."

"I see."

"Yeah. I explained *why* I lied, and he said he understood, but you could see he was still mad. And like, I get why, but it wasn't like I was lying to just him. Lying to you and Don was even worse, but you forgave me."

"We had more incentive," Hera said. "Besides, Amir isn't just angry with you. He's disappointed in himself."

Leia sat up. "You think?"

"Yes. He had considered you in one way, and even though you didn't return those feelings, he thought that his feelings themselves were valid. Now he must be doubting his own perception and understanding in the light of this new knowledge."

"*Really*," Leia said, fixing Hera with a knowing look.

"Ah," Hera said wearily. "A trap. You don't need to trick me into admitting that I'm doubting my powers of perception, Leia. I've had considerable experience there."

"Don isn't like your ex, though," Leia argued, sitting up on her knees.

"You've never met Zeus," Hera pointed out. "But no, they're not very similar, except perhaps for the charm." She tucked her legs up and offered a new conversational topic: "Did you make a decision on a school today?"

"I narrowed it down to two. I think it's going to depend on where Don's living."

"All right."

Leia was watching her narrowly. "He was looking at apartment rentals in his lunch break."

"Leia, enough," Hera said. "Please."

"Okay." Leia patted her shoulder. "Tell me about the Winter Ball."

"I've settled on Dryad's Dream," Hera said. "Start thinking about your gown."

"*I'm* invited?"

"Of course." Hera reclined, unable to hold herself upright another second. This quilt really was incredibly cozy. "I think you'd look lovely in deep green or violet. And it'll give you a chance to look at Midaeion. My alma mater, you know."

"What did you study?" Leia asked, and Hera mumbled her way through a wandering description of her graduate degree. Usually, whenever she thought of Midaeion, she thought of Zeus. He was entwined with all her memories of that time, when she'd believed they were invincible.

He was still in her memories. But the sting was gone.

She didn't feel a sting, when she thought of Don. Just pain, and sorrow, and a childish wish to turn back time.

"Hera? Hera, wake up." A small hand was shaking her shoulder.

Hera fought inertia and opened her eyes.

Leia was looking worried. "You work too hard," she said severely. "Go to bed."

"Good idea," Hera said and pulled herself off Leia's bed. "Leia?"

"Yes?"

"How is he?"

"Not good," Leia said. "But stop thinking about it and go to sleep."

Hera nodded, and staggered off to obey.

***

"Do you want another slice?" Persephone asked.

Don glanced at the cheesecake she was proffering. It was the Portuguese style, burnt nearly black on top. His favorite, but he'd already had two slices. "No, thanks."

"How about a beer? I got the Ninkasi Brewery IPA you like." She jumped up from the dining room table.

"I don't—thank you." He glanced at Hades, who shrugged.

Persephone came back with beer in a can, a bottle, and a tall glass. "I wasn't sure which you'd prefer—"

"Persephone," Don said. "It's okay. You don't need to do all this."

"I just want you to feel welcome," she said, her blue eyes anxious.

Don tilted his head at her. "Do you think that I blame you for what happened?"

"I did sort of push you to confess," Persephone said.

"No, you told me that Hera was going to work it out pretty soon and gave me a chance to make it happen in my own time. It's not your fault it didn't work."

Hades coughed. "What did happen, exactly?"

Don raised his eyebrows. "I'm pretty sure you don't want to know *all* the details."

"Oh," Hades said. "Uh, yes, that's all right."

Persephone frowned, then her eyes widened. "*Oh.*"

"I'm going to go finish my proposal for the DIY classes," Don said, and effected an escape with the remnants of his dignity. Behind him, there was silence.

For a moment. Then the urgent whispering started.

The problem, of course, was that he hadn't just fucked things up for himself. Hades was Hera's brother as well, in all but name, and Persephone was fast becoming a close friend. He didn't want their loyalty to him to make things awkward, but he was worried that it already had.

Don waited for that little voice at the back of his head to tell him that they'd all be better off if he ran again. He could drive out of the city and stop at the first interesting small town. He could head down to the docks and see if anyone needed crew.

He wasn't going to do it. He had too much tying him here.

But the little voice was quiet. It seemed that he wasn't even tempted.

Maybe it was that last scrap of hope, the five weeks of waiting Hera had asked for. Maybe when she said no, once and for all, he'd feel the wanderlust rise again.

But until she actually said it, he was going to make the most of what he had. He smoothed out the scrap of paper with his bullet print ideas, opened the laptop Hades had lent him, and started typing.

***

On Thursday, Hera was going through the list of the increasingly desperate catering options. Neither of the two caterers she'd auditioned on Tuesday had met her usual standard, but she was wondering whether it was time to make a call between waxy petit-four or dry mini-quiche.

"Hera, your one o'clock is here," Cyd said.

"My what?" Hera said, looking up with a start. Had she forgotten to postpone or pass a meeting onto Peter?

Aphrodite Urania bounced in. Cyd withdrew, looking smug.

"Hello, Aphrodite," Hera said, more than a little bemused. "What brings you here?"

"Okay, so, first thing, I'm Team Hera," Aphrodite said. "Persephone has to be Team Don, but she sends her love."

"Oh," Hera said, absurdly touched. "That's very kind of you, but there's no need for teams."

Aphrodite waved that away. "Second thing, your assistants told the assistant group chat that you're working literally non-stop."

"Our assistants are in a group chat?"

"I know! It's terrifying!" Aphrodite said cheerfully. "Anyway, Lina thought I'd like to know, which I did, and I talked to Diana, and she talked to Cyd, and I am now officially scheduled as your one o'clock lunch date every Thursday, except next week, because I'll be in Tahiti that Thursday, so it's the Tuesday instead."

Hera sighed. "I appreciate it, but I honestly don't have the time."

Aphrodite stopped smiling and leaned in. "Leia is really worried about you," she said quietly. "I told her that I could get you to take an hour off once a week, and it made her feel better."

Hera rubbed the tight spot between her eyes. "This is emotional blackmail."

"It sure is."

Hera put her tablet down. "Fine. But we're staying in the office, and I'm sending down to the cafeteria for food."

"Fine with me," Aphrodite said. "Your test kitchens do the best salads in town anyway." She curled up in Hera's sitting area, looking as comfortable as a bee in a flower. "Third thing! You slept with Don. Was it good?"

Hera thought about glaring at her, not that it would have any effect. Aphrodite had apparently once been terrified of her, but the mystique was long gone. "Please tell me *that* hasn't hit the assistants group chat," she said instead.

"No, no. Straight from Persephone to me. Well?"

Hera got up from her desk and joined Aphrodite on the couch. "It was *very* good."

Aphrodite's grin was blinding. "*Yes.*"

"He was...oh, I don't know how to describe it. I was barely thinking for half of it. It was as if my body was doing so much that my mind just shut down."

"Wow," Aphrodite said. "For someone who thinks as much as you do, that had to be really relaxing."

Hera stopped, arrested. "You know, I think it was." The sex had been energetic, but also oddly restful. She hadn't been watching what she said or how she moved, or considering whether her face had made any unsightly expressions or worrying that she smelled too much of horse. None of that had mattered. She'd been so wholly *there*, all of the details had faded away.

"Okay," Aphrodite said. "So, the sex was great, and then afterwards, he tells you he loves you—"

"During."

Aphrodite's mouth dropped open. "Wow," she said. "What a dumbass."

"I don't think he meant to," Hera said. "We were both...a little over-wrought."

Aphrodite pointed at her. "Excuse me, I am the captain of Team Hera, and we don't make excuses for Don. He should *definitely* have picked a better time. Like maybe any time in the last two decades."

"He had good reason not to."

"Sure, but he lied," Aphrodite said.

Hera shook her head. "Not exactly lied."

"But he concealed the truth. A big truth! A really important truth."

"What else was he supposed to do?" Hera asked, annoyed. "Either he's preying on his brother's partner, or he's taking advantage of her when she's grieving her marriage. And there was hardly a good moment to tell me right *before* we had sex. I was practically stripping him down before he had a chance to take a breath."

"And what did you say when he told you?" Aphrodite said.

"I didn't *say* anything," Hera said. "I came my brains out."

"I love it when you're crude," Aphrodite said. "People expect it from me, but from you it's just incredible. Okay, so, he tells you he loves you and you see stars, and...then I bet you started thinking again. And you thought yourself right into this mess."

Hera stared at her. "Are you really on my team?"

Aphrodite leaned forward and took her hand. "Babe, I am Team Hera from now until the end of time," she said, with unmistakable sincerity. "But if the sex is great, and he's already one of your best friends, and your strongest support, and you've already been living happily with him for months, then what is the *problem*?"

"Don wants to know if I can love him, once and for all."

"Don't you?" Aphrodite said, very gently.

"I don't know," Hera said helplessly. "I really, truly don't know. And I have until the Winter Ball to work it out. It's not the sort of thing where I can say, well, let's have more mind-blowing sex and see how it goes. Let's date for a little while. It's got to be all or nothing. Because if I say yes, and I'm not absolutely sure, I am going to break his heart." Her own heart hurt at the thought, and she laid a hand on her chest. "But if I say no, and realize later that I was wrong..."

"Oh," Aphrodite said, sitting back. "Yeah, okay, that's hard."

"And it's all down to me, because Don knows how he feels, and he has for a long time. I'm so envious of that certainty. I'm furious, actually. I could just slap him."

"Don't do that," Aphrodite said, looking alarmed.

"I would never. But it's so strange." Hera shook her head. "I just don't know what to do. I'm half excited, and half terrified and half hoping he'll come back and say 'look, I made a mistake, I can't love someone so indecisive...'" She trailed off.

"That's too many halves," Aphrodite observed.

Hera sighed. "Yes. I'm split into too many pieces."

There was a tentative tap on the door, and Hera looked up. Daphne, the temporary head of Events, was hovering. Hera got up.

"No," Aphrodite said.

"She's holding the proof designs of the invitations that have to leave this building in three hours," Hera said.

Aphrodite grimaced. "All right, but I want it known that I am protesting."

"Your protest is noted." Hera beckoned Daphne in, and cleared a space on her desk to lay the stack of printed cards out. The card stock texture was perfect, a heavy matte with a subtle hint of woodgrain.

They'd finalized the fonts and color scheme that morning and now they had to choose from the subtle combinations of seafoam, mint, silver and dark grey on the text and background.

"Oooh," Aphrodite said, comfortably looking over Hera's head. "Pretty."

Hera glanced at her. Aphrodite was not only her ideal market for these invitations, she was a genuine tastemaker in her own right. "Which one?" she asked.

Aphrodite's focus sharpened. She surveyed the cards, nodded to herself, and pointed unerringly at the seafoam and silver. "That one."

"Done," Hera said, and handed the card to Daphne. "Thank you, Daphne. Please let the design team know how much I appreciate their hard work."

"Thank you, Hera," Daphne said. "I'll start bringing them in for signatures as they're printed and cut."

"See, that wasn't indecisive," Aphrodite said, and before Hera could point out that this was hardly an issue on the same magnitude of deciding whether or not she could love Don forever, she went on without a pause: "You're signing all the invitations?"

"People appreciate the personal touch."

"And of course, Zeus never bothered."

Hera smiled. "Correct."

"Well, your hands are going to fall off," Aphrodite said. "But I personally appreciate everything that smacks Zeus on the nose with his failings. Is he invited?"

Hera shrugged. "He's a major shareholder. He has to be."

"Then you've got to look spectacular."

"I haven't even thought about my gown," Hera admitted.

Aphrodite squinted at her. "Do you trust me?"

"Yes."

"Then let me think about it for you. Oh, good, lunch! Cyd, you're amazing."

"True," Cyd said, and handed Hera a huge sandwich. "Eat that, and I'll let you use my nicest fountain pen and my fast-drying ink for those signatures."

"Bribery," Hera said, and took a giant bite. She was suddenly starving. And considerably lighter in spirit. "All right, lunch was a good idea."

"A win for Team Hera," Aphrodite agreed, around a mouthful of baby spinach. "Let's keep racking them up."

***

"Yes," Doris said.

Don wrestled the holiday sale banner into place, smiled at a customer brushing past him into the Grotto, and cracked his back. "Yes, you're going to hire another part-timer for the holiday rush?"

"I'm hiring two," Doris said. "I've never seen sales numbers like this. Neron's talked me into a holiday bonus for everyone."

"Leia will be thrilled."

"But I meant yes to your classes idea. Book Ara *now* for whatever dates you can get her. That girl is going places, and we won't get a chance at her later. Close your mouth, you'll catch flies."

Don hauled up his dropped jaw. He'd given Doris the proposal that morning. He hadn't thought she'd have even read it yet, much less agreed so quickly.

She read his expression and looked amused. "Don, when are you going to believe you're good at this?"

"I don't—I mean, I don't even have a degree. I've got barely any experience. The Grotto's pretty much my only retail job."

"It's not like you to lack confidence," Doris observed, looking a little more knowing than he would have liked. "But in case you need a reminder, you're great with people, you've got a good eye, and I've never seen anyone learn faster." She paused. "I mean, it doesn't hurt that Neron and I are the ones teaching you."

"No, ma'am," Don agreed humbly. "Well, I guess I'll start sourcing people for those courses."

"In your own time," she said severely. "There's a new furniture delivery out back. Snap to it."

Don saluted. The arm movement rubbed against the breast pocket of his plaid overshirt, and the stiff invitation card inside it, and he pulled it out as he headed towards the back.

Either Hades or Persephone had left the invitation at his place at their table that morning, and then they'd both escaped to Olympus before he could see it and react. Tact or cowardice, but he wasn't sure which.

He ran his thumb over the silver embossing. *Olympus Inc cordially invites you to Dryad's Dream, a winter celebration of the turning seasons.*

A discreet note at the bottom asked the recipient to RSVP and please disregard any previous invitation.

As a major shareholder, Don was always invited. As a constant traveler, those invitations had always been via email, sent months in advance, and accompanied by a personal note from Hera herself.

No note this time. Just this astonishingly substantial reminder of his ties to Olympus, with a peacock blue signature in Hera's firm, flowing hand. Not printed. He was willing to bet she'd signed them all.

Had she hesitated at all when it came to his name? Held the card for a moment of thought? Or had she dashed off her signature and reached for the next?

You're mooning over a piece of cardboard, Don reminded himself, and strode purposefully towards the garbage can in the back dock to toss it.

At the last second, he tucked it back into his pocket.

***

Don wasn't at the end-of-November shareholder meeting. Hera hadn't expected it, or even dared to hope, but she'd been nevertheless disappointed when he hadn't arrived. Missing him was usually a dull ache, ever present, but buried under the relentless workload. Every now and then, though, she was stabbed with a reminder of his absence.

Hades was there, which was good.

So was Zeus, which was considerably less so.

She'd been trying to believe that he had no further gambit up his sleeve. His approaches in the past months had been about her, not Olympus. It was just possible that his resignation as Chair and CEO had been a genuine recognition that he'd lost, or some sort of clumsy overture toward her.

Now he was sitting beside Samuel Janus, who had greeted him like a prodigal son. At least he wasn't smirking. Nobody was smiling, as Hades detailed the financial state of the company.

Olympus wasn't in serious trouble yet. Unfortunately, the downward decline in sales and subscriptions was unmistakable. For half a year, as Zeus floundered and stalled on decisions, they'd returned no profit. Hera's first quarter as CEO had slowed the decline, but not reversed it. Hades was quick to point out that had been part of her original financial projections when she'd first taken the job. In fact Olympus had performed slightly better than the projections had indicated.

But the shareholders had wanted miracles.

And Hera, in her heart of hearts, had wanted to provide them.

There would probably be no shareholder dividends next April. And she'd just pushed an increase to the Winter Ball budget through an emergency Board meeting with much more opposition than she'd expected.

Most of the opposition had come from the Chair. Hera was not pleased with Samuel Janus, and the more time he spent laughing too loudly at Zeus's sotto voce comments, the less inclined she was to charity.

Sure enough, as Hades finished his presentation and sat down with an almost-concealed sigh of relief, Janus took the floor. First, he ponderously presented Zeus with the gratitude of the shareholders, a motion formally passed at the last shareholder meeting.

It was the motion Hera had proposed, but Janus somehow managed to avoid mentioning that.

Zeus raised an eyebrow at her as the shareholders clapped. She politely applauded him, knowing her face was perfectly smooth.

"Now," Janus said, and gave Hera an indulgent little smile. "We're all very grateful to our CEO for working so hard on the end of year party, but I must admit some unease that it might be claiming too much of your attention."

"The Winter Ball is one of the city's most highly anticipated social events," Hera said, without bothering to rise. "A great deal of Olympus's reputation has been built on the ball's success. A number of social commentators have already remarked on this year's slow start and chaotic change of venue. I cannot overstate the importance of a strong and cohesive event."

Hades was nodding along with her, which was very nice of him, considering that attending the Winter Ball made him about as happy as sticking his hand into a basket of venomous snakes would. Actually, given the choice, he might take the snakes.

"I don't doubt it," Janus said soothingly. In a minute he'd be patting her hand and wanting to offer her candy.

"Hera has achieved an incredible amount in a short space of time," Peter said. "The budget increase was unfortunate, but unavoidable."

What the hell, Peter, Hera thought. No one had mentioned the budget increase yet. Janus might have been angling towards it, but there was no need to do his dirty work for him.

"The ball pays considerable dividends down the line," Hades said, which was much more useful, and set the shareholders thinking about *considerable dividends.*

"The most time-intensive stage is complete, and I am picking up my other duties again," Hera said, ignoring Peter's startled blink at her. "I would like to formally acknowledge the work of Peter Atlas as assistant-consultant CEO over the last two weeks, and the excellent efforts of the Events team, who have risen to the challenge in extraordinary circumstances."

Hera smiled graciously at Peter and tapped her hands together, pulling the rest of the attendees into clapping with her. Janus looked like he was waiting for an opportunity to speak again, so she cut in, raising her voice just slightly over the last of the applause. "Now, let's discuss what we have coming up in the new year."

After the meeting proper, as everyone mingled over coffee, Zeus angled towards her. Hera automatically sized up her retreat routes, mentally sighed, and squared her shoulders.

"Are you doing okay?" he asked solicitously. "You look...tired."

There was so much concealer under her eyes that she was worried about blinking, but Hera knew that she *looked* fresh and alert. "Very well, thank you," she said, and bared her teeth. "How are you?"

"Never better," he said breezily. "Hey, I just wanted to say. You're doing great work with the Ball."

Hera decided that was enough small talk. "I cannot believe you slept with Joy," she said through her teeth.

Zeus looked puzzled for a moment, then his expression cleared. "That was *years* ago," he said.

"Yes," Hera said. "Like Aphrodite, and all the other women you forgot to mention when we were going through marriage counseling and you were pretending to be open and honest."

Zeus actually looked contrite. "I'm sorry about that."

"I don't care if you're sorry," Hera said. "But I would prefer not to be blindsided. So if there are any more of your former lovers heading departments at Olympus, please have the common courtesy to let me know."

Zeus frowned. "Will you fire them too?"

"Don't pretend you're concerned for their wellbeing," Hera said. "But no. I need to let them know I know, so there are no secrets hanging over their heads." She bit her lip, but she was too tired to control herself, and the words slipped out. "And by the way, Joy was let go for gross incompetence and deliberate deception. Anyone in my position would have fired her. Don't mistake the real me for the vengeful version you made up to scare young women."

Zeus winced. "I guess I deserve that."

"Well?"

"I'll think about it and get back to you. Maybe over dinner?"

"Grow up," Hera said, just as Hades came to join them.

"Co-signed," he said, deadpan, and Zeus rolled his eyes.

"I hear Don's back on your couch, Hades" he said. "Must be a pain to have him in your love nest."

"I've always got room for Don," Hades said, with just the slightest emphasis on the name.

"And unlike Hera, you're too much of a wimp to kick him to the curb when he wears out his welcome," Zeus said. "Or did he run away again? He's great at that." He sounded genuinely bitter.

Hera wasn't sure what her face had just done, but she was very much hoping Zeus couldn't accurately interpret it.

"Well, always nice to chat," Hades began, but Zeus was staring at her.

"No way," he said. "Did Don actually shoot his shot?"

"Goodbye, Zeus," Hades said firmly, and tucked Hera's hand into his arm as he turned her away. For a moment, Hera was worried that Zeus would simply shout after them, but when she surreptitiously glanced back, he was staring thoughtfully into space.

"Don's actually not staying with us much longer," Hades said quietly. "He's rented an apartment on the edge of the docks district."

Hera nodded. "Very sensible," she said, trying to sound approving. She didn't want Don to put his entire life on hold while he waited for her to make up her mind. She'd have been shocked if he had. But an apartment, apart from her…

"I looked over the lease for him," Hades added. "It's a short-term rental."

Hera should not have felt relieved. "I'll come down to Finance with you," she said.

"That would be nice," Hades said. He was moving his thumb over his fingers in quick, awkward motions. Yes, it was definitely time to get him off the top floor.

Hera smiled a goodbye to a few people and nodded in a mature and professional way at Sam Janus, who was pontificating at Peter. Peter looked up at her, presumably in the hope of an escape route, but Hera ignored him. She was still annoyed that he'd brought up the Winter Ball budget.

"You've got lunch with Aphrodite at one," Cyd said, as she escorted Hades swiftly through the outer office space. "Then the video content people are up here to be guided through the planning of the Winter Ball feature."

"Thank you," Hera said. She had actually forgotten the video. She glanced at her office. She was trying to keep on top of the debris, but it didn't exactly radiate cool, calm and collected. "Would you—?"

"Diana's on it," Cyd said, effortlessly reading her mind.

Gary, the receptionist, had been put to work logging the RSVPs. He briefly glanced up as Hera walked through the reception area and got Hades into the elevator. Gary had stopped the skittish fawning that she'd noted on her first few weeks on the job. He would need to graduate from reception soon. Perhaps she could find a place for him assisting one of the heads of department.

Hades had a tight grip on the handrail. They needed a distracting conversational topic for the journey down. "Hades, would you prefer to suffer through dry sandwiches or tasteless shrimp on toothpicks?"

Hades managed a sympathetic expression. "Still having trouble with the caterers?"

"I have settled on the least terrible," Hera said. "Normally, I'd try to tactfully guide them through a menu improvement, but I just don't think I have the fortitude."

"That reminds me. Are you really going to pick up the rest of your usual workload? I thought things generally got busier just before the ball."

"I wasn't planning to," Hera said grimly. "Peter is carrying much of my to-do list, and the rest isn't as urgent. But I needed to shut Janus down, and since I've said it in public, I suppose that now I'll have to. Don't look so alarmed, it's only for two more weeks."

"You are going to need to sleep at some point during that two weeks," Hades said.

If *Hades* thought she was working too hard, she probably was. They reached the eighth floor, and Hera stood aside so that Hades could step out of the elevator first. She followed him to his office, making small talk as the Finance employees strove to look busy around them.

"I imagine this doesn't need saying," Hades said, as soon as they were safely away from eavesdroppers again. "But if there's anything I can do to help you, professionally *or* personally, you only need ask."

"I'm most concerned that I'm neglecting Leia," Hera admitted. "I'm gone before she wakes up, I get home late, and when I do have a free evening, it's because I'm claimed for one of the social events I really couldn't cancel. I'm taking to her as many of those as I can, just to see her, but formal dinners and congratulatory speeches are not exciting."

"You know we'd be happy to host her, if you're worried she'll be left alone too much."

"Maybe for the final week? I know she's just as responsible as she always was, but leaving a sixteen-year-old on her own feels much more dubious than allowing an eighteen-year-old the run of the house."

"Persephone and I will talk about it," Hades said. "Is there...anything else you'd like me to say? To anyone?"

"No, thank you," Hera said, and left quickly. She wasn't running away from the question, she told herself. She was moving swiftly, because she had just so much to do.

Chapter Fifteen

O n the Sunday exactly three weeks after Don had moved out of Hera's apartment, his ex-boyfriend stopped by the Grotto.

Don spotted him immediately. Jason Auron was short, wiry, and had golden blond hair that curled at the slightest provocation. But it was the gait Don would always recognize; the rolling stride of a man who spent most of his life at sea, with the arrogant swagger that was all Jason.

"Don Kronion!" he called, his voice pitched to carry through the store. Jason could make himself heard on deck through a gale, so even the Grotto's cavernous space wasn't really a challenge.

"Jason Auron," Don said, and walked over to clasp his hand. Jason did the arm grip he liked, grinning as he squeezed Don's forearm muscles. "How're you doing, man?"

"Great," Jason said. "You know, they told me you'd started working landside and gone soft, but I didn't believe it."

"Soft?" Don said, raising his eyebrows.

"On that, they were obviously wrong," Jason said. "But is this really your thing? You work in an interior design store?"

"Come January, I'm the acting manager."

"I thought that if you ever left the sea, it'd be to join that fancy business your brothers own."

Don snorted. "Hardly."

Jason leaned against a shelf. He had also not gotten soft. "The thing is, my current second officer's got a bad case of mono. She needs to stay in port with rest and fluids and I need somebody who can step into the job fast. What do you say?"

For a moment, the idea tugged at Don, like a hook in his heart. Salt and sea, storm and sky, and work that would keep him moving, far away from heartbreak.

But he shook his head. "I'm committed here."

Jason scoffed. "You? Committed?"

"Turns out it's possible."

"I'll believe it when I see it. Well, I'm in town for ten days, loading and unloading. Hit me up if you want to go get a drink." He winked.

"Yeah, maybe," Don said.

"The drink part is a euphemism," Jason said helpfully.

"Uh huh," Don said, and gave Jason another, more careful look. Jason was kind of an untrustworthy asshole, but he could be a lot of fun, as long as you never believed a single thing he said. He was a surprisingly dedicated ship's officer, an excellent sailor, and incredibly good in bed.

Don had long ago acknowledged that he had a thing for competence.

He wasn't sure if he still had a thing for Jason.

"Do you still have the same phone number?" he asked.

"Of course not," Jason said, and pulled a cheap burner out of his pocket. "Get this down."

Don wrote the digits on the back of his left hand.

"Fuck me, that's a nice piece of hardware," Jason said, and nodded at the Submariner. "Did you come into some cash?"

"It was a gift."

Jason grinned. "Hook me up with that gift-giver, would you?"

"Not a chance," Don said. "Okay, well. We're pretty busy, but if I've got time I'll give you a call."

"Great. Would be good to catch up." He caught Don's dubious look and added, "Hey, I mean it. Even if you don't get lucky."

"Don't you mean, even if *you* don't get lucky?"

"Oh, we both know who the lucky one is," Jason said. He gave Don a cheerful leer, then headed out of the Grotto, his rolling stride eating up the ground.

Leia came up beside Don, wiping her hands on her apron. "Who was that?" she asked. She was scowling at Jason's back.

"My ex," Don said. After a second, he remembered that teenagers brought up in survivalist communes with at least some adherence to traditional gender roles might not have much awareness of diverse sexual identities. "Is that a problem?"

"No, no," Leia said. "Aphrodite told me about pansexuality and Hecate told me about being trans, and then I looked on the internet. For the record, I'm pretty sure I'm cis and straight."

"Okay," Don said. "Well, for the record, I'm cis and bi."

"So is Jasmine!" Leia said. "Wait, am I allowed to tell you that?"

"She brought her girlfriend to the last Grotto drinks night," Don said. "I think it's safe to say she's out to me."

"Anyway, I don't care about that. He just seems like he might be—" She stopped, and Don watched a girl who didn't know the word for "fuckboy" nevertheless try to phrase the concept. "—trouble."

"He can be," Don conceded. "He started a bar fight that got me arrested."

"*What?*"

Don shrugged. "Yeah, it wasn't great. He said something smart to someone, someone's friend didn't like it, there was some shoving and punching, someone knocked Jason down and tried to kick him, and then I laid that guy out. I hit him pretty hard, and he was still on the ground when the cops came, so they arrested me."

"Did you go to *jail*?"

"For a couple of nights, yeah. I pled guilty to assault in the third degree, mitigated by the fact that the other guys started the fight and that one in particular was attacking my—well, we said 'friend' to the judge, but I don't think she was fooled. To give Jason some credit, he did make a character statement for me."

"You defended him," Leia said, looking slightly starry-eyed.

"I wasn't being a hero, Leia. I was drunk and stupid, okay? That guy and I were both damn lucky I didn't really hurt him. I got time served and a fine, and it could have been much worse."

Leia rolled her eyes. "It wasn't like I was going to go out and punch the first person I saw."

"Well, good, because I have other plans for you. I've rented an apartment a few blocks away and the car's full of boxes. Come help me unpack after work."

Leia made a face.

"Don't you want to see your room?"

"I get a room?" she said, brightening up, then scowled again. "Why don't you just stay with Hades and Persephone until you move back with us?"

"Because that's not very likely," Don said, and when Leia opened her mouth, he shook his head. "Don't. I don't want to hear it."

"Then you can unpack your own stupid boxes," Leia said, and stomped away.

***

"Turn," Penny said.

Hera took a quarter step to the left, balancing carefully in her heels on the narrow stool Penny had brought up from Wardrobe. Penny slid another pin into the hem of her gown. "Thank you for doing this," Hera told her.

"Thank you for letting me do it," Penny said. "I wouldn't trust anyone else with this dress. Aphrodite picked you a real winner."

"Mark?" Hera said. "Please continue."

Mark Hermes coughed, and looked at his tablet, which he was using to brief Hera at the same time she was being fitted.

It was a week before the Winter Ball, and Hera was pushing multi-tasking to new heights, but she thought her relationships with Mark and Penny were both secure enough to risk a little cross-contamination.

"I've got four potentials lined up for the Events Head position, and can do interviews whenever you're ready," he said.

"Mid-January at the earliest," Hera said. "Daphne's doing all right for now, and I don't want to further disrupt the Events team with a new leader."

"I'll schedule that. Last item. The interns are progressing well. I'm slightly concerned about two of them, but it's not a real problem yet, and I'm giving them some extra support."

"Softie," Penny mumbled, through a mouth full of pins. "Turn."

294

"I think we need a staff morale check," Hera said. She was facing out the window now, and Mark shifted around to keep her in view. "The last all-staff anonymous survey was nearly two years ago, correct?"

"That's right," Mark said. "They're supposed to be annual, but the last one—"

"—didn't get approved," Hera finished with him. "Well, I'm approving one. Can I get a timeline for the project by the end of the year?"

"That should be doable."

"Excellent. Thank you, Mark. Please hand me my phone before you go?" She could at least check her email while Penny did the rest of the adjustments.

The email at the top of the list was from Zeus, marked URGENT.

Hera grimaced, and tapped it.

"Turn," Penny said, and then, after a beat. "Everything okay?"

"Could you go and get Mark, please?" Hera said, staring at the screen.

"Uh, sure," Penny said, getting up off her knees. She had the wit not to ask further questions, not that Hera intended to answer them.

When Mark came back in, looking slightly confused and definitely wary, Hera handed him her phone.

He read the email. Then he met her eyes. "If you're planning to fire her, I quit," he said.

"Of course I'm not firing her," Hera said. "I really wish people would stop thinking I was some kind of revenge-motivated monster."

"Oh," Mark said, looking abashed. "I'm sorry. It's just that when you involve the head of HR in this sort of thing, it usually means—I do apologize. What do you need?"

"I need you to help me make an awkward conversation flow as smoothly as possible," Hera said. "I left you out of the loop when I let Joy go, and I won't be making that mistake again."

"Oh."

"Well?"

"Hm," Mark said, and she could actually see his brain clicking back into gear. She really did like watching competent people work. "Well, my first suggestion is that you approach on her home territory. And that I accompany you."

"Excellent," Hera said, and headed for the door.

"Now?" Mark asked.

"Why not now?"

"Well, you're wearing a fifty-thousand-dollar dress with half the hem dragging behind you," Mark said. "I assumed you'd want to change."

"Oh. Of course. Would you send Penny back in, please?"

"So, how's it going?" Penny asked, as she unzipped Hera and carefully lifted the gown over her head.

"I am losing my entire mind," Hera said.

"I don't blame you," Penny said. "Go. I've got this."

***

Hera knew Olympus very well. There was, as she had neglected to point out to Mark, a sense in which it was all *her* home territory.

Nevertheless, the shiny stainless-steel fittings, clanging pans and endless bustle of Kitchens were their own fiefdom, and the sovereign queen sat behind the desk in her office, her box braids tied around her head and wrapped in a scarf, and regarded Hera with rueful determination.

"I don't need to know the details," Hera said. "But is this true? You and Zeus slept together?"

"Yes," Hestia said. "It was while you were divorced the first time."

Mark let out a slow exhale.

"*Oh*," Hera said. "Well, that doesn't even count as an affair. I'm sorry, Hestia. I think Zeus is playing games."

Hestia shrugged. "It's still something I knew that you didn't," she said, and there was a weary note in her voice. "I should have told you. But I couldn't see the point in stirring it all up."

"I entirely understand."

"Do you? I wish you could explain it to me. I'd never thought I was the kind of person who'd sleep with her boss."

Hera sighed. "It's what he does," she said. "He can be very charming, of course, and he seems entirely confident, but in fact, he's terrified of failure. So he targets younger women, or women who work for him, because his odds of success are better."

"Oh," Hestia said.

"Could I get a glass of water, perhaps? It's rather warm in here." She fumbled at the neck of her blouse, opening a few buttons. "Oh, that's better. Yes, so he's exploiting a power differential, but I suspect he doesn't even think of it as predatory behavior. Because deep down, he's scared. Scared of disappointing his father, mostly. Even though that horrible old man died years ago."

"Are you feeling all right?"

"Mm?" Hera said vaguely. "Yes, I'm fine." She laughed. "Even the charm is a defense mechanism. This is all from my therapist, of course,

I couldn't see this when I was in it." She reached over the desk to pat Hestia's hand. "Don't look so worried. We're fine. Actually, you're wonderful. Do people tell you that enough?"

"Here," someone said, and someone tried to put something smooth and cool in her hand, but her fingers wouldn't close around it and the glass fell, smashing on the white tile floor.

"Oops," Hera said. She bent over to pick up the pieces, and kept going down as her legs folded under her.

"Fuck!" someone said. "Can I get some help in here!"

Someone had grabbed her with strong hands, and it was uncomfortable. She tried to turn away and was restrained.

"Hera!" someone was saying. "Hera. Hera, can you hear me?"

"Um?" she said, and blinked rapidly. Mark's face came into focus, hovering over her. Hestia was issuing calm commands, somewhere nearby.

Hera blinked again. She was lying on her back on Hestia's floor, Mark's hands on her shoulders. "Did I *faint*?" she said.

"You did," Mark said, sounding relieved.

"How absurd," Hera said, and tried to push herself upright. Her hand landed on something sharp, and she jerked away.

Everything went woozy for a moment, and then there was something wrapped around her hand and Mark was talking to someone "—not sure if it was stress or—"

"—her doctor," someone said.

Hera made a tremendous effort and found her voice again. "No doctor," she said. "I'm just a little dizzy, that's all."

Hades's face appeared in her field of vision. "You've passed out twice," he said grimly. "There's broken glass all over the floor and you've cut your hand. The doctor is non-negotiable."

Hera made a more cautious attempt to sit up. The room spun a little, but she made it to a cross-legged position.

"Here," Hestia said, and handed her a tall glass of water with a straw. Hera sipped gratefully. The wrapping on her hand was Hestia's scarf.

"This is terribly embarrassing," she said. "I don't want any fuss."

"Fussing is also non-negotiable," Hades said. "Do you think you can walk if you lean on me, or should I call for an ambulance?"

***

Don was showing Amir how to sand painted furniture when Hades walked into the workshop.

That Hades was at the Grotto at all was unusual. That he was there during office hours, had apparently been granted workshop access, and was wearing a suit and a grave expression was incredibly alarming.

Don gripped the edge of the antique table he was working on and felt it creak.

"Hera's okay now," Hades said, and Don made his fingers unclench.

"What happened?"

"She fainted at work," Hades said. "I got her to the doctor, and there's nothing wrong that can't be fixed. Stress, sleep deprivation, and dehydration. She's resting at home."

"Leia just started school," Don said.

"I know. Do you want me to pick her up after school? If you like, she can stay with me and Persephone for now."

"Fuck," Don said, and covered his face with his hands.

"I'll, uh, just—" Amir said, and scuttled out.

"Okay," Don said, and straightened up. "Okay. Thanks for telling me. Uh, let me talk to Leia."

Hades nodded. "Do you want to see Hera now, or later? You can probably wait until after work. She's asleep at the moment, and might be for a while."

"Did she ask for me?"

"No," Hades said, his eyebrows tilting. "She was barely coherent, Don."

"Then I can't," Don said.

Hades regarded his brother for a long moment. "Okay," he said. "I love you dearly, and you know I'll do whatever it takes to make you happy. But right now, you need to get your head out of your ass."

Don frowned. "I'm not going to push my way in if she doesn't want me there."

"I swear to whatever you hold holy, I have never seen two people so intent on making themselves miserable," Hades snapped, in a tone Don had heard from him maybe once or twice in his entire life. "Pick up that kid, take her to see Hera, and don't be such a fucking chickenshit."

"What the hell?"

"Fight for her!" Hades said. "You've been respectful and given her the time and space and all of that is good, but she fainted into a pile of broken glass, Don!"

Don stared at him. "You didn't mention broken glass."

"I was hoping I wouldn't have to," Hades said, through clenched teeth.

"Fine." Don yanked his apron off with unnecessary violence. "But this is—we're going to talk about this later!"

"I look forward to it," Hades said.

Don gave him the finger and went looking for Neron, who he figured would be the softest touch. School pick-up traffic was predictably nightmarish, especially at Leia's private school gates, where the Camry stuck out like a broken tooth between shiny SUVs. Don spent a lot of the wait time muttering the things he should have said to Hades and consciously not leaning on the horn.

Leia came out at last, flanked by two other girls. In her prep school uniform, she looked her actual age. Don watched her register his presence, wave goodbye to her friends and bounce towards him. She lost her verve when she got close enough to see his face.

"No one's badly hurt," he said. Fuck Hades. But that was still the right way to start. "Hera fainted at work, but she's at home now and she's fine."

"Oh," Leia said.

"We're going to go see her, and you can grab a few things and stay with me or Persephone and Hades, up to you."

"With you," Leia said immediately, and then, "My dad called again today."

"Good news?"

"Still wait and see news. I think he and my mom are fighting about it. But Hera said he already cashed the check, so that will act as a psychological impediment."

Don could hear Hera's cadence in the words. "Well, Minerva's got that emancipation paperwork drawn up," he said.

"Yeah," Leia said. "I *knew* she was working too hard!"

"And now we get to go say we told her so," Don said.

But when they arrived, Hera was sleeping. Samia allowed Leia to peek into the bedroom, and Don peered over the top of her head.

Hera was a small shape in the middle of her enormous white bed, her dark hair ruffled around her pale face. One hand was propped up on a pillow, a bandage neatly tied around it. Minerva Eule was sitting in a chair beside the bed, upright in her grey trouser suit, reading paperwork through round thick-rimmed glasses. She gave Leia a warm smile, then leveled a cool look at Don.

Hera was still. Only the faint rise and fall of her chest as she breathed gave any hint of her usual vital presence.

Don had to back out of the hall and stand in the dining room, taking deep breaths with his fists clenched at his sides.

"I'll get my things," Leia said from the doorway, but she was gone by the time he could turn around. He scrubbed at his face.

There was a stir and a murmur in the bedroom, and when he next looked in, Samia tried to close the door in his face.

"Is that Don?" Hera's voice said muzzily, at which point he would have walked right through the door if he'd had to.

But Samia grimaced and stepped back, and Don went over to the bed. Hera was sitting up. She was wearing an old Midaeion t-shirt, and no one had taken her makeup off; her lipstick was smeared and the mascara had left rings under her eyes.

"One second," Don said, and went to her en-suite, where he found make-up wipes and moisturizing cucumber spray laid out. Samia shot him another look when he came back with them, so he was probably trampling over some housekeeper etiquette, but Hera looked relieved when he handed them to her.

"Thank you," she said, and spritzed vigorously.

"Leia's coming back with me tonight," he told her.

"Oh good," she said, and scrubbed her face clean. "So. Aren't you going to say you told me so?"

"No," Don said, and sucked a huge breath in through his teeth. His eyes were screwed shut, but he felt the small hand landing tentatively on his.

"I'm sorry that I worried you," Hera said.

"You didn't *worry* me," Don said, turning his hand over to catch hers. "My heart pretty much exploded out of my chest. I have been imagining what could have happened if you'd landed face first in that glass from the second Hades mentioned it."

"Precisely," Minerva said, pointing at him.

Hera looked mutinous. "Well, I didn't."

"What did the doctor say?"

"Nothing's really wrong with me," Hera said.

"She needs rest and fluids," Samia said. "*Proper* rest. The doctor suggested a week of leave."

Hera opened her mouth.

"Hera," Don said. "If it were Leia, or Cyd, or Minerva, or anyone else you care about, what would you be saying to them right now?"

Hera closed her mouth. Then she grimaced. "Rest," she said.

"Okay."

"But I can't take a whole week."

"Okay," Don said, and when Minerva scowled at him, he shrugged at her. "Hera knows what she can handle."

"Oh no," Hera said, with the ghost of a smile. "You're trusting me to do the right thing."

"Yup. Is it working?"

"Yes," she said, looking peeved.

Don grinned at her.

Hera's gaze caught on his face, her hand tightening on his. "Thank you for coming," she said quietly.

Don decided that maybe he wouldn't shout at Hades after all.

Hera's gaze softened, and he was suddenly very aware that they were touching. After four weeks of separation, it should have been awkward.

But it wasn't. It was completely and undeniably right.

"Hera!" Leia said behind him, and rushed in to hug her. "Are you all right? I told you that you were working too hard!"

Don let go and retreated to the doorway while Hera reassured Leia and agreed that yes, indeed, she had told her so, and yes, Hera had been foolish not to listen. But her eyes flickered over to Don, with a rare uncertainty.

One week, Don reminded himself. He only had to wait one more week for her decision.

For the first time since they'd parted, he dared to hope that she'd decide in favor of him.

***

Hera slept for three days.

She roused herself occasionally. She got up to pee, and sometimes to stretch. She tried to read, but kept falling asleep sitting up in bed. Aphrodite suggested some audiobooks, and that went better—she still fell asleep, but she didn't wake up with a crick in her neck.

She ate at odd hours, wandering out to the kitchen to find the prepared snacks Samia had left there to tempt her. She drank water and enough black tea to keep the caffeine headaches at bay.

On the afternoon of the fourth day, she tried to change the dressing on her cut hand, and after a sweaty, painful struggle in her bathroom, humbly asked Cyd to help her.

Cyd had installed herself in Hera's study, and was diligently triaging requests and alleged emergencies that required her attention. So far, none of the emergencies had actually required Hera.

Cyd unwrapped Hera's hand, inspected the cut closely, and then rebandaged it.

"It's looking better," she said.

"Yes."

"So are you," she added pointedly, and Hera nodded. She was tired of stubbornly pushing back on everyone's concern.

Especially since they were right. The look of sheer horror on Don's face was still haunting her. *My heart pretty much exploded out of my chest.*

"I feel a lot better," she said. "What do I need to know?"

Cyd picked up a notepad. "Peter's covering most of your meetings. Musicians have been booked, Events are on top of decor, sound and lighting, final total is 532 RSVPs and Penny says the gown will be ready for final fitting whenever you're up to it. The caterers quit, but that's been handled."

"The caterers *quit?*" Hera said.

"Adrestus Argive apparently made them a last-minute, much better offer to staff his family's end of year party."

"He couldn't get away with suing Olympus for breach of promise, so he stole my *caterers*?"

"Apparently."

"Gracious," Hera said. After a moment she added, "I hope he chokes on a dry sandwich."

"Cheers to that," Cyd said.

"Who was booked instead?"

"Kitchens is handling it," Cyd said, so matter-of-fact that it took Hera a moment to realize what she meant.

"Oh, no," Hera said. "Olympus staff shouldn't have to—"

"They're happy to do it," Cyd said. "Or, actually, Hestia's happy to do it, and Kitchens follow her lead like adorable little ducklings."

"But—"

"Hera," Cyd said, and put the notepad down. "Mark Hermes has personally trained the interns to be coat-check attendants. Penny called in a favor from her cousin's wife to make her start their vacation later so that Paris and the Archers could play at the ball. Hestia has designed and tested a presentation cake that is an actual work of genius. The Olympus tech crew have created the lighting scheme, half of Subscriptions has been drafted into handling the phone calls, PR has made sure that every publication of note will be putting the ball at the center of their social reporting, and I have been coordinating it all. We all want to make this Winter Ball sensational, and we want to help you do it. The Events team would crawl through barbed wire for you."

For a moment, Hera couldn't speak. "But why?" she said, her voice cracking.

"Because you're an excellent boss," Cyd said. "Because you didn't fire the Ask Cassandra columnist when that was the expedient move. Because, despite the declining numbers, you haven't discussed layoffs."

"That's just good business," Hera said. "If we want to reverse the decline, we need good people there to do it."

"You work hard and you set high standards. You make sure people get credit for the work they do. Mark Hermes was telling me that in four years as HR head, he rarely saw Zeus acknowledge other people's effort unless he could claim a healthy chunk of the kudos. And even when you're stressed to breaking point, you say please and thank you."

"But I fell apart," Hera said. "I've made so many mistakes."

Cyd's eyes were steady on her face. "You've made so many more brilliant choices. And you're not just good at your job, but good to your people. That counts for so much." She smiled at her boss. "I know you have trouble believing that you can be anything less than perfect. That's all right. We'll believe it for you."

Hera sat still for a moment. "I'll try to believe it," she said as humbly as possible.

"Good."

"And tomorrow, I'm going back to work," she added.

"Great," Cyd said. "Good to have you back."

Chapter Sixteen

On Tuesday morning, Hera walked into her office with a profound sense of relief, tempered only by what she found in there.

"Hera!" Peter said, rising from his seat behind her desk. "You're back!"

"Hello," she said, and accepted his kiss on her cheek. "Were you making yourself at home?"

He smiled ruefully. "For some reason, people are much more impressed when they meet me here than in my office."

"The view does a lot of the heavy lifting," Hera acknowledged. "Thank you so much for all your work while I was on sick leave. Do you have a list of the decisions you made that I can review?"

"Oh, you don't need to worry about all that right now. You've got the ball to focus on."

Hera sat down in the chair he'd vacated, and discovered he'd changed the height. Well, he had longer legs than she did. It was silly to be territorial about a chair. "It seems that the Winter Ball is well in hand, actually," she said. "So I would like to see that list."

"I'll have my assistant put one together."

"Oh, and regarding the ball—do you have your speech written?"

He looked amused. "Do you need to approve that too?"

"Yes," Hera said. "Cyd is proof-reading mine now, so it should be ready soon, if you'd like to take a look at it."

"Uh, sure," he said, looking taken aback. "I'll get right on it."

"Thank you, Peter," Hera said.

He hesitated. "Look," he said. "I was thinking. I know you said you didn't want to date anymore, and that you froze up when we—anyway. I wondered if there was any chance you wanted to give it another shot?"

"I'm sorry, but no," Hera said gently.

"Okay." He took a couple of steps towards the door, then came back. "But tell me one thing. Is it Don Kronion? Is he the guy?"

"That's really none of your business," Hera said, much less gently. "The list, Peter. Please."

***

"And that's how you know if it's a polynomial," Don concluded, and put his pencil down.

Leia scowled at the page. "I might not have wanted to go to high school so bad if I'd known about the homework."

"It'll get easier as you go," Don promised. "Right now, you're still catching up on a lot of things."

"All the other kids are so much smarter than me."

"It only seems that way because they've had more academic experience," Don said. "You're learning a lot faster than you think you are, and you have a ton of skills they don't." He tapped her head. "And you're very smart. Give it six months, and you'll be blowing them all away."

"Hm," Leia said, and for a second she sounded so much like Hera that Don nearly laughed out loud. "Well, we'll see, I guess." She pushed back from the battered dining table. Don had thrifted most of his furniture, and taken advantage of the Grotto discount for the rest. The result was an apartment that was comfortable and interesting. Much like his future, it felt like a work in progress.

"We should unpack more boxes," Leia said authoritatively.

"I suppose," Don said, with no enthusiasm.

Don had been living a peripatetic life for years, and hadn't thought of himself as having a lot of possessions. Every now and then, when he accumulated too many things to easily move on, he'd sent a box to Hades to put into storage for him. When he'd finally gone to clear out the storage locker, he'd been amazed by how much had accumulated.

The oldest boxes were from when he'd gone to college. Don had always assumed their father had ordered his room cleared and his possessions destroyed, but it turned out Hades had quietly arranged for everything to be packed and put away. For over twenty years, Hades had been caring for these physical reminders of his brother.

Now it was time for Don to do it himself.

He kind of hated it, but Leia enjoyed rummaging through the detritus of his life. It had been a welcome distraction for her over the weekend, as Hera rested.

"Hera went back to work today," she said, as she opened another box. "She says she feels *much* better, and I don't need to worry, and I can come back whenever I want."

"She texted me too," Don said.

"Did you text back?"

"Of course."

"What did you say?"

"I don't remember," Don said, which was a lie, because he'd spent ten minutes thinking about his response. In the end he'd gone with "Pleased to hear it, looking forward to seeing you soon." "Do you want to go back tonight? Maybe after dinner?"

"No, I told her I'd stay here until the ball." She shot him a look. "If that's okay with you?"

"That's great with me," he said.

"Because Hera will be busy all day on Thursday anyway, and she'll be at the ball early, so you and I can go in together." Leia frowned at the boxes. "Do you have a tuxedo in here somewhere? I thought you could wear your nice suit, but Aphrodite said no, it was definitely tux energy."

"I'm not going," Don said, startled.

"What?" Leia said. "Of *course* you are."

"I didn't RSVP," Don said.

"So? You're a shareholder! You're a Kronion! Who's going to stop you?" Leia put her hands on her hips. "Don! You're not going to make me walk in there all alone, are you?"

"Oh, sure. Just you, all alone, except for Hades, Persephone, Aphrodite, Hecate—"

Leia actually stamped her foot. "It's not the *same.*"

Don gave way. "Fine. I think my tux is in one of those boxes in that pile."

Leia grabbed a box cutter and got to work, while Don went through a box of his old prep school reports and yearbooks. The reports had been mailed out in glossy cardboard folders, and all had some variation or another of "Don could do much better with more effort." Those went straight into the trash. The yearbooks were more interesting. His senior head shot was labeled with "Most Likely To Run Away and Join The Circus" under a picture of him grinning defiantly at the camera.

Don stared, struck by how much of a *kid* he'd been. Angry, confused, afraid of coming out to their dad, afraid of never being able to meet his standards, afraid he'd let Hades down, that he wouldn't be able to protect Zeus...

He paused, arrested. There really had been a time when he'd wanted to protect Zeus. The impulse had died with their father, when Zeus took over Olympus and very quickly proved that he didn't need or want protection. It was about then that they'd started arguing, every time Don came back to the city. It hadn't been about Hera, Don thought, not really. He'd known he didn't have a chance. It was about who Zeus was becoming at Olympus, about how their father's legacy was poisoning him, encouraging selfishness and greed.

He closed the yearbook and put it in the keep pile.

"Who's this?" Leia said. She was holding a framed photo of three young men. Hades was in the middle, wearing a black gown and cap, looking faintly surprised. Don had half turned toward him, grinning with pride.

"That's Zeus," Don said. "We're at Hades's graduation."

Leia tapped Zeus's blinding smile. "This is Zeus?"

"Yes."

"But I know him," Leia said. "That's the man who was meeting with Peter Atlas, the day we went to his house."

***

312

At six p.m. that evening, Hera was walking around her bedroom with all the lights on, playing Bizet's *Carmen* while she mentally remodeled the room. Three days in the serene white surroundings had been enough to convince her she definitely needed more color. What a shame she hadn't thought to get an Ara Kaney quilt when they'd first been displayed. Now they were this season's hot item, and the waiting list was absurd. It was the kind of list she could probably leap to the front of, if she wanted to, but that seemed unfair to everyone else who wanted one. No, she'd simply have to accept that she'd missed her opportunity and think of something else.

Her doorbell rang, a discordant note in the vibrant score.

It was Persephone, looking worried and angry. And another young woman, who Hera recognized with a jolt of alarm.

"Ms. Cadmida," she said.

Semele Cadmida was wearing dark jeans and a leather jacket, but she wore them like a business suit, standing ramrod straight in the doorway. "I'm sorry to just show up like this," she said quietly. "I know I must be the last person you'd ever want to see, but this is important."

"May we come in?" Persephone said.

"Of course," Hera said automatically, before she could even think about whether she really wanted the mother of her ex-husband's son in her home. But her hostess skills kicked in, and she found herself offering tea and cookies in the sitting room.

The teacup shook in Semele's hand, and she put it down quickly on a side table.

"Is—I'm so sorry, are you all right?" Hera asked. "Is your son—"

"Hades is watching Dio," Persephone said. She was clearly holding her tongue, letting Semele take the lead.

"I'm not all right," Semele said. "I was threatened today. He told me he could make sure Dio was taken away if I didn't do what he wanted."

Hera's teeth clenched. "Zeus," she said.

"No," Semele said, and leaned in. "What would you do? If someone threatened your kid?"

Hera didn't even think about it. Fury rolled up her body and out her mouth, in a voice she didn't even recognize. "I'd *destroy* them."

Semele met her eyes. "Yes," she said. "So would I. That's why I'm here."

"All right," Hera said, after a moment. "I think you'd better tell me what's going on."

***

Finding Zeus's new address had been easy. Making Leia stay at home had been hard.

Don had prevailed in the end, and he was even pretty sure she wouldn't say anything to anyone else until he'd had a chance to confront his brother, but the argument had taken more time that he'd thought, and it was nearly seven o'clock before he was parked outside Zeus's flashy executive townhouse.

It was far too much space for one person, even if you took Zeus's ego into account. But that was Zeus.

Don had considered his options, but in the end, he went for something simple. He knocked on the door, and when Zeus opened it, he barreled directly into him, slamming Zeus against the wall.

"What the fuck have you been planning with Peter Atlas?" he growled.

Zeus tried to knee him in the balls.

Don twisted to catch the blow on his thigh, and bounced him off the wall again. "We could have lost Hera!"

"What?" Zeus said. "Is she okay?"

"Like you give a shit."

"Fuck you!" Zeus heaved, and Don staggered back a couple of steps. "You think I'd hurt Hera?"

"I think you'd do anything to get your own way," Don said, and before he could think about it, the suspicion he'd never once voiced came out: "What happened to Dad, huh? Hades and Hera left, and he was with you, alone and helpless in that hospital bed. He died, and you got Olympus, just like you always wanted."

"You think I *killed Dad*?" Zeus's voice went high and disbelieving.

Don hesitated. Zeus looked genuinely shocked, but his brother was a good liar.

"What happened to Hera?" Zeus said insistently.

"She was so stressed and sleep-deprived that she passed out at work. She was on bed rest for three days."

Zeus went dead white. "I didn't—that wasn't supposed to happen."

"The hell *was* supposed to happen, Zeus? What have you and Peter Atlas been cooking up?" Don's brain caught up. "Fuck. You sold him those shares, didn't you?"

Zeus looked away.

"What's the plan?" Don said.

"I don't know any more," Zeus said bitterly. "He's not taking my calls."

Don clenched his fists, and then consciously relaxed them.

"He was supposed to get close to her," Zeus said, after a moment. He chuckled darkly. "Not as close as he tried to get, but I didn't figure that out until later. Figure out her plans, let me know what was going on. Make things difficult, when he could get away with it. Make her see that Olympus needed me. That she needed me. But she wasn't supposed to get hurt."

"Did he sabotage the Winter Ball?"

"Yeah. He paid Joy to fuck it up. I think he had something on her too. Peter likes knowing people's weaknesses."

Don took a deep breath. "You wanted Atlas to ruin the event Hera's reputation has been built on and you didn't think that would hurt her? She worked herself to the bone!"

"I thought she'd cancel it!" Zeus said. "I didn't think she'd try to keep it going! She turned the entire thing around in five weeks! Who *does* that?"

"Hera Rheczack does that," Don said, and even through his rage, he felt pride bloom.

"Yeah," Zeus said, his voice softening. "I guess she does."

There was a moment when they were simply two men, united in admiration, and then Zeus scowled at him. "While we're on the topic, did you hit on my wife?"

"Ex-wife," Don said. "And yeah, I did."

"And she kicked you out," Zeus said. "Good for her. She knows better than to rely on you." There was a bitter note in his voice.

"This isn't about you and me, you idiot," Don said. "Grab your coat, and let's go."

When Semele finished talking, Hera closed her eyes for a long moment.

"I am so sorry," she said.

"Thank you," Semele said. "But I didn't come to you for sympathy. Can you help me?"

"I think so," Hera said. It was beginning to look as if her collapse had been a blessing in disguise. The days of rest had restored her energy reserves and she was ready to meet this moment. She could actually feel her mind clicking into top speed. "All right. You gave him the impression you'd agreed?"

"Yes. I thought that it would buy me some time."

"Good," Hera said. "Let him continue to think that. I think you're going to have to actually do the work."

Semele made a face.

"I know," Hera said. "But since you know it won't be used, you don't have to worry about exercising restraint."

"That will help," Semele said. Her eyes were brightening at the challenge.

The doorbell went again, and Persephone jumped to her feet. "Let me get it," she said, but she came back a minute later, looking alarmed. "Um, Hera..."

Hera went back with her to peer through the peephole. Zeus and Don were standing shoulder to shoulder in her doorway. Zeus looked handsome and polished and...weak. Sulky.

Beside him, Don looked solid and reliable. Real in a way Zeus couldn't be, for all his posturing.

Hera opened the door.

Oh, she thought, as everything fell into place with the certainty of a key turning in a lock. *There it is.*

"Now, Hera—" Zeus began, and Don talked over him as if he wasn't even there.

"We need to talk about Peter Atlas," he said seriously.

"Yes," Hera said. "I rather think we do."

***

The war council took the better part of two hours.

Zeus, perhaps surprisingly, told his part of the story with a distinct lack of self-excusing bravado. His eyes lingered on the dressing on Hera's hand, and he couldn't meet Semele's eyes. If some understanding of the magnitude of his offenses had finally dawned on Zeus, Hera was distantly pleased about it, but she couldn't waste the brain power on him right now. She was too busy calculating what Atlas knew, and what she could let him know she knew, and what she'd have to keep concealed until she was ready to strike.

She would lay any money that the speech notes he'd give her tomorrow wouldn't bear any resemblance to what he actually planned to say at the Winter Ball. Atlas would be planning to hit her at what he thought would be her weakest moment and roll over her, claiming his victory before she had a chance to regroup and fight back.

But prepared, she had a shot.

"Can't you just confront him?" Persephone asked. "Tell him you're not scared and you won't give in?"

"That sounds nice," Semele said carefully. "But Hera's right. He needs to think he's winning."

"This is going to expose you to retribution," Hera told her. "Even defeated, he'll still have a lot of contacts in the industry. He could blacklist you."

"I'm already stalking celebrities and influencers for shitty little stories," Semele said. "I used to be a real journalist, but Olympus seems to be the only place hiring."

"And you didn't apply?"

Semele met her eyes. "I wasn't sure it was a good idea. At this point, I just want to protect my son. Atlas said he could make Zeus sue for custody. I thought Hades would probably help pay for lawyers if that happened, but..." she shrugged.

Zeus shifted his weight restlessly. Hera wasn't sympathetic to his discomfort, but she might be able to use it. "Zeus," she said crisply. "Would you be willing to formally give up any custody interest in Dio?"

"Huh?" Zeus said, and Hera watched his face flicker through the thought process. He didn't care about Dio as his son—that was obvious to everyone in the room. But Hera saw the moment he realized that giving up Dio would mean giving up a possible lever on Semele. It wasn't a lever he wanted to lean on at the moment, but who knew if it might be handy in the future? Then his eyes went to Hera, and she saw him recognize that she had seen and understood his thoughts. There was anger there, and a touch of amusement, but mostly shame.

She would always see him clearly now, Hera realized. He'd never be able to fool her again.

"Okay," he said, still looking at Hera, not Semele. "Sure. Have Minerva write up the paperwork and I'll sign it."

Semele's face was still, a mask hiding strong emotion. Hera knew what that was like. She probably wouldn't relax until she had the signed paperwork in hand.

And now Hera had a guarantee that Semele wouldn't leave this meeting and go straight to Atlas with the news. She was almost certain that Semele wouldn't have done that, that she'd committed to helping Hera when she'd first contacted Persephone and Hades. But Hera couldn't help being who she was, and she was too canny to scorn an advantage when she could get it.

When the conversation broke up, and Persephone took Semele home to pick up her son, Zeus got to his feet and looked at Don expectantly. "You drove me here," he said.

Don didn't move. "Take a cab."

Zeus's eyes narrowed. "I don't think so."

"Don, can I speak to you in my bedroom for a moment?" Hera said. She kept her voice pleasant, and was not above enjoying Zeus's look of sudden alarm.

"Sure," Don said, and went with her. She'd left the lights blazing, and the white room no longer seemed so sterile and cold with Don in it. He was so alive. So normal and natural, with his easy bulk and the crow's feet around his intelligent eyes, and the scruffy blond hair curling over his worn flannel collar. The tidiest thing on him was the watch she'd given him, a triumph of beauty and practicality clasped around his wrist.

Normally, Hera liked precision, perfection, deliberation.

But not when it came to Don.

"What did you want to tell me?" he asked.

"Two things," Hera said. "One, I need you to understand that I am going to crush Peter Atlas. I am not going to be nice about this. He needs to be completely removed as a possible threat."

"Great," Don said. "I'm fully in. Fuck that guy. What's the second thing?"

"I love you," Hera said.

Don froze.

"I really do," Hera said. "I worried about it for weeks. I wasn't certain, and I couldn't come to you uncertain. I couldn't meet the kind of love you were willing to give me with anything less than my whole heart. But tonight I saw you, and I knew. With no doubt. I know. I love you."

His eyes were locked on hers, but he didn't speak. He barely seemed to breathe.

"Don?" Hera said, beginning to be afraid. "Say something."

"I can't," he whispered. "I might ruin it. Is this real?"

Hera touched the side of his face, feeling his stubble rasp against her fingertips. "It's real," she said. "If you still want me, I'm yours."

He turned his head to the side and kissed her palm.

"Oh," she said, and he went to his knees and gathered her to him.

"I love you," he said in her ear, and the sensation shivered through her. "Hera, I'm out of my mind for you. I've never felt this for anyone else, and I never will. Are you *sure?*"

"*Yes,*" Hera said, and kissed him.

He pulled her in, no hesitation, no control, and she felt that wild electricity surge between them, only it was even better now, because she knew how he felt, and she felt the same, she *loved him.* She surrendered to the heat of Don's mouth on hers, to the motion of his hands on her body, and by the time she came back to herself, she was straddling his lap, rotating her hips against him and making eager little gasps as he kissed a line down her throat towards her breast.

He tore his mouth away. "*Fuck.*"

"That was kind of the idea," Hera said breathlessly. They should probably get rid of Zeus first, but after that it seemed like it would be an excellent idea to really muss up her white sheets.

"No, I mean I can't stay. Leia's home alone. She knows I'm here, but it's already been a couple of hours."

"Oh," Hera said, and climbed off him. "Yes, quite right."

"Tomorrow night?" Don said hopefully, as he got to his feet, but her brain was catching up and saying a number of sharp things to her libido.

"I think we'd better not," she said reluctantly. "Peter is slippery. We're only going to get one shot at nailing him and for this to work, he's got to think I'm vulnerable."

"I make you invulnerable?" Don said skeptically.

Hera smiled. "No. But you do make me stronger. He has to think I'm weak." She leaned in and kissed him again, because she couldn't help it. "I'll see you at the Winter Ball."

"Yes," Don said, and she felt his breath in her hair.

"And all the days after that," Hera said, and pushed herself away with sheer force of will. "We've got a lot of lost time to make up for. But for now, you'd better leave."

He smiled at her, and it tore at her heart because he was so happy. She'd made him that happy, and she loved him so much.

"Yes, ma'am," he said.

Hera pressed her hands to her chest as he left, wondering how her body could contain everything she felt. She could go after him now, catch him in the hallway, kiss him goodbye.

But Zeus would throw a fit.

Perhaps she should have felt a pang for Zeus, who loved her. She'd never doubted that he loved her. But she felt nothing at all, save a weary irritation that she couldn't count on him not to taint the moment. It was Don who was setting her alight, Don who filled her heart and mind.

"All right," she whispered to herself. "All right. That's settled. Next."

Chapter Seventeen

On the way back to his apartment, Don had tried to come up with a good way to tell Leia that he and Hera had worked it all out—two days before the deadline, even—but in the end he hadn't had to. Leia had looked up from her book, put her hands on her hips, and said, "Well, *finally.*"

"Yes, but you can't tell anyone," Don said, grinning from ear to ear. He was pretty sure that this was actually happening, and wasn't just one of his better dreams. For one, his dreams had never involved dropping his sulky younger brother off on the way home.

"Why not?" Leia had said, which had started another, much harder conversation.

Don had wanted Leia to stay at home on Thursday night. If things went wrong, Atlas might target her. But Leia had argued that her absence might be a red flag they knew too much about Atlas's plans, had claimed that she was demonstrably better at keeping secrets than Don was, and had finally, ominously, pointed out that if Don didn't take her to the Winter Ball, she could still find her own way there. Besides, she'd added, with the air of an inarguable triumph, she already had the *dress.*

At that point, Don had found some tardy sympathy for Joe Graham. When Leia really dug her heels in, stubborn wasn't a strong enough word.

He was still concerned. But standing with Leia outside the Winter Ball, waiting for their turn on the red carpet, he couldn't help but be happy at her excitement. Leia was wearing a light violet gown with crystal detailing over the straps and bodice, and her fine hair had been tamed into a demure updo by Aphrodite's own stylist, who had also tactfully redirected Leia's desire for statement eye makeup into something more appropriate. "You want the dress to shine," she'd explained.

And it did, and Leia shone with it.

"How do you feel?" Don asked.

"Like I'm going to blink these eyelashes off," Leia said. "I'm glad Jasmine told me to practice walking in heels. Do I look awkward?"

"Not at all," Don said, surprised. "You look beautiful."

"Yes, but do I have *poise*?" Leia asked intently.

"Buckets of it," Don said.

Leia rolled her eyes at him—apparently "buckets" was the wrong descriptor for poise—and then let out a tiny yelp as one of the attendants beckoned them forward. "Eyes up, chin forward, hand on hip, tongue behind teeth," she muttered under her breath, and then hit her mark as if she'd been doing it all her life. The cameras flashed.

Don registered that he'd been caught smiling at Leia, instead of at the camera, but they were being politely moved on. They weren't important enough for lengthy photoshoots or the red-carpet reporters; this was just a quick shot for the society pages or a social media gallery. But Leia was glowing, delighted with her very first red carpet, even as a jolt went through the media pack and someone started calling "Aphrodite, Aphrodite, this way!"

Leia craned over her shoulder, looking for her friend.

"Nope," Don said firmly, and followed the attendant inside, Leia on his arm. They definitely didn't want to be part of that scrum. Aphrodite on a red carpet was a show all on her own.

And here was the reception committee, standing just inside the wide glass doors to the atrium. Samuel Janus, looking hearty and slightly foolish, flirting with all the women and backslapping all the men. Peter Atlas, smiling and affable, looking like a dashing executive instead of a snake in the grass. Hades, looking agonizingly awkward, which Atlas probably wouldn't read as anything more than his usual social discomfort. And Hera, looking...perfect.

She was wearing a long, sleek gown in rich peacock green, delicately accented with gold embroidery around the neckline and on either side of the high, narrow slit that rose to mid-thigh, showing flashes of tender, luminous skin. Her dark hair was adorned with a diadem, twining golden oak leaves set with subtle moments of emerald and pearl.

Dryad's Dream, Don thought. He certainly felt as if he were dreaming. But this was a waking vision.

"Keep walking," Leia muttered, and he took another step down the line, unable to look away. Thank goodness he wasn't supposed to be keeping his emotions concealed either. They'd decided that it would be all right for *him* to look lovestruck. It was Hera that had to look cool and calm. Regretful, perhaps, but not reciprocating.

He backslapped Janus, shook Atlas's hand and said something bland and forgettable to both. He managed a more sincere greeting for his brother, and stopped again in front of Hera.

"You look *incredible*," he said, the word gusting out of him.

"Thank you," Hera said, her tone remote. She held out her hand and allowed him to shake it, her dark eyes taking him in with one comprehensive glance. Her gaze skipped to Leia, and she smiled with genuine delight, pulling the girl in for one of those arm's length hugs, designed to demonstrate affection, but not muss up hair, make up, or clothes. "Don't you look wonderful!" she said.

"Thank you for inviting me," Leia said shyly.

"Do enjoy the party," Hera said, and gave Don another cool look. "Don."

"Hera," Don said, and gave her a longing look so blatant that it bordered on parody.

For a second, he caught the gleam in her eye and the tremble of a laugh in the corner of her lip. Then she was an ice queen again, and Peter Atlas, smirking, had turned to greet the next guests.

"Oh, *wow*," Leia said as they came out of the narrow space of the landing and walked into the atrium. "Hera went to school *here*?"

"It wouldn't usually look like this," Don said, trying not to goggle too openly. Hera was good, everyone knew that, and he hadn't expected the Winter Ball to look awful, even though it had been a rush job. But this—this was spectacular.

When he'd heard "glass atrium", he'd been expecting something corporate, clean and bland. But whoever had designed this space had gone for a more traditional aesthetic. Instead of aluminum joinery, the panels of glass in the south wall were held in place by wrought iron struts, which rose up the glass and unfurled across the clear ceiling in elegant arcs, suggesting the bare, black branches of a tree in winter.

Hera's people had enhanced that suggestion, with subtle lighting hinting at more branches on the glass panes between. And they'd taken full advantage of the space. Green, vibrant plants flourished in wooden planters. There were actual trees in here, reaching up mere feet from the ceiling. Someone had done something clever to those plants, Don realized, after a puzzled moment. Leaves didn't normally glimmer like that.

Among the wondering guests, servers moved unobtrusively, every platter piled high with canapes that looked more like jewels than food. On the stage towards the far side of the atrium, an all-female band played old music on their modern instruments. Plain black pole heaters, elegant in their austerity, kept the air warm enough for arms bared by formal gowns.

Beyond the glass of the south wall was downtown, the neon signs and billboards softened by night to a haze of distant color, somewhere out there in the cold and the dark. But Hera's guests were inside the dryad's dream, enclosed in a sweet fantasy of warmth and light at the heart of winter.

This year's Winter Ball wasn't just a good fix for a bad situation. It was a genuine triumph.

"I love her so much," Don said. It was mostly to himself, but Leia heard, and jabbed him in the ribs with her pointy little elbow.

"Duh," she said. "Let's go get something to eat."

***

A few minutes after she got off the reception line, Hera became aware that she was hosting something truly special.

People always said nice things about her events, both because she did an excellent job, and also it was just the done thing to say at parties, at least to the host's face. But this evening, people weren't mentioning the food in passing or complimenting her on the decor as a small talk aside. She could barely walk four steps without someone approaching to gush.

And she thought they were sincere, not least because many of them leavened the praise with implicit or outright surprise. This was potentially insulting, but Hera decided magnanimously to forgive them, especially because up until the very last minute, she hadn't been positive they could pull it off.

Demeter Erinyes could put *that* in her pipe and smoke it.

It had been slightly nauseating to stand beside Peter, knowing what she knew about him, letting him kiss her cheek and accept the greetings of their guests when she knew just how much he'd done to sabotage the evening they were thanking him for.

There were ways in which she and Peter were very similar. They were both schemers and strategists. They were both good at psychological assessment and social maneuvering. Soon, they'd both know who was better at it.

Hera was pinning rather a lot on Peter planning his final move for tonight. She'd spent the last two days baiting the trap, deliberately confiding that she was exhausted by the whole ordeal, and making subtle insinuations that the situation with Don had torn at her self-esteem.

And by the way, what right had Don to look so good in his tux? She'd long appreciated the raffish air he cut in formal wear, always with his hair loose, or a top button undone.

But this year, only years of practice in rigid self-control had prevented her from flinging herself at him the moment he appeared. And then he'd nearly made her *laugh*, the terrible man. She couldn't wait to get him alone and do filthy things to him.

Consumed by thoughts she shouldn't really be having in public at all, much less while she shifted the power balance of a major company, she nearly walked right into a solid young woman who was standing quietly near the band.

"Oh, I'm sorry," she said.

The woman shook her head, her bob of thick curls bouncing. "It happens all the time," she said. "I'm a natural lurker. Actually, Ms. Rheczack, do you have a moment?"

"I—" Hera said, and then reconsidered her polite leave-taking. The brown eyes behind the round glasses were intelligent and intent. "A brief moment, yes."

"I'm Cassie Troiades," the woman said quietly. "I write the Ask Cassandra advice column. I just wanted to say that I'm grateful for your support. I heard about what happened with Dammond Argive, and I know it would have been a lot easier to fire me."

"Oh," Hera said, and took a longer look at her. She couldn't remember seeing the woman around, and she had a good memory for faces. "You're a freelancer, yes? Not a full-time Olympus employee?"

"That's right. The advice column is an anonymous side gig. But it's a useful one, and I really enjoy it. It's nice to have a way to help people."

"Do people take your advice then?" Hera asked curiously.

Cassie smiled, her round cheeks lifting. "Not always," she admitted. "But I like to think that even if the person I'm writing to doesn't listen, the others who are reading might."

"Well, keep up the good work," Hera said, and wondered what advice Ask Cassandra might give her. Probably something along the lines of "Don't get involved with your ex-husband's brother,' which she would certainly ignore. "And thank you for coming this evening." Although, come to think of it, she couldn't recall signing an invitation for her.

"Oh, I'm only a tag-a-long," Cassie said, nodding up at the woman singing throatily into the microphone. "My cousin Paris is in the band. Anyway, I don't mean to keep you. I just wanted to say thanks."

"You're very welcome," Hera said, with a warmth that was wholly genuine. Peter had wanted to fire Cassie to appease the Argives, she recalled. *Would* have fired her, without a second thought. Even if she hadn't wanted Olympus, she couldn't allow a man like that to have it.

She'd displayed her ignorance to Peter, acted coolly towards Don, and mingled appropriately. It was twenty minutes before the speeches were due to begin, and she lifted her hand, deliberately adjusting the crown perched on her head.

She had to give some credit where it was due, because Zeus picked up the cue beautifully. He'd been one of the earliest guests to the Ball, glaring at Peter on his way in. Now he marched towards her, making no attempt to conceal his progress.

"I need to talk to you," he said, in a tone that cut through the background chatter. "In private."

In the corner of her eye, Hera caught the quick twist of Peter Atlas's head towards them.

"I have nothing to say," Hera said.

"You *need* to hear this," Zeus insisted, and she shrugged, the impatient gesture of a woman who was too busy for her ex's nonsense, but also didn't want a fuss.

"Very well," she said. "But quickly, please, the speeches are soon." She scanned the atrium, ostensibly looking for a private nook she'd already scouted, well before the doors had opened. It was just to the left of the stage, in the space between two of the wooden planters. Thick, dark green curtains had been erected at the front and back of the walking space between, and the shrubs in the planters screened the sides. The area had served as the band's green room, but was empty now.

Imperiously, she led Zeus there and ducked behind the heavy drapes with him.

"What do you think, ten minutes?" Zeus asked.

"Five," Hera said. "He'll want to limit how much you can give away."

Zeus nodded. They waited in tense silence, counting off the seconds.

"I'm really sorry," Zeus said abruptly. "For hurting you. For everything I did, but especially hurting you."

Hera looked at him. "That might have meant something once," she said slowly. "Now, I find that I don't really care."

Zeus winced, but said nothing else. At the five-minute mark, he left.

Hera gave him thirty seconds to make his way towards Atlas, and then emerged from the curtained area herself, doing her best to look like a woman struggling to control fear and fury. Neither were particularly difficult to portray; she *was* furious, and if this went wrong, she'd be forced to adopt a much riskier strategy, with much riskier outcomes. Hera scanned the crowd, and noted Hades by Samuel Janus in a group near the center of the Ball and Minerva with Aphrodite and Hecate near the bar. Persephone had taken Leia to chat with Penny and her husband, which would neatly remove Leia from the line of fire. Don had disappeared, and she hadn't seen her secret weapon at all, which was also as it should be.

Her expression hardened as her eyes finally landed on Peter, who was smiling pleasantly at Zeus, saying something obviously intended to be appeasing, while Zeus looked equally determined to be unappeased. Peter, she noted with pleasure, had moved much closer toward them in the time they'd been tucked quietly away. She made eye contact with him, and beckoned him over.

And, brushing Zeus off, and smiling, he came.

Hera allowed herself one momentary flash of relief as she returned to the curtained-off space area. It was only the first move, she reminded herself, and set her features to cool frustration as Peter moved aside the heavy fabric and joined her.

"Hello, Hera," he said, looking rueful. "I take it Zeus has been running his mouth?"

"Would you care to explain yourself?" Hera asked. "I'm not sure what to believe, but he claims that you've been working together, working against me!" She forced her voice to go high and shrill on the last phrase.

There was a pause, and then Peter smiled at her, his lips stretching over his teeth, his eyes shining with delight at his own cleverness. "Working together might be a stretch," he said. "Though it was handy to let Zeus think so."

"He said he sold you half his shares," Hera said. "Before I could serve him with my intention to divorce. That was in *March*, Peter! Have you been following his plan the whole time?" She saw that hit the mark. Peter, she was sure, was just dying to be acknowledged for his brilliance. He wouldn't want Zeus to get the credit.

"Oh, Zeus," he said dismissively. "He was on the phone with me minutes after that scuffle in his office, telling me about how he'd fucked it up. He said he had a plan, and if I was willing to take half his shares… Well. I saw the possibilities almost immediately."

"But why would you do that to *me*?" Hera said. "I was going to do my best to get you into any company you wanted."

"Well, that sounds nice," Peter said pleasantly. "But I think I've got a counter-offer. What about co-CEO of this one? We make a good team, Hera. I'd be the first to admit you've got the better connections, and the Kronion name still means something, even if you're calling yourself Rheczack now. And you're good at the job. Much better than I expected."

"*Co*-CEO?" Hera curled her lip. "And here I thought you wanted the whole pie."

"Oh, my first thought was to push you out," Peter said. "The problem was that you had Don and Hades behind you. There was no way to make those numbers work. So I had to find some incentive to get you on side, and I think I've nailed it. Hell, we can even get married if you want." He chuckled. "I won't hold you to that one, of course, but I think you can see all the ways it makes sense."

As proposals went, Hera thought, this one left a lot to be desired. She could see exactly what would happen if she was fool enough to say yes. He'd snatch her connections, work his way into her network. And when she was no longer useful, out she'd go.

"And if I say no?"

"No to marrying me? Then we can keep it strictly professional. I'm not Zeus, Hera. You're terrific, but I wouldn't wreck my life for you."

"No to you being co-CEO," Hera said, and crossed her arms in defiance. "What if I go out there right now and tell everyone exactly what a sneaking little toad you are? What's the *incentive* for me not to reveal you to the world?" This was the crucial moment. She thought she'd presented a compelling bait, but she needed Peter to spring the trap.

"Well, then we'd have a little problem," Peter said, still kind, and Hera felt a flash of triumph that never made it to her face. "Then I'd have to tell my pet journalist to get to work."

Hera frowned at him. "On what?"

"On an expose of you, Hera. She's dug up a lot of dirt. All those rumors about you being a vengeful hell-beast that Zeus put around? There's a lot of people who would still like to believe them. I can get at least one ex-mistress on record that you personally threatened her."

"I assume that's Joy," Hera said. "Who so *conveniently* failed to do her job."

"Oh, so you've worked that out? You know, I barely had to apply any pressure to make her do that. She really dislikes you."

"And that makes it all right for you to blackmail her?"

Peter laughed. "Just makes it a little easier." He gestured at the party beyond the curtain. "I did not think you'd pull this off. I'm impressed, truly."

"People have said terrible things about me before," Hera said, through her teeth. "I can't imagine you think that's enough of a threat."

"No," Peter said slowly. "No, I didn't think it was. But you see, if that story isn't enough, she's got another one about the underage runaway you took into your home at the same time your criminal ex-brother-in-law moved in." He winked at her. "Providing him all the home comforts, hm? I've even got shots of them on the red carpet together, looking *very* cozy." He shook his head in mock sorrow. "Do you think her parents will let her live with you then? They'll take her right back to their Podunk commune, and the courts won't let you do anything about it. Not with this story making the rounds. And Don's name will be mud."

"That's *disgusting*," Hera said, with a repulsion that was entirely genuine.

Peter grinned. "Isn't it? People would talk about it for *years*."

Hera's jaw was clenched tight. "Don has never been anything but a mentor and a friend to Leia, and you know it."

"Oh, sure. But it doesn't matter what I know, Hera. It matters what people think. And Don really does have a criminal record. It's not impressive—a few citations for vagrancy and time served and a fine for a 3rd degree assault. But it doesn't make him look good. And Hades has such a strong moral compass. He's already practically disowned Zeus for his heinous misdeeds. How fast do you think he'll turn on Don and walk away from Olympus altogether? I can probably pick up his shares for a song."

"It might be harder than you think," Hera said, her voice level.

"It might," Peter conceded. "Family is strange, and social engineering always has its limits. But I've got my fingers on your buttons, Hera. You care about Olympus, but you don't want it badly enough to hurt the people you love. That's your mistake, but I'll let you make it."

"Did you have this planned from the beginning?" Hera asked. "Did you manipulate Samuel Janus into offering you the position?"

Peter laughed. "Of course. It wasn't difficult. Sam's stuck in the past. He'll say all the right things, but he still doesn't think a woman can run a company on her own." He checked his watch, the carnelian face flashing orange in the dim light.

"What if I tell him?" Hera asked. "What if I tell Samuel that you set him up, tell Zeus you think he's an idiot, tell Joy you're using her?"

"And admit that you were fooled?" Peter said. "The great Hera Rheczack, actually asking for *help* instead of taking care of your own dirty business? I don't think so. No, Hera, I know you. And what it comes down to is that you've got a choice to make, right now. Do you walk out of here with me and announce to all our guests that to your great delight I've accepted the role of permanent co-CEO? Or do I call my tame journalist and tell her to send her exclusive to one of my contacts at Titan?" He waggled his phone at her. "She's already written the story, and honestly, I was impressed. I knew she was looking forward to getting away from the paparazzi beat, but it might be the best hatchet job I've ever read."

"Yes, Semele does good work, doesn't she?" Hera said. "I was impressed too."

Peter looked at her sharply.

With a sense of theatre she wouldn't have thought he could summon, Hades stepped through the back curtain and pulled it aside. Behind the curtain were the cluster of people Hera had chosen to be her witnesses—the Kronion brothers, Minerva and Hecate, who had identical small smiles, Sam Janus, who was red in the face, and Semele, who was staring at Peter with unrelenting hatred. She held a small black recorder in one hand, and the click of her thumb on the stop record button was very loud in the sudden silence.

"What the hell is this?" Peter snapped.

"In case you're too stunned to do the tally," Hera said, "you just confessed your revolting little scheme in front of an investigative journalist, three major shareholders, two officers of the court, and the Olympus Inc Board chair."

"Stuck in the past, am I?" Sam Janus spat, his eyes furious. He pointed at Zeus. "And you! You worked with this man?"

"I thought better of it," Zeus said, and Hera decided she'd let him have that.

"So, Peter," she said pleasantly. "What it comes down to is that you've got a choice to make, right now. Do you immediately resign as consultant CEO before leaving this city forever? Or do I make sure that Semele's *other* story hits every major news outlet by eight a.m. tomorrow?"

"This is a mistake," Peter told Semele, but the arrogance was shaky.

"You threatened my son," she snarled. "*That* was the mistake."

Peter looked at Hera, and tried to smile. "Look, this wasn't *personal*."

"I'm taking it very personally," Hera said, and let her rage inform her face. "Leave my party, Peter. Leave my company. Leave my city. Leave tonight. Or I will show you exactly what a vengeful hell-beast I can be. You *lost*."

She saw that hit home, and his shock turn to an appalled understanding of just how deep a grave he'd dug for himself. "I—" he said, and paused, evidently unable to come up with anything to say.

Hera stepped towards him. "Also, I'll be buying those shares," she said, and held out a single dollar bill.

Peter's face flushed with rage and humiliation, and he snarled, raising his hand. Hera met his eyes, and wondered distantly if he'd actually hit her and how much it would hurt.

In a rush of movement, Don was suddenly by her side. "Just give me the excuse," he said, sincerity dripping from every word.

Peter's hand fell to his side. After a moment, he snatched the dollar bill from Hera, his face purple. Hera wondered how she could ever have thought him handsome. "Minerva has the paperwork for you to sign," she said, and went up on her tiptoes to kiss Don's cheek. "Thank you, darling."

"You're very welcome," Don said, his eyes catching on hers. Hera shivered. She was aware that Zeus was sputtering, and Hades was talking to him in sharp disapproval, while Minerva went through the shares sales agreement with a morose Peter, but all of it was unimportant background noise, fading away. What was real was Don's face, solemn and bright, and his grip on her waist, and the soft strength of his lips as she brought his mouth down to hers.

"Later," she whispered, and felt him shudder in anticipation.

Then she straightened her crown and slipped out through the front curtain of the alcove to find Cyd and get her notes. After all, she had a job to do.

***

Don was sure that Hera's speech was fantastic—the applause afterwards was loud and sustained—but he couldn't claim he'd heard a single word. He was standing with his brothers, still buzzing with triumph. They'd personally escorted Peter Atlas out of the Ball. Leia was safe. Olympus was safe, which mattered to him because it mattered to Hera.

And Hera wasn't just safe. She was magnificent. He wasn't sure whether he should be going to his knees in worship or tumbling her onto the nearest flat surface.

She'd claimed him, in front of all of them. No hesitation, no doubt, just her mouth on his and the whispered promise of *later*.

When was later? Could later be now? Hera was on the other side of the room, talking to Aphrodite and Persephone, but he could swear she'd caught his eye from the stage...

Someone tapped his shoulder. "Hey," Zeus said, his tone curt.

Reluctantly, Don looked at his little brother. "What?"

Zeus was switching his weight from foot to foot. "I think we get one each," he said abruptly.

Don frowned. Hera wouldn't like it, but... "That seems fair."

"You're both idiots," Hades said, sounding resigned. "At least take it outside, away from the cameras."

Zeus nodded, and gestured sharply towards a side exit. The attendant stationed there to politely encourage guests back inside recognized Zeus, and didn't protest.

It was bitterly cold outside, but they were alone, with no photographers to spoil the fun. Don surveyed the narrow alley, with its ranks of recycling bins and dirty frozen slush, and grunted. "Not exactly a formal dueling ground," he observed.

Zeus punched him in the gut.

It was a solid punch, Don thought, as he bent forward over it. Zeus had missed the solar plexus, but not by much, and he'd put his body weight behind his fist. Don had some significant layers of fat and muscle to cushion the blow, but it still fucking hurt.

"You hit on Hera, you motherfucker," Zeus said. His teeth were bared in a mirthless smile, and his fists were still clenched.

"You betrayed her," Don said, and landed a beautiful right straight to the side of his brother's face.

At the very last moment, he pulled the punch. Angry as he was, he didn't want to permanently damage Zeus, and head blows were a chancy thing. He liked to think he'd learned from past mistakes.

Zeus staggered and went down on one knee in the slush-covered alleyway, but he didn't pass out, and he didn't lose any teeth. "What the hell," he managed, after a second. "You nearly took my head off!"

"Not even close," Don said, and purposefully relaxed his fists. "We good?"

"No," Zeus said, feeling his jaw. "But we're done for now. Fuck, you're strong."

Don extended a hand, but Zeus got to his feet by himself. "I didn't kill Dad," he said abruptly.

"I believe you," Don said. He hadn't, when he really thought about it, considered Zeus capable of murder. But it had been a dark little suspicion, something that had niggled at him for years. Saturnius had died suddenly when he could have lingered for months, and only Zeus had been there.

"But I did watch him die," Zeus went on, and Don's head came up. "He told me to get rid of Hera. He said I needed a woman who could give me biological kids, who could keep the Kronion name going. He said that if I dumped her, he'd cut you and Hades out of the will and give me your shares."

Don stared at him.

Zeus grinned back, blood all over his teeth. He must have cut the inside of his cheek. "He offered me all of his sixty percent of Olympus. I'd have had a controlling interest, all by myself."

"That's insane," Don said. He wasn't surprised that their father had wanted to take Olympus away from him. But Hades had been, if quietly resistant to some of their father's worst impulses, never openly rebellious. Saturnius rewarding dogged, careful Hades with disinheritance would have been the worst slap in the face.

"Oh, he knew what he was doing," Zeus said. "He had a fresh will all drawn up, being that I am of sound mind, etcetera. Told me to get it out of his bedside drawer." He touched his jaw again. "So I did. And then I tore it up, right in front of him, and told him that I'd rather have Hera than a single share in his precious company. He started going off at me, and I guess it was too much for him. He went red, and then white, and then he died." He shrugged, but there was something pinched and haunted about his eyes.

"Dad was a monster," Don said.

"Yeah," Zeus said. "Now, tell me I'm just like him, and we can hit each other again."

"You're not, though," Don said, feeling his way carefully through the thought. "He couldn't love anyone. You loved Hera."

"Still do," Zeus said. "But I don't deserve her."

"No."

"You don't either."

"Probably not," Don said. "But she loves me anyway. So we're going to be together, and we don't need your blessing."

"Good, because you don't have it," Zeus said pleasantly. "I'm going to sit back and watch you crash and burn."

"It's not going to happen," Don said, with absolute certainty. "You can keep sitting back."

Zeus scowled, but he didn't argue further. Instead, he brushed slush off his pants and straightened his bow-tie. "Well, I'm going home," he said sourly. "Enjoy the rest of the party."

"I will," Don said, and watched him limp to the mouth of the alley, feeling unwilling pity for him. "Hey, Zeus," he said, and then panicked a little when his brother stopped and looked back at him. He hadn't really worked out anything to say. He'd only acted on that sympathetic impulse. But after a second, he had it. "You're not like Dad," he said. "He's dead, and honestly, the world is better off for it. But you're alive. You can change, if you want to."

Zeus stared at him for a long moment. "Yeah," he said. "Okay." And then he turned his back and walked into the cold night.

Don let him go. Inside, there was color and light and warmth, the world dreaming itself into spring.

Inside, there was Hera, and the rest of forever.

Chapter Eighteen

"I thought that went rather well," Hera said. She was sitting beside Don in the back of her town car. The privacy partition between the back seat and the driver's compartment was up, but they weren't touching. There was a thrumming line of energy between them, a tension drawn out like a wire strained to the breaking point.

She was looking forward to the snap.

"Are you happy?" Don asked.

"Oh, yes," Hera said, and laid her head against his shoulder. The hard bulk of the diadem scratched her scalp, and she straightened again, gingerly pulling out the clips that held it in place before pulling the golden oak leaves free from her hair.

"The crown suits you," Don said. "I liked seeing you in it."

"Did you?" Hera asked, with some interest.

Don's eyes were hot. "Yes. But I'd rather see you in nothing at all."

Hera felt desire tighten inside her. "It was nice of Aphrodite to invite Leia back to her place," she said.

"Very nice," Don agreed. He drew one finger down her bare arm, so lightly that he was barely touching the skin, and her pussy clenched in immediate reaction.

"Keep that up, and we won't even make it out of the car," she told him.

"Is that a promise?" Don asked, and swept his palm down her arm, firm and possessive.

"Oh," Hera said, and yanked him down by the bow-tie. He laughed softly against her mouth, but there was nothing soft about his big hands, one holding her hip, the other sliding straight to her gown's thigh-high slit. He sucked in a shaky breath as he felt the bare skin underneath, and she bit his lip, flicking her tongue out to ease the bite, then gasping herself as his hand slid further up her thigh, up, up, over—

The car stopped.

"Tell him to go round the block," Don said, and she laughed and tore herself away from him.

"Come on," she said, fumbling for the door handle before the driver could get it for her. It wasn't exactly a graceful exit, but she didn't care. Don was right behind her, equally eager, and they went right past the startled doorman and into the elevator, where Hera caught sight of her reflection in the closing mirrored doors, and stopped. Her lips were swollen and wet, her lipstick smeared. Her hair was a mess, her gown rucked up on one side, and her eyes were bright and wild. She looked totally imperfect and incredibly happy.

"Look at you," Don said, crowding behind her, his voice thick with desire. He reached for her breast, and she watched his fingers move, watched her nipples harden under his skillful touch. "No, don't close your eyes. Look. You're so beautiful." His other hand went to her thigh, sliding through that slit again, tugging the fabric up. She clenched her thighs around his hand, shuddering as he stroked the silky fabric between her legs. She pushed back, working her hips in tiny circles against the thick length pressing against her ass, and watched his pupils dilate until the black nearly swallowed the blue-green of his eyes.

"I love you," she said, suddenly needing to say it.

"I love you too," Don said. "Your bed or mine?"

"Who said we're making it to a bed?" Hera said, and the elevator pinged to a stop at her floor.

"Right," Don said, sounding as if he'd reached the end of his reserves of patience, and Hera found herself off her feet and turned over his shoulder as they exited the elevator. He got them through her front door before she recovered her wits, and started striding towards her bedroom.

Hera grabbed his butt, partly for balance and partly because it was *right there*, and why wouldn't she, and he responded by groping hers, before he flipped her off his shoulder and bounced her right into the middle of her enormous bed.

"We have to discuss this scooping habit of yours," Hera said.

"Later," Don said, ruthlessly divesting himself of his formal wear. "Take that dress off."

"I'll need a hand," Hera said, trying to look demure. It was hard, when she kept staring at the hard length of Don's cock. It bobbed up and down, tapping against the swell of his stomach as he walked deliberately towards her. "Is all of that for me?"

"All of me is for you," Don told her, with devastating sincerity, and she lost her breath for a moment.

She hadn't been lying about needing help to get free of the dress. She couldn't actually reach the hidden zipper herself, and it was hard to tell Don where it was when he kept kissing her, or she kept kissing him—hard to keep track, really. But once he'd found the zipper and peeled the gown off her, she was left in her lingerie set, presented like a work of art to Don's devouring eyes. The green silk was embroidered with a peacock feather motif that wandered over her breasts and dipped between her thighs, encouraging the eye—and the hand—to wander.

"Amazing underwear," Don said.

"I wore it for you," Hera said, and his fingers closed on her breast. He leaned over her, his hand the sole point of contact, watching her face as her nipple tightened to the point of near pain and the answering throb from her clit became unbearable.

"Touch me," she told him, her throat tight with longing.

"I am."

"Touch me *more*," she said, and lifted her hips, hooking one leg around his waist and pulling him down so that his naked cock slid against the sodden silk between her legs.

They both groaned at the contact, and Don's careful touch became an unashamed grope. He thrust against her again, and Hera abruptly lost her taste for the tease. She reached down between them and yanked her panties to one side, so that the next time he moved against her, the head of his cock thrust between her slick folds.

Don went still, his eyes widening in shock. "I—" he said, "Hera?"

"*Fuck me*," Hera said, through gritted teeth, and Don thrust home in one thoroughly gratifying stroke.

Hera snarled her satisfaction and lifted her hips to meet the welcome invasion, matching his intensity with her own ferocity, glorying in the way her body stretched and opened to his, the press of his bulk between her thighs, the heat of his panting breath against her throat and breasts as he kissed them, wet and open-mouthed.

"You're so wet," he whispered in her ear. "So hot and so wet. I can't stand it, Hera. You."

He kissed her, and she kissed back, biting at his lips, his broad neck.

"Are you close?" he said, voice straining. "I'm going to—I can't last long."

"I need—" Hera said, and before she could voice it, he shifted his weight so he was holding himself up with one hand. He was so strong, she couldn't believe how strong he was, and he sucked his thumb into his mouth and then reached between them, reached unerringly to the point where every jangling nerve cried out for his touch.

His thumb pressed hard against the side of her clit, once, twice, and that was it.

Hera felt as if she was exploding, her body becoming a thousand glittering shards of light as pleasure roared through her, from her curled toes to her clenched eyelids. She heard her own startled cry as if from a great distance, as the detonation went off and flung her into the heavens. She drifted back to herself, and opened her eyes to find Don poised over her, teeth gritted, neck and jaw tight. He was rooted inside her, his cock sunk deep while her pussy fluttered against the stiff length in quivering pulses.

"Now," she told him, and he drew in a huge breath, pulled his hips back, and slammed into her, pounding out a frantic, final rhythm as his eyes fixed desperately on her face.

His head snapped back and he gasped something that could have been her name, and that was enough to set her off again, so that she shuddered along with him, bodies and hearts united in that searing ecstasy.

Afterwards, she stroked Don's hair while he rested his head against the hollow of her neck, her fingers tangling in his curls.

"Am I too heavy?" he mumbled.

"You're just right," Hera said. His weight was a pleasant burden, and his skin was a welcome barrier against the cool air. Though his back was probably getting cold. "We should find a blanket. Or get under the covers."

Don sat up. "Oh," he said. "That reminds me. Wait one second." He rolled off the bed and padded out of her room, totally unconscious of his nakedness. Hera took advantage of the opportunity to yank off her remaining scraps of clothing and check herself in the mirror.

She looked thoroughly ravished.

"Excellent," she said, and gave herself an approving smile, as Don returned with an armful of fabric.

"I was going to get Leia to give this to you later, if things didn't work out," he said, and grinned at her. "But since they did..." He tossed the quilt over the bed and stood back to gauge her reaction.

It was an Ara Kaney, of course, and one she'd seen at the exhibit, though it had made little impression then. Now she looked at the design and felt something tighten in her chest. It was an abstract combination of opposing shapes. On one side were a multitude of pointed curves in shades of blue: sapphire, midnight, teal, navy, aquamarine and turquoise, climbing and tumbling over each other. On the other side were green and brown squares and rectangles, neatly piled, carefully articulated and outlined in gold thread. Except where the curves met the squares, the curves became a little less chaotic, and the squares lost their right angles, melding into the boundary.

The design was an ocean rolling over the earth. It was a proud citadel, standing firm against the sea. It was Don and it was her, two very different people, making something beautiful in the spaces between them.

As an added bonus, it was exactly the colorful statement piece her bedroom had been missing.

"Do you like it?" Don asked, his arms going around her.

Hera looked up at him. "It's perfect," she said, feeling the tears prick at her eyes. "You're perfect."

He bent and kissed her.

Presently, they got under the covers, and made more warmth together.

***

EIGHTEEN MONTHS LATER:

Don wasn't an expert, but he thought the Unhoused Youth Community Art Trust inaugural event was going very well.

Hera had been afraid that the stifling June heat would scare people away, but the Grotto was packed with bohemians in fluttery layers, neo-punks in black net mesh, and the city elite in cocktail wear, all of them mingling in apparent amity. Don had opened all the windows to create a cross-breeze and put the sprinklers on in the gardening section, and the promised cool change had come in at the last possible moment. It was still hot, but no one was likely to faint, and he thought they had enough iced tea and punch, served out of the largest glass bowls he'd been able to find in storage.

"How are you?" Hera asked, pausing by him on one of her circuits of the event.

"Stressed out of my tiny mind," he said. "I've no idea how you did so many of these."

"You're doing fine," she said. "Keep smiling, thank everyone for coming, and direct anyone who's looking lost to the auction tables."

In addition to works happily donated by the talents Hera had supported over the years, a number of unhoused youth, former and current, had contributed their own work to the auction they were holding later. Some of them had created pieces in the workshops Hera had funded in the shelters, while others had taken the fees-free places Don kept in the DIY classes at the Grotto. He could make that kind of decision on his own, now—a year ago, with Doris and Neron tacking a second and third cruise onto the end of their first, he'd made them an offer and bought the Grotto outright.

He'd got the money for the purchase by selling Hera his Olympus shares.

It was a perfect solution. Hera got thirty-five percent of the company, Don got to be free of it forever, and Doris and Neron got to take as many cruises as they wanted.

Don didn't pretend to himself that art classes or an auction could fix the lack of equitable housing or care for people in need. At most, they were a creative outlet, and a way to humanize people society preferred to ignore. But an auction with Hera Kronion attracted high profile guests and plenty of publicity.

And Hera had invited literally every politician in her address book and was lobbying them mercilessly for the legislative reform that might create real change.

"We're running out of ice," Leia reported, popping up next to them. "Also, I just met the governor. She's shorter than she looks on TV!"

Don handed her his keys. "Take Jasmine to the gas station on Sumer and Nile and load up."

"Yes, boss," Leia said. "Hera, you look great."

"So do you, darling."

Leia grinned at them and darted away again.

"I'm going to miss her so much," Hera said wistfully.

"She's not going to college until August," Don said.

Hera looked stern. "Don't pretend you won't miss her too."

"Of course," Don admitted. "But we won't have to worry about her walking in on us. Think of all the rooms we can have sex in."

"Hm. That's a very good point," Hera said, her eyes glinting with new thought.

An excited mutter ran through the crowd, and Don spotted the tall red-headed woman walking in, matching her pace to the man in the wheelchair beside her. "Aphrodite and Heph are here," he told Hera.

"Oh, good. I need to ask Heph about whether he'd be interested in bidding on our network restructure project."

"No work talk outside office hours," Don said, with mock sternness.

Hera didn't bother to respond. Don had to admit that she *had* cut her work hours a lot, as Olympus's bottom line improved and she'd felt able to delegate more of her responsibilities. But he couldn't expect her to stop being Hera Rheczack. After all, her drive was one of the many things he loved about her.

"Great party, babe," Aphrodite said, when she and her partner had made their way over.

"Thank you," Hera said. "But really, this is all Don."

"I was *talking* to Don," Aphrodite said, and winked at him. Don winked back.

"Hey, man," Heph said. "Are you still on for *The Binding* expansion drop party next week?"

"You know it," Don said fervently.

"I'm going to destroy both of you," Aphrodite said sweetly, and bent to kiss her boyfriend's cheek. "Where's Persephone? I need to see that ring in person. Photos in the group chat aren't the same."

"She and Hades snuck off somewhere," Hera said, and Aphrodite chortled. "Now, Heph, about this network restructure…"

Don left them to it, and did a circuit of the party. It really was going well, he thought as he circled around the back, and spied a flash of bright floral fabric moving hastily behind a shelf. "Persephone?" he said. "Is that you?"

His soon-to-be sister-in-law popped out from behind the shelf, blushing furiously. Several of the buttons at the top of her dress appeared to be in the wrong holes. "Hello, Don!" she said. "Great party! Oh, I see Aphrodite's here. I'd better. Um."

She rushed off, and Don counted to five before stepping around the shelf, where, as expected, he found a flustered Hades. "Aren't you supposed to be the mature one?" he asked.

Hades's cheeks were stained with red, but he shrugged. "Aren't you supposed to be the careless rebel?" he asked, and gestured at the warehouse, the business, the event that Don had made happen.

"Don't tell anyone," Don said. "But I think I might be responsible now."

Hades grinned at him. "As long as you're happy."

"I really am," Don said. "You?"

"Yes," Hades said immediately. "So happy."

They stared at each other in mutual amazement.

"We made it," Don said, and had to clear his throat. "How about that?"

Hades clapped him on the shoulder, and they walked back to the party. Don watched Aphrodite sparkle and flirt with a grinning Heph, watched Hades and Persephone talking quietly together, and looked instinctively for Hera.

She was walking towards him, her hands outstretched, and he caught them in his, leaning down to kiss her knuckles.

"My Hera," he said.

"My Don," she said, and smiled up at him with no reserve. "I think the speakers are ready. Shall we get started? I want to see what happens next."

About the Author

Kate Healey lives in New Zealand and writes spicy contemporary rom-coms with a mythic twist. Karen Healey, who looks suspiciously similar, lives in New Zealand and writes fantasy romance, science fiction and young adult fiction. They both drink a lot of coffee.

Find more about Karen at http://karenhealey.com and sign up for her newsletter at http://thathealeygirl.com . You'll get the first news on new books, weird research rabbitholes, and occasional freebies!

Now read on for a glimpse of the next book, *Ask Cassandra*!

Ask Cassandra

C assie Troiades is a freelance archivist, but her secret side gig as a popular advice columnist has made her cynical about love and despair for her own romantic future. When Manny Pelopson hires her to catalogue his family's old documents at the Tantalus Vineyard, they begin to find romance and mystery among the archives. But Manny has a secret of his own...

A sparkling new arc in the series where Greek mythology meets *The Devil Wears Prada!*

Dear Cassandra,

Eleven years ago the love of my life left me for someone else. On our wedding day. It wasn't actually at the altar, but six hours afterwards, at the reception.

It's not an exaggeration to say I was destroyed. In the immediate aftermath, I made some stupid decisions that could have had terrible results (they didn't, but I know I was just lucky.)

I know she made the best choice for herself, and I truly don't begrudge her happiness. But I just don't know how to get over her. She was the kindest person I've ever met, with a fantastic dry sense of humor, and she really understood what it's like to grow up in a family of strong personalities when you're the conflict-avoidant one.

Recently, I've tried to get back out there and date other women and I think it's important to be honest about what happened, so that potential partners know where I'm coming from. But every time I tell my dates about the One Who Left, they stop being interested.

Any advice?

Left Behind.

Dear Left Behind,

First, I hope you had (and maybe continue to get) professional help to manage your feelings about what sounds like a truly traumatic event. My entire insides curdled when I read that "the kindest person" you've ever met left you for someone else six hours *after* the wedding. There were dozens of much kinder ways for her to handle that situation, and she should have chosen one of them!

Second, and I say this with all the sympathy in the world, *stop telling other women about her*.

The truth is, the One Who Left story is eleven years old. It is off the bestseller charts, it is being removed from the library collections, it is no longer accepted for trade at secondhand bookstores, and you do not need to bring it out for review on dates. (I am really hoping not *first* dates. No, right? Right?)

As long as you keep telling yourself and other people this story about the woman you don't know how to get over, you are not leaving any space for a *different* story, the one where you fall in love with someone fabulous who loves you back just as hard.

This column is firmly in favor of honesty, but that doesn't have to be complete honesty. I don't tell my dates I have a side-gig as an advice columnist. If I ever meet someone serious, then sure, but until then, not every twenty-minute coffee or casual movie hang needs to come with a side of my life story.

Don't tell your dates yours. See how that goes. And if you feel up to it, write back to tell us how it works out–I know that the readers are rooting for you just as much as I am.

Yours,

Cassandra.

Buy *Ask Cassandra* now!

Acknowledgements

My most fervent thanks to Robyn Fleming, best friend and editor, who truly went above and beyond on fast and thorough editing of what was a very messy first draft, with notes like [horses scene goes here] scattered throughout.

I am extremely grateful to Ben Moxon for sharing his expertise on said horses scene, to Naomi van der Broek for quilting advice and inspiration, and to Jessica Tai, who was not only unfailingly enthusiastic about Don, but helped me brainstorm fine arts examples. Gina Healey applied her excellent eye to the proofreading. AJ Lancaster and Marie Cardno are brilliant writers and wonderful professional mentors in the exciting world of indie publishing. Kristen Smirnov, Carla Lee, Marianne Kirby, and the great folks at the Speculative Collective were always ready to tell me that I got this when I was positive that I did not, in fact, have this.

Don't you love it when your friends are right?

Also by Kate Healey

Olympus Inc. Series:

Penelope Pops the Question (a newsletter freebie, available when you sign up at http://thathealeygirl.com!)

Persephone in Bloom

Aphrodite Unbound

Hera Takes Charge

Ask Cassandra

As Karen Healey:

Movie Magic Series:

"Jingle Spells" (a newsletter freebie, available when you sign up at http://thathealeygirl.com)

Bespoke & Bespelled

Savory & Supernatural

The Hidden Histories Series (with Robyn Fleming):

The Empress of Timbra

The Spymaster's Apprentice

Young Adult:

Guardian of the Dead

The Shattering

When We Wake

While We Run

9 781738 612734